Sea Change

Out of the Box, Book 7

Robert J. Crane

Sea Change
Out of the Box #7
Robert J. Crane
Copyright © 2015 Revelen Press
All Rights Reserved.

1st Edition

1

FADE IN:
EXTERIOR NIGHT

Albert Hammond's "It Never Rains in Southern California" plays over a high shot of the city of Los Angeles. We PUSH IN on a blond girl, BARBARA "BOBBIE" KEEN on Rodeo Drive in Beverly Hills, early twenties, blond, leggy, vivacious, but poor, two steps north of hipster or homeless. PAN AROUND to REVEAL her looking at a shop window, full of hope and California dreams as she looks at diamonds by herself.

                    BOBBIE
'Tis the season.

A guy in his mid-forties pushes past, jostling her as he goes by. The sidewalk is empty; he's just being a dick.

                    GUY
Way to stop and gawk in the middle of the sidewalk, Barbie!

                    BOBBIE
              (under her breath)
Merry Christmas to you, too, dickhead.

Katrina Forrest looked up from the page, her green eyes perplexed. Her brow failed to show a single wrinkle, even while she struggled mightily to show just how confused she was by the pages of movie script loosely held in her small, perfectly manicured fingers. "I don't get it. Where is this going?"

She'd just met the writer of this particular work about ten minutes earlier, hustled into the meeting by her agent and producer, Aaron Taggert. She glanced at Taggert now, and he arched his eyebrows at her, his thin lips pushed together, holding in his thoughts. He sat next to the writer, Bob Humphries. She'd thought it a little odd that the character's name in the script was Bobbie while the writer's name was Bob, but she decided not to draw attention to it, at least not just yet.

"See," Humphries started, gesturing at the page in her hands with a little too much excitement. Caffeine or coke? she wondered as she glanced at the small Starbucks cup in front of him. "It's really an exploration of the seedy underbelly of Los Angeles through the eyes of someone new in town."

"It's practically tailored just for you," Taggert said, arching his eyebrows and breaking his silence at last. He leaned forward on the conference table that separated them, the white walls a pale wash behind his swarthy, orange, spray-tanned face. "You wanted to branch out from the reality TV mold, Kitten? This could be the thing. We could even structure a whole season of your show around filming, make it a great storyline for you. Making a movie can be tough at times, it'd be a great opportunity to show the audience the travails, a little behind-the-scenes sizzle, some Hollywood glam, make them empathize with you even more."

Humphries stared blankly at Taggert then shifted his gaze back to Kat. "Uhm, yeah, sure. I mean, sure, that makes sense. Kind of a cross-marketing thing to tie it in with your TV series. But, anyway, the script, it's like *LA Story* meets

Mean Girls. But there's murder, and Christmas, so it's got a little Shane Black thrown in—"

"Some real grit," Taggert said, his dark eyes flashing. "A chance for you to really act."

Kat felt her face flush hot, like someone had switched on a sunlamp above her. "I act all the time, Taggert."

"You know what I mean, kiddo," Taggert said, backing off a little. "Not for the reality TV cameras, but a performance that could potentially get you some award nods." He smirked. "They're not exactly handing out 'Best Actress' in your current genre, if you know what I mean, even though you're acting your ass off, am I right?"

Kat settled back in her chair. It wasn't very padded, felt kind of hard on her backside. She leaned against the wood and wondered why someone in her entourage—all waiting outside the door, except for Taggert—hadn't brought her something more comfortable to sit on. "But the show's going really well, I thought you said? That some of the upcoming storylines were our strongest—"

"Absolutely," Taggert said, nodding. "And you're tuned in with the tabloids, you got your platform and social media rocking, I mean you've got this thing wired, Kitten, your brand awareness is going up by the day. But it doesn't hurt to move some eggs into other baskets, if you know what I mean, and Bob's screenplay can make that happen. We get you on board, leverage your current successes, and boom, we move you into a new place, the burgeoning actress/reality TV star category. Opens new channels, new opportunities, some more cross-promotion, maybe some doors to some new friends that work in the scripted content universe, get you some guest roles on the popular shows—just raise your profile, you know?" He grinned, his teeth in an even line.

"Yeah, maybe," Kat said after a moment of thought. That drew smiles from Bob and Taggert. Bob wasn't nearly as tanned, spray or otherwise, as Taggert. He actually looked kind of pale. Maybe he spent too much time working on

3

scripts. "I guess it does make business sense to diversify."

"Whoa!" Taggert said, laughing sharply as he exchanged a look with Bob. "Listen to this one! Pretty soon you won't even need me managing your career! You're really picking it up."

Kat flushed, a little embarrassed. "Just been listening to you, I guess." She looked up. "Okay. So, when can we start on this?"

"Uh, don't you want to read the rest of the script first?" Bob asked, looking at her, his pudgy cheeks looking a little bigger thanks to the way he was holding his mouth. The writer caught a searing gaze from Taggert and instantly melted. "Or not. I mean, whatever works for you guys."

"If Taggert says it's good, I'm in," Kat says, letting go of that little bit of reticence she'd had coming in. Taggert had steered her well thus far, after all, from a near nobody—practically a backup dancer to Sienna Nealon—to the star of one of the biggest television shows on cable, and in just a few short years.

"I'll start talking with the studios," Taggert said, his veneer back to placid, his smile returning to his lips. "See if we can get some financing put together and—you know, all that other stuff. Line up a distributor."

"Great!" Bob said, standing up. He stuck out a hand awkwardly toward Kat, who regarded it carefully.

"She doesn't do that," Taggert said, rising up and fastening the button of his jacket. Beneath it he wore jeans and a simple Polo-style shirt. The first couple buttons were undone, and a healthy mat of chest hair peeked out from beneath. "You should know that." It was a step above a rebuke, but the aura of distaste that the reminder had to be issued clouded the air in the conference room.

"Oh, I am so sorry," Bob said, yanking his hand back like it had almost been thrust into a grinder. "My apologies. I forgot—"

"Try to remember who you're dealing with here," Taggert

said, frosty as winter—a sensation Kat hadn't really felt since coming to LA. "This deal could change your life, Bob. Get with the program."

"Right, yessir," Bob said, nodding, now red with embarrassment. He gave Kat a nod. "So sorry."

"It's fine," Kat said, picking up her sunglasses where she'd almost left them on the table, along with her bottle of Fiji water. "Just try to remember it for next time." She turned, practicing the perfectly poised stride-away that she'd been working on. It really played for the cameras, of which there were none at the moment. They were waiting outside with the rest of her entourage, and if needed, they could film this meeting again, staged properly next time. For now, Taggert hadn't wanted it on film, and as producer, well, he knew what he was doing.

"We'll be in touch," Taggert said, hurrying ahead of her, opening the door just before she got there. She stepped out of the conference room into a bare corridor, white walls, not much deco—the place looked cheap, actually. Taggert took the lead as two big guys, Bruce and Bruce, her bodyguards, walked a couple paces in front of her. She hadn't been sure why she needed two of them at first, but then the paparazzi had started showing up. It had taken only a day or two of that to convince her that even two bodyguards might not be enough to control the crowds.

"You're sure this is the right move?" Kat asked as the elevator dinged beneath Taggert's touch. He extended a hand as if to prevent the elevator door from closing as she stepped inside, Bruce and Bruce following. They both turned their backs to her and Taggert, who was much smaller than the bulky bodyguards. Both Bruces looked like defensive players on a football team.

Taggert slipped in to stand beside her. "It's the right move." He took hold of her elbow and squeezed possessively. "There's no downside. If the movie goes sour, you've still got the show."

"What if it all goes sour?" Kat asked, a little tremor of fear running through her as the elevator dinged shut and started to move downward.

"Just stick with me, Kitten," Taggert said, flashing her a wink. "I made you, I can make you again. Don't you even spare the water sweating it."

"Not in this drought," she said as the elevator dinged to indicate it had moved one floor down to the lobby. The doors swept open to reveal the glass lobby of the small office building. It was so tiny it didn't have a doorman, didn't have a receptionist. All it had was a staircase in a twenty-by-twenty open area, with paint that looked years old and faded by the sun that shone in through the immense glass fronting of the building. As usual there didn't look to be many clouds in the sky, and the sun was beating in even now, the metal beams that held the panes in place making harsh shadows on the grey carpeting.

Beyond the double doors to outside waited the paparazzi. Kat fiddled with her sunglasses as she composed herself. They could probably already see her, but the cameras wouldn't be able to catch a very good picture with the reflective glass of this dump of an office building between them. She'd be ready when she came out, though, because the cameras would already be clicking away, capturing thousands of digital exposures. She couldn't risk having a single one of those be a poor shot; they had to be glamorous, they had to be perfect, they had to be composed.

"Remember," Taggert whispered, "you're selling a lifestyle. It's glam, baby. Your life is the best. You're rich, you're powerful, you're jet-setting, visiting places these losers will never tread. Your vacations are beyond their wildest dreams, and your every day is the fantasy of every bored drama queen or king yearning for a better life than the crappy one they live right now." He slapped her lightly on the ass. She didn't blanch; she was used to it by now. "Go sell, baby. Sell."

She did her perfect stride on those stiletto heels. That was not difficult; she had metahuman dexterity, after all, helping to keep her from tipping over. They added inches of height and made her look more regal, after all. The name-brand clothes helped, too—the Givenchy suit was perfect on her, the jacket fitted to her trim figure and the skirt just long enough to be tasteful yet practical for the weather.

This wasn't Minnesota in winter.

This was LA in November.

"Ms. Forrest," her assistant, Karyn, stepped into her shadow and began to whisper. "You have five more appointments today—"

"Cancel them," Kat murmured under her breath as the Bruces swept open the double doors for her and the onslaught began.

"Kat!"

"Katrina!"

"Look over here!"

She kept a faint smile on her lips; she'd practiced it in the mirror for what felt like a thousand years until she loved the way it looked and Taggert had given her the thumbs up. It was her go-to, the thing she did on all occasions. A little mischievous, a little coy, an expression that highlighted her perfect cheekbones. She studiously ignored the paparazzi, heading straight for her car, parked there in front of the curb, motor running, the bastards—err, press—flocked around it like birds. Her driver, Dan, had not hesitated to give the paparazzi a bumping before.

"Kat!"

"Hey, Katrina! Over here!"

The voices were loud enough to drown out the faint sound of waves crashing a few blocks away. The salt breeze was still in the air, though. She could taste it, though she doubted anyone else could. It was kind of a bummer being surrounded by humans. They couldn't hear like she could, couldn't smell the things she could smell. This scent, for

7

example, made her long for the beach. Maybe she'd talk to Taggert and the other producers, see if they could set up some sort of private beach trip for her tomorrow after her *Vanity Fair* photoshoot. She'd had so many meetings lately, it'd be nice to just—

"KAT!" One voice thundered over the rest, snapping her head around and ruining her perfect poise. If she hadn't been wearing her glasses, she might have risked someone seeing exactly how displeased she was all the way up to the eyes. They were wrathful, she was sure, as she searched the crowd for the person who'd yelled so loud as to startle her. She took a breath, trying to let out the bad energy, and her eyes settled on the bastard who'd—

Oh.

Oh, shit. Not—

Oh, wait.

This could be good, after all.

Scott Byerly waved a hand from the edge of the crowd, a little sheepishly, his face flushed at the sudden attention his beyond-booming voice had gotten. Paparazzi were looking sideways at him, shaking their heads at the new guy as she stared straight at him.

"What is it?" Taggert asked, suddenly at her shoulder. "What's the matter?"

"Nothing," Kat said, a warm tingle replacing her surprise as she pondered the advantage, the nice little gift that had just been dropped in her lap like a free Prada purse. She raised her voice, knowing that her camera man, Wayne, had just gotten close enough to get a good angle on her, and that Mike, the sound guy, had his boom microphone hanging overhead to capture her and Taggert's conversation until they could put field mics on them again. She raised her voice so that it could be captured for the show, for her fans—

For ratings.

"It's my ex," she said, trying to put a little horror into the way she said it. "He must be following me."

2.

Sienna

November in Minneapolis was a crappy time to wear a dress, and yet here I was. It was the first week of November, and I was wearing a dress in downtown Minneapolis, freezing my freaking buns off even after having been inside for ten minutes. It was enough to make me want to light off a Gavrikov in the room, but that would have set fire to the spotless white table cloth in front of me, the soft-backed chair under my rump, the classy carpeting beneath my flats— I don't do heels—and probably, eventually, make its way across the table in this all-too-fancy restaurant and light my date on fire.

It would have been nothing but an improvement, I assure you.

My date's name was Ricardo, but he did not appear to be Latin in any way. I know looks can sometimes be deceiving, but his last name was Smith. I think. Actually, I'm not really sure. Maybe he'd said it when he'd introduced himself, but I was already pretty underwhelmed by that point and might have been actively tuning him out. Why? you ask.

I'm glad you asked.

This whole thing was an internet dating setup. Bowing to pressure from some quarters (Ariadne, Reed, Ariadne, Augustus, Ariadne, Dr. Zollers, oh, and did I mention

9

Ariadne?) I had decided to start dating again. It had been a while, after all. Like, years, since I'd last had a boyfriend. "I'm fine," I told them. "I'm a modern liberated woman, who doesn't need a man," I said. Also, it's not like I'd been super lonely or anything. I had my career, I had—well, I didn't have a dog anymore because he'd turned out to be a spy for my enemies shifted into canine form, but I had a new TV! And that was better.

Also, Ariadne was still rooming at my house. Presumably because she felt sorry for me. I had been really nice, too, not bothering to point out that she was like 2.5x my age and heading toward old maidhood *muy rapido*, as Ricardo's non-existent Latin forbears would have said. Is that racist? Why would it be? This dude was whiter than Hollywood director meetings.

Anyway, I was sitting in the fanciest seafood restaurant in Minneapolis across from a douche named Ricardo (just ditch the "o" and add an "h" so you can become the Dick that your name and nature compel you to be, guy), only half paying attention to the menu and wondering how long I'd have to be there.

Oh, I haven't told you why he's a douche yet, have I? My bad.

I arrived at the restaurant early, because that's the classy thing to do. Richard-o showed up fifteen minutes late, and when he introduced himself, he gave me the once over, plainly checking out my ass in this dress (it looks good, dammit) and made a hmmph-ing noise of disapproval.

Also, he'd already tried to order my drink for me, even though I was sitting right in front of him and possessed of all my speech capabilities at the time.

This is why I don't date. Also, because I can consume the souls of my fellow human beings with only the touch of my skin on theirs.

But mostly because of this. And because these sorts of dates make me want to consume the vapid, lightweight souls of dudes like Dick-o here like crackerjacks right out of the gym-toned bodies that hold them.

The waitress, a lovely young lady named Wendy, who wore a shining name badge on her spotless white outfit with sharply creased black pants, meandered over for the third time with our drinks perched on a plate. I eyed them hungrily and she gave me a tight smile. She'd been standing between us at the round table when Dick (let's just drop the pretense that he should be called anything else) had made his bold gambit of telling me what I wanted to drink, and she'd shot me a "Can you believe this guy?" look of solidarity.

Can you believe this guy? No. No, I can't.

"Oh, good," Dick said as Wendy positioned herself once more between us at this itty-bitty little table in the middle of the room. The dining room was pretty packed, all done up with neon blue tones. I half expected them to pull back a curtain at the back of the restaurant to reveal an aquarium where they harvested the fish we were going to be eating. "I think I'm almost ready."

Wendy smiled at me, clearly trying to lead Dick out of rudeness against his natural instincts. "And are you ready to order, ma'am, or do you need a few more minutes?"

"I am well prepared to order," I said, putting the one-page menu down. "In fact, the sooner, the better. Maybe we can even skip the appetizers and soups and just get right to the main event." So we can get the hell out of here as quickly as politeness allows me to.

I know, I know. Why am *I* bothering to be polite?

Because I promised I would, of course. Duh. It's one of the therapy things that Dr. Zollers had me working on, and I could already see the disappointed gleam in Ariadne's eyes if I came home before nine. She'd treat it like a personal affront, maybe even see it as an insult, since she'd been the one to help me pick out this particular Dick. I don't know why she'd take it so personally, she doesn't even like d—

Uhh, never mind. She'd taken over my mom's room, and

11

I was beginning to fear she'd picked up some of the passive-aggressive (mostly aggressive) qualities of its previous occupant.

"Question," Dick said, still staring at the menu. He'd yet to actually acknowledge Wendy's arrival with eye contact, like, you know, a human being would. "Is this lobster locally sourced?"

Wendy blinked away her surprise very quickly. "Uhm, no," she said, and it sounded a little strained, like she was trying to hold in some laughter. "It's freshly caught Maine Lobster. Just flown in this morning."

"Hmm," Dick said, staring at the menu as though it held the secrets of life. "Is it ethically raised?"

That raised my eyebrows, and Wendy's as well. "Ah, well," she said, recovering admirably quickly, "it's fresh, so it was raised in the ocean until it was caught, and then kept alive in a tank in the back—"

"Yeah, but is it ethically treated?" Dick asked, finally looking up to fix poor Wendy with a very serious look that I couldn't take seriously. Was this Dick actually trying to act like he had some sort of conscience? Because thus far, I had him figured for a psychopath. Having known a few in my time *cough cough* Wolfe and Bjorn *cough cough*—

Hey, Wolfe said in my mind.

Guilty, Bjorn said, clearly cool with my diagnosis, maybe even proud of it.

—I felt qualified to at least hazard a guess in Dick's case.

"Well," Wendy said, a smile plastered on her face that reminded me of the way Jackie, my agency's press secretary, looked on camera right before she was about to lose her shit on national television, "once you order one, we're going to drop it, still living, into a pot of boiling water while it screams in pain until it dies, and then once it's cooked, we're going to bring it out and you're going to crack open its shell and eat its muscles, so ... not sure you'd consider that ethical, but ..."

"Mmhmm," Dick said, nodding seriously. Definite

psychopath. "Hm. What about—"

"Okay," I said, dropping my menu on the table. "I have to go to powder my nose." Which was possibly a euphemism for commit suicide in the most painful way possible. Wait, second-most painful. This date was pretty much first-most painful at this point.

"You're not even wearing any makeup," Dick said with a sneer.

There was a slight gasp from Wendy, who grimaced but quickly caught herself, covering her mouth to hide her surprise and giving me a sympathetic look. "I was being polite," I said, barely hanging on to my civility. Think of poor Ariadne, and how devastated she would be if I come home early and with a sad story about disemboweling my date with my bare hands. She'd look at my bloody dress and the smile of satisfaction on my face, and she'd be so disappointed. "I need to take a giant, massive steaming dump and deliver it to the toilet." *And his name is Ricard-o,* I did not add but seriously wanted to. I shot Wendy a look. "Would you mind telling me where the restroom is?"

"I'll show you the way," Wendy said, trying hard to hide a smile as she gestured toward the bar. With deft fingers she picked up my drink and set it on her tray, beckoning me away from the king of all jackasses.

"Thank you," I said, brushing past Dick with Wendy trailing in my wake.

"I'll just wait here, then, I guess," Dick said, spitting sarcasm. "Starving to death or something."

"I think that'd be the ethical thing to do," I muttered under my breath, loud enough for Wendy to hear me as we headed toward the bar. I heard her snicker as we snaked through the crowd of tables toward it, a giant, polished, warm wood contraption that stretched from one end of the room to the other. It was filled to the max, and I could see a corridor beyond, likely the entry to the kitchen, the bathrooms, or both.

"Do you actually need to go?" Wendy asked, handing over my drink, some kind of fruity, delicious-smelling thing.

"Nope," I said, guzzling the sugary, boozy excellence in one gulp. "Gonna need a few more of these if I'm going to go back over there, though."

She made a face. "Why would you even think about going back over there?"

"Guilt," I said. "Not for him. For my, uh, mom-figure."

"Mom guilt is a powerful thing," Wendy said with a bob of her head as she sidled up to the end of the bar with me in tow. "Blanchard," she said, catching the attention of a dark-haired guy behind the bar. "I've got a lady here who needs another." She took my glass carefully from between my fingers and waggled at him.

Blanchard made his way over, his face a little pale. "Did you see what's going on right now?" He chucked a thumb at a small TV behind the bar that was tuned to one of those cable news networks. It was subtly hidden in the décor, a nice little diversion for the crowd at the bar that maybe wanted to enjoy their drink without conversation. I could sympathize.

"What's going on?" I asked, trying to hone in on what was being said; I couldn't quite get it over the roar of a thousand conversations in the bar.

"A plane's about to crash in Milwaukee. They lost their pilot and co-pilot and they're about to run out of fuel." He glanced at me and did a double take. "Hey, aren't you—"

"Is there an exit back there?" I asked Wendy, almost breathless. She nodded, and I was off in a flash, my dress fluttering in the wind as I blew through the back door and out into the frigid Minnesota night.

Dammit. I forgot my coat.

3.

Scott Byerly

The promise of the beach was beckoning to Scott Byerly—salt air, warm sands, a pleasant breeze across the crowded ocean shore. He'd gotten a glimpse of it on the way to his meeting, and the waters had called to him, but he'd done the right thing and gone to the meeting, trying his best not to think of how it'd feel to put his toes in the water and walk on the sand once he was done.

The LA heat was a little much for him, but the crowd he'd seen just outside of his very own meeting—the reason he'd even come to Los Angeles in the first place—had been a weird thing for a Minneapolis native to behold.

"What the hell is that?" Scott had asked Buchanan Brock, a tall, powerfully built man in his fifties. Brock was a man looking to do business with Scott's father, and so he'd been asked to take the meeting. After an hour and a half of pleasantries, he felt like he'd gotten a little swept up in Brock's charm.

"This is Hollywood, son," Brock said, his deep voice laced with some amusement. "Probably some starlet or another." He'd nodded his head when the crowd went into a buzz. They'd been standing just outside Brock's office; his host had walked him all the way out when the meeting was done, engaging him pleasantly the whole way. "Looks like it's

15

that one girl, the new meta one that everyone's talking about." His tall forehead wrinkled. "Say, don't you know her …?"

Scott had lost focus as soon as he'd laid eyes on Kat. *How long has it been since I've even seen her in person? Probably right after the—after … well, Sovereign …*

His feet had carried him, unexpectedly, toward the crowd of paparazzi and flashing cameras. His senses had compelled him in the other direction, toward the beach, toward water—this whole town felt dry as a desert gulch. Normally he could pull water out of air like a magician with a rabbit and a hat. It was an uncomfortable sensation, akin to mid-winter in Minnesota, when the air was this dry. It was like being buried up to his neck in sand, and he was just dying to loosen the tie he'd worn into his meeting with Brock, maybe leave it aside as he dipped toes in the ocean.

Instead, he found himself pulled toward Kat, crossing between a shining, gleaming, glass-fronted building and a black SUV looming just at the edge of the crowd of paparazzi. He watched her graceful crossing; she was moving slowly, though, way slower than she needed to. She was walking funny, too, and it took him a second to realize she was posing for the cameras, her face frozen in a look he couldn't recall seeing on her face at any point in their relationship.

Not that she remembers our relationship, he thought with more than a little bitterness, the reflected glare of the sun off the front of the office building nearly blinding him.

He didn't quite realize what he was doing when he yelled out, "KAT!" at the top of his lungs, booming and heavy enough to jar her out of her artificially posed walk. She missed a step in surprise and looked at him through giant sunglasses that covered her below her cheekbones. Her forehead looked … puffier? *What the hell …? Did she Botox? She's a meta … we don't age like normal people … what the …?*

She whispered in the ear of another man who came up to

her side, loud enough he could almost hear her even over the crowd of paparazzi, loud enough that he realized she was playing to the boom microphone that had been swung over her head like a branch with mistletoe at Christmas.

Kat made her way through the crowd and the paparazzi moved aside for her two mountainous bodyguards. They cut a path through at the behest of the guy who she'd been talking to. He locked eyes with the older man and caught a surprisingly buoyant smile from the fellow, who followed a few paces behind Kat with another woman in his wake. Scott took in the little entourage with a glance and landed back on that guy again. He looked … amused? Pleased? Something uncomfortable that was causing some smile lines to crease up the side of his acne-scarred face.

"Scott," Kat said as her two bodyguards shoved a photographer out of the way to make room for her to stand about a foot from him. The boom mic that followed her swung down perilously, so close that Scott wondered if he needed to duck his head. A man with a shoulder-mounted video camera pushed his way up to film them, perfectly positioned about ten feet away, putting them in the middle of the frame. Scott gave him a look, a very distinct *What the f—?* sort of look of combined horror and disgust. "What are you doing here?" she asked, sounding like she was a little horrified herself.

"Uhm, I had a meeting over there," Scott said, pointing his finger over his shoulder. He looked for Buchanan Brock, figured maybe the man would back up his story, but he was gone, probably back into his office and out of the damned dry heat.

"Really," Kat said, making clear she was not exactly convinced.

"It's been a while," Scott said, feeling more than a little on-the-spot and painfully aware that the camera and microphone combo were recording this awkward and uncomfortable interaction for broadcast to … well, the entire

17

world, really. *All eyes on you and the only thing you can come up with is that?* He stopped short of smacking himself in the forehead.

"It has," Kat said, looking more than a little tense. "I'm a little surprised to see you in LA."

He frowned. "Because?"

"It's not really your sort of scene," she said airily, still hiding behind those dark glasses. Her voice sounded strange, more stilted than he could recall it ever being before.

"Well, I'm only in town for a couple days—the meeting, maybe some lounging by the seashore," Scott said, feeling his discomfort rising but trying desperately to get it under control. *Remember, she doesn't recall any of our history. Not a thing.* Yep, this was just as uncomfortable as he'd recalled it being every other time he'd tried to talk with her before the war had ended. "I'll be gone before you know it," he said, wishing that moment were here now.

"I heard you and Sienna were hanging out again," Kat said, a little softer.

Scott let out a slow breath. "I helped her and Reed a couple months ago, yeah." His mind flitted through possibilities associated with that question.

"Are you two dating?" Kat asked, coolly.

"What?" Scott stifled a laugh. "No. We didn't—"

"Uh huh," Kat said, making a face that played directly to the camera without her once looking at it. *What the ...?* Scott thought for the dozenth time in the last few minutes.

"Need to wrap this up," the sun-glazed guy lurking behind her said quietly enough that Scott barely heard it over the crowd noise. The flashes of cameras in his peripheral vision were blinding. Wasn't it the middle of the day? "Can you get an angry confrontation out of this?"

"What?" Scott looked at the guy, aghast. "'Angry confrontation'?"

"Oh, that's right, he's a meta," the guy said.

"This is Scott Byerly," Kat said, her voice loud and

staged. "He thinks we dated once upon a time."

"Because we did," Scott said hotly.

"Yeah. Okay," Kat said, swallowing visibly. "There's no need to get violent."

"I'm not—what?" Scott's facade of control degenerated. "I'm not violent. What are you talking about?"

"That's good," Taggert said, whispering softly. Scott anchored his gaze on the man's acne-scarred face. "Just ignore me," Taggert said to him, just out of view of the camera that was fixed on Scott and Kat. "Pretend I'm not here."

"If only I could," Scott snapped. "Kat, what the hell is this?"

"I asked you to stop stalking me," Kat said, voice in a low quiver. The flashes of bulbs, the click of cameras were blinding lights to Scott, but he held his eyes painfully open as his jaw dropped. "I know you've got powerful connections, and I'm a just a girl who—"

"What the actual—?" Scott let his head slump in disbelief and disgust. "I'm not *stalking* you. I saw you, and I thought I'd say hello—"

"You've made up all these details of a relationship that never happened," Kat said, shuddering slightly on camera. She adjusted her sunglasses and wiped a single tear off her cheek—her right cheek, perfectly positioned where it would be in frame.

Scott felt himself hit hard boil and his fists clenched. "You gotta be kidding me."

"You don't need to be so abusive," Kat said, taking a step back, her voice quivering.

"Abu-WHAT?" Scott boggled. "This is the first time I've seen you in years!"

"I know you've been following me," Kat said.

"I've been in Minnesota!" Scott sputtered. "It's hard to follow you from Minnesota, unless you count watching the occasional interview, or your TV show—"

"You're stalking me," she said quietly, and her bodyguards closed ranks, positioning their enormous frames between her and Scott. "You're unhinged, Scott, and this has to stop. All these things you remember about our supposed relationship—they're all in your head."

"Uh, no," Scott said, "they're just not in yours, unfortunately, because of your powers draining your memory—"

"You need professional help," Kat shouted from between the two towering bodyguards as they protectively shuffled her away. "You need to talk to a psychiatrist, Scott!" Her voice was all insipid concern, so filled with worry. "You can't keep living like thi—"

A spatter of blood hit her sun-glowing white blazer and drenched her tastefully exposed, bronzed upper chest. The dark crimson was like ink on her browned skin, barely visible between the linebackers who protected her from Scott.

"What the—" he mouthed, and then another splatter of crimson liquid bathed her blond hair, running down the side of her face in beads as her own mouth dropped in surprise. A little blood hit her exposed, bleached teeth.

Her bodyguards fell, leaving Kat exposed between the two of their corpses. Wounds gaped on their sides, holes a few inches wide. A tall, lanky man stood next to Kat. He was pale as snow but freckled, and he had long red hair and a ragged beard that stretched down the middle of his chest. He grabbed Kat by the wrist, fingers sinking into her golden skin and squeezing, hints of white showing around the edges of his fingers as he squeezed and then shook her. She flapped like a paper being waved, dragged by his superior strength as she stared at him in stunned horror.

"Do you know what you do to people?" the man shouted, right in her face, his voice thin and ragged as he was, in danger of breaking. He had sunken eyes, a skeletal, malnourished look. He looked a little like a ginger skeleton, some sort of vagrant who had wandered in from somewhere far up north. Kat's horrified gaze was locked on her bodyguards' fallen forms, blood rushing out of the wounds in their ribcages where something had torn through them. "Do you have any idea?" the man asked with a steadily rising voice. "Do you know?" He sounded deranged, furious, and then Scott noticed the phone clenched in his other hand, the camera pointed right at Kat's horrified face, capturing her emotions with its glass eyes glinting in the California sun. "You kill them," he said, shoving her roughly to one knee and letting her loose as he raised a hand high to strike at her in the same way he'd struck at her bodyguards, his phone still aimed at her, the crowd breathless and still at the spectacle playing out before their very eyes. "And I'm gonna show the world what it looks like when it happens to you—"

4.

Midwest Airlines Flight 404
Milwaukee, Wisconsin

Tara Garcia had been on planes most of the day, starting her morning in New York City with a quick run to Orlando that took off at local 8 a.m. and now finishing her last flight from Chicago to Milwaukee now, local time 9:06 p.m. Midwest Airlines was a mostly regional carrier that had been expanding rapidly the last few years thanks to rock bottom prices. She'd signed on as a flight attendant eighteen months earlier and found it to be mostly enjoyable. There were always a few assholes on any given day, but she'd worked retail before this during the holiday season, and so dealing with only one or two a-holes at a time was a refreshing break given her prior experience.

On the other hand, Tara had never really felt as imperiled working retail as she felt right now, sitting in the co-pilot's seat on this DC-9 that was just about empty of fuel.

"Shit shit shit," the man in the pilot's seat said. His name was Neil Ericson, he looked about mid-forties, and she'd just met him for the first time two hours earlier, under less-than-ideal conditions. He was fighting fatigue and stress of a sort she was feeling more than a little of herself. It had been just that sort of stress that had caused Captain Michael Donowitz to have a heart attack, slipping into unconsciousness about

22

fifteen minutes before their scheduled landing.

Of course, it might also have been slightly aggravated by having the co-pilot, Jason Treadway, pass out into a state of unconsciousness so complete that they'd had to summon a doctor from the passenger section into the cockpit. Captain Donowitz had looked a little white before that, but watching his co-pilot, a man in his early thirties, dragged insensate out of his seat had seemed to push the captain a little more. When he'd gone down just a few minutes later, Tara hadn't panicked exactly. She hadn't had time to. Instead, she'd calmly gone to the back and asked if anyone had had flying lessons, stepping over the unconscious bodies of both pilot and co-pilot to do so. Now this Neil Ericson was now at the controls, a man who had taken three flying lessons some *six years ago* ... was the best-qualified person to sit in the captain's chair. When they'd realized the autolanding systems were not functioning properly only a few minutes later, that was when the first icy tingles of panic had started running down Tara's back.

Since then, Tara had had almost two whole hours of watching the fuel gauge steadily sink to work herself into a complete panic, but she had not ever reached it. She talked low and calmly to Milwaukee tower in the exact same way she'd heard the pilot do on the occasions she'd been in the cockpit, not letting a hint of the panic she should have been feeling creep into her voice.

"Milwaukee tower," she said cheerfully, as if she was putting on her best customer service voice when dealing with one of those inevitable a-holes that seemed to find themselves in her side of the plane, "this is Midwest 404. We are pretty much out of fuel and are going to have to try a landing soon." She looked at Neil Ericson laboring at the controls and wondered if he was going to suffer a heart attack as well. She didn't rule it out, based on the pasty look on the man's face.

There was a pause before Milwaukee tower responded.

"Understood, Midwest 404. We have you on vector—what the hell was—" There was a crackle of static. "Midwest 404, are you still there?"

Tara felt a chill run down her skin as she looked at Neil over in the pilot's seat. The man looked stricken. It was getting to be a usual sensation for both of them. "Why wouldn't we be, tower?"

"Uh, sorry, Midwest 404 … saw a blip on radar moving toward you fast, thought maybe—never mind. We have you at five thousand feet, ten miles out, but your approach to runway one-zero-niner is a little off. Could you adjust and try again?"

The frustration mingled with fear in Tara's throat. They'd been trying for an hour now to line up properly, and Ericson couldn't quite get the plane to do what he needed it to. "We'll try, tower, but—"

THUMP.

"JESUS!" Ericson shouted, coming to his feet before he hit his head on the roof of the cockpit and slammed back down into his seat. Tara lunged for the co-pilot controls to steady the plane as Ericson came back down in his seat clutching his head, blood running down from beneath his hairline.

"What is it?" Tara asked, wrestling hard against the controls. Disengaging the autopilot had been the start of the downward spiral. If you didn't count the pilot having a heart attack or the first officer passing out.

"Look!" Ericson said, his voice ten octaves higher than it had been even when it was panic soaked and exhausted a moment earlier. His finger pointed at the window, which Tara hadn't looked out of for some time, since she was trying to talk with tower and make sense of the instrument panel in case of—

Holy hell.

There were two faces pressed against the front window, perched there like they'd been suction-cupped on like a

24

Garfield cat on a minivan. Both female, both of them with hair blowing ridiculously hard in the wind. One of them, the terrified-looking one, wore the shoulder boards of a pilot, its golden tassels the same color as her hair. She was mouthing the words that Tara herself had been saying only recently, but inside her head.

Oh shit oh shit oh shit oh please please please—

The other looked calm and slapped a hand against the front window as her dark hair blew around her. "Is that …?" Tara blinked, staring out into the darkness above the Milwaukee skyline. "… Sienna Nealon?"

"I think so?" Neil Ericson sounded like he'd fully crapped himself at last. He was just not up to the strain he'd been put under. "And is that a … who is that with her?"

"It's a pilot," Tara said, the first breath of hope coming into her lungs.

"Open … the … door," Sienna Nealon said, rapping on the thick glass of the windshield, her voice inaudible.

Tara jumped out of her seat and headed for the first exit she could find. paused, feeling scared witless, about to do something she'd never had to do before—

Open the hatch mid-flight, five thousand feet above the world below—and save her plane from certain destruction.

I will never fly again, Tara thought as she unlocked the hatch but did not open it, instead moving back and anchoring herself in the hallway. *I will take the damned bus, even if I need to travel from Seattle to Miami. That European vacation I wanted to take? Hell, they make cruise ships for that.*

The hatch opened and the breeze blew hard into the cabin, not enough altitude difference to depressurize at this point. The lady captain was heaved in first, and Sienna Nealon came in second, wearing a dress barely hanging on by two shoulder straps.

Sienna grabbed the hatch and pulled it hard, ripping it shut against the wind resistance. Tara rushed forward to help her lock it back into place, looking breathlessly at the woman who looked like she was dressed for a fancy dinner out rather than a bit of superheroism.

"Sorry I'm late," Sienna yelled, adjusting her voice, looking a little shocked at how loud it came out. Tara could sympathize; the wind blowing as she'd come into the cabin had been deafening. "Dave Grohl wasn't available," Sienna went on, sounding surprisingly relaxed given the circumstances, "so I hope this nice, scared lady captain will land the plane well enough for you."

"Oh shit, oh shit," the captain said, getting back to her feet. Her blond hair was blown back behind her shoulders. "When you said you needed help landing a plane, I thought you meant a Cessna—and that I'd do it from a nice, warm tower somewhere …"

"Yeah, no hero points for that," Sienna said casually, unflappable. Her eyes fell on Tara. "I don't know if she's going to be able to find the cockpit in her current condition; you mind showing her the way?"

"I know where the damned cockpit is," the blond pilot groused, making her way forward on the DC-9. "Get everyone ready for landing. Crosscheck and all-call." She disappeared down the hall and slammed the door to the cockpit. Tara heard muffled swearing from beyond it before swiveling back to Sienna Nealon.

"You just saved everyone on this plane," Tara said, looking at her in awe.

"Yeah, well, we're not on the ground yet," Sienna said, adjusting the straps on her dress uncomfortably as she peeked around into the first-class section. "Got any extra seats or am I standing for landing?"

"Uhm …" Tara said, thinking quickly. "You can sit up front with me. The, uh, captain and co-pilot are both strapped in in first class, the last two empty seats we had before—"

"Yeah, yeah," Sienna said, eyeing the jump seats next to the door. "Okay, then. Gives me an easy exit if I have to jump out and guide the plane down anyway."

"Uh ... in that?" Tara asked, pointing at the dress. It looked nice, like maybe she'd been out for the evening, but it didn't go so well with the hair, which was windblown, to say the least.

"I could do it naked, I guess," Sienna said, "I'm getting kinda used to that at this point, unfortunately—"

"Can I get you anything?" Tara asked as the plane swept wide around, under professional control feeling once more like it was—well, like it was under control.

"I could use a drink," Sienna said, settling back into the first seat with a thud. "It's been a day—or actually, a night."

"That makes two of us," Tara said and grabbed a half dozen of the little bottles out of the storage case, using her skirt to hold them like a parachute as she made her way over to strap herself in for landing, handing the other woman three to start with and watching her chug them lightning fast. "That makes two of us."

5.

Kat
Los Angeles

The red-haired homeless-looking guy had come out of nowhere and killed both the Bruces so fast that she hadn't seen anything but a flash of blood as it sprayed across her white suit. Kat Forrest had seen death—up close and personal, in ways that most people couldn't even imagine, so when the red-haired guy grabbed her by the wrist and twisted it down, her first instinct wasn't to just go along with it. He had a good grip, though, and locked her in place until he could throw her down.

She hit the pavement hard, went sprawling, heard him say something about showing the world what she was, but Kat was too busy trying to not die to pay much attention. Though she might not have anyway, because the dude was a creepy bum with unwashed hair and—let's face it—some B.O. like he'd come straight out of Topanga Canyon. Kat rolled hard, her meta strength carrying her away as the bum's hand descended to the pavement—

And passed right through it like it wasn't even there.

Kat rolled and spun back to her feet, not nearly as gracefully as Sienna would have, but enough to get the job done. The redhead looked up in surprise at her fast motion, blinking away his surprise with dark eyes.

A concentrated spray of water hit him in the side of the face, stunning him for a second. Then his washed-out features suddenly took on an even more washed-out look, like smoke dissipating in the wind as Scott's attack went right through his face, a stream of liquid that tapered off quickly.

Kat shot a look at Scott, his finger extended, the water blast he'd directed at the redhead dropping off to the intensity of a water pistol. "Why are you stopping?" she asked.

"There's a drought," Scott said. "I can't pull water out of the air when there's no water in the air—"

"You're all scheming against me!" The redhead erupted, causing Kat to take a few more steps back. His hair fell in front of his eyes, still ragged and disheveled, though now a little damp from the squirting Scott had given him.

"Dude, I don't even know who you are," Scott said.

"Neither do I," Kat said, holding up both her hands, her Fiji water bottle still clenched tightly in one of them. "I've never even seen you before in my life—"

"Of course you don't know me," he said, his face twitching. "You don't even notice the little people as you step on them, do you? You're just like the others—"

"Other whats?" Scott asked, holding his own hands up now, matching her non-offensive posture. "Metahuman reality TV stars? Because there are very, very few of those, pretty much just the one right now—"

"Leeches," the redhead pronounced, brushing shaggy, stray hairs out of his eyes with a hand. He blew out of his lips, stirring the wild mustache on his upper lip. "That's what you are."

"Listen, Red Lebowski," Scott said, "I don't know what she's done to offend you, but I'm sure it was really bad—"

"I didn't do anything—" Kat protested.

"You just tried to frame me as your stalker," Scott said, glancing sideways. Kat followed his gaze. The cameraman was there, filming, Mike the sound guy had his boom mic extended toward them, catching the whole exchange.

This was going to be great TV. Ratings gold.

If she survived.

"I don't know what you're talking about," she said, shrugging at the camera since she'd already broken the fourth wall without thinking about it. It was a crisis; these things were understandable. She'd just had some crazy man jump out and assault her, after all.

"You know what, angry ginger homeless guy?" Scott said, exasperated. "Whatever she's done to you, you can't have her."

"That's really not very nice," Kat said.

"Which part?" Scott snapped. "Angry, ginger or homeless?"

"The part where you just act like you can decide what I get to do, like I'm property or some kind of gift you'd deign to hand out—"

"You're the worst gift I could imagine giving, like a whoopee cushion filled with nerve gas or—"

"SHUT UP!" the redhead screamed. "SHUT UP SHUT UP SHUT UP!" He shook in the middle of the street like he was about to explode. He extended a finger right at Kat. "I'm telling you this now—you live your life in the spotlight, sucking dry every dramatic bone you can get your grubby hands on—"

Scott frowned at her. "Is this metaphorical or is he talking about—"

"I'M SPEAKING NOW!" the redhead exploded again, jabbing his finger in her direction again. "You live in the spotlight, you'll die in the spotlight—and no one—not your manager," he gestured to Taggert, who was trying his hardest to blend into the crowd of paparazzi next to the SUV, "not your little friend with his little squirtgun action—" He waved at Scott.

"Usually it's a powerful torrent, okay?" Scott said, annoyed. "It's not my fault you people live in the middle of the damned desert."

"—none of your little friends can save you," the man said, shaking with rage. "You're going to die, and the world is going to watch it happen." He waved a hand at her again and then sprinted off in the other direction, passing through the crowd like he was made of smoke itself, people gasping as he ghosted his way through them.

"Holy hell," Taggert said, stepping back up now, his eyes locked on the place where the redhead disappeared into the crowd.

"Kat," Scott said, easing over to her, cautious. "You okay?"

"Tell me we got that." Taggert tossed a look at the cameraman, who gave him a nod before receiving a thumbs up. Taggert grinned. "We got it."

"Your bodyguards are dead," Scott said, wide-eyed, kneeling down next to one of the Bruces. "That guy just killed them—and he said he's going to kill you."

Kat blinked, not sure what to say. There was a faint screaming sensation somewhere in her throat, clawing to get out.

"Kitten, baby," Taggert said, still grinning, "this is ratings diamonds. You'll go up by—"

"Are you kidding me?" Scott stood up. "Kat! Wake up! Your life is in danger. That guy can pass through people, probably through walls—he just ripped your bodyguards' hearts out." He put both hands on her thin shoulders and shook her. She locked her eyes on him, the faint memory of the Bruces' dying gasps echoing somewhere inside her head. "He's going to kill you."

"You can't stop him, can you?" Kat asked faintly, her voice coming back at last. She blinked at him, suddenly acutely aware that her glasses were gone. She felt as brittle as she realized, dimly, that she needed to feel. No awards for this, but it wasn't really hard at the moment, either …

Scott looked in the direction the redhead had run, shaking

31

his head. "Not me alone, no." He held up a hand and it spritzed faintly, causing her to jerk away from him. "I think you know who you need to call."

"No," Kat said, staring into space. "You think she'd come?"

"Your life is in danger," Scott said, looking a little torn himself. "Yeah. I think she would. Old loyalties and all that."

"I can see it now," Taggert said behind her, voice low, the paparazzi closing in and shouting questions she couldn't hear over the sound of silence in her head. "'Special Guest Star—Sienna Ne—"

"ARE YOU KIDDING ME?" Scott bellowed.

Kat for her part, just kept staring, trying to feel the look on her face, and knowing that however it looked, it wasn't composed, it wasn't produced, it wasn't stage-managed. It was the horror of knowing that someone out there wanted to kill her, truly and immediately—and that the only person who might be able to stop them was someone who probably never wanted to so much as hear from her ever again.

6.

I breezed back in through the back exit of the restaurant, my hair a FEMA-certified disaster area, smoothing my dress as I went. I was a little fuzzy on how long I'd been gone. I mean, I'd flown straight to Milwaukee at supersonic speed, but I'd had to stop and retrieve my dress the first time it blew off, then I'd had to find the captain, which basically entailed pissing off airport security by overflying their security checkpoints and finding someone dressed like a pilot, then I had to zoom up to find the actual plane—that one was easy, it was the one circling the airport, looking like a drunken monkey was at the helm. Then I had to get on board, yadda yadda yadda, and then I got drunk with that really cool flight attendant.

Now, however many minutes later, I was staggering back into the rear door of one of the classiest seafood places in Minneapolis, walking unsteadily on my flats, which I'd conveniently left just outside the exit (who needs shoes when they're flying?), and I found Wendy just about where I'd left her at the bar.

"Hey," I chirruped, a little sing-songy.

"Oh," Wendy said, eyes widening, "you came back. Wow."

33

"Yeah," I said, motioning to Branch or whatever his name was behind the bar. "I need another."

"Are you sure?" he asked, looking me over. "You, uh … don't look, uh …"

"She'll have another," Wendy said smoothly, saving the bartender from a drunken punch to the face. "Your date's, uhm … still here."

"Really?" I giggled. "I'm so surprised. Why?"

"I don't know," she said with a little amusement, "I've been kind of … avoiding him. I expect that'll affect my tip, but I'm finding it really, really hard to care."

"God, I'm starving," I said, straightening my dress—probably futilely—for about the ten thousandth time. It flew off again on the way back to Minneapolis, did you know that? And one of the straps was torn, so my bra was showing. The first person who designed a clothing line for unplanned supersonic flight was going to get all my clothing-budget dollars, I can tell you that. I could talk to NASA about it, maybe. "You think Dick will still buy me dinner?"

Wendy turned and I followed her gaze to where Dick-o was still sitting, his back to the bar, an empty glass in front of him. "Only one way to find out."

"Ugh, that involves going over and talking to him, doesn't it?" Bartender boy set another glass next to me on the bar. "Bottoms up, ladies." I raised it to Wendy and then—Blanchard! His name was Blanchard! Yes! I toasted them and drained it to the bottom of the martini glass. "Liquid courage." I stumbled toward Dick and his table in the middle of the damned restaurant, the showy bastard.

Dick's eyes widened when he caught sight of me, which was just about when I rounded the last turn and parked my ass in the chair. Wendy had to catch me, scooting it in behind me like the old-fashioned gentleman my date clearly was not. I was just about drunk enough to start calling him Dick-less—and to his face, no less. "I am so hungry," I pronounced, not lying at all.

"You were in the bathroom for a long time," Dick-less said, horrorstruck, his eyes fixed on my hair. "And ... what happened to your—"

"Listen, your personality is really working against you, here," I said to him, nodding at Wendy as she withdrew to the side of the table with her pad in hand. "So why don't you just shut up and order?"

"I don't have to deal with this," Dick-less said, warranting the removal of the 'less' from my official name for him. "You know I turned down dates with three other women to be here tonight with you." He stood up. "You look different than your profile picture, you know. It's like a lie."

I winked at him. "That's all right. Your profile didn't say you were a complete and utter prick, so I feel like we're even."

He froze, spine straight, face twisted. "What did you just say to me?"

"I said you're a dick, Dick." I glanced at Wendy. "I want a Halibut steak. Those are big, right?" She nodded uncomfortably, clearly not super enthused about being caught in the middle of our little spat. I looked back at Dick. "You gonna order, or am I eating by myself? Not that I'd complain at this point." His lips moved in outrage, trying to form words but coming up blank. "Try, 'Well, I never!'" I suggested helpfully.

"Well, I never—" he said, getting some traction finally. "No one has ever spoken to me in such a way—"

"Your mom should have when you were a little Dick, maybe you wouldn't be such a big Dick now."

His eyes flared at that and he scooped up his coat, knocking his chair over in the process as he sped toward the exit without looking back.

I glanced at Wendy and shrugged. "Something I said?"

"I'll get your order in right away if you still want it," Wendy said, the corner of her mouth twisting up.

"Hell yeah, I still want it," I said, "I just flew to

Milwaukee and back, did you know that?" She nodded, looking a little blank or surprised or something. "It takes a lot out of me." I gestured at my broken shoulder strap. "You see this shit I have to deal with?" I motioned at Dick's empty chair. "And that."

"I'll get your order in right away," Wendy said, stopping to pick up the chair. "This one kinda makes you want to just give up on the species, doesn't it?"

"Best date I've had in months," I said as a buzzing came from somewhere under the table. My phone! I fished for it, apparently lying on the ground where I'd left it. I looked at the lit-up nameplate and my heart sank.

"Wendy," I said, catching her as she started to walk away, jerking her head back around. "I need another drink. Maybe two." She nodded, and I slid the screen to answer. "Hey, Scott ..." I said, as gently as I could.

But what I was thinking was much along the same lines as Wendy's thought: *Men ...*

7.

Karl Nash

Karl walked in the darkness, ignoring the quiet sounds, the rumbling in the distance. He passed through walls on his way to his destination as easily as if they were not there. He could see well enough to move along, his footsteps echoing in the quiet. Being alone in the dark didn't bother him anymore. Once, it had been the worst thing he could imagine, but the trial he'd been through had sorted that out for him quicker than anything else he could have imagined.

He listened for a moment and heard a rattling, shaking noise in the distance. He smiled. It was a more pleasant noise than stark silence, reassuring in its way. He could smell the mustiness of still, uncirculated air, and he pressed on through it, stirring for the first time in probably quite a while.

He recognized his destination by the sight of the spray paint on the concrete wall. It was almost hidden next to long-ago water runoff stains, tingeing the white concrete a darker shade. Karl ran his fingers over the wall, felt the imperfections of the pour, the rough edge of it. He ran fingers through the knotted hair of his red beard and let out a long putrid breath.

"I saw what you did." The voice of his benefactor came out of the darkness behind him. Karl didn't whirl to face him; he was used to this by now. His backer liked playing the man of mystery. Karl just kept his hand on the wall, as though he could draw some strength from it. "It was note perfect, just what we discussed."

"It was ... fun," Karl said, remembering the sight of the bodyguards keeling over after he'd thrust his hand into their chests. It had been an easy thing, slipping in insubstantial and ripping their heart muscles out as he withdrew his fingers in solid form. He'd discovered his ability when he was a teenager, a thin, bullied young boy who couldn't find a friend with both hands and a flashlight. But once he'd found his power—found it and learned to use it—well, he'd had no shortage of friends.

Including the ones that got him into the trouble he'd had earlier this year.

"Well, I'm glad you had some fun," his backer said in a smooth voice, staying in the shadows. "No reason not to, after all. It's revenge; if it wasn't satisfying, what would be the point?"

"To show the world," Karl said, voice hard, anger welling up from within him. "To let the world see them for what they are—exploiters, plunderers of human capital."

"Well, of course they are," his backer said. "This is LA. That's what's done here."

"They just use people up and leave 'em in wreckage," Karl said, rubbing his hand against the concrete. "Don't even care what happens to them after."

"Cheaper to find a new someone to replace them," his backer agreed. "I think you did a fine job of making the promise, though. It'll give them some time to think before you come in and finish the job. Everything's running smooth in that direction, too—"

"Good," Karl said, pushing off the wall. He liked the sensation so much, he put his hand back on the concrete and pushed off again. The sense of resistance, of the firmness, of solid ground, immovable, was reassuring to him in a way that few things were anymore.

He wanted to take that sense away from Katrina Forrest. He wanted the world to see him do it, wanted to watch her scream and die while the entirety of the globe had their horrified eyes fixed, staring, on it, unable to look away.

Maybe then they'd see what she was—what all of them were.

And then, maybe finally, things would change. And even if they didn't … they'd certainly never forget him.

8.

Sienna

He couldn't be serious. That was the overriding thought bouncing around in my drunken mind as I came in for a landing on my back lawn. I could tell I was still slightly hammered because I ended up landing in a stagger-step and almost diving headfirst into the leafless bushes that Ariadne had planted a couple months ago to spruce up the backyard. Admittedly, before that, it had maybe been just a tad, uhm ... overgrown.

Hey, I've got more important things on my mind than landscaping for a house I wasn't even living in until two months ago.

I fumbled for my keys, searching my dress for pockets that weren't there before I broke out into an uncontrollable case of the giggles and remembered I'd left them behind. I knocked on the back door, thumping as lightly as I was capable of. The danger of meta strength was that sometimes you had replace even a steel door.

"Coming!" Ariadne's muffled voice came from somewhere inside. She unlocked the door and opened it a moment later, greeting me with a smile that told me that my cheeks were probably flushed with what looked like triumph but was actually booze. "How did it go?"

"Oh, yeah," I said, remembering why I'd originally gone

out in the first place. "It went well."

"Really?" Ariadne wasn't the sort to get excited enough to clap her hands together, but she nodded, which was like her stoic, Nordic version of that.

"Oh, yeah, it went great," I said, trying to decide when to drop the boom on her about how the actual date went versus the other parts, where I saved a plane and got hammered in two entirely different cities. "How did your night go?"

The first sign of clouds rolled in on her face. "It didn't go great, did it?"

"Why, have you been watching the news?"

She frowned. "No. Why? What did you do?"

"Oh, nothing."

"Sienna ..."

"I had to bail in the middle of the date to save a commuter flight. No big deal, okay?"

You could see the air just rush out of her like a balloon losing air. "This was supposed to be your night," she said, following me as I wandered through the kitchen as I took off my earring. One earring. Must have lost the other somewhere over Wisconsin. Enjoy that $0.37 boon when you find it in a pile of cow shit, dairy farmer.

"It turned out that my date was an asshole, but I partied with a flight attendant and my server at the restaurant, so it's all good," I said. "Also," I paused before dropping a bomb, "Scott called."

That stopped her in her tracks. Well, that or the counter, which she ran into with her left hip when she turned to look at me with eyes wide enough I could have shoved a saucer in her sockets. But I wouldn't do that because I don't have very many good dishes. "What?"

"Yeah, apparently Kat got attacked out in LA today," I said, suddenly beset by another inexplicable case of the giggles.

"Why would Scott call you about that?" Ariadne asked, rubbing herself where she'd slammed into the counter.

"I guess he was there or something? I dunno." My head was swaying gently under the effects of alcohol. Oh, Al Cohol, you should have been my only date tonight. I love you, Al. "I lost interest after hearing that Kat wanted me to come to the coast and defend her honor or something—"

"Wait, she wants your help?" Ariadne's frown became a full-blown dark hurricane on her face.

"I know, right?" I asked with some verve as I curled up in a ball on the couch. It just felt right. "Like … why would she call me after that last crap bomb she splattered me with?"

Ariadne's face darkened even further. I'd honestly expected a slightly more forgiving track from her; she'd always gotten on well with Kat, even though I hadn't. I think that last thing, though, where Kat had called me after the prison break incident and recorded our forty-minute phone call in which I talked about my feelings (I was exhausted, okay?) and got it shaved down to a two-minute exchange for her reality TV show that made me look like a psychopath, had probably been the straw that cracked even Ariadne's strong back. "Well, in fairness, she had Scott call you on her behalf, so …"

"Yeah, that was pretty chickenshit," I said, resting my chin on my bare knees. I tried to pull my dress up to cover them, but it was trapped under my butt. "Such a Kat thing to do."

"I wouldn't say Kat is chicken, exactly," Ariadne said, picking her way around the coffee table in the middle of the room to sit down in the chair to my left. "She's been in battle with you on more than a few occasions, and she never showed a sign of cowardice."

"Umm, except for that time she betrayed us," I said.

"There were other factors at work there. Janus and—"

"Ughhhhhh," I said, feeling nauseous and wondering if it was the drink or the thought of Kat and Janus that did it.

"So what are you going to do?" Ariadne asked.

"Probably puke my guts out if this nausea isn't a

temporary effect of thinking about Janus and Kat—"

"About Kat, I mean," Ariadne said.

"Ummm ..." Was this a trick question? "Watch her dangle helplessly, hoisted on her own justly deserved petard?"

"That's malignantly gleeful," Ariadne said, and I could tell she was judging me. Some from the tone, some from the look she was giving me. "I thought you were trying not to be like that anymore."

"I'm trying not to kill people as much," I said, squeezing my eyes closed as if I could shut this whole uncomfortable situation out and make it go away. "I make no promises about letting people who have screwed me over come to their own unfortunate, mostly natural ends."

"What if she dies?" Ariadne asked.

What if she dies? Aleksandr Gavrikov asked in my head, totes raining on my damned parade.

"That'd be a real shame, and I'll send a lovely bouquet of flowers to the funeral—"

"Sienna," Ariadne said, her head slumping back, her patience clearly at an end.

"A fruit basket would be more appropriate, you think?"

"Sienna!"

"Ariadne, she's not exactly the wind beneath my wings—more like the knife between my ribs," I said. "She made me look like shit in front of the whole world. I mean, it wasn't enough that Ma Clary and her merry band of assholes were trying to destroy me and then kill me—they got aided and abetted by someone who pretended to be a friend." This was all true. In fact, my reputation out in the world at large was such that I got spit on in public sometimes. True story.

At least, it happened once. I think word might have gotten out about what happened to that guy, though; he was still being fed through a tube according to the last court papers I got served with. I maintain that it was a real shame that he resisted arrest after that, but hey, what are you going to do? Spitting on officers of the law is a bad idea in addition to being illegal. Spitting on an officer of the law who can hit like a freight train feels like bad judgment on the level of trying to have a boxing match with a nuclear missile. The destruction is assured, but not mutual.

Wait. I guess that would be mutual, since the missile would blow up ... shit. Whatever, I'm drunk, and my metaphors are like gifts from Bacchus, okay? Shove your literal-minded disapproval.

"What if she dies?" Ariadne asked again, and this time I had no defense. "What if Scott dies, since he's there with her—"

Ugh. That was a valid point. I mean, Scott Byerly was a guy who had come to my aid thrice recently in spite of officially cutting ties with our agency years ago. He'd been the one who asked for my help, not Kat—

Oh, Klementina, Gavrikov whispered in my mind.

"Oh, shut up about your stupid sister, Gavrikov," I said, letting it spill out of my head. "I'll save her, all right?"

"Really?" Ariadne asked. She was used to me talking to the voices in my head by now, and brushed it off like a champ, though I'm sure it looked weird to people outside my head.

"Why not?" I asked, shrugging my shoulders. "Reed and Augustus are still off in—what, Texas or something?"

"Austin, I think," Ariadne said.

"And it's not like I have an office to sit around on a daily basis, waiting for something to happen." That was also true; our office had been destroyed a couple months prior, and no decisions had been made as yet on what was to happen next. My feeling was that it'd be decided after the election next week, probably a quiet announcement telling me to pack my crap and move to Washington, D.C. Most of the time lately I worked from home, which coincidentally was done with the television on. I'd grown tired of watching paternity tests with Maury in the afternoons, but on the plus side I hadn't seen

Andrew Phillips's smiling face in almost two months. Almost worth it.

I stood up definitively, drunkenly, and almost fell over onto the coffee table. Whoops. "All right," I said, putting my fists on my hips. "I'm going to go and—you know, be a hero and stuff."

"I knew you'd do the right thing," Ariadne said. She looked nervously at me. "But, uh, maybe you should change first."

"Wha—oh," I said, looking down at my dress. My bra was still showing, and there was a smudge of dirt across the surface of the dress. "Is that—aw, hell, must have picked it up from the nose of the plane."

"Yeah, I doubt they wash those very often," Ariadne said, giving me a sympathetic look as I left the room.

I put on a somewhat nice blouse, buttoning it up over my new bra holster that concealed the Glock 43 I carried these days as a backup gun. I strapped my new CZ 75 Shadow II onto my hip carefully after I'd put on my jeans and belt, slipped my badge and ID into my jacket pocket, and wondered where my phone had gone as I strapped my boots on.

"Hey," Ariadne called as I walked back out into the living room down the long hallway, "you got a text message."

"Oh," I said, scooping up my phone from the coffee table as I came into the room. "Did you see who it was from?" I swiped and keyed the unlock code.

"I don't know," she said in a voice that told me she was a lying liar.

"Yes, you do," I said, pulling up my text messages as I flushed the guilty look out of her. I knew she'd looked because the message didn't show up under my notifications, which meant SOMEONE *cough cough* Ariadne, had already peeked. I put my finger on the first message in line without reading the preview, and froze as it came up.

Ricardo

You are the most intriguing woman I have ever met.

"I thought you said the date didn't go well." Ariadne was giving me a slight smirk, a sort of I-told-you-so look that was clearly mixed with a little triumph.

Son of a bitch.

9.

Kat

Los Angeles

"What do we do now?" Scott asked, his voice quiet in the expansive environment.

"Karyn?" Taggert asked from his place on the lush white couch in the living room. "Get Kitten a bottle of water, will you?" He looked calm for the most part, especially considering what they'd just been through this afternoon. Kat watched him with slightly lowered eyes, trying to figure out what the man was thinking. Taggert stood abruptly, stalking his way over to the glass doors that led out to the pool deck. "We just need to hang tight. I'll get another bodyguard or two."

"You saw what that guy did to the last bodyguards," Scott said, his voice laced with quiet menace. Taggert had argued against letting Scott come back to the house after the attack. Kat didn't argue with Taggert very often—he was so very often right, and she could see that almost always—but Taggert didn't have experience with metas, not really, and he was operating from the assumption that the two police officers lurking outside would be enough to stop her attacker. Kat was not laboring under such illusions.

Karyn gently placed an opened bottle of Fiji water in Kat's hand. Wordlessly she pressed it to her lips, drinking it down by a quarter of the bottle.

"Ah ah ah," Taggert said, scolding her from his place by the glass doors, "graceful. You're drinking like some dude at the gym; be more birdlike."

"Are you joking?" Scott asked, his temper going right to the top—again. "Someone just tried to kill her and you're worried about how she looks drinking water?" His eyes flashed to the cameraman in the corner. This one's name was Jed, and the sound guy was—well, she didn't remember his name. She was mic'd now, though, which meant he could hold the boom mic closer to Scott, who was the only one in the room not wearing his own microphone. He'd refused.

Taggert made a throat-cutting gesture to Jed, the cameraman, who shrugged. "Fine, we'll cut it later." Taggert turned to Scott. "In case you're as slow as I'm taking you to be, she's always *on*, okay? Any moment could be a moment that makes it onto television, and that affects her brand, her image. Now, we can cut around things that don't look so good, and can even do a little re-shoot here and there if we have to, but if we can get it right the first time, then—"

"Holy shit," Scott said, hands coming up to his tousled, sandy blond hair as he turned away from the conversation.

"Scott, it's okay," Kat said, trying to soothe him before he made himself look like even more of an ass. The way he was acting wasn't going to play well once it was edited, and he probably had no idea. She looked squarely at Taggert. "We still have the party tonight, don't we?"

Taggert met her gaze coolly. "The fundraiser at Anna Vargas's house? Yeah. I was gonna say that you need to be seen there for that. It's a can't-miss."

"I'm surrounded by insane people," Scott said, now talking to himself, but loudly. That wasn't going to play well, either. "Out of your minds, all of you."

"Can't show fear now," Taggert said, looking at her with a glint in his eye. What he really meant was that she couldn't show fear until this episode of the show premiered. Then she could look as scared as she was right now, because it'd look great. All she had to do was put up a mostly brave face in front of the other cameras, and let the ones that orbited her like planets around a celestial body catch her doing a little crying just out of sight, maybe.

"Showing up to a party and dying is cool, though," Scott said. Kat grimaced; she needed to find a way to break it to him—gently, of course—that he needed to think about his image. He looked right at her. "Kat … this guy looks like the type that can walk through walls. I can't stop that. You can't stop that—" He frowned. "Not that you tried real hard to, in any case." She remained silent, and after a moment he went on. "We need to get you out of here. Can't you—I dunno, take a beach vacation or—hang out on a private island or something?" He waved a hand in the air. "Anything, really. Basic security considerations."

Taggert mulled that one, and Kat watched him. "You just got back from St. Kitts. I think we need to establish you working for a bit, you know, build the drama of the season around something. I'm all for the glamour of the high vacation lifestyle, but if we do too much of it without showing you digging into other projects, your brand is going to take some hits on—"

Scott rammed his head against a wall, cracking timbers somewhere within and causing Kat to jump. "Sorry," he said. "Couldn't help it."

"Listen, pal," Taggert said with a sweet smile and a friendly tone that set off every warning bell in Kat's head, "you just don't understand the business—"

"Is it the funeral business?" Scott asked, turning around to reveal a gash on his forehead that was trailing a thin trickle of blood. "Because that's the business you're about to be in—"

A hard knocking at the door caused all of them to jump. "Karyn," Taggert snapped a finger, pointing Kat's assistant to the door.

Karyn looked dumbstruck, even though she regularly opened the door and answered the phone. "Uhh …"

"I'll get it," Scott said, running a hand across his brow. It took a second for things to settle and for Kat to realize that the knock had come from the back door, the one that led to the pool deck, not the front door where guests would normally—

"Wait!" Kat threw up a hand just as Scott came up short of the handle. The door swung wide; it was unlocked. *Oh God … she thought.*

"Apparently you people don't learn from Paris Hilton's mistakes." Sienna Nealon stepped inside, dressed in her usual trainwreck of too-loose to be flattering jeans, a blouse top that looked appropriate for a low-paid teacher, lace-up boots of the sort a construction worker or a Goth might wear, and a leather jacket that was too baggy to be cool and too ugly to fit in anywhere Kat had ever been.

"Sienna," she said, blanching at the woman's taste in clothes.

"Kat," Sienna said, halting just in front of Scott and behind Taggert, who stood there looking at her with dollar signs dancing in his eyes. She made a face, like she'd taken a swig of Diet Coke and gotten the lime by accident. "I heard someone's trying to kill you and I came to help." She paused. "… To help *you*, I mean. Not help them kill you. Probably."

And she grinned in a manner that was not very reassuring.

10.

Sienna

Kat's house wasn't the hardest thing to find. I had to stop for one of those star maps, but once I had it, it was easy peasy to come drifting down in the backyard next to the lovely pool and just invite myself in. The temp was a pleasant seventy or so, a dramatic change from both what I'd left behind in Minneapolis and what I'd experienced flying here.

"You don't look so pleased to see me, Kat," I said, looking past Scott, who seemed relieved, and another guy, to where the object of my ire waited. She did not look relieved or like she'd peed recently at all, really; she looked like she needed to go, mouth wide in a horrified rictus, like she figured I was going to jump over the lushly appointed couches between us, overturning the end tables as I went, just so I could punch her in her scaredy-Kat face.

NYET! Gavrikov shouted in my head.

Relax, Aleksandr, I thought real loud, *I'm not gonna do it. Again.*

Probably.

"I'm ... glad to see you, Sienna," Kat said, convincing me that a Best Actress award was not going to be forthcoming to her anytime soon, at least not for this performance. "Really," she added, not exactly the frosting on the convincing cake.

"Hi, how you doing," the relieving guy said, sliding up to

me. "I'm Taggert." Like that alone was supposed to mean something. "I'm Kitten's agent-producer." He waved a hand to move a couple guys with a microphone and a camera huddling in the corner. They started working their way around the room closer to me.

"Aren't agents and producers supposed to be two different things?" I asked, watching the guys coming toward me with a wary eye. They were filming me, which seemed to always end badly, at least of late.

"I have my fingers in a lot of pies," Taggert said with a smug grin that I wanted to punch off his face, along with all the skin and his neatly ordered teeth. This was surprising to me, because it usually takes at least a few lines of dialogue after their introduction for someone to make me want to punch them. I imagined grabbing him by the back of the head and shoving his face in a pie until he stopped writhing. He moved his head slightly, his spray-on tan looking super orange in the room's surprisingly bright lights. "You're smiling."

"Uh, sorry," I said, ignoring the hand he extended for me to shake. "I imagined you saying you had your fingers in a lot of butts." I brushed past him, still ignoring that hand. Because he probably *had* had his fingers in a lot of butts. I glanced around the room, taking it all in. It was kind of a classic décor, all large windows and wood floors and—I dunno, Persian carpets or something. It all looked really expensive, and I felt completely ill at ease here. "So, I hear I'm not the only one you've been pissing off, Kat."

"People are always envious of success," Taggert offered from behind me. I was regretting not practicing my punch-based dentistry on him already.

"People are also annoyed when successful people stomp on them to become successful," I offered in return, considerably cooler than I might have an hour or so earlier, before I sobered up some on my flight. "Also, I've met a reasonable number of successful people who never had to step on anyone to get that way."

"I doubt that," Taggert said.

"That I've met successful people?" I asked, carefully putting my hands behind my back and clenching them together, forcing a smile on my face, "or that some of them have done that whole 'climb to the top' thing without screwing anyone else over?"

"Maybe both," Taggert said with a ready grin. His hair was all slicked back, his skin more than a little rough from what looked like a few bouts of acne in his youth.

"What's the situation?" I had the good grace to pass on firing back at that jackass as I turned my attention to Scott, who was standing mute near the door I'd just come in. He was looking at me blankly but came back to life when I directed my question at him.

"Did you see the news?" Scott asked.

"Is this on the news?" I asked, inadvertently sighing. I bet this totally knocked the coverage of my saving the plane right out of the spotlight. Not that I'd stayed around to pose for pictures, but still … I get no credit.

"Wall to wall," Taggert said, grinning again as he snapped his fingers, gesturing for a girl in her twenties like he was ordering a dog around. He pointed at the flatscreen mounted above the fireplace, which I assumed was ceremonial or decorative. It was November, but I'd been here for like, five minutes, and I was already wishing I'd worn shorts and ditched the jacket. The girl obediently scrambled for a remote and turned on the TV, and I added another simmering desire to my burgeoning wishlist: all I wanted for Christmas was to knock out Taggert's two front teeth. And then all the rest of them.

Sigh. Being good was such hard work.

When the TV came on, I saw that Taggert was right, though. There was helicopter footage and on-the-scene reportage from Kat's attack. They had the big lighting rigs mounted and everything, since now it was dark and that place looked like it was lit up like daytime. It was some office park on a city street, as near as I could tell, and the place looked way, way different from a Minneapolis street.

"Can we have a minute?" I asked, looking around the room and making a motion toward Kat, who froze at my mere suggestion. "I think we girls need to work something out."

Taggert did not respond favorably to this idea. "Is it just going to be a talk?"

"Yes," I said, sighing again. I had a feeling I'd be doing a lot of this.

"On your honor?" Taggert asked with a healthy dose of sarcasm.

"Well, I damned sure wouldn't bother swearing on yours," I said, turning my back on the bastard. "I just need to clarify a couple of points with Ms. Gavrikov before I make any commitments here."

"Ms. Who?" Taggert asked, his face frowning in a way that looked wholly unnatural. There were parts that just didn't move with the rest of his face, causing me to do a double take while looking at him. Plastic surgery, I realized after a beat.

"Oh, you didn't know that was her original name?" I smirked

"Sienna, please," Kat said, looking more than a little stricken. "Please, Taggert … we need a few minutes."

"Yeah, all right," Taggert said and snapped his fingers at the poor girl who'd turned on the TV. She hurried after him as he swept from the room. Scott, for his part, seemed a little less put off by that shit than I was and paused on his way out of the room.

"Thought you weren't coming," he said.

"I changed my mind," I said. "It's a woman's prerogative."

"If you say so," he said, favoring me with a smile as he headed after Taggert.

I waited another minute for the room to clear, but the camera guy and the dude with the big microphone on a stick did not make any motion toward leaving. I rolled my eyes. "You, Guido, Luigi, get the hell out of here, okay?" They didn't respond, like they were automated or furniture or something, so I mimicked Taggert and snapped my finger at them. "You know who I am?" I asked, summoning my most menacing, commanding voice. They nodded in sync. "Get the hell out of here or I'm going to take your boom mic and your camera and sodomize you both with them—sideways."

That got them moving. Probably in more ways than one, though I wasn't close enough to smell them to be sure. They scrambled through the open archway and disappeared into what looked like a spacious kitchen, one big enough to probably swallow my entire house. Time was, I might have sighed in envy, but that was before I parked a half-billion dollars of moderately ill-gotten gains in a Liechtenstein bank account. Someday, maybe I'd get a house like this. But probably not in California. I already didn't care for the weather. Not my speed. Also, I knew what real estate cost out here. Half a billion didn't feel like it would go far enough.

"So, Kat," I said, tilting my head toward the aperture where Taggert was probably listening in on us with the cameramen, "why don't we step outside?"

She froze then nodded in surrender. "Okay."

"Stop acting like I'm going to murder you or something," I said, opening the door for her, "it's insulting."

"I know you have a temper," she said, just loud enough I knew she was playing for the damned cameras.

"Yes," I said, "and remember that I've seen yours at work, too, including times when you've killed our fellow human beings in seriously unpleasant ways." I spoke loudly too, enough to do a little playing of my own to the camera. "Remember that time in Gables, Minnesota, when you crushed like five guys to death with tree branches—?"

"Okay, let's go outside," Kat said, hauling her bony ass

55

out the door before I could even finish my sentence. I guess emphasizing her war record wasn't good for "brand management." It wasn't like she'd done anything wrong; the guys she'd killed were sure doing their damnedest to kill us at the time.

I closed the door behind us and stepped out onto the softly lit pool deck. Kat looked like she was glowing cerulean from the underwater lights, and I looked up into a sky that was so polluted by light that I couldn't see a single star. "So," I started, "as an impartial observer, I hear you're kind of up shit creek here." I walked along the concrete edge of the pool and tossed a quick look back over my shoulder to the house in time to see the cameraman duck down, framed in the lit window to the kitchen. He was gonna look really funny walking around with that camera hanging out of his rectum.

"Does that make you happy?" Kat asked softly. I suspected that absent the abnormal lighting, she would probably look pale and sick. As it was, she looked a little like one of those aliens from *Avatar*, but shorter.

"You getting the shaft doesn't exactly make me sad," I said, folding my arms in front of me. "Do you have any idea how bad you screwed me over with that crap you pulled?"

"I didn't—"

"If you deny it, I will fly my ass home tonight and drag Scott along with me," I said, throwing up a finger in accusation.

"It wasn't me," Kat said. "I don't have anything to do with the editing of the show, okay? I'm not the director."

I locked my jaw until the last twitch of rage passed. It took a few seconds. "Who is?"

"Taggert," she said, a small surrender.

"That guy really does have his fingers in a lot of butts."

She blanched. "He's just doing what he needs to in order to make the show successful." She straightened a little. "To make my career a success."

"Yeah, well, I remember when I put my effort toward

making sure you lived long enough to have a career outside of a snuff film minus the film," I said, glaring at her. "Though I doubt you even remember that time I stopped your brother on the IDS tower—"

"I remember," she said, muttering.

"Yeah, so do I," I said crossly, "every time that knucklehead pipes up about his precious Klementina—"

HEY, Gavrikov said. It was the favored expression of outrage among the voices in my head, because it always got me to take a moment to respond.

Shut up, Gavrikov.

"Can you please cool it about that?" She looked genuinely worried.

"Why?" I asked. "You worried that your brand will take a hit if people find out you've celebrated your centennial?"

"I did not celebrate a centennial," she said, more than a little irritated, something that Kat very seldom was. "I don't remember any of my life before, and you know it. I lost those memories—"

"In some noble pursuit, I'm sure." I didn't roll my eyes this time, because for all I knew, she had lost them nobly. Kat's power was tied inextricably to life. As a Persephone-type meta, she could manipulate living greenery, which was kind of a cool thing to watch. Her other ability, though, was to heal people with the touch of her skin. Unfortunately for her, if she tried to heal too much, she lost memories. I'd seen her lose all her memories of Scott after an incident in Des Moines, Iowa, when she'd saved his life. They'd been one of those really annoying boyfriend/girlfriend combos, tight as her pants one day, and the next day he was a sobbing mess and she didn't know him from a random guy on the street. It would have made for an awkward Thanksgiving dinner if we'd actually celebrated Thanksgiving that year.

"Sienna, I just want to live my new life—"

"If you'd just wanted to live your new life," I said with grating harshness, "you would have let my little prison break incident pass without inflicting a call on me."

"Well, I haven't called you since," she said.

"Not so," I sniped. "You called me when I was in Atlanta dealing with that business with Tom Cavanagh—"

"Oh," Kat said. "Right. I forgot. Well, it's not like you answered—"

"Hell, no. I had J.J. block your calls."

Her face fell. "What if I needed to get hold of you? You know, for an emergency—"

"You mean like this?"

"Well, yeah."

"Then I imagine you'd call me from a friend's phone—*if you have any of those left.*" I delivered the coup de grâce with the utter lack of remorse it required and watched it hit her like a punch to the jaw. Not one of mine, of course, because that would have required all the plastic surgeons in Beverly Hills to fix, but close. She actually took a step back, looking a little unsteady, and I realized that in my natural, admittedly sadistic, desire to lash out at this person who had caused me so much pain, I had just stumbled on something that I hadn't even realized.

Kat *didn't* have an actual friend left in the world.

I worked that all out in a few seconds and watched her try and blink her way to a response, failing utterly.

"Never mind," I said hastily, suddenly embarrassed for her. I shouldn't have been, because obviously she'd been plenty shitty to me, even trying to come back to the well after knowing how crappy things had gone for me after her first phone call, but … I actually did feel sorry for her.

Because if there was anything I knew after the last few months, it was what it was like to feel like you didn't have a friend left in the world.

"Wait, that's it?" she asked, like she was having trouble coming to terms with the fact that I'd started to walk away from our little argument after less than a round. Of course, I felt like I'd landed my knockout punch and was ready to leave, but maybe she didn't know that.

"That's it," I said. "I mean, probably. I might let slip a little passive-aggressive comment every now and again, some sarcasm, which is the way of my people—"

"Your people?" she asked. "The … Norwegians?"

"Come on, Kat," I said, ignoring her. "Let's get you inside. It's not safe here."

"Okay," she said, watching me warily as she headed for the door, "I have to get ready for the party anyway." She made her way inside past me, leaving the door open, walking like she'd had plenty of the starch taken out of her step, and I didn't think she was acting this time.

"Yeah," I nodded sagely, "you should—"

Wait, *what?*

11.

What kind of idiot goes to a Hollywood party when they've nearly been murdered that very afternoon?

World, I introduce to you Klementina Gavrikov, a.k.a. Katrina Forrest. If fate protects fools and babies, then this girl was clearly being watched over by Clotho, Lachesis and Atropos. They were probably metas, as all those ancient Greeks with power tended to be. I hoped for Kat's sake they had power beyond my own, because based on her level of stupidity, whoever was protecting her would have to work overtime to keep her safe.

I followed Kat's car to the party by flying overhead about a hundred feet, drifting along at what felt like snail speed after my supersonic flight across the country to get here. Before you ask, I did consider arguing with her about going to a party at this exact moment, but my Halibut steak had been burned off during my flight and I was hungry again.

Also, I was kinda hoping Jennifer Lawrence would be there because I had a feeling she would be a fun person to get loaded at a party with.

I set down in front of Kat's SUV just as the valet was stepping out to get the keys from the driver, a guy named Dan who looked like he was not happy to be on the job today. I nearly scared the valet as I appeared, causing him to draw a sharp breath and take a few steps back, almost stumbling on the pristine white brick driveway. "Dude, settle down," I said to him as I walked to the back of the SUV, "you've probably opened a door for Miley Cyrus, don't get all skittish over little ol' me." I grinned like an ass because, let's face it, I was kinda being one.

The door popped open (I didn't open it because, well, I'm not Kat's damned valet) and Karyn stepped out first. I'd learned she was Kat's assistant from Scott just before we left. My reply when he'd told me that: "Are we sure she's not actually Taggert's slave?" He guffawed.

Karyn held the door open as Kat unfolded her skinny, long-legged carcass and stepped down in a gown that was slit up to the hip and made me wonder if she was trying to get some side-beaver photos taken "accidentally." She preened a little, stopping when I rolled my eyes. The two photogs who were on the scene had already finished their pictures and moved down the line to the limo pulling in behind us.

"No press," Taggert said as he stepped out, buttoning up his jacket. The man was wearing blue jeans and a suit jacket with a button-up shirt that looked like it might have come from Hawaii. Like, sold on the street in Hawaii, not from a retailer. "That's good for us."

"What do you mean, 'no press'?" I asked, furrowing my brow as I waved at the two photographers who'd just snapped half a hundred pics of Kat. "What were those guys?"

He smirked—again. "That's like having no press. You'll see what I mean tomorrow."

"Excuse me, ma'am." A guy snaked out in a black suit with a white shirt and black tie. "I'm gonna need to search you."

"I'm a federal agent on a case," I said, flashing my badge and keeping my patience under tight wraps. "So, no, you don't."

He looked ready to argue behind black sunglasses, and I saw he had a companion just behind him. It's night, boys. The "stars" aren't bright enough to justify that look, you jackasses. "All right," he finally said, "Ms. Nealon."

"Thanks for your cooperation," I said, giving him a patronizing smile. "You should totally search her, though," I said, waving to Kat behind me, who probably couldn't have hid a toothpick in that ensemble. I watched with some satisfaction as a woman dressed exactly like the first Secret Service wannabe gave Kat a very thorough pat-down. Not gonna lie, it did my heart some good to watch it.

"Hey," Taggert said with a broad grin as he received a security screening of his own, "you do much more of that and I'm gonna have to charge you." I rolled my eyes. I had a feeling it usually worked the opposite way.

I led the way into the party, drawing a scathing look from a guy with a mohawk who had a chain stretching from his earring to his nose piercing. I felt a little strange being judged by Mr. Slightly Unconventional, but whatever, I guess. Maybe my hair was a little askew. Try flying cross-country without a plane and not being a little mussed.

"Kat!" a woman in a glittering gown squealed. I didn't recognize her, but that didn't mean anything. Kat made a squealing noise of her own in reaction, and I let the girl pass without dislocating her arm trying to stop her, which was what I'd been preparing to do when Kat acknowledged her. I hadn't done much bodyguarding in my time, though I'd certainly acted as protector to people on a few occasions.

"Guarana," Kat said, running her hands lightly and briefly over the girl's bare arms before folding them over each other and returning them to covering her nearly-exposed crotch. I frowned, wondering if Guarana was the girl's given name or if she'd just been a fan of staying caffeinated. "How have you been?"

"Just terrible," Guarana said, holding a hand over her heart. "I heard what happened to you earlier. I felt so bad." She was a terrible actor, too, but Kat's sadface response made her look like an award-winner by comparison.

What the hell was wrong with these people?

"What the hell is wrong with these people?" Scott asked

in a whisper, sidling up to me. Kat heard him and tossed us both a cold look, as though I had anything to do with his simple statement. You know, other than thinking the exact same thing at the exact same moment. What? She's not a telepath, people. She couldn't have known.

"Maybe it's just her and her friend," I said. I glanced at Taggert. "And him."

"Kat!" Another voice called, this one belonging to a guy in a tuxedo that was so new-style I barely recognized it as a tux. "I heard about what happened, and I am so sorry."

"He doesn't sound sorry," Scott said. "He sounds … kinda jealous, actually."

"Whatever," I said, shrugging my shoulders, "at least she doesn't have the film crew following her around right now."

"Yeah," Scott said, his face sort of scrunched up, "I wonder what's up with that. I thought she didn't go anywhere without it."

"Maybe they took my threat to heart." Or anus, as the case may be.

"Maybe," he said, blowing air between his lips, then stopping suddenly when he realized how rude it sounded. "Uhm … should we mingle?"

I thought about that for a minute. "Parties are not really my scene, as you know."

He frowned. "How would I know that?"

I froze. Of course he didn't know that. It wasn't like he could have remembered the awful Christmas gala his family held that he'd made me suffer through only a few years ago. I remembered it clearly, of course, every bit of it, but he didn't. "Do you suppose there's a buffet table?" I asked to change the subject.

"Can't have a party without something to eat," he opined as another guest, this one I recognized from a daytime soap that I might maybe have occasionally watched now that I was working from home—came up to give Kat her not-so-sympathetic-sympathies.

It took three rooms of hunting to find the food, and when I found it, I was actually kind of disappointed.

"Hi," a woman said as she came up to me with a bright, effervescent smile.

"Hi," I returned, already put on my guard by her chipper nature.

"How'd you get here tonight?" she asked.

"I ... flew," I said, blinking.

She threw her head back and laughed. "Out of towner, huh?"

"Is it that obvious?" I looked back and found Scott missing, nowhere in sight. Probably threw himself behind one of the lampshades when he saw this one coming.

"You can always pick 'em out," she said, arching her eyebrows. "What do you do?"

I narrowed my eyes at her. "I'm in law enforcement."

She tilted her head to the side. "You're a cop? No way! My next project has me playing this role as a minor—well, it's not really minor, it's a very integral part—"

"Excuse me," I said, instead of being exceptionally rude and just saying what I meant, which was, "Get away from me before I get sick right in your face." I wasn't feeling sick at all, but it was starting to become a danger because I was really hungry and the so-called buffet was not looking very buffet-y.

I pushed past her and found myself in a kitchen that looked like Kat's, except it was black and kind of brown-toned and ... I really have no feel for decorating, as anyone who had ever seen my linoleum kitchen floors would be able to attest to. Ariadne still looked a little ill every time she lowered her gaze in the kitchen. There was no linoleum here; it was a beautiful wood floor with a white-yellow tinge. I was looking in the other direction when I ran into someone, shoulder-checking them into a marble-topped counter.

"Ow," the guy said, flinching and grabbing at his back. I spun on him, noticing two more of the black-suited security personnel focusing on me and my little disturbance. They even had the earpieces sticking out of their ears, and it made me wonder what nightclub rope line was missing its clown-car full of bouncers for the evening.

"Yeah, you should watch where you're going," I said, giving the guy I'd run into the once over.

"I guess so," he said, sounding genuinely remorseful as he straightened back up. "You pack a full head of steam, huh?" He had brown eyes, chestnut-colored hair, and—

Whoooooops.

I realized after an uncomfortable second of staring that I'd just shoulder-checked Steven Clayton. *The* Steven Clayton. The one who had become Hollywood's leading man in the last couple years, the one who was two parts Chris Hemsworth, one part Chris Pratt, and a little bit of Tom Cruise before the radioactive disaster site that was Oprah's couch.

"Oh, shit," I said, covering my mouth.

"It's okay, I'm good," he said, stretching his back and finally taking his hand off his spine. He still had a pained look, but it was—uhh, well—it was kind of a goooood look. Like, really good. Like, ruggedly handsome, just got done filming an action scene where he did something super heroic and then fell off a building but was totally casual about it and—

I'm gushing. In my own monologue. For shame, Sienna.

"Hey," he said, locking those coffee brown eyes on me, "aren't you S—"

"I'm nobody," I said casually, shaking my head. "Definitely not that, uhh … crazy person." I giggled under my breath and then considered briefly creating a distraction by pulling my CZ Shadow and shooting myself in the foot in order to get out of this awkward situation. It's not like it would kill me, after all. I mean, I'd just giggled, for crying out loud. Who does that?

"That's soooo amazing," Kat said, strolling by with a guy

on her arm, emitting a throaty giggle as she threaded her way past me on the other side of the island in the middle of the kitchen.

Oh, no. I've become *that* girl.

Kat, as if sensing my horror, turned her head and looked right at me then scanned on to Steven Clayton. Her eyes widened in undisguised shock and revulsion, and she promptly rescued her arm from the crook of the elbow of the man she was strolling with, probably dislocating his shoulder in the process. I cringed. That meta strength … you really gotta watch that.

"Oh, hi!" she said, moving around the island toward me with a hustle that I wouldn't have expected to see from her in life-and-death battles, let alone in a kitchen in Hollywood. "Steven, I'm Kat. How do you do? We have so many mutual acquaintances—"

"Oh, uh, yeah," he said, looking a little startled by her sudden offensive. "Nice to meet you, Kat. I'm familiar with your show—"

"Oh, you watch my show?" she asked, the falsely modesty oozing like green phlegm down an upper lip. Yeah. I went there. She was subtle as snot, okay?

"Well, I've heard of it—"

Unasked, she looped her arm around his, faster than he could say anything, and started to lightly drag him along. "You simply must tell me about your latest movie …" She reminded me of something out of a Jane Austen novel, but with a much more predatory air. She shot me a furious STAY BACK! look as she hauled him out of the radius of my … I dunno, my antisocial slime, probably.

"Oh, good, she got to meet Steven," Taggert said, easing up behind me. He wasn't quiet about it, fortunately, which gave me ample warning so I wasn't surprised. Which would have been bad, but mostly for him.

"Why is that good?" I asked.

"Have you seen the guy?" Taggert asked, like I was

stupid. "California's most eligible bachelor. He's not just a flavor of the month, that boy's got staying power. If he could even do a guest spot, maybe as a date for Kitten, we're talking top-shelf ratings. We'll gain five points of share that night, it'd be an event." He squealed a little, under his breath. "Can you imagine the wedding ratings?"

"She just met him."

"It'd be huge," Taggert went on, probably not hearing me over the sound of cash register bells in his head. "And the divorce episodes would be a great storyline for—"

"I like how you jump right to assuming they're going to both marry *and* divorce, mere seconds after they just met for the first time." The former was kind of optimistic, but the latter was the sort of practiced cynicism I would have tended to hang my hat on. If I ever wore a hat.

"You don't like me, do you?" Taggert asked with a grin.

"Oh, good," I said, "I was afraid I wasn't being obvious enough about it."

"Listen," he said, putting a hand on my shoulder. If I hadn't had both a jacket and a blouse on, as well as a bra strap, I think I would have needed to scrub myself bloody just to feel somewhat normal afterward; as it was, I was just going to burn the clothes. "I'm connected out here. I've got a lot of sway ... with the right people, the right causes. I could help you." His grin stretched wider. "Maybe help make you Teflon. We do the editing right, you come out of this season looking like a hero, maybe help you pick up some lost points in the public relations department."

I didn't bother to pretend that wouldn't have been helpful, but I really despised it when people held that particular carrot over my head, because it was always attached to a stick that they tried their best to get me to ignore. "In exchange for?"

Taggert shrugged broadly. "You're doing a favor for Kitten. Maybe you could do some favors for me, too."

He kept his delivery well on this side of randy, but I still frowned. "Such as?"

"We'll talk about it later," he said, patting my shoulder reassuringly. "The point is—I've got power that could help you. Plus, I drive a 1961 Ferrari 250 GT SWB California Spyder. It's the car from *Ferris Bueller's Day Off.*" He grinned, his even teeth practically begging to be punched out. "I'm quite the guy."

"Yes," I said dryly, "you're an amazing human being. Why, you could probably even lift Mjolnir."

"You play ball," he went on, making me feel greasy just being in proximity to him, "you could have a career out here, maybe—"

"Not interested," I said, firmly, ready to walk away. He clenched his fingers a little tighter, enough to stop me and get my evil eye, but as soon as I started to spin on him, he let go and held them up.

"I know the president," he said. "Your boss, technically. I could put in a good word. I've heard you had problems—"

"You know Gerry Harmon?" I gave him a wary eye.

"I do," he smiled even more broadly.

"Tell him he's a dick and I'm not voting for him," I said, flashing him an evil grin. Taggert's face fell in a way that was just—it was like the most beautiful thing I could imagine, and I'd known the guy for all of an hour. I had a feeling he didn't get the rug yanked out from him very often, and it was sweet.

"Tell him yourself," came a voice from behind me, chillingly familiar.

I spun around, and I felt my stomach drop like I was on a Midwest Airlines flight that had run out of fuel. Unfortunately, I was unlikely to save it because I was experiencing something of a falling sensation myself at the moment. It was at that moment that I kicked myself for not realizing—*dumbass, dumbass, dumbass*—that the Secret Service wannabes weren't actually wannabes—they were the real deal.

"President Harmon," I said quietly, with just a hint of

contrition.

"Sienna Nealon," President Gerard Harmon said, staring coolly at me icy blue eyes, a placid look on his face. "How interesting to finally meet you ... and under these circumstances, no less."

12.

Scott

Scott had gotten lost in a hallway, staring at a beach scene painted on a broad canvas. He'd kind of zoned off looking at the scenery for a few minutes, and when he'd turned back to say something to Sienna, she'd been gone. "Damn," he muttered mildly as a thin woman in a black dress slipped by him with barely more than an acknowledgment. He looked down at his slightly sloppy suit, the same one he'd worn to his business meeting this afternoon, and felt a surge of complete and utter inadequacy.

Another beautiful woman passed him by without so much as a look, and he started to say, "Excuse me," but stopped himself. Why did it matter what anyone else thought? He wasn't here because he wanted to be; he was here because Kat's life was in danger.

Yet another starlet came past, walking in such a way that he had to practically crowbar his head in the opposite direction to keep from staring. "Must lead to the bathroom," he said, and made his way back down the narrow hall toward a living room.

The crowd here wasn't too bad, and he could feel a little more humidity in the air than what he'd been dealing with outside. It was actually somewhat refreshing indoors, and he guessed by the green lawn he'd seen when they were driving up that this area wasn't failing to get its fair share of water, even during drought conditions.

"Scott!" came the booming voice of Buchanan Brock, his broad smile obvious from a mile way and way more inviting than any of the other receptions Scott gotten thus far this evening, save perhaps from Sienna. He had his arms open and was waving Scott over from a small group of people in the corner. "Didn't expect to see you here," Brock said, with that drawl of his.

"I didn't expect to be here," Scott said, easing up to where Brock stood with two twenty-something lovelies. He tried not to stare, seeing the much older man with the younger women was like a tickling sensation on his upper lip, making him smile awkwardly in spite of himself. "What brings you to this party?"

"Oh, I took the 405," Brock said casually. "Got off at—"

"I meant—uh, who invited you?" Scott asked. "Not to be rude."

"Oh, that's not rude, I just didn't understand you," Brock said, patting him warmly on the shoulder. "I always get invited to the president's fundraisers in LA."

Scott's eyebrows crept toward the ceiling. "This is a fundraiser?"

"I know, I know," Brock said, "this close to the election? But with our man Harmon trailing Foreman in the polls, he needs some cash to dump on swing states—"

"I meant I didn't know the president was—" Scott felt himself seize internally, like machinery encountering resistance within. "President Harmon is here?"

"Why yes, he is," Brock said with that same grin, motioning toward a passage into what looked like the kitchen. "He just came through a minute before you did, in fact. Would you like me to arrange an introduction?"

"Whoa, no," Scott said, holding up his hands in front of him as if to defend himself from the prospect of just such an introduction. "I'm one of the simple folk, not a presidential hand-shaker. Under the radar, that's where I live."

Brock grinned. "If that's so, you're at the wrong party, friend." He pulled a hand around expansively. "I mean, just look at what we're dealing with here. Starlets, power-brokers, directors—I think I even saw Joss Whedon earlier."

"Ooh," Scott said, looking around, "him I'd like to meet."

"I think it's about time I moseyed on," Brock said, lifting his arms. One of the women with him slid her thin shoulders underneath and he lowered it to protectively encompass her. "I'm sure a young man like you understands." He cast a look back at the other young woman. "You staying, then?" She made a little face and his smirk grew even wider. "All right." Brock extended a hand to Scott and Scott took it, getting a firm handshake in return. "You think about what we talked about. Chew it over with your dad and let me know what you come up with."

"Will do," Scott said, and made way for the big man to thread his way through the crowded living room toward the door. He waited until Brock had walked out the front door before he spoke again. "Now there's a man living the high life."

"Ewww," the woman Brock had left behind said in reply, shuddering as she stood and walked away. Scott watched her go. He didn't need to do too much imagining to figure out exactly what she was talking about.

13.

Kat

The party was buzzing, but the lack of cameras left Kat feeling a little cold in spite of the warm air in the backyard, where she stood in a small circle of her friends.

"Did you see the dress Caitlynn Courie was wearing?" Anna Vargas asked, running a diamond-crusted hand over her face to show off her newest rock. The girl did like to shop.

"No," Kat gasped, pushing herself into the conversation. She was suppressing some minor irritation because Steven Clayton had ditched her as soon as she'd rescued him from Sienna, making some excuse about needing to powder his nose. He'd even said exactly that, and what was she going to do? Tell him not to go do a line? That would have been rude. "What did it look like?"

"You'll probably see it on the red carpet in a few weeks," Flannery Steiner said, holding a champagne goblet in front of puckered, amused lips. "Along with the sides, top and bottom of her tits." Flannery was a former Disney Channel star who had left her childhood image behind in a squeal of tires from a high-speed chase that had resulted in her eighteenth arrest for possession of a controlled substance. The chase was the consequence of her having sex with her boyfriend in a public place and then running from the cops

73

when they'd pulled up behind her while she still on the young man's lap. The tabloid headlines had been exposure that had made Taggert wonder if Kat should feign a drug habit—or even pick up a real one for a bit. It's not like track marks would be a problem for her; they'd heal overnight. The public indecency thing would be a little harder for her to stomach, but Taggert was pushing it, especially if she could get the right setup and partner.

"I'm so jealous of that dress," Anna said, taking a sip of her drink, a pink concoction in a martini glass. "Who is it?"

"Chanel, I think?" Bree Lancer said, brushing her long auburn hair back carefully so as not to disturb her well-designed coif. It was a distinctive look that left a little hair hanging over her eyes.

"By the way," Anna Vargas said, lowering her voice, "I heard what happened to you this afternoon, Kat. That's so terrible. My thoughts are with you."

"Oh, yes," Flannery agreed, putting a hand across her chest. "Just awful, what happened to your bodyguards. I sent you a tweet of support and RT'd Jenny Kline's Tumblr post. So glad you're okay."

"Ooh, I saw Jenny's Tumblr post," Bree said, sucking in a breath that disturbed her hanging hair. "I thought it was, like, so on the nose." She looked to Kat. "So sorry. How are you holding up?"

Kat froze. She wasn't entirely sure what to say in this case. "I'm ... I'm okay."

"At least you're getting a ton of attention over it," Anna said, a little jealously. "And I saw your new bodyguard. Whoever this disgusting vagrant guy that's after you is, I doubt he'll mess with Sienna Nealon."

"Ohmigosh," Bree said, "Sienna Nealon is here?"

"Is that who that was?" Flannery whipped her head around to look back at the house. "Z-O-M-G, ratings. Nice move, Taggert." She turned to look at Kat. "You're so lucky Taggert is working on your show. He's a genius. Meanwhile,

I'm sinking in share by the episode." Her eyelids drooped and she puckered her lips frightfully. "You don't think he'd want to try and turn things around for me, do you?"

"If Taggert takes on any other projects, I want him on mine," Anna said in a huff.

Kat forced a brittle smile. "He's good."

"He's brilliant," Bree said. "The only way I'd consider a reality TV project was if Taggert came to me with it." She cast her eyes skyward in thought. "What do you suppose it'd cost to get something like that off the ground?"

A little dignity and all your self-respect, said a little voice in the back of Kat's mind. "It's easier than you think," was what she said to them, though.

"Hey, did you guys meet the president yet?" Anna asked, looking back toward the house. "It's so cool to be at a party where the president is, can you believe it?"

"Yeah," Bree said, puffing up a little. "I mean, look at the people here. It kinda makes you feel important, doesn't it?"

There was a small chorus of agreement that descended into a conversation that Kat mostly missed. In her head, she was retreating into a circle of thoughts that she didn't want to entertain but felt like she couldn't escape, like the worst houseguest in history.

Does it make you feel important, being here at a party with all these famous people?

Does brushing up against people who are known make you feel good about yourself?

No.

Well, then why are you working so damned hard to do it?

The answer she had didn't satisfy, but instead of delving deeper she pulled away and smiled and listened along to a conversation about Givenchy while those damned houseguests in her head tried their hardest to make her feel like shit about the life she'd worked so hard to build.

14.

Sienna

"You're a dick," I said to the president of the United States as he raised an eyebrow sharply in amusement. "You said to tell you myself, so ..." I waited for a thunderous response, for some hint of darkening around his eyes, for the Secret Service to yank me offstage with one of those hooked canes, but nothing came. The president seemed genial and good-natured, his light-brown hair streaked with hints of grey—but surprisingly few considering that he was in his sixties.

"And so you did," Gerard "Gerry" Harmon said with a nod and that hint of a smile.

"You seem strangely unmoved by it, though," I said.

"Well, it really burned me up the first time you said it, when your back was still turned to me. Probably lost most of its impact in the interval between." He kept his lips in a flat line, deadpan. "Or maybe it lost its sting when I ran for governor of Massachusetts that first time and stupidly wandered into an internet message board where they called me ever-so-much worse." He smiled. When he spoke, his words came out infused with so much personality that I almost felt like I needed to take a step back. "What brings you to the state of California tonight, Ms. Nealon?"

I tried to find an answer that was somewhat appropriate given that I was speaking to the man at the top of the pyramid and I'd already called him a dick and he'd forgiven me. Don't get me wrong, I had a feeling my days on the job were limited, but I wasn't in a hurry to hasten my departure from government service. "Well, there was an incident ..."

"There frequently is when you're involved," Harmon said with a touch of good humor. "Would this be the meta attack against your friend Ms. Forrest earlier?"

"You heard about that, huh?" I asked, feeling a little nervous suddenly.

"I get informed of quite a bit," President Harmon said. "Something about the job I'm in, I suppose. I think people might hesitate to vote for a president who doesn't know a damned thing. They like to save that for senators, see."

"Nice," I said, admiring the shot he'd just taken at his opponent. Senator Robb Foreman of Tennessee had been an ally—maybe kindasorta a friend?—during the war.

"Oh, I think you might have taken that the wrong way," Harmon said with a smile that told me I hadn't. "I didn't mean to insult your friend, especially since he's done so much for you."

I hadn't seen Robb Foreman since early in the summer, when he'd given me a little assistance on a case I was struggling with in Atlanta. That had been just before he'd won his party's nomination in a big, glorious ceremony in the middle of an arena in Raleigh-Durham, North Carolina. I'd caught the replay; Foreman knew how to play to a crowd. Which had been of real help to him when he'd rolled into the first debate with Gerry Harmon a few weeks later and given the president a drubbing unlike the man had ever received in his entire political career. I'd watched that, too, until it had gotten too painful and I'd had to turn it off.

Yeah. It was so bad that I—yes, me—had felt it was an unfair, lopsided, brutal contest and had changed the channel to watch *Agents of S.H.I.E.LD.* instead. The second debate had been marginally better for Harmon, but not exactly a win. Fortunately for him, there was not a third, but he lost ten points in the polls and was heading into election week at a rather significant disadvantage.

He watched me carefully. "If what I hear about you is true, I think can almost sense the sarcasm going on behind your eyes."

"Admire my restraint," I said with some regret. "It's a thing I'm working on."

"And I appreciate that," he said with a little irony. "Why, it's been something like ninety days since you last embarrassed my administration, and don't think we haven't noticed. If you make it to a hundred twenty, I'll send you a fruit basket."

"Ooh, something to look forward to."

"Mr. President." One of the secret service guys strode up. "We're running a little behind schedule."

"Right," Gerry Harmon said, shifting his attention back to me. "I think this is where I leave you, Ms. Nealon." He offered me a hand, and I considered it for a second before I took it. His fingers were a little damp from perspiration, but probably not as damp as mine were. It's not every day I accidentally and then intentionally insulted the leader of the free world.

"You didn't say anything like, 'I hope I can count on your vote,'" I observed as he turned away.

He looked back in slight surprise. "Let's be honest; even if you weren't voting for your friend, you live in Minnesota." He smiled. "It's not exactly a swing state."

"I certainly feel motivated to join your cause now," I said sardonically.

"Well, I don't really need your vote, but it doesn't mean I couldn't use your help—remember, there's a fruit basket in it for you." His eyes flashed in amusement at the inside joke the two of us now shared, and he walked away with a Secret Service detail surrounding him.

"You really are a dick," I said, once I was sure he was out of earshot. And I meant it.

15.

I turned around to find Taggert had apparently disappeared sometime between the first time I called the president of the United States a dick and the last one, and I couldn't have been happier. There was a circle that had formed in the kitchen during my exchange with him, and I caught a few scandalized looks from people who'd heard my last observation. Weak-kneed pansies.

I looked for Kat but didn't see her, or Scott, and since I was sick of people wearing formalwear that cost more than I made in a year looking horrified at me, I decided to leave the kitchen. I spun and started away and promptly ran into someone standing a little too close to me.

"Ow," Steven Clayton said, barely catching himself before he was linebackered over the island in the middle of the kitchen.

"Dude," I said, "you keep getting in my personal bubble. It's not a safe space."

He stretched cautiously. "I'm getting that, believe me. I never even got checked like that when I played hockey." He opened his mouth and I heard his jaw pop.

"You have a surprising number of your teeth remaining considering you played hockey," I said. In Minnesota, playing hockey is almost a religion. I'm not entirely sure, but hockey fans might edge out Lutherans, population-wise.

"I played for like, a season," he said, fully regaining his

balance. His classic tux looked ... uh, classically good on him. He wore it well. "Switched to football. The hits were more manageable, and there were fewer games."

"Couldn't handle all the fighting, huh?"

"Oh, I could handle the fighting," he said with a glint in his eye, "but the first time I got a black eye it sort of messed with my ability to play Hamlet in the winter production, so I had to make a difficult choice."

I tried to imagine him playing Hamlet, all tortured and kinda broody and whatnot. It was not a bad daydream. "Right," I said, coming back from that. "Well, sorry I ran into you—twice."

"These things happen," he said, surprisingly casual about it. That made him smart in my book; other people come at me like they have some sort of grievance, but getting huffy with one of the most powerful people in the world doesn't usually end well. Don't depend on my restraint to keep you from being turned into slurry.

Because I don't have much restraint, duh. Like I told the president, I'm working on it.

"Did you hit up the food?" he asked, seemingly cool about the whole me knocking him around thing.

"Uh, I saw it," I said, wondering why he was still talking to me. Not that I was complaining, it was just ... weird. "Artisanal bread, artisanal cheeses ... figured I'd skip it so as to avoid having an artisanal bowel movement later." Did I just say that?

He laughed, surprising me again. "Nice one."

"I excel at jokes that end up in the gutter," I said a little feebly.

"I could stand to hear a little more about those," he said with a conspiratorial wink that probably sent my eyebrows up into my wildly mussed hair. Why couldn't I have met this eligible Hollywood bachelor like six hours ago, when I was dressed for my date with Dick? I looked nice then, and I hadn't flown thousands of miles yet. I was suddenly self-conscious about my appearance, which, I noted finally, was not so impressive compared to all the other women at this party. Also, I suspected my anti-perspirant had failed over Madison. I sniffed. Yep, that was the wafting scent of failure.

There was a sound of raised voices from the front of the house that caused me to turn. "What was that?" I murmured, almost to myself.

"Holy shit!" some guy said as he came around the corner, reminding me of a teenager in a bad high school movie. "The president just told some dude off and then got into his limo and vamoosed."

"Who says 'vamoosed'?" I asked in a low voice.

"Canadians?" Steven offered helpfully, causing me to turn back around to see him wearing a tight smile. "Because it has 'moose' in it."

"Yeah, I got that," I said with a tight smile of my own. "We have a few of those in Minnesota, too."

"Nice," he said. "I'm from Alaska, and we have … a lot more than a few."

"So you're intimately familiar with moose … es? Meese?" I asked, searching for the plural.

"Yeah, I lost my virginity to one," he said, utterly deadpan. "That was a rough weekend. He never even called me again, the bastard."

Okay, that I laughed at, then surveyed the kitchen and the people stationed around it with a glance. They were all staring at us, talking in hushed voices, casting looks of their own in our direction. I didn't think it was just my hair that they were marveling at, either, and it kind of ruined the joke for me. "Well, it was nice to meet you, uh, Mr.—"

"Wow, you called me Mister," he said, his face falling. "Makes me feel really old."

"Yeah, you're definitely getting up there in the years," I shot back. "What are you, like twenty-five?"

"Closer to thirty, but don't tell anyone," he said with a wink that made me moist.

In the armpits, you perverts. Because of failing anti-perspirant. Yeah. It had nothing to do with a big movie star winking at me. Nooooooo. "Yeah, you're like the oldest person I've ever met," I said. "Except for all those old gods that had lived for thousands of years."

Now it was his turn to raise eyebrows. "You met ... like ... gods? Like the real ones? Like Hephaestus and Apollo—?"

"Don't mix and match the Greek and the Roman deities," I said. "Yes on Hephaestus." I'd actually pummeled the hell out of him about five minutes before he died. "Apollo died before B.C. turned to A.D., I think, though I knew his son pretty well." So did Kat, for that matter, since she'd been intimate—not like Moose-joke intimate, but actually intimate—with Janus.

"Wow, that's—" Steven stopped short, straightening as someone approached behind me. "Hello, sir."

Sir? I wondered, turning to find—ugh, Taggert. Again.

"You don't have to call me sir," Taggert said with that same easy, sleazy smile, but something in his manner suggested that maybe he reveled in being called sir. More than a little, even. "How's it going, Steven? I hear you've got some script problems on your new project."

"It's in rewrites," Clayton admitted a little stiffly. "You know me, I stay out of all that." He smiled faintly. "They just pay me to read it and come up with the requisite emotion to go along."

"Oh, come on now," Taggert said, steering carefully around me to land a hand on Steven's shoulder. "They pay you for more than that—your pretty face and your manly manner, for example." Taggert clenched a fist and made a stiff grimace. "You're one of the only real rugged guys in this generation, you know. We're having to import that kind of talent from England and Australia nowadays by the bucketload."

I thought about that for a second. Hemsworth,

Hiddleston, Cumberbatch—hey, maybe he was right. At least we still had Chris Evans and Chris Pratt. Wait, how many Chris's did this town have, anyway?

"Well, thank you, sir," Clayton said, all mannerly and gentlemanly and—uh, yeah, manly, too. He reminded me of one of those old-timey cowboys from the westerns, like a better-looking John Wayne with his chivalry and manners and stuff.

"That project," Taggert said, acting like he was thinking it over, trying to recall, but proving that he wasn't going to be winning any awards for his performance, "it's like *Die Hard* in a National Park, right? You're the ranger from Yogi Berra?"

"Uh, Yogi Berra was a baseball great," Clayton said with a disarming smile, "but yeah, my character is a park ranger. He's an outdoorsman, and—"

"Yeah, yeah, I got it," Taggert said, making a frame out of his hands and putting Clayton in the middle of it. "All-American guy and whatnot. Sounds like a real stretch for you, really pushing your craft." He grinned, and I beat back my desire to practice amateur dentistry again.

Another round of screams came from behind Steven, out the glass doors on the deck, somewhere below where I saw a pool glimmering. "What's that?" Taggert asked as we all turned. "You think the president snuck back in just to tell someone else off?"

"Well, he's not doing it to me, so I'm guessing not," I said, feeling slightly annoyed. Steven gave me a puzzled look. Another scream sounded in the silence, more urgently this time, and desperately familiar—

Klementina.

"Kitten," Taggart whispered, but I was already flying into motion.

16.

Kat

Kat certainly didn't intend to scream, but it came stumbling out from between her lips anyway, after the others had gone through a round of it. Seeing a man walk through a wall tended to do that, ghostly and incorporeal, like he was smoke passing through solid surfaces.

"Kat Forrest," the red-haired demon of a man said in a harsh, grating voice. His beard and hair were so tangled, so … gross. "I told you I was coming for you."

That wasn't what had prompted the scream, though; no, it was him sticking his hand right through Bree Lancer's chest, then pulling it out, taking what looked like her heart with it—that was what caused the scream from Kat.

Others followed, of course, and then the inevitable flight from the scene, with more screams, more cries, more gasps, shouts of "OHMIGOD!" and the like. Kat didn't move, standing still and staring right into the eyes of the red menace as Bree Lancer's corpse splashed into the pool and sank. The red-haired man stood there, hand extended over the water, and let the drops of crimson fall, disappearing into the churning water.

"What the hell, bro!" someone called as they were running away. Kat kept her eyes riveted on the redhead, watching him for movement, but he seemed more interested in dangling the heart over the pool, letting the blood drip out of it.

"I don't know you," Kat said quietly, keeping herself still.

"You will," the redhead said. "By the end of this, you'll know who I am." He smiled and his teeth looked dark and stained. "The world will never forget my name ... and the only thing they'll remember yours for is how you died."

"That's grim," Sienna said as she shot over the balcony above and rocketed down at the redhead. He looked up at her in dull surprise as she led with a foot in a kick that brought her streaking, unerringly, toward him—

Only to pass through as she rocketed toward the concrete pool deck.

Sienna stopped only an inch before her foot slammed into the concrete, her body mingled with the redhead's, his face sticking out of hers, her legs and lower body jutting out of his waist. She spun and disentangled from him in an instant, causing him to take a disoriented step back. "Well, that was a dipsy-doodle," she said, blinking as she stood in front of Kat.

"A what?" Kat asked.

"Not the moment for explanation," Sienna said, holding up a hand protectively to ward Kat back. That was Sienna, all charging in like the big hero, regardless of whether it did any good or not. "So ... mysterious phasing guy ... I hear you've got grievances against Kat here."

"Not as big as the grievance I've got against you," the redhead snapped, tossing aside Bree Lancer's heart like it was a bad pita chip.

"Have we met?" Sienna asked, voice riddled with confusion. "Because I don't recall running up against a guy who could move through walls and people—" She paused. "Waiiiiit a minute. Didn't Augustus kick your ass after you—"

"Shut up!" The redhead hissed, taking a stomping step forward.

"—put a hand through Taneshia?" Sienna finished, and

Kat could hear the smirk in her delivery. "He buried you, didn't he?"

"SHUT UP!" the redhead screamed and stepped forward again, his pale, freckled face flushed.

"Dude," Sienna said, looking him up and down, "What happened to you? You are looking emaciated as—"

The redhead lunged at her, bloodied hands reaching for her neck. Sienna shot backward; he moved fast. She collided with Kat, knocking her into the pool like she'd just been sidelined by a truck coming at her in reverse.

"Ooof—" Kat grunted as she hit the surface of the water with a splash.

The water was warm, at least, but disorientation overcame her as she spun, nearly weightless, headfirst in the pool. The lights in the water gave the whole world a green coloring, with hints of blue, like lush plants were surrounding her instead of water.

Kat spun, her dress clinging to her and yet still swirling behind her in a trail. Now she regretted going with the slightly longer hem, but at least it hadn't been one of those award-season dresses with a full train. She looked up and could see the dark sky above, the hints of trees that surrounded the yard, and some sort of battle taking place—

She was rocketed out of the water like it had spit her out. It was like stone hitting her buttocks and launching her free from the pool's embrace, carrying her out and onto the deck on the upper floor. She rode the pillar of water up, sputtering as it cleared out of her eyes, where the chlorine had already started to burn a little, and delivered her right into the waiting arms of—

Scott.

He had his hands out to steer the water and to catch her, and he did both, sending the water that had carried her up to him back down with a hard push of his hands. It turned like a living thing, tendrils of moisture that made a U-turn and went right for the man with the red hair as he struck out at

Sienna, who was laughing as she dodged him.

What seemed like the entire pool dumped down on the redhead, and he disappeared under hundreds of gallons of fresh liquid. Scott's hands were moist, light glistening off them as he turned the only weapon he had against the enemy in front of him. He clapped his hands together like some kind of signal, and the water just parked itself with the redhead at its center, as though it were trapped by invisible glass walls.

Sienna stood just outside the wall of liquid, hands up in a defensive stance, and cast a short look up at Kat and Scott. "Nicely done."

"Thanks," Scott said, straining, his hands shaking, as he kept the water in place.

Kat stood next to him, utterly drenched and dripping on the deck, breathing hard as she stared down. Within the globule of water, which was formless, like a droplet of water so small as to hold its shape without borders, she could see movement—

Red hair making its way unhindered through the heart of the globe of water.

The man with the ragged red hair and beard emerged from Scott's trap without having to so much as take a breath. He stood there, facing down Sienna once more, looking just as ragged, just as wary, his shoulders slightly slumped.

"I guess you weren't thirsty," Sienna said. Kat would have rated that maybe a 3 out of 10 on Sienna's repartee scale; it wasn't her best work.

"I'm thirsty for vengeance," the redhead said and came at Sienna once more—no warning, no hesitation—and, Kat suspected—no mercy.

17.

Sienna

Every so often I run into someone and I'm just not sure what to do with them. You probably know what I mean—ever come across someone you knew way back when and you're like, "Oh, hey, it's you!" because you don't remember their name?

This was like that, except that I not only didn't know this guy's name, I also didn't know how to kill him. The redhead was leering at me from beneath that enormously scraggly beard and long hair, reminding me of nothing so much as one of Wolfe's brothers—

True, Wolfe offered.

—ready to take another swipe at me. Only a complete and total moron wouldn't have seen it coming a mile off, which was why, when he came for me, I was ready to evade.

But as I fell back from his ineffectual, rage-driven swipes, I ran through my mental list of things I could do to him and scratched items off the list one by one:

Beat him into a messy pulp—Sienna. NOPE.

Turn into a dragon and bite his head off—Bastian. Not so much. Also, *NO,* said Bastian, embarrassed.

Capture him in a web of light—Eve Kappler. I shot a web at him and it passed through like he wasn't there. Well, that was a negatory.

Burn him to death—Gavrikov. I held up both hands and blasted with a jet of flame that I immediately recalled back to my hands, creating a coruscating field of heat just in front of me. It passed through his face and chest like he wasn't even there. Which he probably wasn't. VETO.

Smartass him—Zack.

No, Zack, I thought, *my smart mouth was getting me into trouble long before I met you, dear.*

Damn, he whispered.

Torture him with a dreamwalk—Sienna. Yeah, that wasn't really applicable here.

Pleasure him with a dreamwalk—Sienna. Uhhh … not really appropriate here, or ever, really. Why was I thinking of Steven Clayton again? Man, was it hot in LA at night or was I imagining things?

Now comes the time for Bjorn Odinson to make his use known, Bjorn said.

Ah, yes. The power of the Odin-type. It was something I tended to overlook because it was really quite—uhm … simplistic? Bjorn had the power to project startling imagery of ravens in one's mind.

The warmind is more than that, it is a power that can disrupt one's very ability to—

Yes, thank you, Bjorn.

I concentrated as the redhead came swiping at me, looking like he was about two seconds from trying to start a full-on slap fight with me, and I let him have the warmind.

Captain Redbeard flinched like I'd legitimately slapped him, or given him a sharp jab to the nose. BOOYAH! Take that, you insubstantial bastard. His skin flickered, phasing back into substance. While he rocked back, I used the opportunity to give him a real jab, and he went flying like I'd strapped a rocket to his face and launched him across the yard. He disappeared into the wall of the house, apparently in control of himself enough to trigger his power to save himself from a rough landing.

Nicely done, Wolfe said. *Now tear out his entrails with your teeth.*

"I don't think it's that kind of party," I said, mostly to myself. Mostly. "Close, but ... no." I glanced up at Scott, wondering if I should go into the house or bash through a wall to go looking for this guy. I didn't want to presume he was one and done on the punching, but he hadn't disappeared behind glass; if I was going to go after him, it was going to require some pursuit, and what with a lot of people already having screamed and fled around the sides of the house, I figured it might pay to wait a second and see if he came back to me for another round since I'd just given him a good what-for.

I looked up and saw like twenty people with their cell phone cameras watching from the edges of the upper deck, and a few more hiding behind vegetation in the back yard, sort of hiding around the edges of the party and—I dunno, filming or Instagraming or Vining or YouTubing or whatever. "Get out of here, you idiots!" I shouted. Not a one of them so much as moved.

Figures. Anyone with brains had gotten the hell out of here before the shit had hit the fan.

"Hey!" Steven Clayton called from next to Scott, who still held his hands up as he ushered the water back into the swimming pool a little at a time. "Are you okay?"

"I'm fine," Kat said, throwing herself against him, once more not winning any acting awards for sincerity. "I was so worried!"

Steven looked a little helpless with her hanging on him; she was stronger than a normal human, after all. "Uhh ... good." She was dripping all over his tux, and he'd noticed. "I'm glad to hear that." He gently removed her from him, like she was the most awkward thing in the world.

Hey, did I just get the attention of the big Hollywood star over Kat? Hehe. That's funny.

And also ... weird, right?

"Thanks, Scott!" I called as he carefully managed the last of the swimming pool's contents back to where it belonged.

"I am your own personal Ron Weasley in a flying Ford Anglia, yes," he said, voice straining a little as he dropped the last of the water off the deck in front of me, leaving not so much as a spot. Boy does good work with moisture, lemme tell ya. Uhh … pretend I said that in a very even, detached tone, and forget that we'd slept together once upon a time. Because otherwise it would probably seem irredeemably dirty. "Should we check on that—uhh … do we have a name for that guy?"

"Seems like he's got a mad-on for Kat," I said. "Typical Injustice Collector."

"Whut?" Kat asked, sounding—well, sounding like Kat. "I don't know who he is." Now she sounded petulant. Also like Kat. "He knew you!" She pointed a finger down at me.

"Everybody knows me," I scoffed then felt a little embarrassed at how egomaniacal that probably sounded. "Not in a good way," I corrected, mostly for the benefit of Steven. Uhh … that didn't really help my cause, did it?

I focused on the shocked look on Steven Clayton's face for just a second too long. I thought he was just reacting to my asinine statement, but by the time I realized he was lifting a finger to point to something behind me, it was too late.

I felt a stunning pain in my shoulder as I started to turn, and the Redhead jabbed a hand through me, right into my arm. I stumbled forward and he pursued, ripping into my other side as I staggered. I lost my balance and fell into the pool, feeling a ripping and tearing like I was getting pecked at by a pack of carrion birds all the while.

Wolfe, I said to myself before the hits had stopped coming, and I felt him go to work with his power to heal me. The pain faded in seconds, and there was a splash as someone jumped into the water to save me. I wondered why Scott would waste his time doing that when could have just had the water reject me right out like he had with Kat. Then I felt strong arms take hold of me and start to lift me out of the water. I wanted to hold tight to my rescuer, but instead I grabbed them by the arm and prompted Gavrikov to turn off the gravity, causing us both to soar right out of the water.

I saw the surprise on Steven Clayton's face as I flew him over the yard and dropped him on the soft grass. He hit and rolled like a man who'd been trained in martial arts quite a bit—which he probably had. He hadn't become an action hero by not doing at least a few of his own stunts.

I swept around, looking for Redbeard, the pirate hobo, but all I found was Kat, shaking on the upper deck, Scott perched at the edge of the railing, watching me. Also, those idiots with cell phone cameras.

"Where's the big noise?" I asked, coming to a landing next to Clayton. "And I do mean 'big noise,' too, because I'm gonna make that little shit scream louder than a metal band when I get my hands on him—"

"Gone," Scott said solemnly. He didn't look nearly so rattled as Kat, who was probably in danger of falling apart, she was shaking so much. It wasn't from the cold either, because I'd just taken a dip in the same pool she had and it had to be like seventy-five degrees out here. "But not before he explained himself a little more."

"Oh, yeah?" My feet touched down on the ground, and the weight of gravity settled back on me. "What did ZZ Red have to say for himself?"

Scott looked at Kat before answering, but she was too busy looking down to answer for herself. "Said there weren't any real cameras here tonight." He looked at the circle of spectators still filming all the action with their phones. "Said it wasn't public enough for her to die here. He said ..." Scott licked his lips, but stopped.

"He said," Kat picked it up, her fear obvious even through her bitter tone, "that he wanted the whole world watching when I died—and you, too."

18.

Karl

There were easier ways to die, but Karl couldn't think of any that would be nearly as satisfying as the end he had planned. He was walking away from the house now, down the hill, disappearing through the other houses and scaring the hell out of people in their living rooms and bedrooms and out on their decks as he ran through without regard for what they were thinking. Their scared and surprised faces were motivation, like fuel or food, the thing that kept him going. He loved the revulsion, the attention. It was like sweet candy after not getting a taste of anything for months.

And he knew how that felt, too.

He stopped down the road a bit, looking back up the hill, pausing in the middle of someone's lush, green lawn. Water glistened on the blades of grass, and not from recent rainfall, either. He looked up at where he'd been, lights coming on in some of the houses he'd taken shortcuts through, and smiled. Their fear was his pleasure, and he was about to take a whole lot of pleasure.

They'd remember his name when it was all over, that was for sure.

He fished his phone out of his pocket, dialing a number he knew by heart. When his benefactor picked up, he asked a simple question: "Now?"

"Now," his benefactor said with a voice heavy with a smile and hung up so Karl could make his next call. It rang once as he sat waiting in anticipation, listening to the barking of dogs and shouts of people in the night.

The explosion at the Vargas house rocked the hills, the shockwave shattering glass in the house behind him. He'd left the bomb under a bed on his way out to confront Kat the first time, and it had sat there waiting for him to do just this.

Sirens were already wailing at his handiwork, and Karl waited, watching, listening to them scream closer and closer. It was a satisfying noise, the sound of notoriety, of his rising reputation. Yes, they would remember him, all right. Just a few more moves and he'd see to that. They'd write his name in the history books for all time.

19.

Sienna

Oh, Redbeard, I thought as the house exploded, showering all of us behind my hastily cordoned-off perimeter with glass, there had to be less painful ways to die than pissing me off.

Standard agency procedure after a metahuman event was to evacuate the area in case there was a secondary threat—usually, that would be another meta. It could, however, include bombs, and in this case, that's exactly what we had, apparently. I had to admit, after meeting our little aggrieved ginger, I had a sneaking suspicion he was the sort that wanted to make his miserable mark as violently as he could, with little compunction for what would happen to anyone in his wake. Turned out I was right.

Yay, me.

"Did you hear?" Anna Vargas, star of some vapid reality show like Kat's, but without super powers, wandered by next to Flannery Steiner, one of Los Angeles County's Least Wanted. Since Steiner had neither cocaine nor a naked man nor a moving vehicle close at hand, I gave them both a wary eye and eavesdropped. "We're already trending on Twitter!" She didn't seem too upset about her house, probably because she figured she was insured and it'd be taken care of. That was going to be a rather rude shock.

"I know," Steiner said, clearly enjoying the publicity and

minimally concerned about the death threats against Kat or the party house that had just been blown up like two hundred feet away from where she stood. "Isn't it awful?" Her tone suggested it was anything but, the harpy.

Steven Clayton came wandering up, looking a little dazed. "You all right?" he asked me again.

"Fine," I said, looking back at the burning house. I didn't know exactly what kind of bomb had been used, but it had made for a hell of a detonation and didn't leave too much fire behind. It was spreading now, of course, but it looked more like the structure had just been demolished versus— well, you know those huge pyrotechnic explosions you see in movies? Yeah. This may have been Hollywood, but it didn't look like that. More bang, less burn. My ears were still ringing a little. I glanced at Clayton and felt a shock run through me. "Why? Do I not look okay?"

"Well, you look like one of the extras from a really bad zombie movie I made in my youth," he said, studying me. I had some holes in my clothing, it was true, and there was more than a little red seeping through.

"I saw that one," I said, nodding. He cocked his head at me, and I shrugged. "It was on Netflix, and I was bored—" I paused. "Also, I think you're still in your youth."

"Got me there," he said with a smile. He didn't grin, I'd noticed, which was a mark in his favor. Smiling stupidly ought to be the province of, well, the stupid.

"Get over there!" Taggert shouted from behind me. I turned around to see him hectoring a guy with a camera— not the same one I'd threatened with sodomy earlier, but a new one—pushing him to lift the camera up so he could get a clear view of the blown up house. "Get some good establishing shots, some clear ones of the aftermath, of the fire trucks when they show up, the cops ..." He snapped his fingers in Karyn, the assistant's face, and her glazed-over eyes snapped out of the trance she was in. "Find someone who was filming the whole thing and get them to sell us footage of the explosion, huh?" He shoved her lightly away, and she scurried off to accost a man with a cell phone in his hand. Taggert caught my eye and grinned. "Gotta think of everything."

"Thanks for proving my point on that one, Taggert," I muttered. Clayton gave me a quizzical look, but we both got distracted by the arrival of the first police cars, sirens doing that WHOOOOOP thing, all digital and annoying and shrieky. "You seen Kat?" I asked him.

"She's right there," Clayton said, pointing about ten feet behind me. Kat was in a little gap in the crowd, Scott standing next to her like a silent sentinel, arms folded. The good news was, I could have hit them with a spit from here. The bad news was that I hadn't realized it. In the chaos, Captain Redbeard could have made another, more successful kill attempt, and I might not have seen it in time to stop it.

"Oh, good," I said, trying to decide if it really was good. Man, I was tired.

"You sure you're okay?" Clayton asked with a frown.

"It's past my bedtime," I said, yawning as the cop car made its way through enough of the crowd to come rolling to a halt. "And do you have any idea how long it takes to do witness statements on these things?"

"Uhhh ... no?"

"Good for you," I said with a tight smile of my own. "But you're about to find out."

Taggert sashayed a little closer, clearly not that upset about what I would classify as a disaster, but which he apparently considered nothing less than a wonderful evening. "You know how long this is going to take? Kitten's got a *Vanity Fair* photoshoot tomorrow in the a.m."

I was too tired to wonder why he didn't just say "morning." "Hours," I said. "You might want to cancel that."

He gave me a dismissive wave of the hand. "We'll just have them fix it with Photoshop if she's got bags under the eyes. No big."

I turned to see Steven Clayton with a full-bore cringe on his face. "There's no business like show business, huh?" He did not answer me, but I had a feeling that I knew more or less what he was thinking by the expression on his face.

20.

Scott

Scott sat with his head down, trying to ignore the flare of the police and ambulance lights. The fire trucks were further up the hill by now, and the whole scene was consumed by people in formalwear being asked questions by uniformed emergency personnel. First aid was being administered, and by Scott's reckoning, about a thousand photos were being Instagrammed per minute.

"You know," he said to Kat, who was sitting on the ground next to him, "for a bunch of people who had a decently close brush with death tonight, your friends don't seem overly concerned."

Kat stirred out of her torpor, her dress still damp from where she'd gone in the pool. He held out a hand and drew the moisture to him, pulling it free of the fabric and out of her hair. He pulled a stray tear as well, though he didn't say anything about it as it glistened through the air toward him, reflecting the red and blue light.

"That guy—the red-haired bum guy—he really does want to kill me, doesn't he?" Kat asked.

"Seems like," Scott said after a pause for thought. "I mean, he's following you around with intent."

"What did I ever do to him?" she asked, blinking. Another droplet came oozing out of the corner of her eye, subtle and small.

Scott shifted uneasily where his ass met the hard concrete curb. "You exist. Some people don't need any other reason."

"At least Sienna did something to him," she said, sniffing slightly, "you know, to make him mad—"

"I don't think she actually did …"

"—I've never even met him before and he hates me enough that he wants to kill me," she said quietly. She averted her gaze, watching her cameraman taking shots of the house as the firemen turned their hoses on it, streams of water sailing through the night to put out the small blaze still burning in the wreckage of the home. "I'm sorry I treated you like a stalker earlier."

"Hm?" Scott roused himself out of a perfectly good stupor. He hadn't gotten used to Pacific time yet. "Oh. Right. Yeah, I'm sorry you did, too. Any chance you'd be willing to fix that in edits?"

"I'll talk to Taggert about it," she said, staring blankly at the scene and all the chaos unfolding within it. "I'm sure he'll want to portray you and Sienna both as heroes trying to protect me. I don't see how you could look like my enemies after coming to my rescue like that."

"Maybe," Scott said. He had his suspicions otherwise. He lowered his voice. "I'm sorry I seem like a stalker."

"You're not," she said, shaking her head. "You never did. You just … you remember things I don't." She met his eyes carefully, her green ones still glittering with heartfelt emotion. "I'm sorry that I can't. I've seen the pictures … we seemed happy together." She looked around until her eyes alighted on Sienna, and a hint of jealousy marred her pretty features. "Not as happy as the two of you seemed before I left, but still … It can't be easy to watch her catch the interest of a guy like Steven Clayton."

Scott felt his skin tighten around his eyes, his lips twisting up into an involuntary smirk. "Sienna? Why does everyone keep saying we were together? We're just friends." He nodded his head toward her, where she stood, very uneasily, next to Clayton, answering the questions posed by an African-American woman in a suit with a badge hanging out of her front pocket. "If she, uh, y'know, ends up dating America's most eligible bachelor—"

"He's *People Magazine's* Sexiest Man of the Year," Kat said with a dash of impatience.

"Whatever the case," Scott said, "I'm happy for her."

Kat made a face like she'd swallowed a lime slice. "Yeah. Happy for her. Me, too."

21.

Sienna

Detective Meredith Waters of the LAPD had the sort of long-suffering look that I suspected I'd worn on more than a few occasions myself. She watched me with dark, wary eyes as I answered every question she asked, and she still kept a close watch on me when she started directing her questions toward Steven, who answered them with a lot of florid expression, the sort of thing he probably learned as an actor.

"... when I came out of the pool, the guy was gone," Steven finished, his voice a low, smooth, sexy rumble. "Sienna rounded everyone up and got them to a safe distance from the house. A few minutes later—boom." He made an exploding gesture with his hands.

I waited for Detective Waters to quibble, to ask another question, to pick at his story like she'd picked at mine. "All right, Mr. Clayton," she said, a lot more warmly than she had at any point during my 'interrogation,' "you're free to go."

I wanted to be offended by her offering preferential treatment to the pretty boy over the federal agent, but—let's face it, I was a disaster with a reputation for chaos and he was an upstanding famous person with an ass you could play racquetball on.

Oh, shit, did I just say that?

Detective Waters turned her attention back to me. "Now,

you say you've had contact with this particular villain of yours before?"

I rolled my eyes. "First of all, he's not *my* villain, I don't—you know, personally own him or anything—"

"But you've had an encounter with him before," she said, "in Atlanta?"

"No." I shook my head.

She gave me that doubting look. "Listen, Ms. Nealon, I've heard stories about you. Every cop has. This Atlanta thing you were involved in—"

"I was in one of the Carolinas when that mess kicked off," I said, "I got there at the end. One of my associates, Augustus Coleman, he was the one who took on Captain Redbeard." Which was my new name for this dude with the phase-powers. Eat your heart out, Cisco Ramon, I can name villains, too.

"Uh huh," Detective Waters said. At least, unlike a lot of the other people I'd dealt with tonight, she was sincere—she sincerely did not like me or want me to be here. And hell, if I'd been her, I would have sincerely wished my troublemaking ass out of town. "Does your ... associate ... know this man's name?"

"Well, I think he kind of dug up the earth and buried him in it, so ... maybe?" I shrugged. I'd put in a call to Augustus, but he and Reed were off on an assignment and on Central time. Presumably they were both sleeping right now, because I hadn't heard back from him.

"Maybe?"

"I don't know if names were exchanged before he started ripping the ground beneath the Captain's feet," I said, keeping it just this side of snotty. "If he followed the clearly laid out Conventions of Metahuman Battle, as well as Ms. Manner's Simple Rules for Introductions, then we're golden. If, on the other hand, he was in a desperate fight for his life against about a dozen metas all at once," crossing the snotty line at about supersonic speed, "he might not have gotten the name before he closed up the earth on this guy."

Detective Waters took a sharp breath, and by the way her lips were pressed together, I knew she was counting the hours until she could go home. "Uh huh," was all she said, though.

My phone buzzed, and she and Steven looked at me. I let it go a couple times before I made a show of checking who was calling. "Oh, goody," I said when I saw the screen read "Andrew Phillips," "this night just keeps getting awesomer. How could it possibly get any better?"

"You want to get a drink?" Steven asked nonchalantly.

My phone buzzed in my hand about five times until Detective Waters, the ire rising in her voice said, "Are you going to get that?" I heard jealousy, but I'd also just heard the hottest guy in Hollywood ask me out, so it was possible I was suffering auditory delusions. Could Wolfe change his voice to play ventriloquist to the stars? A fleeting image of him with his hand up—

Oh, snot rockets. (That was what Dr. Zollers was telling me to say in place of my old standby, OH SHIT. Neither of us was holding our breath on me quitting swearing. Besides, I had more pressing personality issues to work on.)

"I'll be right back," I said, probably sounding more shell-shocked than I had after the battle. I stepped away from the two of them and pressed the answer button on my phone. "Waffle House," I said.

"What?" Andrew Phillips's voice came through the speaker, a little tinny. I heard him shifting around, checking to see if he'd called the right number. "Oh, ha ha."

"No, seriously," I said, "if you're calling to place an order for waffles, press one. For all non-waffle related inquiries, please hang up and call someone else."

"I heard you met the president," he said in the same dull tone of voice he always used.

"Did you? What did he think of our waffles?"

"Will you knock that off? I know it's you."

"Jeez, you must be the only guy in the world who doesn't like waffles—"

"If you think smarting off to the president of the United States was a good idea—"

"—maybe a blue waffle for you?"

"—you're even closer to the edge of getting fired than you ever have been, you realize that?" Phillips said, ignoring my rather crass reference.

"Oh, noes."

"What are you even doing in California?" Phillips asked. "I don't remember sending you on assignment to LA."

"Yeah, well, you didn't have to reimburse for my travel so I didn't think you'd notice," I said, looking at my fingernails. They were dirty. "We received a credible threat of meta attack, so here I am, as fits my job description."

"You're not supposed to go on assignment without permission," Phillips said, the tension evident in his voice. "Your assignments are up to my discretion."

"Yes, but your judgment is suspect," I said lightly. "I mean, you don't even like waffles, for crying out loud—"

"You need to get to Washington," Phillips said. "DC," he clarified, probably wisely.

"Too bad, I was totes heading for Seattle as soon as we hung up. Maybe lunch with Bezos or something, bum around Pike Place Market, get some Starbucks right at the source—"

"Stop."

"You want me to ignore the fact that a meta attacked someone on national television?" I asked, having a little fun with this. "I mean, this mess is trending on Twitter right now. Instagram photos of the carnage are spreading like blue waffles across the internet as we speak—"

"What the hell is a—nevermind," he said, his frustration with me reaching—if not a peak, at least a recent high. I'd missed this. "You cannot operate without oversight."

"Fine, oversee me," I said, shrugging my shoulders. "Come to the coast, we'll get together, have some laughs, watch a guy with a really epic beard of red try and kill a reality TV star, and possibly me—"

There was a click, and I said, "Hello?" I felt my eyebrows go up and nodded in silent respect, mostly to myself. I'd never gotten Phillips to hang up on me before. Maybe this day wasn't so bad after all.

I wandered back to Detective Waters and Steven, who were both watching me, Waters with that same jaded look and Clayton with some dim interest that, uh … well, I didn't know quite how to take it.

"Drink?" he asked me again.

I stared at his handsome face, his straight brown hair, perfectly framed for a magazine cover, and I sighed like Princess Anna. "I probably need to make sure Kat doesn't get murdered in the night," I said. *Unfortunately*, I did not add.

"Wow," he said, still sincere as anything. "That's a good point, I hadn't even thought about that. Good for you, keeping your commitment, prioritizing it above petty stuff. You're a good friend to her."

I kept from laughing at the suggestion that Kat and I were friends, but only just barely. "Well, you know," I said a hell of a lot more airily than I felt, "you gotta do the, uh, heroic thing and … whatnot." I'd been up for like, twenty-four hours and had just declined a date with easily the most handsome man I'd seen since I first went running out the front door of my house at age seventeen. I'd dated some reasonably nice-looking guys, but none of them were movie stars, if you catch my meaning.

"You really are a hero," he said. "Maybe some other time." He gave me a nod and started off down the hill. I didn't know where he was walking, but I was watching him until he disappeared into the crowd.

"You really are an idiot," Detective Waters opined once he was gone. I turned my head in time to see that her eyeline was still following him down the hill. She shook her head and wandered off to handle the scene.

I tried to decide which I was, but ultimately just landed on "tired," before I headed off to collect Kat and Scott and hopefully find a place to collapse for a little while—preferably somewhere that the menace of Captain Redbeard wouldn't follow me.

22.

Sienna

I walked into one of the slickest hotel suites I've ever seen in my life, one that rivaled mansions I've cannonballed through the windows of (what? It's not like anyone would invite me into a swank place like that—you know my rep for destruction) and stood admiring the view of Los Angeles before me, all lit up at night like I was in the middle of a city of stars.

"Ugh," Kat said, as though these accommodations were the most substandard she'd ever had inflicted upon her beleaguered, long-suffering person. "Is this the best they could do?" Somewhere in poorer regions of the world, they would be burning the lovely furniture that appointed this suite because fuel was more important to survival than pretty things.

Here in Los Angeles, California, though, Klementina Gavrikov had completely lost perspective and thought this marble-floored, multi-floored palace was completely unsuitable for her more-than-modest needs.

"You've come a long way from that shack outside Kirensk," I quipped, but she looked at me blankly because she couldn't remember that. I could, though, thanks to her brother being in my head. I liked her better when she wasn't too good for everything and everyone.

"Best we could do on short notice, Kitten," Taggert said, mildly apologetic, as poor Karyn struggled in carrying a half-dozen bags while Scott followed behind with a half-dozen more. None of them were his, of course. I would have carried something, but honestly—pro tip—you don't tie up your hands when you're on bodyguard duty. Doing so means you waste valuable seconds dropping whatever it is to either draw your gun or—if you're me—shoot a web of light, send a flaming blast at someone, etc. I also drew my gun frequently, because it looked more intimidating to the average meta than just holding my hand up menacingly. Surprisingly few people made the connection in the heat of the moment, realizing that they were more likely to die from one of my flame attacks than from a bullet. Go figure.

Also, I was nobody's beast of burden, let alone Kat's. If she'd asked me to carry a suitcase for her, I would have shown her exactly where she could carry it, but it would have required the removal of the stick already residing there first.

"I'll be in the master suite," Kat said, making a noise that told us just how put out she was by having to leave her rental house behind in order to hide here in this posh hotel. There were no cameras present, either; they were still gathering footage of the cops and firemen back at the site of the attack. I'd overheard Taggert telling her to do a "confessional booth" video on her phone before she called it a night, and a little piece of my already shrunken soul died.

"Umm," Scott said, gesturing to the suitcases in his hands.

"Follow her up," Taggert said, making an obvious motion toward the staircase Kat was already climbing, Karyn following meekly behind her. "You can drop my bags here." He unbuttoned his jacket. "Then when you're done bringing Kitten's up, you can come back and put mine in my suite." Awww, Taggert. So close to genuine humanity there for a quarter second, but not really.

Scott, however, did nothing more forceful than shoot me

a disbelieving look before shrugging and doing as commanded. I watched with a little disbelief of my own, and then my phone buzzed.

Ricardo

A glorious woman such as you should not spend the night alone.

"Oh, if only I were, Dick," I muttered and then felt the awkward presence of Taggert sidling closer to me, grinning. "Whoa. That's close enough." He stopped as though nothing were unusual about what he was doing. For all I knew, there wasn't anything unusual about it. He was likely a weird creeper to everyone.

"We should talk," he said nonchalantly, placing his hands on his hips and pushing back his jacket. It was kind of a Superman pose, but he really lacked the classic good looks to pull it off. Also, the decency of Clark Kent. Or even Grant Ward, come to think of it.

"So talk," I said, eyeing him like he was going to slowly ooze his slime-puddle self over and mess up my boots. It was a real danger, I judged. "I have ears and can hear you from here."

"Why don't you come into my suite and we can talk a little more privately?" he asked, still grinning. My boots were safe, but the rest of me was feeling crawly at the mere suggestion.

"This seems like a fine spot. Kat will probably have Scott and Karyn unpacking for her, and that'll take at least a year."

"We need to talk about the security precautions for tomorrow's *Vanity Fair* shoot," Taggert said.

"Oh, I've got that covered," I said. "She's not going."

Taggert raised an eyebrow. It looked painful, like he was warring hard against the botulinum toxin to make that happen. "The hell you say."

"The hell I say," I agreed. "She needs to keep a low profile." I shot an appraising glance around the suite. "This isn't helping, but at least it's not public and totally exposed." Well, sort of. For a guy who could walk through walls, nothing was all that private.

"We checked in under a false name," Taggert pointed out.

"Yeah, no one will ever guess that Pamela Isley is actually Kat," I deadpanned. They for real had done that at the check-in desk. Reed would have shat upon the Persian carpet just before the desk had he been here.

"There are a lot of nice hotels in this town," Taggert shrugged, taking off his jacket while he was making the motion. He casually tossed it over the arm of the velvety couch and stretched, showing off his utter lack of pecs under his polo shirt. Less yoga, more weight, dude-bro. "What are the chances he'd find her at this specific one?"

"I don't know," I said sourly. "Ask me in the morning if we haven't had a sudden case of Kat euthanasia."

"No cameras here anyway," he said, shrugging like it didn't mean a thing. "If he was gonna attack, he'd be better off waiting until the shoot."

"Thank you for making my argument for me," I said, arms folded in front of my chest. "Cancel the shoot."

"Can't," he said, smiling impishly. Much like that elf from Rudolph, I was going to be a dentist yet. "Do you know how long this cover shoot has been in the works? Months and months. Everyone wants it. It's a big get."

"You know what else is a big 'get'? Death. It's huge. Pretty much consumes the whole rest of your life, damages the plans you've made for the coming weeks and months and years. Cancel the shoot, or be prepared to cancel a whole lot more stuff in the future."

"I'd rather die than cancel the *Vanity Fair* shoot," Kat said stiffly, staring at us over the balcony above. She had a look on her face telling me she was serious.

"Be careful what you wish for," I said.

"We're doing it, and that's final," she said. She sniffed and then disappeared back toward what I presumed to be her room. I could hear faint noises up there like drawers being opened and closed. It would appear my sarcastic prediction of her putting Scott and Karyn to her unpacking had held some water. Uhh … no pun intended. Poor Scott.

"Yes, it might end up being final," I said, staring at the balcony where she'd stood. "So very, very final."

"Come on," Taggert said, beckoning me forward as he slowly started to make his way to the open double doors to the room behind him. "We'll talk about it a little more."

"What's wrong with right here?" I asked, a little afraid of the answer.

"There's no shower here," he said, grinning again. "And I need one. You, too. We can talk while—"

"Okaayyy," I said, one step from throwing up my hands (to keep me from knocking out all his teeth). "Yeah. No."

He broadened his grin and took a step closer as I mentally drew a circle around myself that I determined would constitute the point where the law would consider him to be crossing into the territory of a threat. "You know what I need right now?"

"I don't know, a lifetime supply of Valtrex?"

He actually grinned wider, the bastard. "Are you slut-shaming me?"

Oh, God. By the look on his face, I realized that not only had he tried this routine with other women before but it had actually *worked*. And probably often, judging by how casual about it he seemed; there was no nervousness, no hand-caught-in-the-cookie-jar guilt, not even the playful illusion of it that anyone with decency might have tossed out as a defense. Just a wry admission that he was a horny old man hitting on a much younger woman. And this bastard didn't even have any power over me. It occurred to me that given his position, that likely wasn't the case most of the time.

The circle of violence I drew around myself broadened in an instant. "If the micro-penis-sized condom fits," I said, low and menacing.

"Oh, you don't want to play," Taggert said, looking hurt. "Such a shame. That's all right, though. I was hoping maybe you and Kitten could show me how good a friends you are later—"

"OH, YUCK!" I made a vomiting noise that was drawing nearer to being real with every passing moment. I should have realized that this lecher would prey on anyone, but somehow the realization that Kat—I didn't even like her, but EWWWWW—at least Janus I could sort of understand, because he was a decent enough guy underneath the old. "You and Kat?" I asked before realizing that I didn't actually want to hear whatever came next.

"She understands how it is," he said. "She's—well, you know, she's just great. She's got an old soul—"

"You have no idea."

"—Sometimes a man just needs a favor, and I've certainly granted her more than a few—"

I wanted to vomit for realsies. You know how right before you're super nauseous, you almost pray for the vomiting to happen, just to get it over with? And how sometimes, afterwards, it feels better, like maybe you expunged the horror from your system? I really hoped for that moment of purgation, even though I didn't think that the sickness of the mind that Taggert's revelation had just forced upon me had even a chance of being purged through vomiting. If I had, I wouldn't have even hesitated, I would have stuck my finger so far down my throat with meta speed that I might have given myself an accidental tonsillectomy.

"I can see you're thinking about it," Taggert said with that same grin.

"And I wish I wasn't," I said, "I wish I could take away my own memories with my power, instead of just being able to take away other peoples'. I would give away my powers and let someone else take this memory and then shoot them in the head with high caliber hollow-points until their brains were splattered all over the floor, and then I would mop them up, douse the bucket and the floor and wall with gasoline and burn it, then nuke the building afterward just to be sure the memory was gone from this earth for good."

Taggert had his lips pressed together tightly; I had finally wiped the grin off his face. "So ... no shower, then?"

"Even if you weren't absolutely the most appalling man I've met even tonight—and that's saying something, because you're in the running with Captain Redbeard the invidious man and Dick-o, the worst first date of all time—I am still not getting Kat's sloppy seconds." Scott appeared at the balcony above and started making his way across the windows, ending up in the room across from Kat's. I made a face. "Again."

"Have it your way, then," Taggert said coolly and strode off to the doors of his suite. He closed them both on himself, mustering a grin again, but this one seemed more ... fake? "If you change your mind ..."

"Then I'll be sure to throw myself out the window over there," I gestured toward the plate glass to my right, "and not use my powers."

He shrugged like it was no big thing and closed the door. I didn't hear the click of a lock, and it bothered me.

My phone buzzed again.

Ricardo

Call me. We should do breakfast. You are captivating and I must see you again.

"Oh, for—" I said, tossing my phone, surprisingly gently, onto the nearest chair. I turned, expecting to find my room under where Scott's was, but—

Aw, hell.

There was nothing but a kitchenette there.

Karyn came down the stairs just then, all mousy and head-down. "Umm," I said, trying to intercept her, "this suite is short a room."

She didn't stop. She was beelining for the door after what was probably a long and degrading day which doubtlessly had her questioning her life choices. "There's a couch," she said, not bothering to stop and do something for me like—I dunno, kill Taggert and burn his corpse and personal possessions so I could have his room, or tell Kat she could have the couch, because the person protecting her should be treated like a guest, or just give me a half-second's commiseration about being treated like the ass end of this shit show—anything, really.

Nope, Karyn went out the door and didn't even bother to tell me to lock it behind her. I did it anyway, though, loafing around, not quite willing yet to accept the hard truth that my logical mind was forcing on me. I didn't want to, not after this night.

Ughhhh.

I was the bodyguard. I was protecting Kat, whom I loathed but thought of as a victim now that I knew— EWWW EWWW EWWWWWW—what price she'd paid for fame.

And now I had to sleep on her couch.

"You'd at least better be comfortable," I muttered to the couch, as if it could hear me.

It wasn't.

"I hate this town," I said, the lights glittering at me from beyond the window even after I'd turned off all the ones in the suite. The honking of an angry car horn somewhere below seemed to agree with me, and I passed out before the kink in my neck from the shitty pillow could give me a neck-ache.

23.

Karl had a house set up in the Elysium neighborhood, a perfect little hidey-hole, or a bolt-hole as his benefactor called it. It had almost no furniture, but the air mattress he had to sleep on was in the middle of the smallest room in the house, and that Karl found immensely soothing.

It was a perfect little lair for scheming his schemes, for imagining how things were going to go. He'd already seen his face on the news, the footage blurry and all shaky-cam, like these people had never filmed an action scene before. It didn't make him happy, exactly, because Karl didn't really feel happiness anymore, but he got a rough sense of satisfaction out of it, a cold feeling of victory, like he was rubbing it in their faces even now. It wasn't the big triumph yet, the one that would show them all, but it was pretty good.

The air mattress was a nice touch. He could have slept on the floor; it was nice to have even that kind of surface to rest on after months of—well, of what he'd dealt with. It was springy enough, light enough, especially in its half-deflated state, to mimic a little of what he'd learned to love.

He still couldn't sleep, though. No, he was too wired. Months of planning had led up to this day. And even though this day was over, the next ones—the ones of reckoning— they were going to be even better.

When he closed his eyes, he pictured the looks on their faces—Kat Forrest's had been good, a mixture of stunned disbelief and terror. She was a leech. She was disgusting.

Sienna Nealon's hadn't been quite so satisfying, but ripping her up had been. It had been so good, dumping her in the pool and then leaving her behind to watch as he blew up the house. She'd been so damned smug through their whole tête-à-tête; it had been nice wiping that off her face when he'd ripped into her muscles. Hopefully she was a little scared now, that she was feeling wronged like he'd been. It was just a taste of what was to come.

He was the righteous one in this exchange. Her little puppet, Augustus, had imprisoned him in the earth for months. MONTHS. He'd been doing his job, and that shit had just ripped the ground out from underneath him—HIM.

What had followed had been hell. What he'd been through was something no one else had been through. The horror was a raw nerve, easy to touch but hard to handle, searing, irritated skin left burnt and hanging in the wind. Or, no, not the wind, not really.

Karl felt the shame, the acidic singe in his gullet as his heartburn flared again. He heard a gunshot in the distance, and he sat up on the air mattress, looking down at his gaunt, emaciated arms, naked under the sheet. He pulled it off, the warm night making it irrelevant. His thighs were painfully thin, even now, like forearms. He'd been a big guy once, well put-together.

Now he was horror. A skeleton looked back at him from the mirror.

They'd all pay for this. All of them. They'd see who he was, what they'd done. He'd make them feel the shame of helplessness, of being done so very damned wrong.

Yes, they'd all see. The whole world would. They couldn't ignore him anymore, and they were talking about him even now, as he stood in the shadows.

He could imagine their faces when he stepped out. Then they'd never stop talking about him.

24.

Scott

Dawn found Scott still awake, staring out over the city, but he didn't want to venture out into the living room area because he'd realized, a little belatedly, that Sienna was sleeping out there. He'd gone out in the middle of the night when he couldn't sleep and found her curled up on the couch. She'd shifted at the sound of his footsteps, and he'd felt bad; here he had taken one of the bedrooms without even giving it a thought and she was stuck on a sofa. At least it looked comfortable, he justified it to himself.

He stared at the dawning day breaking over the city of Los Angeles and took a breath of the clean hotel air. It was better than the hotel his dad had put him up in, but he didn't have a change of clothes or any of his toiletries, so it was kind of a wash. Normally he would have taken a shower, but instead he'd turned on the TV as background noise. They were still talking about the drought, how they hadn't had rain since last fall, when it had deluged a few times and then quit. That didn't seem like the atmosphere to take a long shower in. It would have made him feel guilty.

The taste of morning breath stuck on his tongue, and he tried to remember when he'd last had an actual meal. Had he even had finger food at the party? No, he'd run into Brock before he'd found the food, and now whatever was left of the spread was ash. He tried to smile, but he didn't really feel like it. He had a sense of malaise in this whole thing that was unsettling, but it had settled—on him. On his bones, in his bones. It wasn't just the dry air, either. It was everything, a feeling that had followed him from Minnesota.

Why had Kat said that he and Sienna were together? They'd never so much as gone on a date. He racked his memory; he'd seen the articles, the gossip rag stuff that said they were boyfriend and girlfriend, but that was gossip rags. It wasn't like they ever got anything right. They made shit up for a living, like the weatherman or politicians.

There was a feeling in his mind that he quite couldn't identify, though. Like something stuck in his teeth that he couldn't work loose with his tongue, no matter how hard he tried.

Scott went into the bathroom attached to his room and ran water. It wasn't exactly a shower, but it would do. He ran his hands under the tap, drawing the water in. He could store it inside—retain water, he always joked—and he needed it right now, in this town. After he'd had his fill, he let it run a little longer. It was like taking a drink on a hot day, like quenching a thirst.

He shut off the tap and didn't bother toweling off his hands. They were already dry.

He eased over to the suite door and opened it. He took quiet steps up to the balcony and looked over. Sienna was still on the couch, slobbed out—there was no other way to describe it—mouth open, a little bit of drool running down her chin. He cringed and assisted it back into her mouth from above, then tiptoed down toward the kitchen, hoping they had something in the mini-fridge.

He was almost to the kitchen when the knock sounded at the door. He froze, like someone had whacked him in the back and forced him to stand upright. Sienna stirred on the couch but did not wake. He adjusted his course to the door, reaching it in a half dozen steps as the next pounding came.

He flipped the lock quickly, the word "SHHHHH," already building to be let out from his lungs, threw the door open to deliver his message—

And froze when he saw what was standing on the other side.

It was man wearing a black ski mask with an ovoid hole to allow his eyes to look out. He was massive, a mountain in the hallway, enormous, dangerous—and before Scott could say anything, he pushed his way into the suite.

25.

Sienna

I woke to the sounds of a scuffle, that funny after-sleep taste in my mouth and one leg hanging off the couch. It was a rude awakening; not the rudest I'd ever had, but not exactly a gentle kiss from Steven Clayton—errr, I mean Prince Charming. (I might mean Steven Clayton.)

I rolled my head to find Scott being put in a headlock by a dude in tactical gear with a black mask covering his face. I blinked twice, Scott's neck trapped beneath a hammy forearm, and stopped myself from rolling off the couch just in time.

"Guy Friday!" I snapped, and the black-masked idiot looked right at me. "Let him go."

Guy Friday did as I asked, well-trained chimp that he was. Scott bolted away from him as soon as the grip lessened enough for him to escape, and he turned and raised his hands like was going to give the monkey a bath. "What the hell?" Scott asked, trying to clear his throat.

"I wasn't apprised that you were involved in this situation," Guy Friday said in a thick voice. "It wasn't in the briefing materials."

"You just worked with him like, two months ago," I said, cracking my back as I got to my feet. My leather jacket slid off me where I'd been using it as a blanket, and I caught it deftly. "Maybe give him the benefit of the doubt next time?" Under the mask, I thought I could see Guy Friday thinking it over, but it wasn't easy to tell. He wasn't exactly a brain trust. "What are you doing here?"

"The director sent me," Guy Friday said, hands at his sides, his muscles fading a little now that he considered the danger over, I guess. He was a Hercules-type, able to grow his muscle mass in times of crisis. Or when he wanted to head to the beach and show off, probably still wearing his ski mask the whole time. It was good for all occasions, I guessed, whether hitting the slopes or robbing a liquor store. "I was ordered to find you and keep an eye on the situation, manage the crisis."

"Well, we're managing to crisis just fine, thanks," I said. "Why, we're crisis-ing like pros here."

"Crisis is not a verb," he said stiffly.

"It could be," I said, a little resentful. "Let's crisis, fools!" I said experimentally. He just shook his head. "It's gonna be a thing. You wait and see."

Kat's blond head appeared at the balcony, took one look at Guy Friday and screamed before turning and running back into her room. I heard the slamming of a door and the bolting of a lock. "They're going to have to Photoshop the brown spot out of her yoga pants," I said.

"What?" Guy Friday asked.

"She's doing a photoshoot for *Vanity Fair* today," I said with a forced smile.

"That's stupid," Guy Friday said.

"Yeah, the timing is dumb," I agreed. "I tried to talk her out of it, but she and her manager/producer/lover are immovable on the subject."

"I meant *Vanity Fair* is stupid," Guy Friday said, suddenly an expert in magazines. "Adhering to a scheduled event when someone has declared their intent to kill you is suicidal."

"At last, something upon which we can agree," I said. "And here I thought we had nothing in common."

He perked up, looking at my hip. "Is that a CZ Shadow II?"

"Oh, wow," Scott deadpanned, "you guys have so much in common you should get married."

"No, thank you," Guy Friday said, sounding as serious as if I'd just proposed to him for real, "I quite enjoy the single life, and wouldn't care to be chained down just yet." He wandered toward the staircase and looked out the window, and I thought, just for a second, he was admiring the view of the skyline. "This is a disaster."

"I agree," I said, "urban planning hasn't really improved since the skylines of—"

"I meant the window," Guy Friday said. "You could put a sniper outside and pick the target off with ease."

I looked out the window. There were no other towers of similar height for well over a mile, and in fact anyone trying to shoot up into our room would have a beast of a time making that shot due to the angle, what with us being on the top floor. "Ummm … I'd be more worried that someone would come through with a helicopter and a Gatling gun, but okay … sniper. Will definitely consider that." And file it under "I" for "Idiot." Captain Redbeard was more likely to ride the elevator up and just walk in, do his thing and drop off a bomb while we were all sleeping. Which I had considered but was too tired to take very seriously. Bodyguarding is not really my jam. "Someone should go calm down Kat before she dials 911," I said, and looked to Scott.

He looked back at me for a moment then realized I meant him. "Oh. Right. Yeah." He started toward the staircase, paused, looked like he wanted to say something, then dismissed it and headed on his way.

"Any idea why this target was picked?" Guy Friday asked.

"The suspect is a guy Augustus had a dust-up with in Atlanta a few months back," I said, watching Guy Friday's eyes for a trace of reaction. "You know, Augustus?" He stared at me blankly. "Black guy? Can use earth powers?"

"I know of him," Guy Friday said without a hint of emotion.

"Yeah, well, this guy put a hand in his girlfriend—"

Guy Friday's eyes narrowed. "He did what?"

"He—he can make himself pass through solid matter, and he kind of stuck a hand in Taneshia's back and like, ripped a hole in her body—"

"He ripped her a new one," Guy Friday said, but sounded strangely unamused, like he was filling in a blank. "The body already has several holes," he went on to explain, oh-so-helpfully.

"Yeah, well," I said, "Augustus dealt with him at the time, dragged the ground out from under his feet and buried him in a hole—" I paused a second to track this with my experience. Redbeard could make himself totally insubstantial, walk through walls, dodge through punches, all that, but he didn't fall through the earth when he did any of that. Yet Augustus had yanked the ground from beneath his feet.

How?

I looked around for my phone and found it on the nearby chair. I had notifications out the wazoo. Six were from Dick, a progressive spiral of jealousy and anger as he realized I was apparently not meeting him for breakfast, but the seventh was a missed call from Augustus.

Thankfully, he left a voicemail. Which I immediately pulled up and put on speakerphone.

"Hey, yo," Augustus's youthful voice came, "got your message about that phase-shifting dude. Yeah, I remember him, bald man, red eyebrows and goatee, and a shit attitude. I thought I'd seen the last of him after what he did to Taneshia. Reed and I are in the middle of something pretty big at the moment—yeah, okay, it's actually just the world's longest stakeout, we're talking like, a week going on now—anyway, when this wraps up I'm heading to LA for sure. Anyway, this guy, he's got the ability to slink through solid matter, but he's got to keep the bottoms of his feet solid when he does this stuff, or else he'll slide into the earth. So just, y'know, aim for the flat foot. I don't know." There was a sound in the background, Reed muttering. "Okay, gotta go. Just hold him off and I'll be there to help you—I'm just kidding. I'm sure you'll have him all wrapped up by the time the Austin, Texas, version of *The Longest Day* is finished over here. Later."

"Bottoms of his feet," Guy Friday said, reminding me he was there and annoying me in one go. "Got it."

"Why did the director send you here?" I asked, tucking my phone back in my pocket.

"Because the election is days away," Guy Friday said, "and if you screw this up, it's going to make the president look bad." He paused for dramatic effect, or possibly just because it took the thought that long to rattle through his brain to be dispensed out his mouth. "Again."

"It was super subtle the way you rubbed that in just now," I said. "How'd you find me?"

He nodded to my phone. "The geek tracked you down."

I looked down and found a message from J.J. buried among Dick's multiplicity of texts:

J.J.

Guy Friday is heading directly to you. Director's orders. Sorry.

"Should have slept with my phone by me," I muttered. Then I saw one of Dick's messages:

Ricardo

I am at Al's, and have two stools at the counter. Where are you?

"No, I shouldn't have," I said under my breath and pocketed the phone. Some things could wait. Like crazy. Crazy could wait.

"Do you always talk to yourself?" Guy Friday asked, watching me like I was a science experiment worthy of study. He still had his arms folded in front of him, all forbidding.

"Only when there's no one else worth talking to," I quipped. "Speaking of which, since you're on guard duty, I'm going to go take a shower." And it was going to be long and luxurious, and then I was going to … put on exactly the same clothes I was wearing right now. With no anti-perspirant, because I didn't have any. "On second thought, I'm going out for a bit."

"Where?" Guy Friday asked, squinting at me through his mask.

"I need some stuff to wear," I said, rolling my eyes at him. "Figured maybe I'd go out, get a mask of my own, y'know. Tactical vest and all that."

"Good luck," he snorted. "I picked this baby up online at—"

I closed the door without waiting for him to finish. I doubted I'd be able to find a ski mask in Los Angeles anyway.

26.

Kat

Kat was working it for the camera, and she knew she was kicking this photoshoot's ass. The photographer was a little stiff, his assistants weren't exactly responsive, Karyn hadn't shown up this morning before she'd left the hotel, and Taggert was still sleeping through the effects of Ambien, probably, but she was here and giving it her all. Sienna and Scott were watching with vague disinterest, keeping more of an eye on the crowd around MacArthur Park Lake, where she was parading around in the water looking spontaneous as hell and good while doing it. The other guy, the one in the black mask that Sienna kept calling "Guy Friday," he was watching too, though now he was all swelled up like he should be working out in Venice Beach. Had he been that big earlier? She didn't think so.

"Beautiful, beautiful," the photographer said in a flat tone. She was expecting someone with a European accent, because didn't they all have European accents? This guy didn't, though. He sounded like a Valley boy, all flat and dude-bro. Kat kicked water per his command, and the camera clicked a dozen times. "Yes, yes, that's it—attitude. Give it to me."

Before she'd come to LA, she'd always thought of photo shoots as a thing that happened quickly, but all the ones she'd been on took hours. Hours of costume changes, of make-up and wardrobe, of posing in the least comfortable, most unnatural ways, ways that crimped your muscles afterward and required a damned Valium to get the damned knots out.

"Let's take a breather," Valley Boy said, and Kat froze where she stood in the lake, her legs a little chilly after an hour in the water. "Don't go to wardrobe, though. I want to reconsider, think for a bit, maybe blaze a J for some inspiration." He handed his camera off to a waiting assistant and walked away without another word.

"You taking five?" Sienna asked, hovering closer to the concrete edge of the lake now that the kicking of water was done. She was wearing a black suit with white shirt like she was dressed up herself, playing one of those Secret Service agents she'd sicced on Kat just last night. She was standing upright, arms folded in front of her stomach, black sunglasses reflecting Kat's own cold and nearly shivering image back at her. It was the perfect Sienna pose; looking down smugly from on high with her guard up.

"Maybe," Kat said, throwing her hair back. At least she hadn't gotten her hair wet yet, though that was almost certainly coming. "Why?"

"Because I'm bored, obviously, and was hoping you were done with this stupidity on parade," Sienna said from behind a pair of way-too-small sunglasses. Didn't she know that big frames and lenses were the in thing now?

"You don't have to be snotty about it," Kat sniffed, sloshing water around. The sun glared overhead.

"Umm, excuse me?" A young woman, probably no older than twenty, came wandering up, a streak of bright blue coloring half her otherwise dark hair. She shuffled closer, a pad of paper and pen in hand. "I was just ..." The girl reddened. "Can I have an autograph?"

Sienna watched her out of the corner of her mirrored sunglasses, arms folded in front of her, so serious she looked like she should be in New York, not LA. "I fear for our future."

"Sienna, relax," Kat said, laughing. She looked right at the girl. "Let me just—"

"Umm, I meant from her," the girl said, blushing, looking straight at Sienna. "You ..." she said in a tone of poorly concealed awe, "... are such an amazing badass."

Sienna did not stir behind the mirrored glasses, but Kat suspected she was blinking furiously, flattered. She would be. "Maybe there's some hope for the future after all."

Kat felt her face twitch around the eyes, in a place she had thought was immune to twitching for at least a few more weeks. Apparently her meta powers had eliminated the botulinum toxin. So sad. "Well ... isn't that nice?" she asked as Sienna took the paper and fumbled to sign it with one hand for some reason, keeping her right—which is the one she always used to write anyway—out of the whole process. It looked awkward, like she was trying to slight the girl, and Kat was sure it left her with a really sloppy autograph.

"There you go," Sienna said, still looking out from behind the mirrored glasses. "Uhh ... don't do drugs."

"What?" the girl asked, looking up at her, perplexed.

"I don't know," Sienna said, shrugging, "I was trying to think of something inspirational."

"I've got a pharmacy card, though," the girl said, looking crestfallen. "It's medicinal. For my—"

"Whatever," Sienna said. "Party on, then."

"You're a really inspirational figure," Kat jeered as soon as the girl had wandered out of earshot.

"We can't all slop in around in concrete lakes all day while people take pretty pictures of us," Sienna shot right back in a meta whisper. "Some of us protect people too stupid to defend themselves. Also, the world."

"Which part of that included beating Rick Gerasimos to death with his own chair?"

"Well, I sometimes take breaks to have a little fun,"

Sienna said, deadpan.

"You *would* think murdering people is fun," Kat spat at her.

"According to your TV show, it's one of my strengths," Sienna replied coolly. "I assume that's why you had Scott call me, because you didn't want to subvert the California trees to do your murdering for you." She looked around. "Although … I guess I'm not convinced that palm trees would be as effective at that as … y'know, trees with branches that can deal out a good whacking …"

"What do you know about dealing out a good whacking?" Kat taunted.

"Less than you do, apparently," Sienna taunted back. "But, seriously, though—Taggert? Really?"

All the mirth vanished from Kat's face in a hot second. "How did you …?"

"He was going to try and get us in a three-way last night," Sienna said, her mouth twisting in disgust. "I let him know in no uncertain terms that I was not interested. Also, if I were you, I would get my hands on some sulfuric acid and apply a generous dose to all the places he touched you, and maybe bathe the spots where he lingered or happened to leave behind drippings—"

"Shut up," Kat hissed, her voice still in a whisper. "We can't all be Sienna Nealon, who gets her job handed to her along with enough 'Get Out of Jail Free' cards to put Parker Brothers out of business."

"Hey," Sienna said, looking only mildly annoyed, "at least I didn't have to sleep my way to my current levels of success."

"What success?" Kat hissed. "I think you mean failure, because that's what you are. I read the news—"

"Gawker does not count as news in any civilized society. Maybe in LA, but not—"

"You're what?" Kat asked, rolling her shoulders, the straps of her dress moving along with them. "One last good screwup away from a nasty firing? And then who's going to hire you?"

"Maybe I'll get my own hit reality show."

"You wish." Kat looked down her nose at her, smiling sweetly. "Do you know how hard I've had to work to make this happen?"

"I can imagine. I mean, just the thought of sleeping with Taggert makes me need anti-nausea meds. I can't even fathom how brave you had to be to actually go through with it, and more than once—"

"I work twenty-hour days," Kat said coldly, ignoring her. "Bust my ass trying to get every ancillary business deal I can. Have to work with the producers to try and come up with viable storylines for my show, things that will interest the viewers—"

"I like how you call them 'storylines,' even though it's *supposed* to be reality TV, like you don't even waste your time with the pretense that anything real happens on camera for your show."

"You have no idea how much work goes into this," she finished, "the sacrifices I've had to make."

"You mean beyond sleeping with Taggert?" Sienna watched her through those reflective lenses, unamused. "And, of course, completely shitting on me with that phone call." She looked to either side. "Yeah, no one has suffered like you have. Starving kids in third-world countries all say to each other—you know, before they go to bed at night with empty bellies— 'At least we're not Kat Forrest! Now that girl has it rough.'"

Kat felt her hands shake, her face redden in the heat of anger. "You have no idea."

"About sleeping with Taggert?" Sienna pursed her lips in disgust. "You're right. Don't share, and let's keep it that way. Some things are best left to the imagination." She paused for comedic effect. "On the other hand, maybe the imagination is worse than reality."

"You're always so smug, so smart, so sure you're better than everyone," Kat said. "I've watched you get away with murder, things that would land any of the rest of us in jail—"

"Or on reality TV, sleeping with that slug of a producer—which, honestly, I think is constitutionally in the realm of cruel and unusual punishment. I mean, I'm no lawyer but I feel like you may just have a case—"

She wanted to scream in frustration, but instead she plastered the practiced smile across her lips. Even now, Kat couldn't let her feelings show, not here, not in public. "This is just how you are."

"Yeah, this is me," Sienna said, without a care in the world.

"Nobody likes you," Kat said.

"Uhmm, hey."

Kat wheeled at the sound of the familiar voice to find Steven Clayton standing there. With his boyish good looks, his jeans-and-t-shirt style, and general hotness, he looked as earnest and well put-together as if he'd spent the morning in wardrobe. It was just the right amount of devil-may-care, but the hair was perfectly done, which meant he'd *prepared* for this encounter—

"Steven," she said, feigning surprise. Of course he hadn't wanted to leave it like he had last night, rushing away from her before the party had gone all to hell. "How did you find me?"

He looked slightly taken aback by her question. "Uhm … everyone on Twitter knows where you are. You tweeted 'Behind the Scenes' pictures of the shoot. I saw Anna Vargas RT them." He held up his phone. "She called you 'So Brave.'" He turned his head to look at Sienna. "And I saw you in the background on one of them, figured I'd stop by."

Sienna stared behind her sunglasses, the top of her eyelids twitching like she was blinking. She did that a lot. It was really annoying.

Wait.

Did Steven Clayton—Mr. Eligible Bachelor—*People's* Sexiest Man of the Year—Steven FREAKING Clayton, who she'd been trying to get her picture taken with last night—did he just show up at HER photoshoot and ask for—

Kat held in the scream that threatened to burst out of lungs that suddenly felt filled to capacity and more. She kept that smile in place, that seductive look that the cameras loved, because oh, there were cameras out there, even now, a thousand people with phones seeking their brush with fame, with her, and STEVEN CLAYTON was HERE—

For Sienna.

And Sienna was just standing there, looking like he'd spoken another language to her. "What?" she asked, as though she had taken one too many hard hits to the head. Which she surely had.

"Can we ... step over here and talk?" Steven asked, gesturing toward a spot a few feet away from the fountain but not quite to where the production assistants were congregating while they waited for the photog to finish getting high.

Sienna just stood there stupidly for at least ten seconds. "Okay," she finally said, and with a glance back at Kat, she followed Steven Clayton away from the lake where Kat stood, up to her thighs in water that felt colder by the minute.

"To hell with this," Kat whispered to no one in particular. No one in particular heard her, either.

27.

Sienna

I followed Steven Clayton away from where Kat had spent her morning (I use the word "morning" loosely, because by now my body clock was so screwed up that it felt like it might be midnight even though the sun was high in a blue, cloudless sky) frolicking in a fancy dress in a concrete reservoir that they called a "lake" while some dude with a foot fetish took pics of the whole experience. I didn't exactly miss the grey clouds that had covered the Minnesota sky when I awoke yesterday, but the fact that over the last twenty-four hours I'd had both fight (Captain Redbeard) and flight (anything related to Taggert) instincts triggered had me feeling like I was on an uneven keel that even a shower and new clothes hadn't been able to fix.

Also, LA, just FYI, this shit is not a lake. Minnesota has like ten thousand of them; I know what they look like.

I'd had to go with the Secret Service look, because none of the fashionable stuff in the stores I'd looked at in the ten minutes I'd allocated to finding something to wear had been the sort of thing I felt comfortable in. That dress I'd worn on my date last night? A nun would have chosen it from the lineup of the dresses I saw this morning, and she would have felt it was perfectly modest by comparison, too.

"What's up?" I asked Steven once there was a few feet of

distance between us and Kat. The photographer's assistants were looking at us with interest, the paparazzi behind the rope line were agitating for Steven to look their way, and I heard the click of about a thousand pictures being taken—of us, which was weird—but other than that, we were totally having a private conversation.

"I wanted to see you again," Steven said, and he looked … nervous? "I didn't want to just … you know, leave it after last night."

I looked around to make sure he was still talking to me, that Kat hadn't seeped up over my shoulder like a noxious, invisible gas. "Dude," I said, feeling very California as I said it, though I was pretty sure I'd been saying that since long before I came to this state, "what is the deal here?"

He blinked at me in surprise. "I'm … interested in you. I'd like to get to know you better."

I pressed my lips together in amusement before I dared speak. "Look … I've dated some nice-looking guys in my time. Very handsome fellows. I know I don't totally look like something … y'know, scraped off the bottom of a boot—err, some of the time," I checked my hair subconsciously. I hadn't flown this morning, so it was in place. "But …" I waved a hand toward where Kat was sitting sullen at the edge of the fountain, staring resentfully at me. "Objectively, she is so much prettier than me. I mean, I don't even worry about it. She just is, she always has been—hotter, prettier, more … uhm … warm, human—"

Steven laughed nervously. "Okay, that's—that's a … that's an interesting note. So here's the thing—I've been in town for a while, right? Came when I was eighteen, fresh out of high school, all the dreams and whatnot—"

"Oh, a classic American story," I said, managing to avoid sarcasm for once. It was a near thing, but I pulled it off.

"There are some really nice people in LA," he said. "Like anywhere else. Normal people. Wonderful people. Amazing, endearing, hilarious, loyal—just great people." He lowered his voice. "If they're in show business, most of them are behind the camera, I'm sorry to say. Like doing the more menial stuff. Something about becoming an idol of normal America, of attracting celebrity and attention, of having people ask you your opinion about even the most mundane of things and assuming that you're some kind of god because you have that opinion—it changes people."

"Power does that," I said. Maybe a little deadpan that time. "That's not exclusively an LA thing."

"No, it's not," he said. Humble, smart ... I mean, the guy was just—he was the real deal. I ate up what he was saying like it was ice cream being spoon-fed to me. "But I'm familiar with LA and with small town Alaska, because those are the two places I've lived. People with a platform to stand on—people that have this much authority, this much attention paid to their every word and action—it's not healthy, psychologically, for most people. It gives them an outsize sense of importance, I think." He sighed. "And ultimately, it's a competitive business, and ... that's the other problem." He frowned. "I'm rambling, aren't I?"

"You're fine," I said. Meant it, too, in every way possible. *Please tell me more, handsome man.*

Uh oh.

"I don't know who said it," he went on, "but I once heard that there are two ways to have the tallest building in town—to go out and *build* the tallest building, brick by brick." He shrugged. "Or to tear down all the buildings taller than yours. In my business—show business—it's competitive like nothing else. Whether it's because everybody thinks they're vying for a limited number of great roles per year or just because—I don't know, they want to feel important by knowing things others don't—a lot of stuff gets said behind your back that's ... not flattering." His eyes glimmered. "You know what I mean?"

I watched him with a flutter in my stomach and on my skin. "Strangely enough ... why yes. Yes, I do."

"I knew you did," he said quietly with a soft smile that did not help my flutter. "Kat plainly would love to go out with me."

"That is true." I tried to keep my voice even.

"I don't really know her," he said, not daring to look her way, keeping his eyes fixed on me, "but would I be out of line in assuming she might marry me just to drive up her ratings?"

"Well …" I said, feeling a little twist of uncertainty, "… I mean, I don't know, probably not 'marry' …" She slept with Taggert, FFS. She'd marry this dude for ratings in a heartbeat and film the conception of every one of their children as a bonus.

"I don't like that feeling of doubt," he said, frowning. On him, it didn't look unattractive. "Worrying if someone's just wanting to be on your arm in order to get something out of you, you know?"

I thought about Kat calling me back in January and again in the summer, just to try and boost her own profile at my expense. "I think I know what you're saying, yes." What the hell was I doing here again? Did I really turn down a drink with this guy last night in order to protect THAT? I found myself turning to look at Kat, who was now standing, very alone, in the lake, not another soul anywhere close to her.

Here she was, super famous, a crowd of people here struggling to get a look at her, but other than the manager who was basically trading her fame for sexual favors … I doubted she had even a single friend she could call on in a pinch. I felt more right about my assessment made in the cool green light of the pool last night by the minute.

"You know what?" I said, turning back to Steven, who was still looking surprisingly nervous, "I'd love to get a drink with you sometime. Soon, I hope, in fact. I just—I don't want to leave Kat exposed to possible death just so I can … uhm … hang out with a—well, an awesome guy."

"I commend you for your loyalty," he said with a nod.

"Pretty sure we could work something out—"

The screams tore across MacArthur Park, and I was left to turn in a flash, and as I spun I realized that there were definitely cameras here, now, both for Kat's show and for all the paparazzi watching.

Dammit.

There he was, standing in the middle of the fountain, red hair and beard hanging wildly around his face, the color bleached by the sunlight so that it looked strawberry blond. "Now's the time," Captain Redbeard said, his legs insubstantial, like ghosts in the water as he stood opposite a fearful Kat, who looked too stunned to move away from the man who wanted to kill her.

28.

Scott

"Oh, shit," Scott breathed at the appearance of the man with the red hair. At least he was standing in the middle of a fountain, so there was something to work with, instead of choosing to stage a fight in a dry gulch or something. Or … pretty much anywhere else in LA.

"Time to rumble," Guy Friday said, bulking up even bigger, like he'd just gone Bane or something.

"Wait—" Scott didn't even get a chance to get out the full sentence before the big man went rushing forward, leaping into the fountain.

"Sonofa—" Sienna said over the screams of the crowd. The air smelled faintly of smoke and water, all the stronger for the minor humidity that the fountain put into the air. The grass around the park was a little brown, but not totally dead, but the hot sun was beating down on the back of Scott's neck as he sprinted toward the fountain, toward Guy Friday and Kat.

Sienna made it first, flying in a hard hover that caused a stream of water to split in her wake as she shot protectively in front of Kat. "Not so fast, Captain Redbeard," she said.

The red-haired man glared at her. "That's not my name."

"Well, since we haven't been formally introduced," she said, "I've gone ahead and nicknamed you Captain Redbeard.

You're welcome."

He looked offended. Really, really offended. "For what?" he asked, his voice thick with outrage.

"For not calling you something worse, like 'The Disappearing Man,' or 'Dirty Ginger,' or 'The Red Lebowski'—" Redbeard kicked his foot in fury, sloshing water that Sienna easily dodged. "Hey, I'm just saying what we're all thinking. If you want to control your own supervillain name, you really need to get ahead of things, maybe issue a press release after your first attack, I dunno—"

"You people are the worst," Redbeard said, his eyes shining with fury. "The absolute worst."

"You seem to have lost all connection with reality, like it was dial-up internet or something," Sienna said. "Let me re-introduce you: you're trying to kill people because you think we've wronged you in some way." She pointed to herself then to Kat. "We haven't really met you before this, but even if we had, here are the rules of polite society—you don't get to just kill people who piss you off."

Kat coughed loudly, drawing Sienna's attention to her. She shot Sienna a pointed look. "Well, it's true," Sienna said. "I don't make these rules, trust me. I mean, I chafe under them, too, like, they give me a rash, but seriously—" She stopped. "Anyway, killing people who wrong you? Inappropriate response. Unless they try and kill you first. This lesson in polite society has been sponsored by—"

"You think you're just so damned funny, don't you?" Redbeard asked, looking at her with pure, furious spite.

"I try to make the best of bad situations," Sienna said, still hovering between him and Kat. "Like this. You've got a murderous grudge against people who haven't actually done anything to you. Most people might find themselves disturbed to be in that situation. Might call it unnerving. You know what I call it? Sunday." She paused, thinking about it. "It is Sunday, isn't it?" She glanced at Scott for support.

"Uh, yes," he said, jarred into speaking. "It is."

"So," Sienna said, staring him down, "Captain Redbeard ... is this how you want to spend your Sunday?" Guy Friday was standing in the fountain a good ten feet from Redbeard, and Sienna was closer still.

"You think you have me outnumbered?" Redbeard said, voice louder, playing to the rolling cameras. "You can't stop me."

"Oh, you'd be surprised what I can do when I put my mind to it," Sienna said, playful as ever when she was bantering. She always did this, smarting off to people just before a fight. The thing that amazed him was that they just stood still and took it, like they were psychologically working themselves up to fight her. *I guess by now people have seen her beat down enough people that it'd give even the man who can walk through walls a moment's pause*, Scott thought.

"Everybody's watching us now," Redbeard said. "Everybody can see."

"Yeah," Sienna said, and now she was tense. "You won't be quite so jazzed about that when my friends and I beat your ass all over this park and it makes the national news tonight."

Redbeard smiled, and it was cold. "Do you think that'll play well this close to the election?"

Sienna tilted her head, looking at him. "What did you just s—"

The first explosion behind them distracted them all. It was louder than the one the night before, and the human mind was psychologically predisposed to looking toward whatever the most immediate threat was. Scott turned, watching a billow of dust fly into the air, the explosion once again lacking the pyrotechnics of a movie bomb and relying entirely on force and debris. He couldn't tell exactly where it came from; there were trees in the way, but it was at the far end of the park and the shockwave came a moment after, toppling the people in the crowd like it had happened just behind them.

He watched the crowd of humanity fall over and braced

141

himself just in time, kneeling to lower his center of gravity and taking the force of a fierce blast of wind following a moment later. Reed might have been able to dispel it, but Scott was almost powerless against that particular threat. Debris showered down around them. Scott's ears rang like someone had slammed a hammer on a bell next to his head.

Somewhere at the far end of MacArthur Park, something had exploded. Something big, something loud, and the force had been such that the whole crowd was feeling it. For his part, Scott watched the dust swell over him and hoped that wherever she was in this mess, Sienna was all right.

29.

Sienna

Captain Redbeard was a sucker-punching, bomb-laying little asshole, and when he did both those things within about two seconds of each other, it really challenged my new resolution about trying not to kill people. It was a flexible resolution, I told myself. After all, hadn't I started out all sweetly naïve, unwilling to kill, before Old Man Winter showed me how stupid it was to draw that line? Sure, I might have pulled back from that later when the government lawyers suggested I stop leaving quite so many dead bodies behind me. I'd gone with that until a guy named Philip Delsim in London had reminded me what a proper villain looked like. My enemies weren't out to take me prisoner; that much was certain. Captain Redbeard wasn't just going to knock me unconscious and go about his business. Unless he was lying, he definitely planned to kill me. And since he'd just bombed people and sucker-punched me, I was inclined to take the low-down bastard at his word on this one.

The point is, holding back with this guy was starting to look like a bad idea, especially given his enthusiasm for explosives.

Also, he landed his punch a quarter inch inside my jaw before turning his fist solid again and pulling it out. Bone, blood, skin, all of that came ripping off. I may be the world's foremost badass, but that kind of thing staggers even me for a step or two.

And stagger I did, Gavrikov fleeing from my mind in the cacophony of pain and screaming nerve endings. I fell to the earth, knocked back from the lake's edge by Redbeard's attack. I landed badly, twisted my ankle (not that I really felt that, given I'd just had part of my lower face forcibly ripped off) and came to rest on my side, dust and debris from the bomb sweeping over me like a low-flying cloud.

Stupidly, I tried to speak and felt nothing but pain, like someone had—oh, I don't know—shoved a fist into my jaw and ripped it the hell off. Because that's what he'd done. My mandible was hanging like it was operating independently of the other side of my face, and I couldn't help but feel that this particular injury, if left untreated, would derail my fantasies about giving Steven Clayton a good kissing. He looked like he needed one, didn't he? Let's go with yes.

Wolfe, I said in my head, because my mouth was unable to produce so much as a noise other than a gross sucking sound as I bled profusely all over my fancy new suit.

On it, Wolfe replied. Not the squeamish sort, that one.

Bjorn, I said, and he answered me by shooting a burst of the warmind in every direction. It was a short, focused pulse, and I heard cries of pain that gave me my first hint of joy as the pain of my jaw started to fade. Because one of them was Redbeard and the other was Kat, and if anyone in this park deserved a murder of psychic crows pecking around in their heads, it was those two.

I lashed out blindly in the direction of Redbeard's cry. He was close, way too close for comfort, as he'd apparently left his dreams of murdering Kat behind to climb back on dry land in order to finish me first. I hit him as my jaw pulled tight to my face, the skin lashing it back where it belonged. New nerve endings formed, and they screamed at the incompleteness of my jaw line. Blood gushed, squirting into the murky cloudiness with every beat of my heart.

Yeah, it was gross. I also didn't care. I saw red, and not just from being bloodied up. I was ready to kill right here, end this threat to humanity—or at least Los Angeles—once and for all.

My forearm slammed into his calf muscle and hooked his leg out from under him with meta force. I heard another scream, high-pitched, then felt the gentle impact of a human body against the ground next to me. I rolled over to him like I was trying to dodge for my life under a passing streetcar, and ended up straddling Captain Redbeard.

Anyone who has ever suggested a primal link between violence and sex would probably have been able to write reams about the position I occupied on Captain Redbeard. I pinned his hips to the ground, my knees against the hard, packed dirt under MacArthur Park's browning grass, and I started to just work out my frustrations on the Capn's face.

I broke his nose on the first punch.

I drove the cartilage into his face on the second.

I smashed his right orbital socket with the third.

Any psychologist not studying the link between sex and violence by watching this particular tableau would probably have shifted to the spectacle of just how much I was enjoying the very specific injuries I was inflicting on him. Enjoying would probably be a strong word, though. I'd enjoy sitting on my balcony with a cup of hot cider and a cinnamon stick back in Minnesota more than this. This wasn't enjoyment.

This was cold, vicious satisfaction, which was a totes different emotional creature. Totes. Different.

I raised my fist for the fourth strike and held it up, planning to do my level best to reciprocate what he'd done to my jaw when he went insubstantial and dropped right through the grass, leaving nothing but a not-so-faint outline of his body in the soil, the grass and dirt disturbed around his head where I'd just pounded him hard enough to till the earth.

"Fhiiiit," I said, my jaw not quite back to normal. The air

was starting to clear, but the sound of screaming was still present. What else could anybody do? It's not like the bomb had gone off close enough to us to cause actual injuries, but that never stopped the human mind from interpreting it as a brush with death anyway. I mean, for crying out loud, most of us don't deal with bombs exploding in our proximity on a daily basis.

I mean, I did, but I was special. My mother never said so, but I know it's true, because I'm a millennial.

I sat there staring at where Captain Redbeard had disappeared into the earth for a few seconds too long, expecting him to come back and finish our fight. "Huh," I said, and started to get to my feet. That kind of assault, those injuries I'd just inflicted on him? They would have killed a normal person. They would have put a low-level meta out of the fight, period.

Which made it very disquieting that Redbeard had gotten away, because it suggested that he was not a weaksauce meta who'd fold easily.

"Sienna!" Steven came out of the cloud, hands in front of his face, eyes squinted against the dust. "Are you okay?"

"Yeah," I said, doing a little squinting of my own, my eyes feeling the burn. "Bad guy rabbited."

"He had a lot of babies?" Steven asked.

"He *is* a baby," I said, trying to look around, get a clear picture of the situation. I looked back toward the lake, where Kat was still standing knee deep in water. "I don't think he should have any. Besides, he's dickless."

"Ouch," Steven said, peering at me through the dusty air. "What now?"

"Well, he's stuck in the earth, I'd guess," I said, "so—"

"Are you sure about that?" Steven asked, and now he was squinting at me in a way that suggested doubt rather than dust in the eyes.

"Umm, yeah," I said. "We're close to sea level, aren't we, so—"

"The LA subway has a tunnel that runs under this park," Steven said, lowering his hands.

"What?" I asked, in utter disbelief. "LA has a subway?"

"Yeah, I think a lot of the locals are clueless about that one, too, based on the rider numbers—"

"You live in earthquake city," I said. My jaw fell, but not on account of a flesh-ripping sucker punch this time, "why would you build a subway here?"

"Uhm—"

Something grabbed hold of my ankle with furious force and tugged me downward. Suddenly it was like my feet lost all touch with the ground, and my eyes got dragged along with me. Darkness filled my sight and I drifted down, my sense of gravity all screwed up by the fact that I knew I was passing through solid ground. It felt like I'd been pulled out of an airplane, or fallen off a high step in a dream, or accidentally backed into a hole.

Before I could so much as scream "GAVRIKOV!" in utter panic, I hit metal and wood, their distinctive sounds and sensations filling both the air and the nerves in my back. Steel ran across my shoulder blades and wood slammed into my tailbone as I hit rail tracks. At least, I assumed they were rail tracks. I also assumed they were steel and wood, because my mind was filling in the blanks that the dark around me wasn't providing any insight into.

I lit my hand as I called Wolfe to the front of my mind again. *Be wary, Sienna,* he offered oh-so-helpfully as my left hand flared into fire and revealed—

Captain Redbeard standing over me with a broken nose, blood caking his mustache and beard, crazy fury in his eyes as he leered down at me.

I thrust my hand up as he dodged, and all I caught was his beard. I grabbed with my flaming hand and he screamed like a little boy who'd gotten kicked in the crotch, dancing away from me as I lit his stupid beard on fire. I struggled to my feet in spite of the pain in my back, and I had a feeling he'd dinged my vertebrae during the fall.

Wolfe, I groused.

Working on it.

"Now there's no audience, stupidass," I said, staring at him in the dark of the subway tunnel. "Which is fortunate for me, because I need another YouTube video of me obliterating you into dust like I need my jaw ripped off."

"You do need your jaw ripped off," he sneered, beating at the little embers of fire still left in his beard. He circled me warily, watching with thinly concealed fury. "You need to shut your stupid mouth."

"It doesn't surprise me you want a woman who's stronger than you to shut her mouth," I quipped. "This whole scheme of yours is like a giant Freudian article on airing your inadequacies. Apropos of nothing, I just read a study the other day that said that monkeys with the smallest testicles howl the loudest."

"SHUT UP!" he screamed.

"You're really just backing up the research here," I said. My hands were up, in a defensive position, and I was ready to fly at him. *Gavrikov*, I said in my mind, *ready the fire. We're gonna burn the soles of his feet off.*

Aye aye, Keptin, Gavrikov said, reminding me that he probably spent a lot of time in seedy motels in the sixties and seventies watching whatever was on television.

I had a life before you, he said sullenly.

Never tell me about it, Chekov, I fired back, turning my attention back to Redbeard. "Time to dance, a-hole," I said, watching him fade away and drop about six inches into the ground. He cringed in pain, his lower lip wavering. "What the hell?" I asked the air, not really expecting a response from him; he'd just anchored himself to the earth, after all, buried his feet in the earth, where presumably the concrete under the metro line had just merged, painfully, with his feet just below the surface of the floor.

"I don't feel like dancing," he said smugly, pulling

something out from behind him, something he must have grabbed before pulling me down here. It turned solid for a second as he pushed a button, on the oblong, cylindrical object that he held in his hand. It would have taken a dunce, or someone completely unfamiliar with movies, not to recognize the theatrical object in his hand, but I didn't quite get it in time to stop him from doing his thing with it.

It was a detonator. It didn't have a glowing button or anything, but I heard the click when he pressed it.

And then I heard an explosion go off behind my head, filling the tunnel with dust.

It was only enough to stagger me, the force of the shock. My eardrums blew, true, and that hurt like a bastard. I could feel the blood running out of the canals, but I had my eyes open and locked back on my threat a moment later, just in time to watch the detonator hand go insubstantial.

"You think that's going to stop me, turd monkey?" I shouted, unable to hear myself over the damage to my ears. *Wolfe, get on that, will you?* It wasn't likely Redbeard would say something useful, but the sound of me screaming into the void without being able to hear it was kind of annoying.

Redbeard said something, something I couldn't understand because I don't read lips and his were covered by that stupid scraggly beard anyway. I could see the satisfaction in the way he'd said it, though, and it was enough to make me dart a look behind me—

Just in time to get hit by a knee-high wave of water from MacArthur Park Lake as it came rushing into the subway tunnel.

For a second, I thought I was going to be okay; I was strong, after all. I could have just flown out of the water and shot down the tunnel, escaping before it became too high or too fast for me.

Unfortunately, I had forgotten something that Redbeard had not.

Subways run on electricity. Electricity that comes to them

via a third rail.

The water rushing down engulfed the subway's third rail and carried that electricity straight to me. As it hit my legs, it didn't feel like a normal rush of water, like the tide coming in the way I'd once felt it while on a job at Galveston Beach. No, it felt like a thousand stings—

—like pain forcing itself behind my eyeballs—

—like every muscle in my body locked up at once—

Wolfe, I cried helplessly, but I could feel his panic. We hadn't trained for this, this outside possibility of getting struck by lightning. I should have; it's not like there weren't metas out there that could shoot lightning at me, but I'd prioritized using my healing powers to acclimate my skin to gunshots, the more common danger I ran up against.

Ten thousand volts of electricity ran through me, attacking my muscles, attacking my heart, frying my nerves and my brain. The last thing I felt before I was rendered unconscious was the flood behind me carrying me away down the tunnel helplessly as I slipped into death like it was an old slipper, waiting for me at the home I would never see again.

30.

Scott

The second explosion had caught them debating what to do—Kat still in the water, Guy Friday looking all around like a war zone was going to drop down on him at any second, and Steven Clayton frozen like he was completely clueless.

What followed, though, that was a sound that rendered all of them clueless. That or speechless, and Scott didn't really know which it was.

The rumbling of the explosion shook the earth, harder than the one across the park, a little more oomph to it. But this time there was no physical sign, no cloud of dust, no debris in the air. People were screaming, the few that hadn't run off by now, and Kat looked more uncertain than the rest of them.

"Let's get out of here," she said, looking around nervously. With good reason, Scott figured.

"Where's Sienna?" Scott asked, as though she'd coming popping out of the ground any second, dragging Redbeard's beaten carcass behind her like she was returning from a triumphant mole hunt.

"In the ground," Steven Clayton said unhelpfully. "Hopefully in the subway tunnel beneath the park."

"There's a subway tunnel?" Scott asked. "In LA?"

"Metro Rail," Guy Friday pronounced. "It's actually the

descendant of two different railway companies that started in 1901, if you can believe it—"

"I can't," Scott said, focusing all his attention on Clayton. "You think Sienna's in the subway?"

"Well, hopefully she'll be able to catch a ride on one of those cars," Kat said, making a face as the ground shook once more beneath her. The sound of something rushing was faintly below the screams. "Maybe meet up with us later, back at the hotel?"

"This guy could have left her in the ground," Clayton said, looking right at Scott. "I mean, if he just wanted to be done with her—"

"He doesn't just want to be done with her," Scott said, speaking with a certainty he didn't totally feel, hoping he was right. "He wants to kill her in front of an audience. He wants to humiliate, to shock, to destroy—"

"I don't get that," Guy Friday said. "I just kill my enemies. They're dead, they can't talk back anymore, it's great."

"You're really creepy," Kat pronounced like it was coming as a sudden surprise to her. "Why are you so—" She was cut off mid-sentence by the rushing turned to a roar as she snapped her read around to look.

Scott figured it out at last; the lakebed was draining behind her, the water level dropping rapidly.

"Wow, this drought is so terrible," Kat said sagely, sounding like she was about to launch into a lecture. "When are we going to learn—"

"Oh, shit," Steven said, and Scott couldn't help but agree.

The lakebed beneath Kat's feet disintegrated, and she disappeared like she'd dropped into a pit—which she had, he realized, gone in a flash of darkness before he even had time to react.

31.

Kat

She fell into the hole in the ground without anything to cling to, the earth ripped from beneath her so quickly she didn't even have time to scream before she plunged. Water fell with her, ringing her ankles, wetting her dress up to her buttocks. She passed through it as she fell, and it drenched her as she went down, dropping into the darkness.

Kat hit the ground without any water to break the fall, and it hurt. Not as much as it maybe would have if the water hadn't slowed her fall, but it still hurt. She sat up slowly, rubbing her back where she'd landed, and stared into the bizarre spectacle above her.

The water hung suspended above like it was trapped behind aquarium glass. It pulsated, sloshing back and forth behind an invisible barrier as it lifted up off the tracks like it was a video being rewound, water pouring up instead of down. It was the strangest thing she could recall watching, maybe ever, as the tunnel ahead of her cleared, the water lifting off the train tracks, sucked up into the sunny sky that shone above the liquid roof that separated her from the sky above MacArthur Park.

Kat stared into the semi-darkness, a lamp on the wall her only guide. "Sienna?" she called experimentally. Her eyes were still adjusting.

"What the hell?" came a distressed, malevolent voice from somewhere in the darkness ahead of her. She heard the sound of pained grunts and something like cloth tearing hard in the distance.

Kat felt the edge of panic that ran through her. She reached out with all her senses, feeling for plant life; naturally there was none, and even that which she felt in the park above was desperately muted, rendered nearly insensate by the lack of water. The trees were suffering from the drought, and the grass was near dead, its roots too shallow to be of any help anyway.

She backed up, her dress catching on a metal rail. She didn't even hesitate—she slipped it clean off in a second with her meta speed. She had seen enough of this guy—Redbeard, as Sienna called him—to know he wasn't going to be content to let her stumble in the dark with her sopping dress, hoping for mercy. She'd seen his eyes. There was no mercy there.

Kat walked across the painfully rough concrete floor, deftly stepping over the rails as she made her way to the side of the tunnel, out of the light streaming in through the watery ceiling above. Drips of water fell all around her like light tears falling from the sky. Somewhere up there, Scott was holding back the flood as best he could. For now, anyway. That might change, and soon. He'd never been the strongest guy, at least not as far as she knew. Her earliest memories of him all involved tears of some sort, his moaning about a relationship between the two of them that was as alien to her as the thought at this point of living a life without kale smoothies or hot yoga.

She bumped against the cold concrete wall and ran her palm over the rough surface texture as she tried to rein in her breathing. She couldn't hear over the sound of her frightened breaths, coming one by one, ragged, as she stared into the dark unknown. That lone light had winked out suddenly, and all she could see was that the tunnel curved somewhere ahead.

Her eyes played across the dimly lit ground, the sunlight fading the deeper into the tunnel she looked. The raised rails were evident, but somewhere ahead had to be—

She saw the shadowed lump on the ground, the human-sized figured draped across the tracks, and she started to move without thinking it over first. *Sienna*, she thought, recognizing the wider hips of the body turned on its side, draped over one of the rails, insensate—

She heard the sound of a foot scuffing across the concrete just in front of her a second before Redbeard landed a punch to her temple that sent her staggering sideways. Kat's cheek hit the rail. What little light there was faded out, going black as she slipped unconscious.

32.

Scott

Scott was pretty sure he was going to break something, and soon. He wasn't exerting any actual muscles to keep MacArthur Park Lake from draining into the giant abyss that had opened underneath it, but it felt like he was at serious risk of being dragged into the ground by the sheer volume of the weight of water he was holding up. From where he stood on the concrete quay, he had a feeling that that the ground beneath him wasn't exactly stable, but he felt so drained, so taxed by what he was doing that the thought of even walking a few steps to get the hell away from the sucking hole in the ground that led into the tunnel below seemed impossible.

"Nice lift, bro," someone said from behind him, and Scott wondered if it was Guy Friday. The sky was bright, and yet the world was dark around him, like the exertion was causing him to squeeze off the blood vessels in his brain. "What is that, like a hundred thousand gallons?"

"Something … like … that …" Scott muttered through lips he could barely force apart. The entirety of MacArthur Park Lake wanted to rush out to find its level, which was down in those tunnels. He couldn't hold all that water, no chance.

But he could hold the foot or so at the giant gaping hole in the lakebed, pressing the molecules so tightly together that only a trickle could slip through into the tunnels.

Maybe.

It felt as though he was lifting, though, didn't it? Like he had a train on his back, as though he was testing his meta strength by physically lifting a car. His head felt like it was going to explode, like it was going to blow off—like that guy Sienna had kicked in the back so hard his skull blew up. At the time, Scott had sort of admired that—from a strictly detached point of view, of course.

Now, though, he had a certain newfound respect for that poor bastard.

"What are you gonna do, bro?" the voice asked again. It felt like someone was reaching into his chest now, squeezing his heart, like Redbeard had come up here, unnoticed, and just put a hand through his chest and was casually giving it a hard clamping. "Kind of a big concrete pond here. That's a lot of water. You think you can lift it all?"

"No," Scott murmured, feeling the water pressing tighter as gravity fought against his efforts. It was just so much water. So much water. An ocean, practically. And if it had just been a normal pond, with banks that went right up to the edge in a gentle slope, maybe he could have made it rise up the bank a little. But, no, MacArthur Park had to have a nice little concrete edging all the damned way around, a whole drought-induced foot of empty space that he'd have to make the water climb if he wanted to move it out like he'd done—hopefully—to the subway tunnel.

He had done that. He could feel it. He'd reached in and scooped the water out, impossibly, like he'd turned back the tide at the ocean's edge—which was a thing he'd never tried, but was pretty sure he couldn't do.

Or could I?

Scott felt the rising pressure, like the whole ocean had settled on his shoulders, and he knew what he had to do. Water always found its level, and it was damned sure trying to go down right now. He could feel the pressure, the exertion, and knew that somewhere down there, below the water he was barely holding back, were Kat and Sienna.

How do I hold back this water?

How do I ... get rid of this water?

"You look like you're ready to collapse," the voice said. Scott heard it clearly even as the world seemed to fade around him, and he was not entirely sure he wasn't talking to himself. "What are you going to do, bro?"

"I need to ... get rid ... of this water," he said, eyes fluttering as he struggled to stay conscious. It felt like everything was slipping out of his grasp.

"No reservoirs for miles. Just lots of houses, stores—you know, places where people live, schools, all that. You start pulling the water out and rolling it down Wilshire, you're gonna see a lot of people drown. Cure's worse than the disease, bro."

"Stop calling me bro," Scott said, and he hit his knees, the concrete hard, echoing in dual shocks of pain down his shins as the weight of the water threatened to drag him into the abyss. It loomed below, so dark and inviting. All he had to do was take a step off, into the water's loving embrace, and it'd be done ... "I need help."

"I dunno, bro. This town's pretty dry. Been a long time since the rain, you know what I mean? The *air* doesn't feel like it has a drop of moisture anywhere in it ..."

"Reed," Scott whispered, a faint idea forming somewhere in there, at the mere thought of the name. *If Reed were here, he could help me ...*

... help me ...

... how could Reed help me? It's water, not ...

... there's no water in the air.

0% humidity.

But ... air can take water.

And I can—

—if I can take water from the air, maybe I can—

He came to his feet in a rush, dragging in a breath as he

pulled water from MacArthur Lake into his fingers, into his skin, and expelling it out a little at a time in a mist through his mouth.

Too slow, he thought.

Way too slow.

But maybe I can—

Can I …?

No way to know unless you try.

And slowly, painfully slowly, Scott lifted his hands and watched the first layers of moisture start to lift off MacArthur Park Lake like a fog, rolling over the edges of the concrete basin that kept them contained, as easily as if Reed himself were steering the moisture away.

33.

Kat

"Looks like we've got a Kat-a-comb here," Redbeard said in a low, whispered voice right into Kat's ear as she woke up, catching his little pun as she stirred back to motion. She stiffened as she realized her danger, and he punched her in the back, a hard fist to the kidney that drove her face into the ground, bloodying her lip from the impact. "Ah ah ah."

"Ow," Kat said, a faint gasp in the dark. The light was occluded from above now, like clouds had moved over the sun, blotting out hope with it. She could feel warm, sticky blood on her forehead, at the beginning of her hairline and rolling down her temple as if syrup had been poured down her face.

"Did I hurt you?" Redbeard asked. He didn't sound sorry. "Good. You should feel it."

"What did I ever do to you?" Kat asked, her voice shaking more from pain than fear. She'd helped face down the world-ending threat of Sovereign and his hundred lackeys, after all. This guy was a punk with an aversion to shaving.

"What didn't you do to me?" Redbeard asked, yanking her to her feet, twisting her arm and forcing her up painfully. "What didn't you and your kind and your friends—what didn't you do to me?" He spun her around and shoved an

160

invisible hand through her throat. "You took everything, that's all. You heroes. That's what you think you are, isn't it?"

"I'm not a hero," Kat said, swallowing, as though she could feel the intangible presence of the fist that was passing through her skin as easily as if it had no mass at all, as if her throat were not even present to stop it. "I'm just a—"

"You're right about the 'not a hero' part," Redbeard said with a snort, his foul breath hitting her in the face. His face was a mess, blood dripping down and making dark spots in his beard and mustache. "But people think you are, don't they? In World War II, you know how many celebrities joined the army? You couldn't even count them all, and I'm not even talking about Audie Murphy. It's not like that anymore, though, is it? You're all cowards, safely lecturing behind your podiums in your air conditioned rooms and benefit galas and Twitter accounts, and if you go overseas to see how the rest of the world lives, it's with a dozen bodyguards to protect you from the locals." He sneered. "How many little girls are watching you now? How many want to be you? They look around the world and they don't see Malala Yousafzai and look to her for example—they look at you, you hog. You sun-blocking cancer—"

"Sunblock prevents cancer," Kat said evenly, unwilling to give Redbeard the satisfaction of thinking he had her in any way rattled.

"They think you and Kim Kardashian are the way, the truth, and the damned light!" Redbeard said, pushing her against the sloped wall of the tunnel. "You sell yourselves like whores, open up your lives and present what you do as some glorious version of reality when really, you're selling them a bill of goods. You and Hollywood, you're all false, liars, holding up ideals you don't espouse, your perfect lens and your Photoshopped pictures making everyone think you're flawless and great when really there are no heroes left out here in Hollywood—"

"Step away from her!" The shout echoed down the

tunnel, and Kat turned her head to see Steven Clayton with a gun his hands, standing just down the tunnel, a million gallons of water over his head, a little dribbling down on him like he was filming a scene in the rain. His pants were covered in dust and behind him in the dark she could see a small mountain of debris where the tunnel had fallen in on the tracks. *He must have climbed it*, she thought.

"Steven," Kat breathed a sigh. "Where did you come from?"

"MacArthur Station," he said, taking careful aim at Redbeard. "Back away from her."

"Lol." Redbeard actually said, like it was a word. "Where'd you get that? The prop department?"

"I said step away," Clayton edged a little closer.

"Or you'll what?" Redbeard leered. "Shoot me?"

Clayton's features were barely visible in the dark, but his lovely mouth was a hard line. "Yep." He dipped the gun barrel low and fired a string of shots that made Kat jump in fear, the flashes lighting up the tunnel and echoing with deafening noise.

When the sound and light faded, Redbeard was on the ground, grunting in pain. "You ... son of a ...!" He was fumbling for the bottoms of his feet.

Steven fired again, one last time, a seventh shot, and Redbeard screamed in pain, his shoulder bleeding profusely.

Kat stared down at him, watching him writhe, the bottoms of his feet bleeding from circular-shaped wounds that tore right through the soles of his shoes. "How'd you know?" she asked Steven, but he was already snaking his way down the tunnel, taking a wide dogleg around Redbeard.

"Move away from him!" Steven said, beckoning her. He was moving steady, his gun still clutched in one hand, the slide racked back. It was a small one, smaller than the full-sized ones she had used when she was with the agency. He picked his way carefully over the rails and hurried down the tunnel. Kat followed him, not daring to be left behind with

Redbeard, who was stretched across the tracks, writhing and crying softly in pain.

"Where did you get the gun?" Kat asked, catching up to him as he stopped in the middle of the tunnel.

"What?" Steven's head snapped around and he glanced down at the pistol in his hand. "Oh. I don't have bodyguards, and I got a stalker threat last year, so I got a permit."

"That's yours?" Kat looked at him in disbelief then turned to look back down the tunnel at Redbeard, who was on his knees now, hand pressed against his chest.

"Yeah, it's a .380," Steven said, kneeling down. "Doesn't exactly have the knockdown of the 9mm, but I was worried about a crazy lady from Fresno who thought we were supposed to be together forever and couldn't understand why I had a date with Taylor Swift. I didn't think I'd be going up against a metahuman." He fumbled in the dark, and she realized he was crouched over Sienna, running his hands over her. He stopped as he found what he was looking for. "This, on the other hand ..." he squinted in the dark. "Ooh, CZ Shadow II. Fancy." He stood and brandished Sienna's gun, pointing it at Redbeard in the dark. "It's even got the tritium sights. I'm surprised the government sprang for one of these; I was thinking about getting one after my next movie gets done, sort of a reward thing. You know if she rolls with hollow points?"

"What?" Kat stared at him with her mouth slightly agape.

"Hollow points," Steven said, keeping the pistol leveled at Redbeard, who was now almost back to his feet, though he was still clutching at himself. "You know what? Never mind."

"You know what?" Redbeard said with a rasp. "I never liked your films."

"That's a really chilling insult from a guy who goes around trying to murder women he doesn't even know," Steven said, looking down the sights with both eyes open. "That's the sort of review that's going to haunt me for hours.

I'll be taking a shower and it'll be like a PTSD flashback—remember that time the guy with the crazy red 'stache and beard told me he didn't like my movies? Way, way worse than that time my best friend died in a crab fishing accident."

"I'm going to kill you now, too," Redbeard said calmly.

"I'm gonna fill your feet with enough holes that you won't be able to confuse them with the marks of crucifixion anymore," Steven said sharply, "you ginger loser. Your martyr complex is so staggering that the old joke applies—you know what the difference is between you and God?"

"Shut up," Redbeard warned, standing a little limply, the water still suspended over his head. Kat prayed for Scott to drop it, all at once, just to wash him away.

"God doesn't think he's you," Steven finished. "And Jesus actually was persecuted, he didn't just fantasize it. You just—I don't know, maybe your mommy put your diaper on too tight."

"I'm not a kid anymore," Redbeard said, his voice sounding dangerously unhinged. Now there was sound coming from down the tunnel, beyond the shadowed pile of rubble that lay just past him.

"I figured you were actually still wearing diapers," Steven said. Redbeard took a threatening step forward, and Steven fired a shot, eliciting a grunt of pain from Redbeard, who paused and whimpered before steadying himself. "I have seventeen more rounds in this puppy. How much skin do you think you'll have left by the time you get over here?"

"How fast do you think you can aim, smart guy?" Redbeard asked menacingly.

Steven fired twice more, bringing Redbeard back to his knees. A third shot seemed to do nothing at all, and Kat realized Steven had fired at Redbeard's body, hoping to find it corporeal. No such luck. "This is an exquisitely designed target pistol," Steven said, voice heavy with admiration. "I can fire it fast enough that you'll be walking on bone if you take a few more steps."

"I won't stop," Redbeard said, tired but with a thin reed of craziness run through it; Kat was sure he was telling the truth.

"Neither will I," Steven said, and he moved his left hand, something else clutched in it where he'd had it pressed against the butt of the gun. "Want to see me do a combat reload? I've been practicing."

"You're an ... actor," Redbeard said, thin disbelief oozing out like the blood Kat could see him tracking with every step. "A play artist. A bro from California who couldn't find his balls if they got served to you in the middle of a plate of foie gras."

"I'm method, mofo," Steven said, voice hard. "And I'm from Alaska ... *bro*. I've skinned grizzlies twice your size, and they had less shit in their fur, too."

The sound of faint rumbling in the distance was growing louder, and Kat eyed the water above uneasily. It was just hanging there, after all, and had been for long, painful minutes. Was Scott losing control? Was it going to come surging in any minute now, dropping down on them all?

No ... this was coming from further down the tunnel, a low sound like metal on metal, like—

"Oh, God," Kat said under her breath.

"Yesssss," Redbeard said, the pain vanishing from his face in an instant, replaced by rough satisfaction, his canines bared like he was a vampire about to feast.

"What?" Steven asked, not taking his eyes off Redbeard, keeping his aim level and steady in the dark tunnel, unflinching. *Because he doesn't know*, Kat realized. *Because he can't hear ...*

That somewhere in the near distance, a subway train was barreling down the tracks toward them.

34.

Scott was lost in the mist rolling off MacArthur Park Lake, coming off it in waves like the cloud of dust that had flown from the explosion earlier. This time, though, it was a steady rush of humidity, the heat of the Los Angeles day running through the damp air. It was surreal, dreamlike, reminding him of times he'd run through the misting machines that were designed to keep you cool on the hottest day. For him, they had always held an extra power; a dose of refreshment that he didn't understand until he'd manifested his powers.

"Bro," the voice from behind him said, "you're wearing out. How much water you gonna move before you pass out?"

The world shook around him like someone was giving the world a heavy shake. "As much … as it takes …"

"Uh huh. Yeah. This little thing you're doing here—it's not going to be enough to impress her. You know that, right?"

The world swam in front of Scott's eyes as he tried to stare down into the depths of the lake, but the mist was too thick. "Who … what?"

"Sienna. You know this won't get her back, don't you?"

The throbbing in his head was like a drumbeat, like someone had started pounding on it with one of those pedal drums, a steady cadence that caused his skull to expand and contract with each hard thump. "I don't … know what you're talking about …"

"Sure you do." There was a flash, and suddenly Scott could see people in the water, like he was watching a docudrama projected in it.

It's like you don't even care anymore, his own voice said, dripping frustration the way the air was dripping moisture around him. *It's like you've given up on anything but doing the job, putting your head down and trying not to get called on the carpet.*

What do you want from me, Scott? Sienna fired back. She was all done up, hair styled in a way that it never was. *We have this same argument all the time, and I'm a little tired of it. You made your choice—*

I chose to have a life! he shot back, hot indignation pouring out, hotter than any of the other times they'd argued about this. *You, though, you've chosen to give all that up in order to—to what? Be the world's meta policewoman?*

Someone's got to, she said bitterly, her arms folded in front of her as if to protect herself from his words.

It doesn't have to be you, he said, the anger fleeing, replaced by fear, like this was the argument he couldn't lose—couldn't afford to lose.

She had a dead look in her eyes, empty of feeling. *There's no one else.*

"Yeah, that's the stuff," the voice came again from behind him as the figures in the water vanished.

"I don't know … what this is …" Scott muttered, the pain in his head overwhelming. The air was so thick with clouds that he couldn't see anything, and the world had a red tinge to it, like blood was pouring out, mingling with the water vapor.

"It's the past, idiot. It's the place you'd be living—if you could remember it."

With that, the clouds opened up below him and Scott could finally see into the gaping hole that had opened up when the bomb had blown up somewhere between the subway tunnel and the lakebed. It was long, like someone had reached in and rent the earth, displacing concrete and dirt, opening a cavity into the ground below. "It looks like an open grave," he whispered to himself.

"It looks like a fine place to be put to rest, doesn't it?" The speaker stepped up finally. Scott felt a cold tingle roll up his skin, and it wasn't from the chill mist that infused the air.

The person who was speaking was himself, dressed in a suit and tie, the uniform he'd worn when he'd worked for the Directorate—and later, the agency.

"In fact," the other him, the suited him, said, stepping up to the edge, "I think this is where I leave you." He crossed his hands over his chest like he was in already in a casket, and fell backward into the darkness, disappearing below.

Scott fell to his knees at the edge of the abyss, the pain in his head finally too great to fight any longer. He dipped toward the darkness, losing his balance, tumbling in, just as the sound of something roaring and distant came rumbling along below like a train …

35.

Kat

The sound of squealing brakes was like a knife to Kat's ears, like a scream in the night, and it tore through her with all the resonance of a gunshot. It echoed down the tunnel, losing some of its power at the open area just before them where Redbeard stood, his arms spread wide, as insubstantial as the misty light around him, waiting for the train that was coming—

"Come on!" Steven said, yanking her by the arm and pushing her toward the darkness of the tunnel. He was already scooping up Sienna, lifting her in his arms like the movie star he was, running down the middle of the tracks without a care for Redbeard or what he was doing.

"See you later!" Redbeard screamed as the train bore down. "I'll catch you! You know I will! Next time we'll have an audience and you'll—"

The sound of the train hitting the concrete and debris from the bomb site was unmistakable, metal smashing against tons of obstruction, the echo in the tunnel like a hammer banged against steel, again and again, raised by a meta hand and turned against something that wouldn't yield.

Kat ran faster than Steven, her meta speed granting her the power to outpace him with greatest ease. She tore off down the tunnel in fear for her life, bare feet slamming against the hard concrete floor. Bullet wounds she could heal. Broken bones she could mend.

A train running her over, though? That was a career ender.

She sprinted even as the sound of the crash started to recede, the tangling sounds of metal splintering, of concrete breaking under impact, of glass shattering faded in the distance behind her. She ran like she had a fire at her back, like it was chasing her away, like there was a flying man following behind her meaning her harm.

She ran as though her life depended upon it, and she did not stop until she heard Steven Clayton telling her to do so from very far behind her.

"Stop!" His voice echoed. It was light, airy, so far away it was almost inaudible. The sounds of the crash had faded, lost somewhere behind the bend in the track. Kat stopped and turned. There were lights on the wall now, still lit, enabling her to see once more. She blinked at the circular tunnel, at the faintly illuminated tracks at her feet. She stared, perplexed, wondering how far she had gone.

Kat turned and looked back. Steven was at least the length of a football field behind her, just coming around the corner in the distance now. He looked tired, out of breath, struggling under the burden that was Sienna. He clutched her close to his chest, and with a last look back, he stopped, setting her down in the middle of the tracks.

Kat ran back, hesitantly at first. What if Redbeard was waiting? What if he'd changed his mind? What if he'd decided he wanted to finish her anyway, was coming back even now to do the job?

Well, then she probably wanted to be near the guy who had the gun, didn't she?

She ran back to Steven, who was hunched over Sienna now. She felt it when his demeanor changed, when he realized that something was truly wrong. Kat increased her pace, broke into a nervous run, her bare feet slapping as she ran, a sting of pain in her toes. She was leaving a trail of blood behind; she'd run holes in her feet and hadn't even noticed in the rush to get away.

Kat closed on him, was ten feet away when Steven put words to the struggle he was going through. He was shaking Sienna, roughly, jarring her, trying to wake her, putting his hands on her cheeks and—

"Don't do that!" Kat said, shouting at him like she was warning a child away from a hot stove. "Her skin!" He did not look up. "If you touch it, it'll—"

Steven's head snapped up, and she shut her mouth at the mere look on his face. It would have been enough to silence someone more forceful than her; anguish and fear rolled into one with more emotions lurking beneath the surface. It was pain, pure pain, of a sort that she recognized even at this distance, and it told her what he was going to say a second before he spoke, before he delivered the knife right to her soul.

"She's not breathing," he said, voice numb with shock. "She's ... she's dead."

36.

Karl

The train crash was pure pleasure: the sound rattling off the walls of the tight tunnel, the screaming of metal and the crash—oh, yes, the crash itself—it was pure joy, the best present he'd gotten in years. Karl didn't really think of happiness as an achievable possibility for himself at this point, but the sound of the wreck was as close as he could recall feeling it in so very, very long.

When it came crashing through, smashing aside the debris that his bomb—carefully left in the strata just between the tunnel and the bottom of the lakebed—had dropped into the subway, the train had jumped up and hit the remainder of the ceiling. It had been coming kind of fast out of the station, but not nearly fast enough. It hadn't been exactly the kind of high-speed impact he'd hoped for, and when it came to rest, he was standing right in the middle of the first car, buried up to his chest in the floor.

The air in the car was damp, the mist pouring in from somewhere above—he still wasn't sure what was going on up there, but that damned idiot Scott Byerly was responsible somehow, that much he knew. The train had lost a few windows, and the white clouds were coming in, giving the wreck a dark, moody atmosphere as the mist caught the reflection of the flashing red emergency lighting. The sound of water tapping against the roof was unmistakable.

"What ... happened?" A woman asked from a few feet away. She sounded dazed.

Karl was standing with his hands parted, no part of him solid except for the bottoms of his feet, which hurt agonizingly from where he'd been shot. He'd clearly left too much of himself exposed, and that shitty actor had shot him for the mistake. His face throbbed where Sienna Nealon had smashed his nose and eyebrow, and he could taste blood mingling with the mist coming into the train car. "You wrecked," he said simply.

The woman blinked at him in surprise, taking him in, all of him, from the waist up. "Are ... are you all right?"

Karl looked right at her and smiled as he reached for his phone. "I'm fine."

She looked around as though she were just waking up. Down the seat from her, a mother held her child tight to her chest, praying under her breath. Karl couldn't hear the language being used, but the intent was clear. There were probably twelve people scattered around the car, minor scrapes, little injuries. Survivors with a story to tell of a harrowing experience.

"But this is so ..." Karl lost the words, unsure of what he wanted to say. "Placid? Disappointing?"

"We're all alive," the woman said, staring at him, clearly not putting together what she was seeing with regard to his chest sticking out of the flooring. "We should be thankful." She looked around, her dark hair almost black in the flashing red light. "Is everyone else okay?"

"There should be horror," Karl said, thinking it through out loud. "Revulsion. Fear. We need to turn up the volume."

"What?" The woman fixated on him, her eyes narrowed in the dark like she was trying to see him. "Did you hit your head?" She staggered to her feet, unsteady, like a baby horse, the floor tilted at an angle. She came over and peered at him, realizing for the first time that his body just ended at the floor. "What …?"

Karl pushed the button to start recording on his phone, then turned on the flashlight so that it lit her up. "We're on the wreckage of the train outside MacArthur Park Station," he said calmly, narrating. "Everyone survived, thank goodness."

"Are you sure you're all right?" the woman asked, kneeling down next to him. "Your torso, it's—"

Karl shone the light right in her eyes and watched her flinch away from the brightness. "What's your name?" he asked.

"Amanda," she said, peering through the light at him. "Listen, it's going to be okay. We'll get EMTs down here to take a look at you, they're probably already on their way—"

"Goodbye, Amanda," Karl said, and he buried his free hand in the side of her head and then turned it solid. When he pulled it out, half her face came with it. What was left sagged as though he'd cast a palsy upon it, and he caught it perfectly on the little 5" by 3" screen clutched in his hand.

There was time for a quiet breath before the screaming started, and Karl enjoyed it. Once the screams did start, once the fear spread, the panic, it was like caged animals with no way out. They were locked in with him, and no matter how they tried to escape—and some went for the windows, others went for the emergency exits, others just quivered in the corners or played possum—he made sure not one of them survived.

The whole time, the camera was watching—his own quiet record of human sacrifice.

37.

Scott

The first slap against his cheek was a sharp awakening for Scott, the second was like shit gravy on top of the already rude wake-up. The third hurt like hell, and the fourth was overkill.

He caught the fifth as it was about to land on his cheek and stared up into dark eyes that were peering out from a black tactical mask of the sort the SWAT teams wore when out in the field about to kick down a door. Scott got the feeling from the eyes staring out at him that the wearer of that mask was a guy who wished he was about to go into action instead of a guy who was standing on the edge of a concrete walkway ringing a lake, slapping him in the face.

"Knock it off," Scott snapped, his head aching only slightly less than his cheek. He threw Guy Friday's hand away, and the bigger man let him. "I'm awake."

"You don't come out of it so easily," Guy Friday said, pulling up to his full height and leering down at Scott. "I bet you need a loud alarm clock for a wakeup."

"I don't think I was sleeping," Scott said, uncomfortably aware that he was awfully close to the edge of the lake. "I think I passed out." He turned over slowly, the world around him shrouded in a fog, the sun hidden somewhere overhead, a yellow sphere barely visible in the thick atmosphere. He braced on his knees and stared down into the gaping hole below—

"Holy shit," he muttered.

The wreckage of a train lay exposed in the gash at the bottom of the lakebed. Its roof showed some signs of folding, of scraping damage, like it had hit something hard enough to pop it up into the ceiling of the tunnel.

Also, the lake was gone. Entirely.

Scott put a hand to his head, the pain a tangible thing. "How long was I out?"

"A minute or two," Guy Friday answered in that deep, rough voice. It was nothing like the one that had been speaking to him when he'd been pushing the lake from liquid to gas. "You were talking to yourself for a long time before that, though, ranting to the air and waving your hands around. Your face was so red you'd think someone had hacked your nude selfie collection."

"But they didn't, did they?" he deadpanned, pushing up onto his hands. He stared down at the train below, and the sound of shifting metal reached his ears, ever so faintly. "Any sign of Sienna? Kat?"

"No on the first," Guy Friday said, looming over him, "and I haven't seen the blond chick since she fell in."

"Oh, shit," Scott said, getting to his knees. Red and blue lights were flashing in the distance, sirens screaming. "I really drained the whole lake."

"Yeah," Guy Friday said, and Scott stayed on his knees, staring out at the wet mud that remained on the bed of the lake. "I wouldn't have called that one, personally, you know, first thing this morning. If someone had come up to me and been like, 'What do you think is going to happen today?' I would have probably answered—'Naked photos of the blond girl.' Like that would be the most extreme outcome to today I could have envisioned."

"What is it with you and naked pictures?" Scott asked, not ready to get to his feet yet.

"Does seem to be a theme at the moment, doesn't it?" Guy Friday mused. "Must be on my mind for some reason."

"Really?" Scott wondered aloud, staring over the empty lakebed and down at the wreck of the train below. It was like a little reminder that beneath all that was going on was another layer, something he'd caught a glimpse of in the vision of himself when he was clearing the lake. "Because my mind … is not anywhere near that at the moment." He pressed his lips together tightly, wondering if Sienna and Kat were alive or dead, but powerless to act either way, the energy gone from his limbs. "Not anywhere close to it."

38.

Karl

Karl cleared three cars in a row before he stopped to rest. It had been messy work, and his hand was drenched in the blood of these people.

These people he hated.

They were sheep, they were clueless. They weren't even people really, they were just going through the motions. It wasn't even like they were really living; they just weren't dead until he came along.

But now he had a record of their deaths. It was the sort of thing that might wake a few kindred spirits up.

He had settled down to rest on one of the benches in the third car. He could hear movement in the fourth, the sound of survivors who wouldn't be surviving much longer. He just needed to catch his breath, really, and he could go on about the business at hand—the business of his hand, actually.

He let a grim smile spread across his face. He hadn't anticipated this, getting personally involved in this way, on this day, but really, it was perfect. He'd needed to create the frenzy, to make some more noise, and nothing was quite as noisy as killing an entire trainload of people who had just survived a wreck and catching it live on video.

The air had turned heavy and thick in the train cars, the smell of blood and gore going stale on him. That was all right, though, Karl reflected as he got to his feet. He wiped a bloody handprint on the metal wall and started toward the next car. "Miles to go before I sleep and all that," he said to himself, still wearing that grim smile, as he went back to work making a name for himself.

39.

Kat

Kat stared down at Steven Clayton's earnest face in disbelief. If he was a liar, he was worthy of hearing, "And the Oscar for Best Actor goes to ..." followed by his name this year and every year until his own death. She stood over him, staring down at Sienna's pale face—even paler than usual—and looked for a sign of breathing, of the rush of blood, of anything... but there was none.

"Do something," she said, not sure exactly who she was speaking to.

"Isn't this more your department?" Clayton asked, adjusting Sienna's motionless form in his arms. His statement was pointed, like he had pointed Sienna's gun at Kat's heart and shot her right in it.

"I ... I can't," Kat said, shaking her head, not closing her eyes, not daring to look away. "Wha ... how ... do you think she ... did she drown?"

Steven blinked, as if suddenly recalling something. "Maybe," he said and pushed her off his lap. Sienna's head lolled limply, her eyes not quite shut, a crack of white and blue and black showing through the gap. Her lashes were dry and straight, perfect and full and lengthy without a hint of mascara. Kat had to extend hers, because they were blond and faded into nothingness without cosmetic aid.

"What are you doing?" Kat asked in muted horror as he laid her flat and used a finger to push her mouth open as he tilted her head back.

"I was a lifeguard at the pool in Sitka in the summers," he said, all business. "I'm certified to perform CPR." He put his hands, crossed, on her breastbone. Her black suit jacket was dirty and damp and flopped open. He ignored any impropriety in the placement of his hands as Kat stared, dumbstruck, as he pressed hard down on her chest. A sound came like cracking bones, like Rice Krispies with milk just poured over them, and Kat gasped in disgust. "That's normal," he said, but he hesitated before resuming his up and down pushing on her chest. A few more cracking sounds followed, but fewer each time. After several pushes, he paused for a second, took a deep breath, and seemed to steel himself. "Okay, here goes." And he plunged his face down to hers, pressing his lips against Sienna's, breathing into her mouth.

Kat watched, still stunned, not even sure what she could do, what she needed to do. The whole scene was playing out with a distance between them like it was happening on TV or a movie screen. It was almost like she'd come to the premiere of a new and unseen Steven Clayton movie at Grauman's; here he was, a hero for the ages, stepping up to save the life of some derelict who'd drowned in a storm gutter. The atmosphere in the tunnel was just the right combination of seedy and claustrophobic to set the scene for a dark tragedy.

Except it wasn't a scene, it wasn't a movie, it wasn't on a screen at a theater and she wasn't dressed for a premiere, soaked from head to toe and wearing no dress or shoes, her bloodied feet torn from hard running on the concrete as she stood watching Steven Clayton perform CPR on Sienna Nealon.

It was here.

It was happening, right before her eyes.

Sienna was dead.

"You can't be dead," Kat breathed.

Steven was resuming his attacks on Sienna's already-broken breastbone and ribs after another round of invasively shoving his lips against hers, but he stopped long enough to weigh in. "Well, she is," he snapped, "and she's going to stay that way unless either you or I can bring her back."

Kat stood back. Seven times, she counted, he jerked as he pushed down on her chest, before he stopped and dove down again. It looked almost he was kissing her, kneeling to deliver the waking kiss to Sleeping Beauty, a Prince Charming nearly any woman would kill to have giving his attention to her in this way. And someone *had* died, had been killed, in order to get his attention in this way, hadn't they? That was ironic, even to Kat, watching in her stunned state, her mind not even fully processing what she was seeing before her.

You can't be dead, she thought. *You faced Wolfe and Aleksandr, beat Omega assassins and vampires, fought a man who could control the flow of time itself and killed the strongest meta on the planet.*

You can't be dead.

Nothing can kill you.

You were supposed to live … longer than anyone.

I was supposed to fear you for the rest of my life.

The tunnel's cold air chilled Kat through the water still beaded on her skin. The sun's light seemed miles away, though it was probably only twenty or thirty feet to the surface. She could feel the roots of trees above her, somewhere, the near-dead grass hiding behind the concrete-lined tunnel ceiling. She felt much the same, dormant in the face of what was happening, a drought of emotions that deadened her inside.

You were practically going to live forever. I was always going to have to look over my shoulder for you. That's why you came, wasn't it? I haven't forgotten, Sienna. I never forgot, though you thought I didn't know. I know, though. I know how you looked at me …

But you can't be dead.

Steven was pressing again, and Kat had lost track of how many times he'd administered the hard shoves to her chest. That was what they looked like; like he meant to press her into the earth, shove her through the concrete floor like she was as insubstantial as Redbeard. Her body jerked faintly with the motion, with the force, but her face stayed pale, her breath did not come, and Sienna's body was still in the silence of the subway tunnel, as though it had been laid to rest in a tomb.

You can't be dead.

"This isn't working," Steven said, after two more hard breaths. He cast a glare at her angrily. "We need help here. Can you …?"

It was a desperate plea, a question in the air. Her answer came back instinctively. "No."

I know what I have to fear from you, Sienna.

Steven dove back down to work, pushing again, desperately, on her chest. Her neck jerked with the motion, no muscle control to stop her. He swooped down for another breath, another kiss …

And this time, Prince Charming woke Sleeping Beauty.

Sienna coughed back to life, her eyes squeezing desperately shut, that half-lidded gaze now closed off completely. She jerked to motion, limbs flailing as she came back to herself. Steven straightened, slumping back on his haunches as she swung an arm around, just missing his face. "It's okay," he said, reassuring. "You're fine."

Sienna's eyes fluttered open, dull, unfocused. "Wha …?"

"Get Wolfe, Sienna," Kat said, equally dully.

"Wolfe …?" Sienna asked, staring into the distance. Her eyes snapped clear in a second, and she sat up like the monster she was, come back to life. "Oh … gahh …" She brought a hand up and laid it on her forehead, covering half her face. "What just happened?"

"You died," Steven said. "Drowned, I think—"

"No," Sienna said, shaking her head. "Electrocuted.

Water on the third rail."

"Oh," Steven said. "Explains the lack of spitting up water when I performed CPR."

Sienna froze, hand that had been pushing hair out from in her face. "You … did what?"

"I brought you back," he said, leaning closer to her. "How do you feel?"

"Not like I just died," she said, pulling her hand away to reveal a suspicious look. "At least, not anymore."

"Because of Wolfe," Kat said softly, the answer coming to her so naturally.

"Where's Redbeard?" Sienna asked, already getting to her feet.

"Whoa," Steven said. "Hold your horses—you just got over being dead."

"You're right," she said brusquely, "I just did. I am over it now. I am not, however, over Redbeard, not by a long, Chris Kyle-type shot." She looked around the darkened tunnel. "Where is he?"

"There was a train wreck—" Steven said.

"You got that right," Sienna said, all self-righteous fury waiting to be unleashed. Her shoulders slumped and she deflated a second later. "Oh, damn. You mean a literal train wreck, don't you?"

"Back that way," Kat said, pointing down the tunnel. "It hit the debris on the tracks that fell through the hole in the—"

She was gone in a flash, in flight, shooting back down into the darkness the way Kat had pointed.

"Damn," Steven said with admiration. "She really is a hero, you know?"

"Hero, monster," Kat said, staring into the darkness where Sienna had disappeared around the light curve, "I guess it's all a matter of perspective, really."

40.

Karl

The rage had lasted through the whole train, had fueled him through every horrible thing he'd done to every living person on that train. It had carried him down the tunnel, back to the station on a slow walk. It had led him to kill eight people on the platform, a few of them before they'd even realized what was going on. He'd murdered two police officers who had already been on the scene, trying to contain and assess the disaster area. Their blood was on his hands, the seething anger fueled by the slick feeling on his fingers. He could have let it drop off if he'd wanted; could have gone insubstantial but let the blood stay physical, and it would have slid off and hit the ground.

He kept the blood on his hands, though. It was a reminder, it was fuel, it was what he needed to keep going. This was his rage, his fury against the machine that had been set up against him, against so many of the sheep. The whole thing was the slaughterhouse, really, and he was supposed to be a sheep, like the others. Karl didn't like being a sheep, but the slaughterhouse, like any slaughterhouse, wasn't run for the benefit of the sheep. They didn't get an opinion that counted, did they?

He walked up the stairs in MacArthur Park Station and found the world shrouded in mist. It was a nice little metaphor for the lack of clarity most people were living with. Shrugging, he made his way over to the cop car that was running just a few feet away, doors locked, and slipped inside. He wiped the blood on the passenger seat and put the car in gear. He even signaled his turn as he drove off, sirens blazing, back toward the Elysium neighborhood, back to his bolt hole, where he would upload his newly made videos while he watched the day's events unfold on the news. Yes, that would be fun, watching the videos show up on TV. Virality was his way to reach the masses. He would sit and watch the horror and ready himself for the next phase of the plan, laughing all the while as they struggled to reconcile his seemingly random acts of violence.

41.

Sienna

I flew back down the tunnel, expecting the worst. When I'd gone out, everything had been flooding, after all, and it wasn't like water would just U-turn and buck gravity to go the hell back to where it had come from.

So imagine my surprise when I got to the hole in the tunnel and found nothing but some residual hints of water on the tunnel floor, like maybe it had rained a little through its new sunroof, and that was it.

I paused to look up, and saw a thick, heavy mist that was starting to clear, hanging like a pall over MacArthur Park above. There was no sign of a lake, though, which normally I would have found worrisome.

There was, however, a commuter train wrecked not fifty feet away from me, and so I had other things on my mind besides seeking out the source of miracles like an amazing evaporating lake, especially when I had a member of my team that was able to control the flow of water. For all I knew, he was still desperately holding back the tide, and I had minutes to rescue the passengers on the train before we'd all get washed away.

Urgency. I had it. Always. Especially, apparently, after I'd just died.

I flew over the rubble, which had knocked the train rather

187

soundly off its tracks, and I peered into the darkened compartment. I could see more compartments down the train, all jammed up and crooked in the small tunnel, like a zigzag pattern from their sudden stop.

It didn't look like a terrible crash, as far as these things went. It wasn't like any of the cars was lying on its side or anything. They were all still upright, though the lead engine had certainly been smashed in.

I flew above the first and second car and found a really minimal gap there. Someone as skinny as Kat might have been able to fit through, but there was no chance I was going to be able to, not with these hips. I decided to take another tack and flew all the way to the end of the train, the last car in line, and it was there, as I was about to rip the back door off, that I realized something was terribly, terribly wrong.

There was blood splattered on the windows. Like, many, many of the windows. I'd seen car wrecks that had done things like that. I'd actually seen a lot of blood in my time (hold your surprise). My mind raced to fit what I was seeing in the rear compartment with the evidence of the crash. It hadn't exactly been a delicate stop into a cushion of pillows, but it wasn't a plane crash, either. The train was probably only going twenty or thirty miles an hour, tops, when it slammed to a halt. Maybe less.

So why were the rear compartment windows covered in blood?

I ripped the door off and found my answer and wished I hadn't.

The holes in the passengers within were almost perfectly hand-shaped, as clear evidence of Redbeard at work as I needed. I hovered above the crime scene—because now that's what this train was—careful not to touch anything, or anybody. When I was certain that there was no one alive in that car, I carefully made my way to the next one, and the next one, with greater and greater urgency, simply opening the doors between carriages where I could, smashing my way through a window where I couldn't.

There was not a single survivor on the entire train. Every single one of these people was dead at the hands of a madman.

A madman I couldn't stop.

42.

Scott

"I don't know where Sienna or Kat are, exactly," Scott said to the jaded, slightly exasperated Detective Meredith Waters. The scene was a disaster area, the mist finally starting to clear and revealing a scope of wreckage that Scott wouldn't have guessed at. On the far side of the lake, where the bomb had gone off, it looked like a series of storefronts had been ripped open by a giant's fingers, their flat roofs and internal structure exposed to the light of day.

"You didn't see anything?" Detective Waters asked, one eyebrow slightly above the other.

"Well, they went down there," Scott said, waving toward the hole in MacArthur Lake, "but I haven't seen them since. I was a little busy trying to keep them from drowning."

Detective Waters eyed the still-damp air hanging around them suspiciously. "You did this?"

"You think a whole lake evaporating is a natural phenomenon?"

"Could have been the drought for all I know," Waters shot back, "I don't get down here all that often."

"Explains the state of the neighborhood, I guess," Guy Friday added, standing with his arms folded just behind Scott. As if to punctuate the point a homeless man in an overcoat went strolling by just then, rolling a shopping cart filled with ripped-up, dried brown grass sod.

"What happened here?" Waters asked, her notepad open. The sun was shining through the light mist still hanging over them.

"A bomb," Scott said, "another bomb buried in the lakebed, the lake started to drain into the tunnels, and then a train wrecked down there. There was also metahuman-on-metahuman action taking place throughout all of that."

"*Hot* metahuman on metahuman action," Guy Friday added, still not helpfully.

Waters seemed to deflate. "Well, you got the train wreck part right, at least." She shot a glare at Guy Friday. "Why are you wearing that mask, sir?"

"That just what he does," Scott said with a sigh.

"It's eighty-seven degrees," she said. "And sunny."

"I'll vouch for him," Scott said. "He's a federal agent, and he's with me."

That did not seem to appease Waters. "That may be, but as I understand it, you're *not* a federal agent. When did you last see Sienna Nealon?"

"When she went down there," Scott said, pointing at the hole again. "Well, not exactly there. She got dragged through the ground—"

"Never mind," Waters said, now holding her head, pen dangling loosely from her grip. "Just … don't leave yet. I need officers to get statements from both of you, once we have this scene secured." She let out a ragged breath. "It could be a while."

Scott took it all in with a look. The crime scene, if that's what you could call it, stretched from the site of the first bombing all the way over to him. MacArthur Park was filling up with lookie loos. Between the park, the bomb site, the tunnel and the train crash, it was miles of scene to sift through. He didn't envy the LAPD today. "You don't say."

At that moment, movement out of the crater in the lake drew Scott's gaze. He turned to see Sienna rise out of the empty remains of MacArthur Lake, her hair frizzed and ragged, hanging off her in twisted locks, slightly wilder than if she'd taken a high-speed flight. Kat and Steven Clayton were both holding each of her hands, ripped material from Kat's dress—which looked torn and awkwardly worn—wrapped around their hands to keep them from touching Sienna's skin. She brought them up and let them both loose a foot over the concrete. They both landed adroitly, though Kat stumbled slightly on her bare feet.

Guy Friday spoke first. "What happened to your dress, Blondie?"

"I had to take it off for a while," Kat said, brushing her hair back like it was no big deal.

"Go on," Guy Friday said.

"Shut up, Guy Friday," Sienna snapped.

"Hey," Guy Friday said in plain annoyance, "my name is Yancy, okay?"

Sienna blinked. "I can see why you go by Guy Friday, then."

"Are you all right?" Scott asked before Yancy Friday had a chance to reply.

"I'm fine," Sienna said, a little too abruptly even for her.

"She died," Kat said, "but other than that, she's right as rain." Kat puckered her lips. "Which doesn't really fit here, does it? Because it doesn't rain, I mean."

"Did you check on the train wreck?" Waters asked, pushing forward, bumping Scott as she did so.

"It's … bad," Sienna said, her face paler than normal. "Really bad."

"How bad?" Waters asked. Her walkie-talkie beeped, interrupting her, and she held up a finger to silence Sienna. "Go for Waters."

"We have eight—repeat eight fatalities at MacArthur Park Station," the voice over the radio said. "Two officers on scene. No need to hurry on ambulances."

"Son of a—" Waters said, and let her finger off her

walkie. "What the hell happened down there?" She fixated on Sienna.

"The bad guy," Sienna said with a visible gulp that showed on her thin throat. "The train? He killed everyone on it."

A stunned silence fell, broken only by the sound of sirens, the flashing of lights that surrounded them, the voices of emergency workers and a crowd that was barely being held back by the all-too-few officers currently on scene. Detective Waters's walkie-talkie beeped again. "Go for Waters," she said as she clicked the button once more.

"Detective," the voice came, "Chief requires your presence at headquarters."

"I'm managing a disaster scene right now," Waters said, voice straining to break out of the calm inflection she was clearly trying to layer atop warring emotions. "What the hell is so important?"

The answer was a moment in coming. "Apparently the perp has uploaded video footage of massacring an entire train and those people at MacArthur Station. It's going viral as we speak."

43.

Karl

The hateful chaos caused by the carrion birds who were the media was like a feast for Karl's senses. It fed the righteous rage, gave him a warm sense of accomplishment, even delight, as he watched the stunned reactions start to pile up. Even the news anchors—ghouls if ever there were any, people who practically prayed for a tragedy in order to make their names—were stunned into silence after watching his videos live on air.

"All the 'Graphic Content Warnings' in the world can't prepare you sheep for what you're seeing now," Karl crowed into the silence of the nearly empty living room. He sat on the floor, his laptop set up on a coffee table. His mattress was in the corner, out of the way, and the bathroom down the hall. Other than the bedroom he used to store his explosives, the house was empty. Just a three-bedroom in the Elysium neighborhood that would have gone for over a million dollars if it were a mile to the east or west. But instead, he was here, in Elysium, where it was "only" worth a half million dollars.

The system was plainly rigged.

That was the best part of all this. The power structures of the day fawned over each other in a self-perpetuating system of reinforcement. The party he'd broken up the other night, with its elites lording their importance and superiority over the common people, they were watched like hawks by the media elites, who also fawned over the political elite, yet all of them were incestuous with each other—loving to cross paths, to measure their own excellence by all the famous people they knew. They had to confirm their own importance because without that confirmation, they'd just be impotent little weasels preening self-importantly without anyone to watch them.

Karl hated them all, hated all they stood for, and was hard pressed to decide who he hated most of all of them. Everything bad flowed from them—it was all just one lock-step theater show, Kabuki on parade, a show for the people who thought they had a say but didn't realize that really, when it all came down to it, their vote counted for less in the world than their viewing habits and internet clicks. Money ruled all, but the elite provided the distraction that enabled it.

But this … this play of Karl's, of his benefactor's … this was going to reverse the course. This was going to pull things in a different direction, make noise of a sort that the chattering classes wouldn't like. It would take the gaze off the distraction and put it firmly where it belonged—on the elite, the ones who needed to die in order for this grotesque system of oppression to pass.

And who were better symbols of that power, that elitism, than the world's foremost guard dog—bitch, really—Sienna Nealon, and the most-loved meta celebrity in the nation, Kat Forrest?

Their tangential connection to Augustus Coleman was just the cherry on top, really. He wasn't the power behind it all, anyway, he was just a guy who got caught up doing what Sienna Nealon had ordered him to do. He was a soldier, a sheep. These two were the real problem, the face of the enemy. It didn't matter how pretty it was; once you destroyed that face, people would sit up and take notice.

Change was coming, Karl reflected, a smile twisting his

pale face. Oh, yes, it was coming. And every step he took closer to the goal was like a return to that happiness he didn't even think he could feel any more.

44.

Sienna

Disaster scenes weren't the sort of thing that you could easily walk away from, especially if you were heavily involved in their creation. I was tired, ragged, and looked like shit, I was sure, but unfortunately the LAPD did not want me to leave MacArthur Park until I'd given a full statement. They didn't even want me to see if I could help with rescue efforts—which I couldn't, really. The shops that had been bombed had been hit with a pretty straightforward explosion that originated under the sidewalk outside. It had collapsed the storefronts, but most of the people caught in that had been killed straight up. I could see them dragging the body bags out and piling them up on the street for transport, leaving the ambulances sitting there with lights flashing, hoping for survivors they weren't finding.

It was grim as hell, so I found a bench and sat down, waiting for my turn with the police. They'd assigned one officer to take statements, probably because that was all they could spare. The whole place was crawling with LAPD, enough to make me think the rest of the city was probably like Candyland for criminals today. I'd seen SWAT descend into the subway station, followed by a bunch more cops and emergency workers, and now I could hear their voices faintly as they surveyed my findings in the tunnel below.

Steven Clayton was giving his statement to the lone officer assigned to watch my little carnival, and I was just sitting on a bench, staring out at the muddy floor of the lake that was already starting to dry in the sun. The mist was gone, clearly evaporated enough that the air barely felt humid anymore. This place needed rain like it needed Redbeard to die: desperately, urgently, and as soon as possible.

Scott was positioned at a bench about a hundred feet from mine, Guy Friday lurking behind it, still standing, arms folded, in his most serious bodyguarding posture. He was watching Kat pace back and forth at the edge of the lake, as though he was worried she was going fall off and end up in the mud below. Personally, I wasn't worried about that. I would have welcomed it because I'm petty. If she came close enough to me, I can't guarantee I wouldn't have given her a good shove myself.

"Stop looking at me that way," Kat snapped, orbiting closer to me on her next pass. Her green eyes were narrowed, and I didn't even know she'd seen me. She was pacing furiously, her feet leaving the occasional bloody stain on the concrete path ringing the empty lake.

"I'm supposed to watch you," I said mildly, "you know— in case someone tries to kill you. Again."

"You're not watching me like that," Kat snapped, slowing her walk, lingering about ten feet from me, apparently so she could get whatever was off her chest—it was a pretty minimal chest—uh, well, off it.

"How am I watching you?" I asked, my tone wending toward dark amusement. "Like Yancy over there? Because I think he might fancy you, Kat. Yancy fancies." I chortled. "Come on. That's good."

"I can hear you," Guy Friday said.

"And so?" I called back.

"None of this is funny," Kat snapped back.

I looked over the ruin of the park. While it hadn't exactly been the classiest of places when we'd arrived that morning, I couldn't find fault with her assessment. "You're right," I said, accepting my chastening, "it's not."

"I'm not talking about this, either," she said, waving a hand around to encompass all around us.

"Because … this *is* funny?" I asked her uncertainly, now without a clue as to what she was driving at.

"I'm talking about how you look at me, Sienna," Kat said, and now she was almost spitting fury at me. I wanted to laugh again, from exhaustion and from the image of this little stick getting pissed at me after I came to LA and died trying to fight the guy who wanted to kill her—not really sure which of those was the worst part of this whole ordeal.

"How do I look at you, Kat?" I asked, my cynicism settling in for a good laugh. "Like you're an idiot? Because that one's really more on you than me—"

"Janus told me," she said, puffing up with a sense of satisfaction like she was confronting me with my own personal kryptonite.

"Told you what?" I asked, more tired than curious. "That you were special? Because he sold me that line of bullshit, too, but fortunately he didn't try and use it to sleep with me afterward—"

"He told me that you know," Kat said, arching her eyebrows as though plainly I was aware of the big dramatic important thing of which she was speaking.

I racked my weary brain and camp up with goose eggs. "Kat … I have not the first clue what you're on about."

"Bullshit," she said hotly.

Kat didn't really swear very much so that one woke me up a little. Also, calling me a liar on a normal day was not wise. On a day like today? I envisioned myself making a speedy exit from this town, but not before clearing the ten seconds on my calendar that it would take to drop her down the big hole in front of me as I made my way home. I pictured her screaming as she disappeared into the darkness, skinny limbs flailing, and it calmed me enough to respond without violence. "Okay. Tell me what I know that you know that Janus told—" I paused, trying to disentangle what I'd just said. "Just tell me, Kat, so we can get on the same page with this argument you clearly want to have."

"You're painting me as the villain," Kat said, snotty, turning her face away from me and looking to the heavens for either intervention or rain, neither of which forthcoming. "Typical."

"This is why I look at you like you're an idiot, by the way," I said, probably not salving the situation much.

"You look at me like I'm a damned steak and you're hungry, Sienna," Kat snapped.

I sighed. "Kat ... I wouldn't eat you if you were the last cut of meat on earth, all right? I'm not a cannibal, you don't look very filling, and if you're suggesting that I'm in any way harboring same-sex tendencies for you, you're out of your damned mind. Also your ego is huge-normous. Like, it couldn't fit in the Metlife Blimp, or the Metrodome, or Canada—"

"You know what happens if you absorb me," Kat said, almost like it was a threat—to me, not her.

"Absorb you?" I stopped short of laughing. "I can barely stand to be around you for a day. If you think I want to live with you in my head, you're even dumber than I've always suspected. I'd rather deal with Wolfe—"

Grrr ...

"—or Bjorn—"

I am a tasty Nord. All meat—

"—or Eve—"

Ach du—!

"—or your irritating brother—"

HEY!

"—point is," I said, "I don't even like you, Kat." I watched her face fall. "You're a treacherous whore who's thrown me under the bus with meta strength for her own good while pretending to be a friend. Want to absorb you?" I scoffed. "If Scott wasn't here right now, if there wasn't an obvious and imminent threat to innocent people, I'd let you die a cold and ugly death at the hands of Redbeard."

"You can't lie to me, Sienna," Kat said, cold indignation breaking through her brittle facade that I'd just chipped away at. "If you absorb me ..."

"I get an annoying voice in my head forever?" I snorted. "What a prize. Do I get your chlamydia, too, because, if so, bonanza—"

"You keep acting like you don't know," she said haughtily, "but he told you. I know he did. Acting like you don't think about it—well, let's just say you're in the wrong town for bad acting, okay?"

"Or the very right one, considering how much of it you're doing right now." I paused, thinking about Janus's conversation with me about Kat, about absorbing her. Oh. Wait, he had said—

Ohhhhhhh.

Right.

Something must have showed on my face, because Kat puffed up a little bigger. "Yeah. No need to fake your way through the scene anymore."

I rolled my eyes. It was utterly genuine. I'd filed away the rest of what Janus had told me regarding what would happen if I absorbed Kat because—frankly—I didn't give a shit. Absorbing a Persephone meant I could control my skin-based soul absorption powers rather than just have them work whenever I touched someone. And while that would have been kind of useful, I supposed, it wasn't something I gave a lot of thought to anymore, because—well, I had better things to do, and I didn't really want to absorb anyone, ever, let alone Kat Forrest, Queen of People-Who-Piss-Me-Off Town. "What you attribute to fakery might be better chalked up to not caring."

"I know you look at me, thinking about it all the while," Kat said, running a hand up herself in a very *ewwww* sort of way. I'm sure it would have looked great on film if her hair, makeup and dress weren't almost as bad a wreck as the train below, but *Vanity Fair* and their wardrobe, hair and makeup people had long since fled this scene. "About how you could just live a normal life if you did that one thing—"

"Yeah, I'm sure that's the only thing separating me from a normal life," I muttered under my breath. "Just absorb you and it's like a magic tonic that will make everything better—I won't be a workaholic hated by the world anymore, sitting on the edge of being fired from my job and declared a public enemy, and all my relationship woes and baggage will miraculously be fixed because I'll be able to have unprotected sex." I nodded smartly. "It'll probably bring my parents back from the dead, as well—"

"You're such a bitch," Kat said, utter loathing in her eyes as she turned to walk away.

"I'm sure it'll fix that, too," I called after her. "Come back! Let me absorb you, Kat! We will have a magical, extra-special awesome life together!" She stalked off past Scott, who watched her go with a frown, and Guy Friday, who met my gaze with arched eyebrows. "Ugh," I said, and folded my own arms in front of me. "Why do I get stuck working with difficult people?"

"Law of attraction," Steven Clayton said, stalking silently up behind me.

"I am not attracted to Kat, no matter what Yancy over there might be fantasizing—"

"That's not what the law of attraction is about," Steven said with a chuckle. "It's a philosophy thing that went big a few years ago—'You attract what you are.' Therefore, positive, excited people attract themselves to positive, excited people and negative, angry folks—"

"Find many opportunities to punch the shit out of positive, excited people," I finished for him, drawing a smile from him. "Sorry," I said. "I'm in a bit of a mood."

"You got PTSD?" he asked, jerking a thumb over his

shoulder to indicate the hole to the tunnel. "Because that strikes me as the sort of thing that would do it."

"I'm fine," I said, broken record that I am. "Don't you have ... I dunno, work or something?"

"Let me tell you about my profession," he said, cracking a smile, "when I work, it's like ... epically long days. But then I may have a month or two off in a row before I have to go and do a round of press tours and stuff. Right now, I got nothing until my next movie starts table reads next week."

"Yeah, you look bored and idle," I said, surveying him. "Thanks for the ... uh ... breath of life, I guess?" *The life-giving kiss,* I didn't say. All remarks regarding slipping me the tongue were similarly not mentioned, though I was tempted to throw on a Guy Friday-esque expression and let one loose.

"You're welcome," he said. "You're going to need to reload your gun, by the way."

I frowned and felt instinctively for the Shadow in my holster. "Did you steal my sidearm?"

"That thing shoots like a dream," he said by way of explanation. "Smoothest thing I've ever shot."

I raised an eyebrow. "Wow. I didn't expect you to ..."

"Haven't you seen my movies?" He grinned. "I shoot all kinds of guns in those. All loaded with blanks, but still."

"Yeah, well," I shrugged, "you're an actor. You're supposed to be able to pretend with the best of them." I eyed him warily. "Also ... you keep coming to my rescue."

He gave a shrug of his own. "I was a lifeguard as a teenager. You keep falling in the water. This is just instinct for me."

"Feels like more than that," I said. "I mean ... I'm not exactly the most popular person in the world at the moment. The tabloids alone—"

"Yeah," he said, cutting me off. "About that ... if truth were peanut dust, the tabloid stories I've read about myself wouldn't even trigger the most allergic person on earth. So ... I'm assuming that the same applies to their coverage of you."

"Really? Because most people seem to operate from the assumption that where there's smoke, there's Sienna Nealon setting fire to something." This was true.

"Don't let 'em get you down," Steven said with a smile that was warm and engaging, and made—uh, maybe just a little—one of my own spread slowly across my lips. "And about that drink …"

I fumbled for my cell phone and thumbed it on to exchange numbers. It did not light up, and I doubted it was from failing to charge it. "Dammit," I said. "Lost another one."

He pulled a little notebook and pen out of his jean pocket and opened it, ready to write. "Now, normally, my mother would kill me for giving a girl my number instead of asking for hers. But, since your phone is clearly inoperable, probably due to being fried by electricity, I'm just going to give you mine and passively wait by the phone until you call." He finished writing with a flourish and then tore out a little rectangle of cream-colored paper and handed it to me. A phone number was written on it in nice handwriting. I took it tentatively, like a clown car was going to drive up at any second, run over my foot, and a whole circus full of the bastards was going to pile out and laugh at me for thinking the Sexiest Man in Hollywood was actually giving me his number.

"Uh, thanks," I said, taking it and folding it carefully before realizing that if I slipped it in any one of my myriad pockets it would get soaked because they were all still damp from when I fell, shuddering with electrical current, into the water. I pinched it between my thumb and forefinger and nodded at him once. "I will call you when I get a chance to, uhm … not be bodyguarding and also not dodging Redbeard's wrath."

"Redbeard's Wrath sounds like a really epic pirate movie."

"It kinda does, doesn't it?" I nodded. "Or a really gross

porno."

He pressed his lips together in a narrow line. "Uhhhhh …"

I closed my eyes instead of slapping my forehead. "It was nice to meet you again, Steven. Thank you for saving my life. And possibly, Kat's." I paused. "I mean, obviously you saved Kat's, I'm just not sure whether I should thank you for it."

"You're an odd one, Sienna Nealon," he said slyly as he started to walk away. "I think I like you."

"That's good," I said, "because otherwise you just gave your personal, private phone number to me for no reason."

"Wouldn't want to do that," he said with a grin, walking away backward, depriving me of a hell of a view. The grin was nice, though.

45.

We left the park at four in the afternoon, almost on the dot. Turns out the bomb squad had to give the SUV we drove in a once-over before we could leave in it. The driver, for his part, swore up and down that no one had been near the vehicle, that he'd been parked a couple streets away the entire time, waiting for the call to pick us up. I believed him, because he looked too bewildered to be lying and Redbeard didn't strike me as the type to have a well-ordered conspiracy behind him. He was a lone gunman sort, but without the gun. Lone bombman? Lone phase-through-peoples'-chests man? Doesn't have much of a ring to it, does it?

We got stuck in traffic, which I had more or less worked out was a feature of LA, not a bug. It was a feature I hated, like the distressed look in clothing or customer service help lines that automatically route you to a robot for a "Dial 1 to Induce Bone-Chilling Rage At My Lack of Understanding Your Very Basic, Slow-Diction Speech!" Something like twenty-seven hours after first stepping into the car, we made it back to the hotel. I think the sun had risen and set multiple times, but no one had spoken, Guy Friday and myself squeezing Kat into the middle of the backseat, Scott in the front. She squirmed like a petulant child, acting like a black hole trying to collapse in on itself to avoid touching either me or Guy Friday, which was probably wise in both cases, but for very different reasons. When I let her out of the back of the car at the hotel, she stalked off in a huff, not even daring to look at me. I didn't complain, but it did make for an awkward elevator ride.

When we got to the room, she disappeared upstairs, stomping the whole way. Taggert emerged from his suite next to us as Scott, Guy Friday and I stood uneasily in the living room. Well, Scott and I stood uneasily. Guy Friday …

"I should go watch the blond girl," Guy Friday said.

"You mean stand guard by the door of her room, right?" I asked, raising an eyebrow.

"What if someone sneaks in?" Friday asked, making his way up the stairs. "We can't take that chance."

He disappeared up the balcony, and I started to interject, but Scott spoke first. "I need to talk to you in a bit," he said, eyes a little downcast. "Privately."

"Uh, okay," I said, my eyes making their way up to where Guy Friday had just disappeared. "You mind going up and taking a look to make sure Guy … err, Yancy … doesn't get out of line with Kat? I'd go myself, but—"

"Yeah, I heard the dustup in the park," Scott said with a nod. He seemed uncomfortable, and he wouldn't look at me. "Just come find me in a few, okay?" He made his way up the stairs slowly on wobbly legs, without waiting for an answer.

Whatever I might have wanted to say was drowned out first by Kat's slamming of her door upstairs and then Taggert's next words, which were both booming and filled with excessive amounts of TMI. (Too Much Information. It's a slang thing.)

"Look," Taggert was saying into his cell phone, shrugging his shoulders at us, clearly his understanding audience, "this is your problem, not mine. She was fully legal at the time— you know what? I can see we're not going to have a productive resolution to this. Get in touch with my lawyers if you have something else to say. Don't call me again, I have no time for a loser like you." He hung up the phone and took a deep breath. "What a day, huh?" he asked us. Like he'd been there.

"What was that all about?" I asked. I closed my eyes at my mistake upon realizing it a second later, because unfortunately, Taggert was the sort of guy who would probably assume interest.

"Well, there was this girl," Taggert said with that same loathsome grin. "She's eighteen, and she and I had a little thing going on here a while back, nothing major. A fling, you know. Anyway, it's just a daddy, mad that his little girl grew up and started making her own decisions."

"Terrible ones, clearly," I said, "and surely based entirely on mutual attraction and having nothing to do with any perceived favor she could receive from you in return."

His grin grew wider and my skin crawled. "You ever heard that old Churchill quote?"

"Well, I wasn't alive when old Winston was around and running things in Merry Old England," I said, "but since you clearly were, why don't you tell us what your oldest friend in the world said?"

"He's at this party," Taggert said, my dig at his age not slowing him down a whit, "and he's talking with this lady. 'Would you sleep with a man for a million dollars?' he asks—"

"They use pounds in England, so I'm already doubting the veracity of your anecdote," I said. "Are you sure this isn't you talking to every woman ever?"

"And she says, 'Of course,'" Taggert went on, grin broadening to the point where he was reaching Glasgow smile territory, and I was wondering exactly how much plastic surgery he'd had on his mug, "So Churchill, keen observer of human nature that he was, says, 'What about for five dollars?' and she has a shit fit. 'What kind of woman do you think I am?' she asks, fit to be tied—"

"Stop dragging your fantasy life into this."

"—and he says," Taggert paused before delivering the punchline, "'We've already established what you are, madam'—'cuz he was a classy guy—"

"Yes, I always think of men who call women whores as classy, that's the first adjective that comes to mind."

"'Now we're just establishing the price!'" Taggert belted out the last bit with a sort of gusto that made me want to punch him in the face and give him a real Glasgow smile. It was entirely possible that in anyone else's hands, told for anyone else's purpose, this joke could have gotten at least a chuckle out of me. However, coming out of the mouth of a man who was a blatant, unrepentant sleaze, I couldn't help but feel he'd just opened the window to his soul, and I wanted nothing more than to shut said window and brick it up like I was Montresor. For the love of God.

"Yes, that's a keen insight you've got there," I said, as dry as MacArthur Park's Lake. "You sure know women. It's no wonder you're such a highly in-demand guy in the dating pool."

He shrugged with a self-assurance that I found so disgusting that I was tempted once again to burn everything around me preemptively. "I do all right for myself."

"Not so well for anyone else, though."

He shrugged, uncaring. "So, I saw what you did today. Good work. I'll say it again, though—I could make big things happen for you, just say the word."

"The word is still 'Ewww,' followed by a gagging sound."

He was undeterred. "I know they're looking for contestants on 'The Biggest Loser' right now. I could get you on, no problem. I know the producer, we go way back."

I blinked, stunned. Did he just …? Scratch that. What I really wanted to say was, *'OH NO HE DIDN'T!'*

"I know, I know," he held up both hands to ward me off, "it wouldn't be like the real show, more like a favor to help you drop a few pounds—"

"I could help you drop a few pounds, too," I said coldly in order to keep from turning it into 'hotly,' as in burning flames of Gavrikov consuming the minimal soul and wrinkly flesh of Taggert. "How much do you figure all your limbs weigh, ballpark? Because I could rip them off one by one and it'd be instant results, no diet, no exercise needed. I mean, I know your dick is insignificant, but still, every little bit—and I do mean *little*—helps, right? You could start a new fad diet—the SoCal douchebag limb amputation plan. There could be a cookbook and everything."

"I think Hannibal might have written that cookbook," he said wryly. "But hey—I'm just trying to help you."

"You know what would really help me? Like, really, really help me?" I asked. "You not being a creep and gross and making incredibly unwanted advances or non-helpful suggestions about my weight—actually, just not talking to me in general. That would be a huge help."

"Did I hurt your feelings?" He was actually leering.

"Please. It takes a lot more than an asshole like you to hurt my feelings." Now I was sneering. "I'm just going through an adjustment process, categorizing you as the worm you are, making peace with that and trying to work around it."

"Women love assholes," Taggert said, now back to placid. Everything I'd said was water off a duck's back to him, he cared so little. "Assholes and liars, they're your bread and butter."

I couldn't even stop myself from making a face. "That is … the dumbest, most revolting, insulting thing—"

"It's true," he said, "or they wouldn't go for them ten times out of ten."

"How has no one snatched you up yet?" I asked, feeling strangely euphoric, like my efforts at restraining myself from murdering Taggert had resulted in a psychotic break from reality. It was a heady feeling, like I was floating away from my body. But since I hadn't absorbed Redbeard's ability to go insubstantial and since even Taggert had just remarked that I was far from weightless (the prick), I had to chalk it up to fatigue and dealing with this a-hole.

"Well," he said, and I braced myself for what was surely

going to be crass and horrific, "I think I've snatched—"

"Hey," Guy Friday called from above, interrupting, "Brunette Girl. You've got a call."

I blinked, staring up at him on the balcony. "What are you, my secretary? Because, if so, you should at least know my name." I adjusted myself and glared at Taggert. "Everyone else does."

Taggert arched his eyebrows. "You've got good brand recognition. It's just that your image is shit—"

"Girl, call," Guy Friday said, annoyed, and tossed something at me. I caught it with one hand as he disappeared back over the balcony and closed the door to Kat's room. I wondered if I should worry about what was going on in there, but since he was still wearing a mask and Kat was apparently sleeping with Taggert at least some, I tried to put the whole thing out of my head.

I looked down at the object Friday had thrown at me. It was a phone, but an old one, like from the mid 2000s, an old Nokia of the sort that had a grey screen about a half-inch wide and tall. "What the hell is this?"

"Hello?" came a muted voice out of the earpiece, blaring out at me, barely audible save for my powers. "Sienna, are you there?"

"Crap," I muttered and looked up at Taggert. "I have to take this, and not just because I'd rather talk to anyone than talk to you."

"Brand image," he said, shaking his head sadly. "This is part of the problem, your interactions. You need to always play to the camera, like I always tell Kitten—"

"Fuck off, Taggert," I said, more resigned than angry at this point. He shrugged broadly and headed back to his room, no doubt leaving a slime trail across the floor like the slug he was. I sighed as he closed the door then pulled the phone up to my ear, bracing myself for something that would probably be horrific, but was at least destined to be less crass than anything Taggert had to say. "Director Phillips? I'm here."

46.

I was all prepared for Andrew Phillips to lambast me, for an eighteen-minute epic rant about how evil I was as a person to let civilian casualties go down the way they had, for a speech on the virtues of public property and how we ought to make sure that it's not destroyed. I was ready for all of that, for a general screaming of the speaker in the cell phone.

What I got was none of that, and I'll tell you, it shocked me. "Are you all right?" Phillips asked. He didn't sound concerned, because he didn't really have many emotions to display, but he didn't sound angry, either, and he didn't open with, "What the hell were you doing/thinking/up to?" which was his normal go-to when he spoke to me.

"Well, I died," I said, taken aback enough that I answered honestly, "but other than that … yes?" Phillips asking me if I was all right had me wondering if I was still dead, passed on to Valhalla or something.

"… Died?" Phillips actually sounded shocked.

"I got better," I said. "CPR and whatnot."

"That's not on the news," Phillips said, and for him, it sounded like panic. "Don't let that leak. It'd be bad."

"Yeah, well," I said, frowning, "it wasn't exactly a picnic when it happened to me, either. I had broken ribs and—"

"Are you okay?" he asked again, and now I could tell I was straining at his patience a little.

"Fine," I said, letting it go. "What do you want?"

"I was about to ask you the same thing," Phillips said.

I thought about it before answering. "Well, I'd like to beat Kat about the face and neck like an actual cat playing with a ball of yarn—"

"Seriously."

"I am serious," I said, "but failing that, I could use an In-and-Out burger."

I could hear Phillips take a breath on the other end of the line. "How do we get this guy?" he asked, clearly shifting to another conversational track in order to not lose his shit with me.

I was still scrambling to understand how he'd come out of the gate of this conversation without being an a-hole for once. "Uhmm ... that's a good question," I said, "unfortunately, I'm a little busy bodyguarding to run an investigation at the moment. Kat keeps exposing herself to stupid situations that give this bastard opportune shots at her."

"Okay, that needs to stop right now," Phillips said.

"I agree," I said, "which is why I really want to beat her around the face and neck like—"

"No."

"But I guarantee she'd stop when rendered unconscious—"

"No ..." He paused. "Still no."

"I like that you had to think about it for a minute."

"Do we have any clues?" Phillips asked.

"Well, Augustus faced this guy down in Atlanta," I said. "Buried him in the earth. I put in a call to him to try and get his take, and he gave me a good pointer on how to hurt him, but we've still got nothing on the guy's identity."

"You didn't answer your phone," Phillips said. "Can I assume another replacement is in the works?"

I pulled out my phone and looked at it before trying to push the on button. "When I died, it kinda got—I dunno, either electrocuted or waterlogged or maybe both—"

"Okay, don't tell me that," he said, "I don't really want to make an official report on that up the chain." I rolled my eyes. Presumably he was worried, again, that if he had to make an official report on me dying, it would eventually make it out to the press and get covered—well, probably poorly. Your champion dying at the hands of the evil villain is not the most inspiring news, I suppose. "I've got J.J. working on this, and the rest of the agency is digging in now. It's all hands on deck. We'll get this guy."

"What about Reed and Augustus?" I asked.

"They're still in Austin," Phillips said. "If you need them desperately, I can pull them back, but they've been on stakeout for a hundred and ninety two hours. I mean, there's a murderer at work on their case, too—"

"Leave them in place for now," I said. "If we can keep Kat from exposing herself to the public—both literally and figuratively—we won't need them. We'll hunker down. That might give me a chance to poke my head up and see if I can nail this prick to the wall."

"Got it," Phillips said. "Get that phone replaced and call me if you need anything else." He hung up without saying goodbye, of course. He was still Phillips, after all.

I pulled Guy Friday's phone away from my ear and stared at it. "This is just weird," I said aloud to the empty room. Why was Phillips not being an asshole? Phillips was always an asshole. It was like an iron law of the universe. Gravity pulls down. Fire burns. Andrew Phillips is an asshole.

My world was crumbling around me.

My phone buzzed and lit up, displaying a text message.

Ricardo

You are as beautiful as you are mysterious.

"And suddenly the world makes sense again, in all its rampant and infinite bizarreness," I said and started upstairs to return Guy Friday's cell phone before I went to have my little chat with Scott.

47.

Kat

Kat was pacing in her room, the big guy with the mask watching from the door, immovable, his arms folded like always. She didn't mind having him here. He was just another servant, like a piece of furniture but one that could speak if necessary.

"Can you believe this?" she asked, practicing her poise as she walked—no, stalked, because she was furious. "She acts like she doesn't remember. As though absorbing me wouldn't be the fulfillment of her dreams, as though being able to touch anyone she wanted wasn't her greatest ambition."

"My greatest ambition is to visit the Santa Monica pier at this point," Guy Friday said. "I wonder if they have Skee-ball?"

Kat stalked on. This was important. "Well, she may be fooling herself, but she doesn't fool me. I'm a tasty meal, like fries with truffle oil after she's been eating McDonald's for years."

"Or like a USDA prime filet mignon when you've been eating canner grade meat for years," Guy Friday agreed.

"Yes!" Kat agreed, though she hadn't had a steak in years. Red meat was too unhealthy for her to consider it. "Exactly that. But good luck getting anyone else to see it. It's always *Sienna, Sienna, Sienna.*"

"I think you mean, 'Marsha, Marsha, Marsha.'"

Kat made a face and ignored him; she had no idea what he was talking about and it didn't matter, anyway. "Do you know how long it took for me to step out of her shadow? She was the face at the front of the war, like me fighting— like I had nothing to do with it?" She placed her ragged nails on her t-shirt, which was a $250 lime-green, all-cotton original. She needed a manicurist terribly. "When we were at MacArthur Park, did you know some ragged fashion victim came up to her asking for an autograph? From *her.*" Kat scoffed. "She's probably never taken a headshot in her life."

Guy Friday paused, thinking it over. "I think she's taken a few headshots. She's pretty good with a gun, I doubt she makes all her shots for center mass—"

"Not that kind," Kat snapped, seething. "We all know she's good with a gun—like that's some sort of virtue. How many people do you think she's killed?"

"Hundreds," Guy Friday said. "Maybe thousands—"

"That's just ..." Kat felt her skin crawl. "I could be one of those thousands, you know. Sometimes I'm surprised I'm not, that she didn't just kill me in the war and call it an accident." She wandered toward the bed and threw herself lightly onto the bedspread, letting her mussed hair get trapped under her neck as she reached for the remote and turned the TV on. "And then no one would even know me."

The TV picture resolved after the brand name showed on the screen for a few seconds. A news anchor for one of the local stations was talking in a hushed voice. "... Fans of Bree Lancer are in mourning today, still shocked by the sudden death of the—"

"Ughhhh," Kat said, lifting her head for a second and then driving it back into the bed as she rolled over onto her face. "Yes, poor Bree, who got killed by the murderer who's *still* after me, by the way. Way to bury the lede, guys. *Her* problems are over."

"I think this is about her fans," Guy Friday said as Kat

tried to push her face further into the fluffy bedspread. It smelled like cotton but like something else, too, and she wondered when last it had been washed. She pulled her face out immediately. "Yeah, look at them. They seem really sad."

Kat managed to cast a look over her shoulder at the TV. There were people with posters of Bree, with signs, with tears running down their cheeks. They looked like they were near the police barricades that had been set up last night, the wreckage of Anna's house in the background. "Yes, it's so sad. Bree was a saint, Bree was an angel." Kat snatched up the remote and turned the channel. "What they really ought to report is that Bree loved pills more than she ever loved another human being, and that when she was high, she was nasty enough to go down on a leper, or Pauly Shore."

"Did you ever see her do it?" Guy Friday asked, voice raised with curiosity.

"Not Pauly Shore, no," Kat said, gripping a pillow and pulling it down so she could curl up in the fetal position with it. "But I saw her give head to a Gawker reporter one time, which is probably worse than Pauly Shore *or* a leper."

"Hmmm," Guy Friday said, standing a little straighter.

Kat turned her gaze back to the TV. "The city's insurance carrier is already refusing to pay," the anchor said, live at the scene, with a shot of the drained MacArthur Park Lake behind him, "citing the recently ruled-on court case terming metahuman incidents as 'Acts of gods.' The city is pledging to fight it in court, but one of the legal scholars we spoke to suggested—"

"Should have gone with Lloyd's of London, guys," Sienna said, bumping Guy Friday out of the way as she opened the door. "And speaking of which," she looked directly at Kat, "you should insure your back with them, since you're literally making a living on it."

"What do you want?" Kat asked, pulling her head off the comforter enough to look at Sienna. She still looked terrible, of course, the ruins of her suit hanging tattered about her.

Redbeard dressed better than her.

"Came to return the big guy's phone," Sienna said, slapping a mini-brick of a phone into the center of Guy Friday's chest. It made a thumping noise as it hit him.

Guy Friday grunted. "Careful."

"Because it's an antique?" Sienna snarked, a nasty smile on her face. Kat wondered if she even knew how ugly those looks made her. She used them all the time, every single occasion she made one of her little jokes. "You're a phone hipster, I get it." She stood there for a second, looking around. "Well, as much fun as this has been, I wouldn't want to interrupt your scintillating conversation." She snapped open the door. "Au revoir."

"I hate her so much," Kat said, clutching her pillow so tight it felt like it might explode.

"A lot of people feel that way," Guy Friday said, and for some reason, Kat found that very comforting.

48.

Scott

"Come in," Scott said when he heard the knock at the door. He'd been sitting on the bed, waiting, hands sweating, reabsorbing the perspiration and then letting it seep out again accidentally when he lost himself in thought. He stood nervously, wiped his hands on his pants, then reabsorbed the liquid through the cotton trousers into his legs.

The door opened smoothly, quietly, and Sienna came in, looking haggard. "Ugh, Kat," she said. "Can you believe ..." She sighed. "Never mind. What's up?" She stood expectantly, her back against the suite's beautiful paneled door.

"I wanted to ..." He paused, feeling as though there were a fork was through his center, twisting him like spaghetti noodles. "I wanted to have a talk with you ... about something that happened at the park."

"Well, thank you for not being Kat about it," Sienna said, coming in and looking around the suite. The floor to ceiling windows at his right offered a pretty nice view of the darkness falling over Los Angeles.

"Go easy on her," Scott said instinctively. "She's had a rough day."

Sienna looked amused when she answered rather than upset. "*She's* had a rough day? I *died*."

"And you're taking it so very well," Scott said, brushing

that right off. "Listen … when I was … evaporating the lake, I saw … something."

"What kind of something?" Sienna asked, brow furrowing with interest. "Like, something related to Captain Redbeard? Because, boy would I like to sink his ship."

"No," Scott said, afraid to look at her for fear of losing his nerve. "You know … all those rumors about you and me … as a couple?" He chanced a look.

Sienna was watching him carefully, frozen in place. "Uh … yeah?"

"Kat said something funny about that, too," Scott said, splitting his gaze between the carpet pattern and Sienna. "That we were together. And then … today, when I was draining the lake … I saw … like a vision."

"A vision?" Sienna was holding very still, her face carefully neutral.

"Of the two of us," Scott said, struggling to get it out. "Having an argument. And the way it was … it looked like we were … like a couple." He looked her right in the eye. "Do you know what I mean?"

"I don't typically have a lot of visions, no," Sienna said a little too flippantly, but with just a hint that she was experiencing something else, some other feeling, as well.

"I don't feel like it was just a dream," Scott said, looking away again. He stared off at downtown in the distance, the lights coming on in the Bank of America tower. "It felt real, this argument between us."

"We've known each other for a long time," Sienna said quietly. "We've argued in the past."

"This was different," Scott said vehemently, shaking his head. "This was us clashing over—over life choices. Not the sort of thing I'd call you on as a friend." His face tightened. "Sienna … why don't I remember the rest of that conversation?" He waited for an answer, and when it didn't come, he prodded her. "Do you know what I'm talking about?"

She watched him like she was carved out of stone, her eyes frozen in place. "Yes," she said finally, the facade cracking enough to show some uncertainty. "Yeah, I remember ... I remember that."

"When did it happen?" Scott asked, taking a few steps toward her. His head felt foggy just from the effort of trying to jar a memory loose, of trying to pry it out of some dark cranny in his mind.

"Probably the night of my abortive, horrible interview with Gail Roth," Sienna said matter-of-factly, lowering her gaze as she did so. He was presented with a view of the top of her head, and the frizzed, barely-dry, electrified mess of her hair. "That's when it happened."

"Why can't I remember that?" Scott asked. "I mean, I remember seeing the Gail Roth interview on TV, obviously, but—" He shrugged. "I don't remember seeing you that night."

"Well, you were there," she said.

"Where?" Scott asked. "At the interview?"

"Yeah," she said. It felt to him as if he were wrestling something valuable out of her grasp. Her whole body was filled with tension, and she held herself back slightly, like she was preparing for a blow from an unseen source. "You were watching it unfold live."

"How I do not—" He blinked, trying to remember. "How can I not—I don't even recall—" He looked at her, could read the guilt in the way she held herself. "Did you ... *Eternal Sunshine of the Spotless Mind* me?"

Her brow creased, her lips turned down. "Did I ... what?"

"It's a movie," he said. "About a couple that has the memories of their relationship erased from their minds." He watched her like he was waiting for her to bust out a signed confession.

"Oh, well," Sienna said, rubbing a hand along one of her exposed forearms, "then no, I did not." She waited a second, fidgeting, then went on. "Because, uh … I only erased …" her voice fell to a much softer timbre, "… your memories."

Scott felt like a baseball had streaked through the window, broken the glass, and clubbed him right between the eyes. "Do … do you think is funny?"

"No," she said, the answer coming fast, with a rapid shaking of her head. "I don't now, and I didn't then, either. I thought it was tense … horrifying … painful … all of those, for both of us, which was why I took the burden of our failed relationship entirely on myself." She looked straight at him.

"What?" Scott took a step back, like he really had been hit. "What the hell were you thinking?"

"If it didn't come from Phillips, it clearly had to come from somewhere," Sienna muttered. "Stupid universal laws."

"Are you trying to play the hero?" Scott asked, the rough horror settling in on him. "'Taking the burden' on yourself for our—our—failed relationship? Like stealing my—messing with my mind—gaslighting me—is some kind of—of—noble act?" he sputtered with rage, the clouds that had been fogging his mind darkening, like a storm. "People have been saying things for months about you—my parents, my friends—and I've been like, 'No, we were never together'—and they'd look at me like I was nuts." He felt the fury course through him. "All along, it turns out you—you just—" He ran a wet hand over his hair. "And now you want to play the hero."

"I can play the villain if you want," Sienna said quietly. "I've certainly had enough experiences with them—"

"Don't!" He pointed a finger right at her. "Don't—don't think you can just deflect away from—from—you stole my memories, Sienna!" He put a hand on his forehead again, sodden and wet, sweat dripping off. "These—these are the things that make me *me*, and you just made a—a unilateral decision to take them when we were—done, I assume?" He waited until she nodded, slowly, once. "We broke up?" She nodded again. "And you just … stole any memory I had of our … relationship?"

"I did," she said quietly. "I'm—"

"Don't you dare say you're sorry," he cut her off with quiet menace. "You say 'I'm sorry' when you step on someone's foot. You say 'I'm sorry' when you do something that you're actually sorry about, like—I don't know—steal someone's favorite shirt in the post-breakup move. You don't—you don't take someone's—" He buried his head in his palms, dampness seeping out, "—everything, it was like you just—took everything—" He looked up, feeling feverish. "You're not actually sorry you did it, are you?"

She looked stricken. "I'm sorry that—"

"That you got caught?" His voice rose. "Because I have to guess this conversation wasn't going to happen organically, since it's been—" He tried to think about how long it had been, how long people had been asking him.

"Four years," she finished for him, raising his ire even further. "And I was going to tell you. But I haven't seen you since that night after the Clary family reunion wrecked the campus, and I've been busy, and you've been busy, and it's not exactly something I'm super eager to bring up, no. 'Hey, remember that time—oh, that's right, you can't'."

"You made an idiot out of me," he said quietly, the realization fully sinking in. "Everyone must know except me."

"No," she said.

"Does Reed know?"

"… Yes."

"Does Zollers?" Scott asked, keeping a thin leash on his anger.

"… Yes, but—"

"Who doesn't know? Would that be a quicker answer?"

"Those are the only two," Sienna said, looking even more weary, more damaged, than before. "There is no one else who knows what I—"

"That you ripped my mind apart?" Scott kept his tone surprisingly even, his own anger spent—for now. "That when you were done with me, you just … left me in a heap on the side of the road without even the—the common decency not to—to completely destroy me before you left?"

"I didn't pull the trigger on the breakup, okay?" Her voice was husky and full of emotion. "And I left you completely functional when it was over, which was a far cry from how you would have been if I hadn't done what I'd done. You just went back to living your life, without a clue, and I had to—"

"Oh, pause for tears," Scott said. "Let's get them all out there." He glared her down, and she quit speaking. "No, go on. Tell me how hard it was for you, carrying the burden of our couplehood all on your lonely own. Of course, you wouldn't have had to if you hadn't shredded my mind on your way out. I really feel sorry for you—oh, wait, I don't."

"I made my choice," Sienna said. A single tear rolled down her cheek. She wiped it on her sleeve, her eyes hard even now. "I'm not asking you to understand—"

"Good, because I don't. Maybe if I still had my memories, but—hey, someone took care of that for me. Now I'll never understand."

"All right, well," Sienna headed for the door, "this isn't going anywhere good—"

"Are you going to play the martyr now?" He locked his gaze on her, filling his stare with all the fury he felt, soul-deep. "Because I thought you were okay being the villain."

She froze on her way out the door, face half-obscured. She pulled herself back in and looked up enough to make plain she was looking at him, but not anywhere above roughly his knees. "If that's what you need." And she walked out, closing the door behind her.

He wanted to scream behind her in fury, to shout something about how cheap and ugly it was to play that card on her way out, something about how she wasn't really accepting any responsibility for anything at all, but his mind—again—locked before he could say anything, as though a fog had rolled into the space between his mouth and his brain, and nothing came out. Instead, he listened to her urgent footfalls as she retreated down the steps of the hotel suite, and he felt water roll out of every pore, dripping down, masking the tears that flowed freely from his eyes.

49.

Sienna

Well, that was about the most uncomfortable conversation ever, and I include in that the time that my mother decided she had to give me the sex talk. I was nineteen and her boss when it happened, which made it even worse than it probably sounds. I was also not a virgin when it happened, so it had the added bonus of being pointless.

I didn't storm down the stairs in the hotel suite. I made my way tentatively, feeling pretty smacked down. I'd just been involved in an incident in plain sight with an incredible number of civilian casualties, after all, and that was following another one at a house party that had resulted in the death of a pretty famous starlet. I didn't exactly know who Bree Lancer was, but that was because I was a social outcast. I'd seen the news on my phone before it died. She was known. Probably better now that she was dead, but she was known.

I felt a lot worse about the people in and around MacArthur Park, though, and I couldn't decide if that made me a better or worse person. It was probably neutral, since—as Scott had just illustrated—I might already be so terrible that there was no more moving the dial in that direction.

"What's going on?" I asked as I took the last step down into the living room. Taggert was standing with a big, black guy who was built like he went to the gym every day for hours.

"This," Taggert said with some pride, "is Kitten's new bodyguard." He beamed at the musclebound man, who was probably like 6' 6" and three-hundred-and-fifty pounds of solid muscle. "Say hello."

The new bodyguard nodded at me. "Yo," he said, soft-spoken, "My name is Butler."

"Uhh," I said, "nice to meet you, Butler." His hair was very tightly styled around the sides and top of his head, maybe a quarter-inch of curl. His chest was just huge, like Guy Friday's halfway through a bulk-out using his powers. I doubted I would even be able to wrap both my hands around his biceps. "What are you doing here?"

Butler and Taggert looked at each other. Taggert shrugged, still smiling. "I'm Ms. Forrest's new bodyguard," Butler said to me patiently and still softly.

"Dude," I said, looking at him in disbelief, "you know what happened to her last bodyguards?"

"Ah, the Bruces," Taggert said, shaking his head as though mildly wistful that the last guys had had their hearts ripped out their backs. "Such a shame."

"I saw it on TV," Butler said. His voice was smooth, like he should have been recording Grammy-winning soul albums.

"Are you metahuman?" I asked, proceeding down my line of inquiry unbowed.

"No ma'am," Butler said.

"Then are you deranged?" I viewed him with all the skepticism of a doctor in an asylum examining a patient who has been caught eating his own feces. "Suicidal?" I pointed at Taggert. "Did this dipshit tell you what we're up against here?"

"Hey," Taggert said, mildly annoyed, using the exact same word of protest as the psychos in my head. Coincidence? I suspected not.

HEY! my psychos chorused, yes, in protest.

"Mr. Taggert spelled out the threat," Butler said. "But if you're going to be a bodyguard to the stars, you have to be prepared to take on a few stalkers, you know?"

"Exactly," Taggert said, pearly whites just crying out to be removed. He clapped a possessive hand on Butler's shoulder, which was about as far as he could reach. Butler was huge.

"Captain Redbeard is not some loser who haunts the Walk of Fame looking for someone to attach his damaged psyche to," I said, staring at Butler in disbelief.

Butler frowned at me. "'Captain ... Redbeard'?"

"It's what I'm calling this douche." I paused. "Because of the beard and the hair—"

Butler just kept frowning. "Yeah, no, I get it. I just—he looks kinda more like Zach Galifianakis in *The Hangover*, I think."

I had to concede on that one. "Maybe," I said, "but 'Red-headed Zach Galifianakis' doesn't exactly roll off the tongue the way 'Redbeard' does, you know?" I shook my head. "You seem like a bright guy, Butler. What are you doing here?"

Butler shrugged. "It's a career move."

"It's a career-ending move, I think you mean, and also a life-ending one."

"Butler's got this," Taggert said. "He's got experience with bodyguarding."

"Does he have experience with people who can rip his heart out with their bare hands?" I folded my arms over my chest. "Because that's what we're dealing with. A guy who can pass through bone and rip your innards out. He did it to a whole subway train full of people just today, in fact."

"I heard," Butler said. This guy was a cool customer, I'd give him that.

"I don't understand," I said. "You don't exhibit any obvious signs of a frontal lobotomy, so let me spell this one out for you—this guy is murdering people by the train-load. The police can't stop him. *I'm* having some trouble even stopping him. You will be a tragic footnote in this whole thing, a number in the official report if you persist in taking this job."

"I know what this job entails," Butler said with a nod. "I get to do my first work on-camera."

I felt utterly dumbstruck, maybe even dumber-struck than I had been a few minutes ago when my ex had confronted me about the fact that I'd ripped all his memories of our relationship away when we ended things. *"Pardonnez moi?"* I asked, in French, because English wasn't getting the point across.

"I made him a deal," Taggert said, making me want to wipe the perpetual smile off his face with a hammer of the sledge variety. "The crew is gonna be here in a few minutes. Butler is on-camera for this, the new face of Kat's human security detail. It's a choice role, brings some diversity to our otherwise lily-white inner circle—"

"It's going to bring some red," I said, "as in blood, when he gets killed—"

"You're such a pessimist," Taggert said, dismissing me.

I wanted to act like a college girl for a minute and say, "I CAN'T EVEN," but I couldn't even (ha ha) muster that. I felt drained, maybe even more drained than I'd felt when I'd been brought back from the dead by Steven only a few hours earlier. "Forget it, Sienna," I muttered to myself, "it's Los Angeles."

"Ah, the Chinatown quote," Taggert said, brightening, "and nice delivery, by the way. We'll make a star out of you yet."

I couldn't figure out how to answer, and a knock at the door meant I didn't have to. Taggert yanked it open before I could suggest otherwise, revealing Flannery Steiner, the former Disney Channel star turned just-above-juvenile delinquent. "Hey, is Kat here?" Steiner asked, the very image of what I considered to be a Valley girl—perfect nails, short skirt, hair beautifully done, and an expression like all the Botox she pumped into her face couldn't eliminate the stink of something unpleasant. She looked right at me, and I realized that I was the reason for her distaste. I mean, I hadn't been until that moment—before it was probably the nubs of the stick up her ass—but seeing me all ragged and dirty was what was ailing her presently.

"Yeah," I said, weaving around her on my way out of the suite. "She's here."

"Hey!" Taggert called after me. "Where are you going?"

"Butler's got this," I said, on my way to the elevator. "You said so yourself."

I made it to the elevator just before the doors closed, not waiting to hear any reply from Taggert, Butler, or that druggy whore Flannery Steiner, either.

Screw this town.

Screw Scott.

Screw Kat—Klementina Gavrikov—Forrest, too.

Screw it all.

"I quit," I whispered to myself. But I didn't quite believe me.

50.

I'd barely gotten my new phone activated at the store when my first voicemail came through. Activating a new phone was a process I was quite familiar with by this point. I kept hoping someone was going to make a waterproof, fireproof, shockproof, physical damage-proof, basically invincible phone. But apparently the industry thought insuring phones was the way to go.

I'd cure them of that silliness yet, I thought, slipping phone six hundred and eighty five into my pocket. Fortunately, cell phone companies hadn't tumbled to "Acts of gods" as an excuse for denial of claim yet.

When my phone buzzed with the first message, my contacts hadn't quite synched from the cloud yet, so I wasn't really sure who it was from. Knowing that was critically important, because if it was Dick-o, I was totally going to ignore it. In fact, as soon as I figured out how, I was going to block all his texts and calls.

But for now, I listened to the voicemail on speaker, and immediately called back after hearing only a fraction of the message.

"Yo yo yo," J.J. said as he picked up the phone, the sound of explosions going off in the background behind him.

"J.J.?" I asked, frowning. It sounded like I was visiting him with five hundred of my closest enemies. "What the hell is going on?"

"Oh, sorry," he said, and I heard fumbling, then the sound disappeared. "My bad. Had the speaker system cranked up, playing some *Halo* multiplayer."

I felt my eye twitch. "Aren't you supposed to be helping track down Redbeard?"

"Who?" J.J. asked. "Ohh, is that your name for the guy? Public enemy number one? Not bad, not bad. I would have gone with 'The Red Lebowski,' personally, because he looks kinda like Jeff Bridges, but younger and ginger, you know?"

"I toyed with that one, but—hey, did you find anything?" I turned on a dime, realizing that if I didn't, I was bound to get sucked into J.J.'s world, and that was not a place I wanted to be. He was not exactly my own personal Cisco Ramon.

"I did find something," he said with exaggerated confidence, "which is why I am playing *Halo* right now instead of scouring the 'net for signs of your Red Duck Dynasty." I held my breath. "Red—"

"Does J.J. stand for 'Jar Jar'?" I asked.

"Ohhh," he said, sounding wounded. "Owww. You have cut me to the quick, madam."

"I'm about to fly up there and cut you about a foot lower if you don't tell me what you know, you little geek."

"Okay, so," J.J. said, all business again, "no idea who this guy is, but I used traffic cams, GPS and satellite imagery to track him back to his bolt-hole. Turns out he stole a police cruiser in his escape from MacArthur Park and ditched it in a parking garage near downtown, but I got him exiting the structure driving an Oldsmobile, of all things—"

"J.J.," I said.

"I mean, who drives an Oldsmobile?" J.J. asked. "They don't even manufacture them anymore. It's a dead brand. It's like he's trying to draw attention to himself, but he's blending in at the same time—like a cry for help, but whispered—"

"J.J.—"

"—but like a stage whisper, you know? Because why not drive, like, a Jeep, or a Tesla—hell, in LA, why not a

Lamborghini? You can't tell me he couldn't just reach into the ignition with a formless finger and trip the switch—"

"J.J.!"

"Oh, right," J.J. said. "Texting it to you. It's in the Elysium neighborhood, though, so watch your back."

"The—what?"

"Elysium neighborhood," J.J. said patiently. "You know, one of the highest crime areas in LA, yet surprisingly close to both downtown and the beach, right off the freeway—"

"What the hell? Are you secretly an LA realtor when you're not gaming and tormenting me?"

"*Million Dollar Listing LA*," J.J. said casually.

"What?"

"One of my numerous lady friends enjoys the program," he went on. "Naturally, I'm an accommodating host, so I watch it with her. You can learn a lot from—"

"J.J.," I said with rapidly thinning patience, all nicety gone, "if you've ever had a lady friend that wasn't a cat, I'll eat my phone."

There was a long pause. "You're just not nice at all," he said in a choked whisper and hung up on me.

"And so say all of us." I stared at my phone, willing it to buzz. It did, a moment later, with an LA address. I started down the sunny street toward the clothing store where I'd purchased the destroyed suit I wore, intending to purchase some form of replacement, when the first hint of remorse struck. "Dammit, J.J.," I muttered to myself, feeling sorry for how I'd just bombed him.

I did that sort of thing. Dr. Zollers had told me it was a defense mechanism, as though I hadn't known that already. Keeping emotional distance between myself and others was a trick I employed to avoid feeling exposed in my relationships. Psycho-babble aside, the doctor had a valid point. I didn't feel comfortable with people, really, which was probably why I did everything I could to get them the hell away from me. It wasn't that I objected to them on a theoretical level—I liked people. Some people.

Well, I liked Reed and Augustus and Dr. Zollers and mostly Ariadne and sometimes J.J. And Scott, once upon a time.

And me, said Zack.

"And you," I whispered.

And me, said Bjorn.

"Screw off, Nord." That one drew a dirty look from a tall, blond-haired guy passing me on the street. "Wasn't talking to you, skinny Dolph Lundgren."

I was about to text J.J. my apology when my phone buzzed again, and I figured he was going to hit me with a worthy return volley. J.J. wasn't the type to take an insult sitting down, after all. The little geek might not be able to throw a punch, but he could—

Aw, dammit.

Ricardo

I am lying in bed naked, thinking of you as I—

SON OF A BITCH.

51.

Instead of immediately flying back to Minneapolis, tracking down Dick-o and beating him to death with my bare fists in what could only be described as the most satisfying thing I had done recently, I went instead toward the address J.J. had steered me to. I did this mostly because it was the right thing to do.

Also, because since I had just alienated J.J., tracking down Dick-o would probably not be the easiest thing to do at the moment. I mean, I could just text him back with, "Where are you?" and coming in the wake of his last message to me, he'd probably ecstatically give me his location, but I'd have to text him back without vomiting on my new phone, which was a hell of an imposition.

I could have apologized to J.J., I guess, but following it up with a request for some random schmoe's location would have made it sound like a self-serving apology, and I meant to give him a sincere one. At some point.

Anyway, I went to the address J.J. texted me, taking advantage of my phone's GPS and maps. Confusing the hell out of the program was always fun. "Off route," it told me as I flew over a lake that looked like it was way down from its usual level.

"No shit," I muttered to it as I flew over a neighborhood of houses that were probably worth umpteen-billion dollars just by virtue of being not so far from downtown. I passed over what seemed like an invisible wall in the middle of the city, and suddenly the streets were not so well kept, the houses were not so nice or modern, and the sidewalks and avenues were kind of broken.

I set down on a pretty run-down street and flipped through my contacts, hoping that Detective Waters' number had made its way into cloud storage before my phone had suffered its tragic fate in the subway tunnel. A city bus rumbled by, lights glowing in its interior, people slumped down inside, graffiti painted along the sides. I ignored the beeping of the GPS program vying for my attention as I scanned my contacts.

"Hey!" some guy called as I walked up the street. The houses here were all showing their age. The guy who'd called out to me came walking up, wearing baggy clothes, more than a little lumpy beneath them, his face lit by a phone clutched in his hand, pale light on a tanned face, a couple days' worth of beard growth blending with a sorry mustache and goatee. He looked late twenties, maybe. "What are you doing here?"

"Walking," I said, looking up from my contact search. "It's this new thing. All the rage, really. You should try it sometime." I looked him over. "Probably soon would be a good idea."

He gave me an icy look. "How about you give me all your money?"

"How about you give me a pony?" I asked.

He blinked his surprise away after about ten seconds of struggling with it. "What?"

"I figured since we're making requests," I said with a shrug.

"I ain't giving you no pony," he said, informing me about the state of his education.

"Well, I'm not giving you my money," I said, "so it would appear we're at an impasse."

"Pshhh," he said, making a face. "Bitch, I said—" And he

went for a gun under his saggy clothing.

I drew mine first, because—well, because I'm me. His eyes widened in surprise as he stared down at Shadow. "Uhm," he said.

"'Uhm,' yeah," I said. "Now, about that pony ..."

His eyes widened in panic. "Yo, I ain't got no pony."

"I'm going to count to ten," I said calmly, "and then I'm going to shoot you if you don't give me my pony."

"I got no pony!" he said, panic starting to shine through. He held up his hands, pushing them toward the sky like maybe if he could just reach a little higher I'd believe him. "Yo, do you see a pony anywhere on me?"

"You could be hiding one in your pants—oh, no, never mind, you definitely aren't hiding anything down there." I made a show of looking and being disappointed. "Maybe in your shoes?"

"You think I got a horse in my kicks?" He looked at me in disbelief.

"I suppose not an actual horse, just a horse's ass."

"Hah," he said without mirth. "How long we going to stand here?"

"Empty your pockets," I said, "and carefully. Toss out your gun, and if I see a finger go anywhere near the trigger ... well, I'm a dead shot, and that lack of pony you're hiding in your sweatpants is going to become a quarter-horse."

He wordlessly emptied his pockets, carefully placing a shitty revolver on the pavement along with a beat-up wallet, a new-model cell phone, and a set of car keys.

"Now take off all your clothes," I told him.

"I told I ain't got no pony in—"

"I believe you," I said, still holding him at gunpoint, "but I don't want you to walk away from this encounter thinking it's totally okay to just rob people on the street, so I'm going to teach you a lesson your mother apparently failed to." I thumbed back the hammer on Shadow. "Now ... clothes off. I promise you, I'm not going to enjoy this any more than you are."

"Pshhhh," he said, clearly bummed, but he stripped down right there in front of me. I was right; he wasn't hiding a pony. He wasn't even smuggling a toy horse. He stood there fidgeting, covering himself with one hand. "You happy now?"

"About as happy as you are," I said, nodding at his easily concealed manhood. "I didn't realize it was cold tonight."

"Now you're just humiliating me for the fun of it."

"Yes," I said, "duh. That's what the lesson is—don't steal from people, especially in the form of armed robbery, because at some point, as my mother was fond of saying, no matter how bad you are, you're eventually going to meet someone badder than yourself." I pointed my hand at his little pile of clothes, phone, gun and wallet and sent a burst of fire at it that caused his eyes to widen explosively as he jumped back. "Tonight's your night, Sparky."

"Shit!" he shouted, legs trying to withdraw into his chest as he leapt back from the little bonfire I'd just lit. He looked like a cartoon character trying to scramble away. "What the— who are you?"

"Someone who's badder than you," I said, holstering my gun as I started on my way to the address J.J. had given me. I thumbed through my contacts to find Detective Waters' number, leaving my mugger behind to watch his personal effects burn, his eyes haunted, like he was imagining himself in the flames instead. A different night, a different me, it probably could have been. But tonight, I just left him naked in the street, too dumbstruck by what he'd just seen to even reply.

52.

Kat

Flannery had paraded herself into Kat's room in the suite with all the flair needed to make an impression for the cameras, but the cameras weren't here. They were coming, Kat was sure, because Taggert would want to capture footage of her post-attack, but they weren't here yet.

That didn't stop Flannery from acting like they were, which Kat fully understood. She was trying to keep her guard up as well, preparing for the moment. Sometimes the camera guys gave her ample warning, and sometimes they just snuck in and filmed. They probably wouldn't get past Guy Friday without a stop; even her new bodyguard had been given the careful once over by the big Guy—and so had Flannery. She hadn't protested, but only because she was playing to nonexistent cameras.

"I just, like, have so much sorrow for you right now," Flannery said. "So much sorrow. My thoughts and prayers are with you." She paused, looked around then lowered her voice. "Do we still say 'thoughts and prayers'?" she asked at a whisper. "Or is it just 'thoughts' now?"

"I ... don't know," Kat said. "Do you ... actually pray?"

Flannery's eyes flashed with mischief. "I mean, I shout, 'Oh my God!' a lot, but usually—"

"Probably just go with 'thoughts,' then," Kat said, feeling

a little worn out and melancholy. Flannery wasn't who she needed to perk her up right now. It had been just such a long couple days, with all the attempts to kill her, and the photo shoot for *Vanity Fair*. She only hoped some of the photos had turned out usable. "Hey … about Bree …"

"I know, right?" Flannery lit up again. "Do you know how many interviews I've done today?" She smiled brightly. "I had to actually carry some diluted pepper around under my fingernails so I could rub it in my eyes toward the end, you know, just to keep the crying going a little."

Kat stared at her. "That's … uh …"

"But you," Flannery gushed, "you had that whole park thing today. I mean, that had to keep the spotlight going. What marvelous luck!"

Kat froze. "I don't know if I'd call it—"

"Excuse me," the new bodyguard said, breaking in tentatively, like he expected to get hit for it. "Ms. Forrest?"

"Yes," she said, "uhm … what was your name again?"

"Butler, ma'am," he said, his dark skin a brilliant contrast to the white and cream décor in the room. "I just … wanted to introduce myself before the cameras came up, because Mr. Taggert, uh … wanted me to also introduce myself on camera."

Kat felt a peculiar twinge. "None of my bodyguards have done on-camera work before. I mean, they get seen sometimes, but we don't do … on-camera."

"Well, that was the deal he gave me when I took the job," Butler said, clearly uncomfortable.

Kat looked at Flannery, who gave Butler a pitying look. "Get used to conflict," Kat said, remembering what Taggert had told her the first week of filming. Butler straightened. "You're going to see a lot of it. Nature of the business is conflict, caught on camera."

"Yes, ma'am," Butler said, like he was taking some energy and encouragement out of what she'd said. "I'll—I'll get used to it fast. Just nervous, I guess."

"So you're on-camera talent now," Kat said, thinking it through. "Taggert wants to put this threat front and center in the storyline this season, of course, and he's having you do on-camera stuff because …"

"It was our deal," Butler said simply, and Kat almost kicked herself for not seeing it before.

"Of course," she said with a nod and a fake smile. It was all she could do; it wasn't like she could tell him what she'd just figured out.

Taggert is having you introduce yourself and be an on-camera role so that when you die, it plays to the audience. The Bruces weren't known to the audience because they weren't part of the story, and so when they died, it got us nothing. But you …

Butler smiled faintly in reply to her. He was a handsome young man, and so well built. She felt a twinge of guilt. "I appreciate the opportunity," he said sincerely.

"Welcome to the team," Kat said to cover up the faint screaming of that little voice that she hated in her head.

The knock at the doors was the camera and microphone crew for the day—Mike on the microphone, Mitch or something on camera. As they set up the shot, everyone fell into silence—Kat and Flannery were pros at this by now. Kat watched Flannery go through her mental preparations as Kat did her own. Butler just looked nervous—of course, it was his first time on camera. Guy Friday just stayed the same lump in front of the door, unmoved by the sight of the cameras setting up.

When they were rolling, Flannery launched right into it, laying out her reason for being here in a way she hadn't before the cameras showed. "So … are we going to the premiere party tonight?" She had a devilish grin.

Kat blinked; she'd forgotten about the premiere. "Which one is it?"

"The new Nick Elfman movie," Flannery said, enthusing for the camera. Kat knew Flannery couldn't stand Nick Elfman; he'd turned her down when she tried to nail him in a closet at one of Seth Rogen's parties. "I forget what it's called. Some superhero movie, I think? It's at Grauman's, and it's probably a snooze, but the after party is in the penthouse at the Hotel Luxuriant." She said the hotel's name with a French accent and made a pouty face. "Come on, Kat. You can't let this terrorist push you around. We should make an appearance. Put up a strong face."

Flannery was totally playing to the cameras, and Kat knew it. It didn't stop her from being at least a little right, though. "I don't know," Kat said, hedging. She didn't want to look too reckless, either. "So much has happened," she let her voice quiver a little, "I just don't want anyone to get hurt." She closed her eyes and bowed her head slightly. That was the right tone—worried, conciliatory, fearful for others.

"Being afraid of this guy means he wins," Flannery said, answering perfectly. She even sounded sincere. "And you can't let the guy who killed Bree win." She added just the right amount of feeling to Bree's name. It was perfect, and it gave Kat the opening.

"It'd really be disrespectful to Bree's memory to let him get away with it, wouldn't it?" Kat asked, looking to Flannery for support. She hoped the camera didn't catch the glimmer in either of their eyes.

"Totally," Flannery said, just a hair too eager.

Kat didn't need much pushing; her alternatives were to stay here all night and film moody scenes of brooding, or to go out to a kickass party where she could maybe dance the night away. It's not like the killer would be able to find her there; she hadn't even really been invited. She was just going with Flannery, after all. "Okay," she said, drawing in a breath and trying to sound resolute, "let's do it for Bree."

53.

Sienna

I found the house without too much trouble, a small, one-story, nondescript house in the middle of a nondescript block. There were bars on all the windows, though, which seemed apropos given what I'd seen of the neighborhood thus far. It wasn't exactly MacArthur Park, but that was only because I hadn't run across a mentally ill person juggling their own feces. Yet.

I walked down the sidewalk with my ears focused on the sounds around me. It was harder in a city environment, with all the ambient noise for blocks and blocks. It wasn't as disruptive as New York City, but it wasn't easy, either. In New York, the tightly packed nature of Manhattan meant I could almost always hear sirens going, even a mile or two away. Something was always happening, someone was always requiring an ambulance, people were always shouting. It wore on me. I could feel it, could taste it, and it was overwhelming to my meta senses. London was similar, at least close to the city center. At the edges of the sprawl it was less intense.

Los Angeles was different, though. This city was all spread out to hell, and even though I could see downtown from where I stood, it seemed like the city just went in all directions for a hundred miles. For all I knew, it was a hundred miles. It had certainly looked huge when I'd flown in the night before. The population density wasn't as compactly layered as New York or London, and so it was a little quieter, though I could hear lots of hushed voices around me. Still it wasn't midtown Manhattan, and for that I was grateful. So were my ears.

I ignored some of the ambient noise—the nearby freeway and its rush of cars, the plane flying overhead at my one o'clock, the two guys lighting up three doors down on the porch, watching me walk and snickering as they admired the gentle sway of my hips. That wasn't exactly how they said it, but since it was one of the less creepy comments I'd received lately, I took it that way.

I focused in on the house, listening for anything within. I couldn't hear much through walls—meta senses aren't like psychic powers, after all—but I listened anyway. I walked past on the sidewalk once, sneaking peaks at the front windows, all of which were dark. Either there were blackout curtains hanging inside, or the occupant was sleeping, or there was no one home.

I dialed up Detective Waters and got a sleepy answer on the third ring. "Hello?"

"Hi, Detective," I said, awfully chipper. "Guess who?"

"Who?" she asked, mind chugging along a little slower than I would have liked. I didn't have all day.

"It's Sienna Nealon," I said, doubling back to pace in front of the house. I looked closer this time; there were no blackout curtains, as near as I could tell, just the normal variety. "I've got an address on our suspect."

"We'll need a warrant," Detective Waters said, coming to life now.

"I actually don't," I said. "I've heard screams from within the premises and am moving to enter. I just wanted to let you know as a courtesy. I'm texting you the address."

"Wait, you can't—" I hung up on her before she had a chance to reply with what I'm sure was going to be a whole diatribe about civil liberties, blah blah blah. I debated that stuff with Reed, I didn't need to get up to the hip waders in it now with an LAPD detective just before I kicked down the door on a random house. I was waiting for laws to catch up with my agency, but Congress was curiously deadlocked about us and our mission. It had resulted in some great debates, some serious arguments in the courts—really fascinating stuff, if you were a boring lawyer type.

Me, I had a job to do, and I was intent on doing it until they told me I had to follow normal rules. I had a feeling that the way things were going now wasn't the way they would go forever, but much like if there was a terrorist with a WMD on American soil, some rules might get bent or broken in order to bring that person down before they leveled a major US city. I didn't set the tone, but I didn't mind having a little leeway in doing this job. It wasn't like you could contain a metahuman in a normal prison population. Hell, most people were still trying to wrap their brains around what we could do. And it wasn't like America had a meta on every corner. There were like five hundred of us left in the entire United States. We were rarer than albinos.

If you went by strictest interpretation of "a jury of your peers," a meta trial would be a real bear to set up.

All of this was just my way of justifying to myself that I was about to kick down a door that I didn't have a legal warrant to do so on, nor any real probable cause to believe a crime had been committed by anyone in this house. What I had was J.J., illegally accessing passive surveillance footage in public locales for the purpose of tracking a very bad guy back to his hideout. In any court of law, I'd be laughed out.

And yet, Captain Redbeard was out there killing people for fun and sport, and the law had about as much chance of catching him as I did of catching a cold. (I can't, by the way. Zero percent.)

I crept along the concrete wall that ran along the side of the house and made my way around to the back door. I drew Shadow (I like that my gun has a nickname) and prepared myself to knock down the door.

I took a long breath in the still night, the sounds of the Elysium neighborhood playing all around me, and when I heard the first hint of sirens, I raised my leg and kicked my way into the house.

54.

Karl

Karl had fallen asleep sometime after all the videos had been uploaded and played back time and again on every station from ABC to ZZZ. Well, not ZZZ, but—well, sort of, since he had fallen asleep, finally. Karl didn't sleep well anymore, but he'd slept like a baby after the massacre. It was like the mere act of putting the film on the internet had been a release of the sort that aided sleep. It had been a long time for Karl in that regard, too—sex didn't interest him anymore—but he remembered the after feeling, and this was like that, only way more intense.

When he woke up, he found the networks still playing it like crazy, still hashing it all over. It wasn't as satisfying now, though. It wasn't like there was any breaking news, any new detail, any cool new stuff to pore over, just the same old shit they'd been reporting before he'd fallen asleep, stirred up so that it looked different. Victim interviews. Politician reactions. Doctors in a press conference talking about the surgery one of the bombing victims had undergone. Panels weighing in on Karl's motives, his identity.

Well, the last part was fun, anyway.

Karl sighed. Even at its reduced level of entertainment, he could still watch this all night.

Then his phone rang. He glanced at it and scrambled to

247

pick it up immediately. "Hello?"

"Karl," came the voice at the other end of the line, "That was some fine work today. Fine work."

"Thank you," Karl said, feeling the warm rush of accomplishment. "It was … fun."

"Good, good. Hey, I've got something for you," the voice went on.

"Oh?" Karl quirked an eyebrow.

"Yeah," his benefactor said. "This Kat girl, she's supposed to be going to a party tonight at the Luxuriant hotel. Big soiree. Thinks she's going to be safe. Should be a lot of cameras, though, in case you want to … make an appearance."

"Oh," Karl said, nodding along. "Okay. Are you thinking—"

"Yes," the answer came immediately. "I think it's time to be done with Kat Forrest. Make it big. Make it showy. Don't let anyone forget it, Karl—or you." Karl heard the sound of the click at the other end of the line.

Oh, yeah. Karl would make it memorable, all right. No one would ever forget how Kat Forrest ended. Not the way he was going to do it. Not even if they tried.

No, they'd be talking about this death for years and years to come. Karl could pretty much guarantee it.

55.

Scott

When he'd answered the knock at his door with a simple, "Come in," he'd expected it was going to be Sienna.

It wasn't.

Kat had a hopeful look on her face, and a shining, shimmering red dress. A camera was lurking just behind her when she opened the door, capturing every moment of their conversation. Scott immediately pulled himself together, making the uncontrolled wash of perspiration that he'd let out after Sienna left dry up into his skin immediately. "Uhm, yes?" he asked, trying to smooth himself out.

"We need to party, Scott," Kat told him seriously, her eyes alight as she said it. "Get dressed."

Scott felt his lips part slightly. "Uhh ... what?"

"We're going to a party," Kat said, hovering just outside his door, enough that she could lean in and the camera could capture them both. "Enough of this sitting around moping. We need to get out of here and have a moment, you know? Remind ourselves we're alive and not dead like those—" her voice cracked, and then she caught it, "those poor souls in MacArthur Park, or," she sniffled, "like Bree."

Who is Bree? Scott wondered but did not ask. He started to say no, but a thought occurred—Sienna would say no.

"Come on," Kat wheedled. "You know you want to.

There's going to be dancing. Stars." She stopped. "But not *Dancing With the Stars*, because—well, because it's a movie after party, not the show." She smiled a little brighter. "Flannery would probably love to have you escort her."

Flannery he knew. Hell, everyone with a nodding acquaintance with reality knew Flannery Steiner at this point, probably even the residents of nursing homes. "Really?" Scott asked, giving that one some thought. He'd seen the cop's dashcam video. That girl was wild. She hadn't even climbed off her boyfriend while the cops were chasing them at high speed.

"She'd love to spend some time with you—war hero and all that." Kat made a face that was a little more suggestive than Scott was used to seeing from Kat, at least since—well, since she'd lost her memory. Hell, even before that. "You could both use a distraction, right?"

"Boy, could I," Scott said, thinking of Sienna even as he said it. *To hell with her*, that's what he was thinking. "All right, I'm in."

56.

Sienna

No one was home, but boy was I glad I didn't knock.

The door was booby-trapped, because of course a guy who plays with explosives is going to booby-trap his house. When I knocked it off its hinges it blew up around the frame. It would have killed any human who'd tried to enter at that moment, but I heard the click of the fuses over the door crashing inward and shot back twenty feet in an instant.

The explosion echoed in the night, the roar eclipsing the sound of sirens, setting off a million dogs within a ten-block radius, and causing local residents to crap themselves. If a SWAT team had been standing where I was when I knocked down the door, they would have suffered some death and injury. You can thank me later for going without you, LAPD. Send me a note or something, maybe a fruit basket since the likelihood of the president sending me one was dropping by the second.

I hovered about a foot off the ground in the middle of a brown yard, waiting for the smoke to clear and trying to get my ears to stop ringing. The bomb going off was an instant drop of adrenaline into my bloodstream, triggering my fight or flight response. Obviously in this case, flight had won out, but fight was right there, ready to take over now that I'd dodged the explosion.

I activated the flashlight feature on my phone and swooped into the smoky back door. Clearly Redbeard was not into rear entry, I noted as I looked at the damage. This door had been wired shut so that no one could come in. I could see the front door from where I hovered, and it was similarly wired. Of course. Why would a man who can walk through walls need a door?

I searched the house in a flash, finding the windows were all set to blow as well, and one of the rooms had an epic amount of explosives just lying there. It was clearly his cache, or his surplus, because I doubted he was sleeping on plastique.

Other than that, a computer, and an air mattress for sleeping, the house was empty. The fridge was as empty as mine at home, but at least I had expired ketchup.

I heard the first sirens and flew out the back, looping over the house and coming down on the lawn. The first cop car was swiftly followed by eight more, and I stood there with my hands up after identifying myself to the first pair of officers.

Detective Waters arrived on the scene about ten minutes after the first cop, wearing a scowl and looking like I'd dragged her out of bed. "You didn't have probable cause," were her first words to me.

"The back door just exploded," I said, shrugging lightly. "I *probably* did not *cause* that."

"You could have, for all I know," she shot back.

"I can burn things, but I can't, like, blow up a tree," I said. "This place is wired to make a boom. Front door, all the windows. Might want to get your bomb squad on this."

She made a grumbling noise. "They're on their way." She dialed the hostility back a notch or two. "He's not here, I assume?"

"Nope," I said, shrugging.

"Ma'am?" One of the patrolmen got Detective Waters's attention. "We, uh … picked up a naked pedestrian on the

252

way in. He ran when officers caught him huddling over a small fire on the sidewalk. Said he got mugged, someone set fire to his clothes and his possessions."

Detective Waters just stared at him, open-mouthed, before turning to me with an accusatory look. "Weird," I said, "Who would do such a thing?"

"I wonder," Detective Waters said. But I could tell she wasn't wondering too hard.

"All kinds of perverts in this town," I said with a shrug. At least that was true.

57.

Kat

The arrival was perfect, a red carpet appearance that allowed her to hold her head high as she came into the party. They got footage for the show, the paparazzi got their dish, and Kat got to shrug off a million questions, all of which told her that the narrative was going to be exactly what she wanted—that she was a fearless, bold hero for stepping outside her own door tonight.

"Ms. Forrest—"

"Kat—"

"Kat, who are you wearing tonight?"

"Ms. Forrest, how are you feeling after the incident at the park?"

"Kat, do you want to say anything about your friend Bree, how wonderful she was? Her fans are listening!"

"Ms. Forrest, do you have a message for the man who's been terrorizing you?"

Kat stopped on that last one, a strange twinge running down her back. Her gown ran full-length, split up the side to show leg. It was a classic look for a classic occasion, and she turned to see the questioner, waiting.

"Yes," she said and broke away from the line she was leading into the party. Flannery and Scott were a few steps behind her, Guy Friday and Butler a few steps in front of her.

Both groups scrambled to catch up to her, probably afraid she was going to dive into the crowd or something. "I have something to say to him." She looked right into the lens of the camera. "You're a coward."

A silence fell over the red carpet, and Kat pushed her perfectly sculpted hair back before continuing. "This is a man who hides himself, who hides his identity because he knows the world will hate him, will hate what he stands for, who he is." She was going unscripted, improvising, but this was the sort of thing Taggert would approve of. She needed to look brave, to put on the brave face. "This is a man who's been rejected, for good reason." She brushed her hair back again. "He's a murderer. He's a man with powers who preys on the powerless. He's a coward, as gutless as they come, and his days are numbered." She stared right into the camera. "We're not afraid of you. You're doing what you're doing because you didn't want to do what it would take to make yourself heard without violence. You didn't want to play nice, you didn't want to be nice, and you thought you were better. You're not. You're the worst of us, and people saw that in you before you ever did what you've done now. Enjoy the attention you're getting right now—and we all know that's why you're doing it, because you need attention—because your mommy didn't love you or whatever. Try therapy, loser, instead of impotently taking out your pathetic issues on everyone else in the world."

With that, she swept away from the camera, and a hundred media people seemed to all catch their breath at once.

"Ms. Forrest!"

"Kat!"

"Would you care to follow up on—"

"I thought we were supposed to be low profile," Scott said, easing up behind her, Flannery still on his arm. "No one was supposed to know we were here."

"Oh, relax," Kat said, smiling for the cameras. "We'll be

out of here in less than an hour—just enough to make a splash, not long enough to give this guy a target."

"You know what you're doing, Kat," Flannery said coming up next to her as they came into the lobby of the Luxuriant. "That's probably going to trend in like, five minutes."

Kat did not look at Scott. "Good," she said. Because it was good, wasn't it?

58.

Karl

Karl heard every word Kat Forrest spoke, and without exception, every one of them boiled his blood, even the "the's" and "a's." He stood in the middle of the crowd, his beard concealed by a long coat that held more than a few explosive packets, and his hair pulled back under a beanie. The sunglasses did the last part of the trick, oddball frames that were designed to make the shape of his face look entirely different.

He listened and he boiled, but the hot fury ran cool enough for him to realize that there were so many cameras, so many opportunities here. There was even a camera crew following Kat Forrest right now, soaking up her every move, her every word. There'd be more cameras at the party itself maybe, and if not, boy, wouldn't it be fun to let her do another interview, and then right as she delivered one of the bits of gusto, he'd just rip her heart out. He would have done it right now if he hadn't been shaking in quiet rage as she spoke.

No, there was a little time now. He'd make a circle of the perimeter, watch things unfold, and wait for his chance to pull Kat Forrest in front of the cameras for another interview.

And this one would be her last.

59.

Sienna

Detective Waters didn't like me, this much was plain by now, but then, I wasn't giving her a lot to like. I was basically just causing her migraines, after all, breaking into houses, discovering bombs, getting other places bombed, being involved in fatal train wrecks and celebrity party—uhh … catastrophes? Yeah, that's probably the word for it. Couldn't blame her for not liking me, but the truth was, I wasn't *causing* any of these things. An argument could be made that I was causing them to *escalate*—I could even agree with that argument, because people with powers tend to cause havoc when they fight—but I wasn't truly responsible for any of this. It's not like I was running around threatening people or planting bombs.

My eyes fell on the back of the lone, occupied cop car at the scene, the one with a naked man in the back who was staring at me with a spiteful look in his eyes. Okay, well, I wasn't planting bombs, at least.

"You're going to be the death of me," Detective Waters said, shaking her head. I got the feeling she was mentally counting the years until retirement. It looked like it'd be a while for her.

"I sure hope not," I said. "I generally try to be the death of criminals, not cops."

She made that noise again, the one in her throat that hinted at a deep well of exasperation. "Uh huh," was all she said. "Where are your friends tonight?"

"I don't really have friends," I said, giving her an opening that I hoped she would exploit to take a shot. I figured it would give her a little bit of catharsis, and I was sure she sorely needed that as I watched the bomb squad guy stuffed into one of those protective suits waddling his way into the back yard a hundred yards away. They'd evacuated the houses on either side and pulled back the perimeter to give those guys room to work.

"I can't imagine why," she grunted, and I could almost feel her tension dissolve a little.

"Maybe it's the hours," I said, giving her a commonality we shared. "Tough to keep friends when you're working eighteen hour days."

She gave me a sidelong look that turned a little grudging. "Uh huh," she said again, but lighter. *Thank you, Dr. Zollers.* "Fine," she went on. "Where's your posse? Ms. Forrest? The others?"

"Tucked safely into the hotel," I said, folding my arms and leaning back into a police cruiser. "Out of harm's way."

"You talking about Kat Forrest?" A thin cop was standing a few feet away from us in a patrolman's uniform, dark hair and pale eyes. "I heard she just showed up at the Luxuriant at some party. Sounds like a real shindig."

I felt like I'd gotten struck by a bolt of lightning. "No. That's not possible." No one could be that stupid, not even Kat.

"Really?" Detective Waters brought her phone up and touched the screen a couple times. "Hmph." She held it up so I could see it.

KAT FORREST ATTENDS PREMIERE PARTY, HAS BRAVE MESSAGE FOR HER ATTACKER

I wanted to slump right there on the street, to bury my face in my hands, to slam my head in a car door, to drag the naked mugger out of the back of the police cruiser and slap him around for a little while. I did none of these things, however, instead counting silently in my head to ten as I took a deep breath—bad feelings outttttt, good feelings innnnn …

"You gonna be all right?" the patrolman asked.

"Where is this Luxuriant?" I asked, trying to come back to myself. "Also, that's a dumb name for a hotel."

"It's right there," Waters said, pointing at the LA skyline. Of course it was the one lit up with searchlights. Because this whole town was so tailor-made for Kat and her attention-seeking idiocy. It was a perfect marriage, like Ike and Tina, alcohol and vomiting, meatloaf and my tastebuds.

I shot off into the sky, unable to leave my rage behind on the ground, flying off to save my idiot "friend" from herself.

60.

Kat

"This is so fun, isn't it?" Flannery asked, breathless, dancing with Scott in the middle of a sea of famous bodies—celestial bodies, really, stars through and through.

"Yes," Kat said, faking that smile on her face. The cameras were rolling, were catching everything. Scott's forehead had sweat rolling down it profusely, and she was even breaking into beads a little bit here and there. It was hot in here, wasn't it? "So fun."

The music was turned up to eleven. Kat snagged a drink from a waiter who passed by, halting in the middle of the dance floor, her camera crew responsible for a five-foot section of empty floor to her right. The waiter passed right through, conveniently, not looking at the camera but doubtless hoping to get his face noticed. She stopped him, perfectly timed, and handed glasses to Flannery and Scott, flutes of champagne. Probably pretty fine stuff, but she didn't know names for these sorts of things. Crystal? Was that a kind of champagne? It was bubbly and kind of sweet and she tipped it back in one, not even making a toast. Flannery shouted, "Woo!" and drained her own, beckoning the waiter forward for another. Scott did his with a cringe, like a shot, making a face as it went down. He was such a beer guy; champagne was probably a little too sophisticated for his palate.

"Woo," Kat said, under her breath. "Yeah."

"We should mingle," Flannery said, her shoulders under Scott's arm. He looked like he was struggling a little bit, like weight had settled on him, or he'd brought baggage. Well, she knew he had brought some baggage; that was how she got him to come, after all.

"Yes, we should," Kat agreed. Flannery didn't have to say the rest—this was a place to see and be seen. She took her retreat from the dance floor gracefully. The gown was a real bitch to dance in anyway.

"Is that Kevin Feige?" Flannery asked, looking through the crowd. "I need to introduce myself. I could totally be Captain Marvel."

"Don't look too desperate," Kat said, bringing her champagne flute up to her lips. It exploded in her fingertips, showering her with glass. A little too much strength, and she hadn't even noticed she was squeezing the glass. A thin trickle of blood streamed out of her thumb, no wider than a paper cut. It oozed once, then stopped.

"Wow," Flannery said, admiring her finger. She grabbed it and held it up, and Kat held back to urge to slap her hand away. "I bet that constant healing thing could really mess with a good Botox."

"Ugh, tell me about it," Kat said, gently pulling her hand back. "It does almost nothing, I swear. Also, that labiaplasty I wanted—"

"Whaaaaaaaat?" Scott butted into the conversation. "A what?"

"Labiaplasty," Flannery said, rolling her eyes. "Maybe you'll see one later if you don't embarrass yourself. They're big nowadays. Makes everything so much more … put together."

Scott was staring off into space, pondering that one. "Hummm." He shook his head. "Oh, hey, there's Steven."

"Steven Clayton?" Kat spun and sure enough, there he

was, lurking near the edge of the party, threading his way through the crowd. "Oh! Hey! Steven!" she shouted. He was about twenty feet away, through two thick knots of conversational circles, one of which included execs and a star of a movie that had just topped the box office for eight weeks running. "Steven!" she shouted.

He froze, turning to see who had called his name. When he locked eyes with her, he looked …

Disgusted?

He turned away and headed back along the path he'd been treading before she'd called out to him, toward the elevator. "That's weird," she said, watching him go. "That is weird, right?"

"Just ignore him," Flannery said. "He's probably gay. That's why he's interested in your friend with the touch disorder. No one would expect him to do anything with her."

"Ohhh," Kat said, nodding along, a smile breaking across her face. "Yeah, that's probably it, right?"

"Ouch," Scott said.

"Oh, whatever," Flannery said, brushing it off. "Did you hear what she said to the president?"

"No," Scott said. "Why?"

"I just figured maybe you heard," Flannery said with a shrug. "She met him right after you did."

Scott's brow furrowed. "I didn't meet the president."

Flannery made a face, petulant and irritable. "Yeah, okay, whatevs—"

Whatever Flannery had meant to say, she was interrupted by a crack somewhere outside on the balcony, and Kat felt her pulse quicken, looking around. She looked for shots, for gunfire, for the threat, but nothing more than a mild ripple of surprise passed through the crowd. "What was that?" she asked. Everyone's head was pointed toward the enormous balcony.

"Oh, wow," Flannery said, her eyes riveted. "Just … wow. Nice entrance."

"What are you—" Kat caught sight of her just a second later, a flash of movement just outside, motion against the background of the night sky.

Sienna.

"Party's over, I guess," Flannery said, more than a little amused.

"No, it's not," Kat said, feeling the bitterness roll over her at the sight of her last bodyguard. "No, it damned well is not."

61.

Sienna

I set down on the balcony outside, scanning the party for Kat. The place was packed, filled with people dressed entirely too nicely for a Sunday night. I suppose it was always Friday out here or something, kind of like how they had summertime all year long.

As soon as I landed, I started forward, figuring I'd find my subject somewhere inside. It was kind of a breezy night; she probably wasn't hanging out out here. It'd mess up her hair. Mine, on the other hand, was perpetually wrecked. I'd thought about getting a pixie cut, but I just wasn't ready to embrace that yet.

"Heyyyy," a guy said, making his way over to me, clearly oblivious to the single-minded purpose with which I was cutting through the crowd. "I know who you are." He arched his eyebrows at me.

"You and everyone else with one of those idiot boxes," I said, looking past him. It was tough to see much, though, because I'm so short. "Hey, was the idiot box named after you? It's all starting to make sense now."

"Ooh," he said, grimacing a little. "Okay. You live up to your rep, so I'm just gonna get right to it. I've got a proposition for you, something maybe to get your foot in the door in the biz—have you ever thought of having sex on camera before?"

My head snapped around on him, all thought of finding and beating Kat gone in favor of giving this guy two seconds to explain himself before I beat him instead. "You want to film a snuff movie? With me as the star? What is *wrong* with you?"

"No, no," he said, holding up his hands. "I'm in the industry—you know, adult movies. Succubi are a big fantasy and—I mean, there are things we can do, tricks we can use, when we're filming—you know, in post—but there's stuff we can do on the day to capture usable footage without endangering anyone—"

"'On the day'?" I picked one phrase out of the shit he was spewing. "On what day? The day I murder someone on camera while filming a sex scene?" I shook my head. Why was I letting myself be drawn into this conversation?

Oh, right. Because letting Wolfe run my life meant killing douches like this instantly.

HEY.

True, Wolfe. You know it, too.

Maybe, he grudgingly conceded. *Okay, yes. But it would be so much more fun.*

Also true. But new. This was brand new me, embracing change for the better.

"On what day," the guy said, amused by my question. "You're new, I forgot."

"I'm getting older by the second," I said, "and so is this schtick." Change isn't an instant thing, okay? It takes time.

"Hmph," he said, making a face. "Yeah, you're not very nice. This is totally why you don't have a boyfriend."

"Oh, no, it's not," I said, shoving him hard out of the way. He went face-first into a potted plant, shattering it with his cro-magnon skull. "That's probably why. And as a sidepoint," I said, lecturing his insensate body, "whatever will I do if I don't have a man like you around to validate and approve of all my choices?" I held myself back from curb stomping him into the shards of pottery, deciding it might be just a bit too much. "Why, I might have to live my own life. Gasp." And I left him in the wreckage, with at least a couple hands of scattered applause behind me. Not enough to indicate overwhelming approval, but enough to cool my anger a few notches, at least until I found Kat. Then, I had a feeling, my anger was not going to be cool any longer.

62.

Karl

Karl had wandered around the basement parking garage of the Luxuriant, doing his thing, making his mark. It hadn't taken too long to set things up the way he'd wanted them, just a few minutes, really, and then he'd decided to wait in the hotel lobby, lingering at the fringes. The paparazzi and the press were outside, and he was in here, just sitting with a copy of the *LA Times* stretched out in front of his face, the edge bent down so he could watch the elevators for her inevitable arrival.

It certainly didn't bother him that Sienna Nealon hadn't shown up yet. Her part in this whole thing wasn't anywhere close to done yet, after all. His backer had one last hurrah in mind for her before this thing came to its finale, and Karl was waiting for the moment that it did. He felt like killing Kat Forrest was sort of like the warm-up; killing Sienna Nealon, that was going to be the real satisfaction.

Because then he would have cut down two of the most famous metas in the world, the powerful one and the one everyone loved, and his legacy would be complete. He could go out with a bang knowing he'd never be forgotten, in LA or anywhere else.

He glanced to the side and saw a little cooler of orange-peel infused water chilled, with cups waiting for the hotel guests. It was a lovely little touch, one that made him wish he could add a dollop of poison. It wouldn't matter, of course, but this was the shit he hated. When was the last time someone in a poor neighborhood got orange-peel-infused drinking water? They were lucky if they got clean water at all.

He looked over his newspaper, back at the elevator with renewed fury. It dinged, and he felt a thrill of excitement, peering over it to see who it would spit out.

Then it opened. He locked eyes with the lone occupant within for a split second, and that was all it took.

SHIT.

Steven Clayton saw him, knew him, realized exactly who he was in the instant their eyes met, no beanie, overcoat or sunglasses fooling him. Karl just sat, stunned, for a second longer than he needed to, mind locked as he wondered what the Hollywood pretty boy would do with that knowledge—

Then Steven Clayton pulled a gun from his shoulder holster as smoothly as if he'd practiced it a thousand times, and fired it right at Karl.

Three shots tore through the paper, the sound of paper ripping lost in the roar of gunshots. The bullets whipped through the spot where Karl was sitting, slapping into the couch behind him.

Karl threw the paper aside and started to get up as Steven Clayton advanced on him, altering his aim just as Karl started to get to his feet. Clayton fired down, and Karl felt something sharp rupture the skin of his right buttock where it had been pressed against the couch only a second earlier, a feeling like fire that caused him to arch his back in pain.

NO.

Karl triggered his power and went entirely insubstantial instantaneously, passing through the floor within a second, disappearing into the darkness below, swearing under his breath and vowing revenge on all these fake heroes.

63.

Sienna

"Oh," Kat said as I strolled up to her, leaving the usual levels of mayhem and broken people in my wake, "it's you." Like she didn't see me coming or hear the disturbance with the snuff porn film guy out on the balcony.

I bypassed Guy Friday, who lifted an eyebrow, and Butler, who apparently had the sense to stay back. I left the crowd behind and entered the small circle of people around Kat, which included Flannery Steiner and Scott. Scott looked a little flushed, embarrassed and maybe defiant, but not in equal measure. Flannery just looked like she was ready to spectate a cat fight. Or a Kat fight.

"It's me," I agreed, keeping my voice neutral with heroic levels of restraint. I wanted cookies for this. All the cookies. And maybe a pie or two for good measure. "Time to go."

"No, it's not," Kat said snootily.

"This party is so happening," Flannery said, and I couldn't tell whether she was trying to throw gas on the fire or not. "We just saw Steven Clayton a minute ago. He took one look at Kat and bailed for the elevators with the nastiest look on his face."

Kat flushed, looking at Flannery like she'd been betrayed. Well, that answered that. "He probably had somewhere else to be."

"So do you," I said. "Let's go."

"I'm not going anywhere," Kat said, sticking her nose up in the air. "Why don't you go find Steven?" She smiled nastily. "He's clearly looking for a beard."

I gave her a stony stare; that was a low blow, even for Kat. "I don't care what he's looking for—"

"Of course you don't," she sniffed. "You'd probably be totally cool being his side piece, sponging off his fame."

"'Side piece'?" I looked at her in thinly layered disbelief. "You're a piece of something, too." I glanced at the camera crew filming her dramatic attempt to draw me into a verbal brawl. "... Which I will not say on TV."

"Oh, no, you're good," the cameraman said, shoving his lens into my face, "we can totally bleep it out in editing, like what I'm saying right here. Fire away."

"Get real, Sienna," Kat said, drawing my attention back from the shitshow that was currently making us its stars, "the only reason Steven probably wants anything to do with you is because he's got a squeaky clean good guy rep to shed or because he's gay and needs a plausible reason not to have sex with his girlfriend."

"Well, I have sex, as you well know, so that's right out," I said, flushing. She did a little flushing, too, and I got the feeling Kat was in way over her head on this one. "Alternatively, did you ever consider he might just be a good guy who's got questionable taste in women?" Yes, I insulted myself. On television. Dr. Zollers suggested some humility in public spaces, and I was working on that, too.

"Oh, sweety," Flannery chimed in, "you're in the wrong town. Go back to podunk America before you get hurt, please."

I didn't punch her, but it wasn't easy. "Not everyone is a user, even here in Los Angeles." Pretty sure my eyes were rolling from the exertion of still not killing Flannery as I said that.

Kat bristled like ... well, a cat. "Oh, come on. You're

here because you still think of me as a meal."

"I don't want to eat you, Kat," I said. "I don't even want to be around you, but this is how screwed up you are—you're complaining about how I look at you but you let Taggert use you sexually without a thought."

Kat's face flushed scarlet with heat, looking sidewise in alarm at the camera before turning, fully enraged, back to me. "You don't even know. You have no idea. You don't even try, and you get attention."

"Yes, negative attention," I said, staring back at her in stunned disbelief. "People hate me."

"I can't imagine why," Flannery Steiner said, all snotty, playing to the crowd.

"Because I'm impulsively violent and have problems controlling my anger," I said, leveling my gaze on her. She squirmed and I liked it. "Neither of which either of you are helping at the moment." I snapped my attention back to Kat. "There is a psychopath out there bombing houses and parks—anywhere he can that you are, all in a desperate bid to get attention of his own. Now you've come to this—this—atrocity of a party, held in the middle of a multi-story grand hotel, exposing everyone here and in the building and around it to danger because—*why*, Kat?"

"We're not afraid of him," Flannery said, putting a hand on Kat's shoulder in support. "And he ought to know it."

"Yeah," Kat said, ghostly quiet. "I'm not afraid of him."

"You're so brave," Flannery said, nodding along, lip almost quivering.

I slapped my forehead. I couldn't help it. "You are so. Very. Stupid."

"Lot of that going around," Scott said with more than a little resentment. I looked right at him and he looked back, unbowed.

"Yeah, I'm stupid," Kat said, getting huffy again. "I'm stupid and you think you're God. That you know better than everyone else, that you can just do whatever you want, whenever you want because you're Sienna Nealon."

"Not to go quoting Spider-Man to you," I said, "but with power comes a level of responsibility, and you're being so damned irresponsible right now—"

I froze when I heard the muted sound of gunshots. It was floors below us, wafting through the crowd that was silently watching, silently judging us for our public spat, and enjoying it all the while. The sharp cracks rang over the whispers, so far away that I wouldn't have heard them save for my meta hearing. Sharp, staccato, and definitely gunfire.

"Party's over," I whispered.

64.

I shot over the heads of everyone at the party and zoomed over the edge of the balcony toward the ground below. I could see the red carpet still laid out, although all the guests of honor had presumably already arrived for this blowout party that was probably about to turn into an actual blowout. I held my breath as I descended at high speed, listening for further sounds of gunfire.

The red carpet was lit up like a landing strip, and I made use of it as such. The crowd on either side had a skittish feel, uncertain. They'd clearly heard the noise and had a feeling about what it was. Gunfire was a universal sound that tended to set people on edge, after all. Then I heard something else—sirens, klaxons, a fire alarm at work, howling somewhere in the hotel.

I touched down as the doors to the hotel's main lobby opened up and Steven Clayton spilled out, a Glock 17 clutched in his hands, pointed in low rest at the earth.

"Sienna!" he called, breaking into a run as he headed toward me. He looked like a cop, like a really well-dressed cop but without a badge and—you know—hotter. Worry lines creased his face and lips. "He's here."

"Is that yours?" I asked, nodding at the pistol in his hands.

He glanced down at it. "Yeah. I took a few shots at him. Think I mostly missed."

"Where was he?"

"Sitting on a couch in the lobby," Steven said, his mouth a stiff line. "Like he owned the place, wearing a beanie and sunglasses, just waiting, looking at the elevators. He saw me as soon as I stepped out." The corners of his mouth turned upward. "I don't think he was expecting me to start shooting, though. He went through the floor in a half second."

"Damn," I said, rolling that one over in my head and coming to the obvious conclusion. A mad bomber running loose around the foundation of a massive hotel—

"He was wearing a trench coat," Steven said, back to worried. "Could have been carrying anything with him. I pulled the fire alarm, but—"

"Yeah," I said and shot upward again without waiting for him to spell out the rest. I zoomed up the intervening floors to the balcony, knowing full well what I had to do.

This hotel wasn't going to evacuate itself, after all.

65.

Kat

"Wow," Flannery said, voice dripping with irony right after Sienna had left them behind, "that was a scene. So embarrassing."

Kat knew she was lying, knew that she'd probably enjoyed it in a way that Kat couldn't have, but saying so wasn't something her character would do. Because that was really what she'd become—a character she played for the camera. Like that movie script she had been reading when all this had started. What was the girl's name? Bobbie? She'd come to California with hopes and dreams, figuring with luck and hard work, she'd make her name, become famous. That was why Kat had come here, after all, wasn't it? She tried to remember the arguments with Janus before the end. What had he said about fame being fleeting but power lasting?

It didn't matter. What mattered was that she delivered her lines and hit her mark, and right now she had a very definite mark to hit. "Sienna thinks she's in charge of everybody," Kat said, and then the sound of the fire alarm howling cut her off.

"What the hell?" Scott asked, looking around with everyone else in the party. Heads were swiveling. Not that there was much to see, just white lights flashing on the walls where the red alarm stations were mounted.

"That was gunfire, wasn't it?" Butler edged in close to them.

"Yep," Guy Friday said, appearing out of the crowd, bowling over one of the premiere agents in all of LA as he did so. "Time to leave, people." He grabbed Kat by the waist before she had a chance to protest.

"Whoa!" Kat said as she was lifted into the air over Guy Friday's shoulder. "What are you doing?" The crowd started to surge around them. Someone screamed.

Sienna flashed into view over the balcony again, shattering windows as she blasted into the room. "We've gotta get everyone out of here!" she shouted over the already-beginning-to-panic crowd. She swooped down and grabbed Guy Friday by the waist and yanked the both of them along, Kat struggling.

"What the—" Kat started to say, and then she felt Guy Friday's feet touch solid ground again, the shudder of a hard landing running through his body and into hers. She blinked and looked around; they were on the pool deck of the hotel on the opposite side of the street.

"No time to chat!" Sienna shouted as she blasted across the street again, disappearing back over the balcony a story or two above them. She reappeared a moment later with two more people, one under each arm, dropping them in the pool and then zooming away again.

"Well, at least she didn't drop us in there," Guy Friday said, looking on the bright side.

"Probably didn't think of it," Kat said, sullenly. Why did Sienna always have to ruin everything?

66.

Sienna

I was grabbing people by the arms and legs and hauling them into the air, dragging them over the gulf between the Luxuriant and the tower across the street, chucking them into the swimming pool and flying back for more.

Yes. That's right. I was grabbing some of the most powerful people in Hollywood by the suit jackets and expensive nightgowns, flying them across the street, and tossing them into a swimming pool as quickly as I could.

In spite of the shitstorm going on at the hotel, it was probably the best night ever.

"Don't leave the camera—!" Kat's cameraman barely got out before I dragged him and the sound guy out of the penthouse and across the street. They made a satisfying splash—minus the camera, which I had made sure he dropped by "accidentally" running it into the balcony doorframe on the way out. Oops.

Sometime after I tossed Grant Gustin into the pool (which I actually felt bad about, because he seemed nice—still, TAKE THAT, FASTEST MAN ALIVE, shown up by a woman), I realized I hadn't grabbed Scott yet.

I made a conscious effort on my next pass to try and find him, but when I was halfway across the street I heard the first explosion go off.

67.

Karl

There was a sharp pain running through Karl's backside, worse than the other wounds he'd suffered in the last couple days. Those had been mostly superficial, that last layer of flesh he'd made whole to keep him from falling through those surfaces, through earth, ripped open. A centimeter of epidermis at most, a tear in the skin. It hurt, definitely, but it wasn't agony. Even the punching Sienna Nealon had inflicted on his face had been extremely painful, but was nothing compared to this.

This was agony. He'd caught the full impact when he'd fallen through the floor of the lobby, landing in the first sub-basement parking garage. He hadn't landed on his feet, either, it had been a hard, crushing landing where everything but his skull bounced against concrete floor. The impact had reverberated, his whole body bouncing a foot up before coming down again. After he'd settled, he'd lain there for a minute, taking stock of the pain.

The sound of dripping in the distance was a reminder he was in an underground garage. There was no sound of cars moving, no engines running, just the quiet solitude of being underground. Not as quiet as the time he'd spent months in the earth, but not nearly as loud as the gunshot- and chatter-filled lobby he'd left behind.

The pain ran the length of him, from ass to the top of his spine and spread up into his skull, bouncing around in there like someone had fired a bullet that had gotten trapped. He tasted blood in his mouth and wondered how hard he'd hit.

He grunted and it echoed in the silence. He turned his head and saw one of the big concrete pillars that supported the hotel standing there, looming in front of him. He'd walked past it only an hour earlier, planted one of his bombs in it, it and five others like it. He'd done all he could to make sure that this building was going to come down when the moment was right.

And the moment? As far as he was concerned, it couldn't get any righter.

He strained against the aches in his body and fumbled for the detonator on his belt. Raising it up, he fought his way to his feet, drawing in a sharp breath of the damp air, and pushed the button, running toward the wall, nothing but the soles of his feet making contact with the ground, the sound blotted out by the explosion echoing through the garage behind him.

68.

Scott

Flannery Steiner's perfectly manicured nails ate into Scott's arm as the panic swept through the party. People were crowding the elevators, crowding the balcony, and Sienna was flying in and out at a blurry speed, almost like an afterimage of her was present for a second then gone, a couple more people removed from the thinning crowd with every appearance.

"What do we do?" Flannery asked, drawing a sharp breath, voice barely above a whisper. "Should we go for the elevators?"

"That's a fight to the death." Scott looked over his shoulder. It was a grim sight, people in formalwear shoving, elbowing, nearly throwing punches every time one of the elevators dinged and people scrambled to get on. The shouts, the cries, the squeals of triumph—they all blended into cacophony. It was too loud by half for Scott, and it was almost drowned out by the screamed pleas from the masses of people on the balcony who were begging for Sienna to save them. "Balcony," he decided, without even having to give it much thought.

"There are like a hundred people out there," Flannery said, nails gripping deeper into his arm, drawing blood, "there's no way she's going to get them all." She looked at

281

him with horrorstruck eyes. "Is she?"

He had to bite back the anger that came from even thinking of Sienna. "If anyone can …"

A hard smell of fear had settled over the party, the parting of the two sides—one bound for the elevator and stairs, the other to the woman flying every person she could to safety—left an enormous gulf, a no man's land that Scott stood squarely in the middle of. For now, it looked like an even divide, the elevator and stairs swallowing just as many people as Sienna was evacuating via the balcony.

What is going on here? Scott wondered. The fire alarm screamed. *Because this doesn't just seem like a fire. The sprinklers aren't even going.*

"Screw this," Flannery said, bolting from his arm. "You may trust that crazy bitch, but I don't." She stared at him for a split second, eyes wide with fear. "I'm saving myself." And she was off, kicking off her heels, shouldering her way toward the crowd for the nearest elevator.

"I …" Scott faltered, like his mind clouded in that instant. *Do I trust Sienna?*
If it comes down to it … is she going to save me?
Or would she leave me behind?

Before he could get to the answer, the first explosion rocked the hotel, shaking the ground beneath his feet and spelling out for him exactly what was happening here. The second followed a moment later, then a third, and the walls and ground started to crack all around him.

69.

Sienna

The explosions came one after another, like gunshots in the night, but louder and more forceful. I could tell they were happening somewhere beneath the hotel; maybe Redbeard had been an architectural engineer in a previous life. A cloud of debris washed out of the first floor, and I knew that nobody had survived down there.

Worse than that, every single staircase in the building had just been cut off. The ground floor had just ceased to exist, and the rippling shockwave was now running up the facade of the old building.

The art deco tower shuddered under the force of the explosions running through it. Plaster cracked, dust came flying off like billowing clouds, windows shattered on the first four floors in quick succession. The sound of metal straining was faint, but audible somewhere beneath the stunned silence brought on by the explosions spilling out onto a Los Angeles street.

The tower started to buckle, and I surged into motion. With no time to waste, I shot back to the balcony. I put all thoughts of the lower floors out of my mind. I had seconds to rescue as many people as I could, and anyone who wasn't within grabbing distance was—tragically—out of luck.

I swept back to the party balcony and found screaming

chaos. People had been pleading to get my attention before, but now desperation was setting in. It would have been impossible not to feel the shocks from the explosion, and no one—I don't care how many earthquakes they've been in—likes to have the ground beneath their feet get unsteady.

I dropped low and snatched up two people immediately. More grabbed onto my thighs, and for the first time I wasn't sorry that they were a little wider than standard. Screams filled my ears, and I realized one of them was a guy clutching tightly to my ankle. It was Mr. Snuff Film, and as I jetted back off the balcony, I reflected that truly, saving lives was my business, because apparently I was saving this douche, and I'd already saved Kat.

I dumped them in the pool and shot back for the hotel. The tower was crumbling now, splits running up the plaster, the last moments heralded by all the damage that was showing in the exterior lines. I froze for a second above the balcony as I dipped low, my eyes locking on Scott's, way at the back of the crowd, his look one of stricken disbelief.

My hands were full, though, and I had six people clinging to my legs and my pants, making me really glad I invested in that leather belt this afternoon. I flew over the edge of the balcony, not losing his eyes as I went.

The hotel started to fall behind me, the top floor collapsing onto the one beneath it as I flew away, carrying as many complete strangers as I could, and leaving behind the man I had once loved.

70.

Scott

There's no one coming to save you, the voice came again, a surprise like before, though at least this time he recognized his own voice, unlike at MacArthur Park.

The balcony was falling, the whole building coming down, and Scott had just shoved to the head of the crowd, right there with a front-row view of the whole thing as Sienna flew off, people hanging from her. There were probably thirty people still on the balcony, and now their screams were almost deafening, the screams and the sound of a building falling around them.

"If only you'd faced this kind of thing before," he said. "Maybe jumped out of a plane or something."

With a flash, Scott saw tumbling skies around him, felt the weightless sensation of falling, saw Sienna in front of him, the ground racing up—

"I've done this before," he said to himself and vaulted over the balcony, flinging himself clear of the falling building.

"Yeah, you're old hat at this," the voice said in the rushing wind. "Too bad you can't remember, thanks to her."

The street below rushed up at him, and Scott threw his hands out as if to catch himself. The memory came back to him again, the feeling of water spraying out of his hands, draining him, hitting the ground enough to—

Break my fall, he willed, shooting out his hardest spray. It bounced against the concrete, the solid, coherent stream splashing against the pavement. It was like a cannon out of his fists. His arms jerked from the impact, slowing him …

He drifted to the ground in a cloud of dust as the hotel smashed to the ground behind him. The screams in the night were lost in his own, which faded to the sound of sirens, and he stood there, in the dust, in the cloud, lost in himself, his own thoughts, trying to remember a memory that had been stolen.

71.

Sienna

I hovered over the wreckage of the Luxuriant with a steadily growing fury, an anger that compounded the longer I stared at the ruin of the building below. I could have gone and checked on the people I'd thrown in the pool, could have gone down to talk to emergency personnel, could have studiously avoided Scott, who was milling around on the street below with the other survivors, could have given an angry interview to the local TV news that was showing up on the scene—I could even have started the fruitless rescue attempts, trying to pry survivors out of the concrete and rebar coffin that the hotel had become, but I didn't feel remotely qualified to do that. They had cranes for that sort of thing, and the odds were good I wouldn't have been a very effective team player at the moment, since I didn't want to play as a team.

What I wanted to do was find Redbeard and pull his heart out through his ribcage. Not like he did it, with an insubstantial hand, but my way, where I busted through skin and bone with superior, furious force and just ripped his heart out in a very literal sense.

I watched the streets, hoping he'd show up. I had a feeling that even with what Steven had done to him, he'd made it out somehow. He'd hit the detonator, after all. For some reason, I didn't think he'd made this building his gravesite. Probably because I didn't think he had the decency or the balls to just end it. I mean, when you want to kill everybody, start with yourself, asshole, because odds are good that's going to solve the problem. Don't inflict your baggage on the rest of us. That's just selfish.

But then, people were selfish, weren't they? I was staring out at a smoldering monument to selfishness, watching the firefighters set up to douse it with water in the spots where fires had broken out in the collapsed rubble.

I swung around and looked at the pool deck behind me. It was filled with soaking refugees too stupid to clear out, to get the hell away from the epicenter of a disaster that had nearly claimed their lives. They stared on in stunned silence like sheep, maybe counting themselves lucky and trying to avoid going into shock. There was a little jockeying for position at the edge of the railing, and it made me sick.

Kat was near the front, of course, Guy Friday and Butler lingering behind her, presumably doing some gawking of their own, too caught up in the spectacle to see with clear eyes that she should be escorted far, far from the scene—and now. I drifted down until she noticed me. She looked more than a little stunned herself, but unlike her fellow partygoers, she at least wasn't dripping water.

"What are you still doing here, Kat?" I asked, my voice raw with emotion.

"I'm ..." she searched for an answer like she was giving it in front of a camera. "... I'm just taking a moment for the fallen—"

"Don't give me that bullshit," I said, snapping at her so hard she jerked in surprise. "Why did you come here tonight?"

"I was ... being brave," she said, finding her spine about halfway through her answer. "I was doing what you would have—"

"I wouldn't have come to a crowded public place unasked

if there was a mad bombing meta after me," I shot at her, remorseless. She flinched. "It's not brave to expose other people to your danger. It's the opposite. It's chickenshit. And if you have to keep telling yourself how brave you're being when you're really acting selfish and self-laudatory, it kind of makes you a pathetic human being."

"Hey," said a guy in the front row with a soaking plaid jacket, "who are you to judge her?"

"I'm the one who just saved your life," I said, glaring at him so hard he took a step back from the edge, "in case you're as short on memory as she is on reason." I turned my gaze back to Kat. "You got a lot of people killed tonight and earlier today because you were so damned focused on being famous, on making yourself look better and not caring about what happened to anyone else. This guy wants to kill you, publicly, and instead of being a human being and keeping yourself away from danger, from giving him opportunities to kill you and lots more people, you keep showing him your ass and daring him to come after it." I lurched closer to her. "Well, it's not happening again."

"Hey—!" Butler said, making a grab for me as I came over the rail toward them.

I snatched up Kat before he could do anything to stop me, lifting her kicking and struggling into the air. "I'm sick of you acting like a child," I said, wrapping my arms around her waist and streaking into the heavens. "No one else is going to die for you, Kat."

The air whipped past both of our faces, and I felt her go still in my grasp after she realized that if she broke free of my hold, she'd plummet to her death. "What are you going to do with me?" she asked, voice quivering.

I didn't answer her as I altered our course to carry this albatross, this selfish infant, this negligent murderer away from Los Angeles. Far, far away from Los Angeles.

Somewhere that she'd never be found.

72.

Karl

Karl walked through the wall of the burger joint without stopping, passing through and ending up in the deep fryer, grease spitting from the boiling surface. He didn't even feel the heat as he moved. The kitchen was all streamlined metal surfaces and ugly brown tile, like this place might have been a McDonald's or a Wendy's before shutting down and returning to life as a boutique locally owned establishment. The employee uniforms, polo-style shirts and no hats, were a half step up from fast-food chain standard,. He couldn't smell the food, not when he was out of phase, so he made his nose solid for a second and took a deep whiff.

Oof. Truffle oil. He took a deeper sniff and caught all the little aromas—mushrooms, Swiss, maybe some pineapple from a Hawaiian-style burger, he wasn't entirely sure. It was a sweet, sharp aroma. Karl closed his eyes for a second, his crotch buried in the middle of the deep fryer, the scent of fries permeating the air, and he just took it all in.

Yeah. This was the place.

Karl opened his eyes to see a young woman in the restaurant uniform staring at him in openmouthed horror, her jaw down at about her ankles. He locked eyes with her, stared right back, and smiled. "I want one of those mushroom and Swiss burgers, and one of the ones with pineapple on it, plus a standard, good ol' fashioned one with lettuce, tomato, mayo, onion, cheddar or American cheese, whichever goes best, and fries—you listening to me?" He wobbled his head to look at her, break her out of her trance.

She took a sharp breath that sounded like someone had hit her in the gut. "You're him," she said after a moment of struggling.

"Yeah," he said with a careful smile. So this was what it was like to be known.

"You ... you killed those people," she said.

"Yeah," Karl said, and angled his head toward the wall he'd just walked through. "I just blew up the Luxuriant hotel, too. Probably hundreds dead there. Can't believe they named it that." He smiled. "Yeah, that was a good time." He let the smile fade. "You gonna get my order?"

Tears ran down the girl's broad face. She had blondish brown hair and a pug nose. "I ... are you going to kill me?"

"Get my burgers and throw in some fries and you'll be fine," Karl said, stifling a yawn. His ass still hurt where that stupid prettyboy actor had shot him. "Hurry about it, will you?" He looked to the side; whatever renovation this place had experienced after its start as a fast food joint had caused them to cut off the kitchen from the restaurant itself. He couldn't see the dining area, leaving his encounter with this employee pretty private. He looked at her nametag. "You gonna help me ... Amy?"

She snapped mechanically into motion, going toward the fryer and then stopping herself, staring at him, standing in the middle of it. "The—the fries—I need to—they're done cooking ..."

"Oh," he said and stepped to the side. Now he stood with a griddle in the middle of his chest, three all-beef patties sizzling somewhere inside him. He imagined them in his belly, and it felt weird, even though that's where they were sitting. Amy lurched toward the fryer, still watching him in horror, pulling the fries out of the vat. They dripped grease, stuck in their little wire-frame cage.

He watched her do her work, ignoring the sounds in the front of the restaurant. It sounded like patrons, like people, like cattle, like meat—they *should* serve people here, like they were the main course, he thought. No, wait, that was society's job. People were the product, and they never even realized it. That was the funny part of this whole thing.

Amy was putting the burgers in buns, putting the condiments on them, then shoving them, wrapped in paper, into a brown paper bag. She carefully scooped fries out of the cage and dumped them into a large cup, dusting them with a salt shaker as she did so. She was torn between watching what she was doing and looking at him, and she made no effort to look anything other than scared witless the whole time. Karl didn't mind that any more than he minded having the griddle hissing somewhere in the middle of his crotch. It didn't bother him a bit.

"H-here you go," Amy said, curling up the top of the bag and offering it to him.

"Thanks," Karl said, taking it from her and immediately unrolling the top. He picked one of the burgers and unwrapped it, the one that had the strong smell of onions wafting off of it. "Where are you from, Amy?" He took his first bite. Greasy goodness, a little drip rolling down into his beard, crumbly pieces of the perfectly toasted, buttery bun got caught in his mustache.

"Uhmm …" she looked around as though the answer were written on a wall. "I'm from, uh … Montana?"

Karl studied her as he chewed his burger. His stomach was empty, rumbling, furious. He was used to it by now; it was nothing like what he'd gone through after that Augustus bastard had locked him in the earth. "Where in Montana?" he asked. Talking to her felt … weird? But all right. Little flecks of the burger came out as he spoke, but not enough to lose the flavor, thankfully.

"Uhm, Great Falls," she said. "It's … it's …"

"Yeah, don't worry about it," Karl said, taking another bite of the burger and then wrapping it back up. He opened the next one, the one that smelled of pineapple, and took a bite. The slight tartness of the fruit went perfectly with … was that teriyaki sauce and mayo? He chewed experimentally, decided he liked it, and then took another huge bite before he'd even finished chewing the first. "What brought you to LA?" His words came out garbled by the food in his mouth.

"I'm sorry?" She really did sound apologetic. "What … I didn't … I didn't understand, I'm so sorry." Fresh tears spouted from her eyelids, running down her face like tiny rivers. He could see grease on her face, the rivers rolling around some of the thicker patches. It wasn't the sort of detail most people would have noticed, but he was meta.

"Yeah, that's fine," Karl said and waved at her with the hand that held the bag of his food. She made a face like she still didn't understand, so he chewed faster. "Don't worry about it. It doesn't matter."

The more he spoke, the redder her face got, the more she squinted, crying now, her face balling up with her cheeks stretching out. She started to hang her head, her eyes pressed closed, scared to even look at him.

He didn't like the look of that at all, so he turned around and walked through the wall, leaving her right where she was.

Karl walked on, into the night, with a slight limp, still nursing the wounds done to his feet and his ass earlier. Those would still be a while healing, unfortunately. Yeah, he needed a car, and he'd probably find one soon. Then it would be time to go home, to plan for the next—hopefully the last—phase, and bring this show to its bloody conclusion. He chewed his burger as he contemplated it. The pineapple really elevated this concoction to the next level.

73.

Scott

The street was chaos, as one might expect after a meta attack and a building collapse. People were milling around, emergency personnel were scrambling to and fro. Firefighters were still trying to put out some of the fires that had sprung up in the wreckage of the Luxuriant, police officers were trying to get witness statements and keep the press from over-running the scene, and EMTs were trying to tend to all the wounded. A pretty tall order considering how many people were walking around covered in dust and blood, looking like they were in shock, faces grey and eyes wide.

Scott felt a buzz in his pocket and looked down. He fumbled and came up with his phone, eyes catching on the scratch marks Flannery had left on his forearm before she'd gone for the elevator. That hadn't gone so well for her, he guessed, though who knew how long it would be until they found a body. She'd been too far up to survive without a miracle, after all. All of them had.

He stared at the glowing screen, the caller ID pronouncing that Buchanan Brock was calling him. Not really sure what else to do, he answered. "Hello?"

"Scott," Brock said on the other end of the connection, booming voice deep with concern. "How are you?"

"I'm standing in the middle of a rubble-strewn street

surrounded by bloody and scared people," Scott said, his words coming out in a rush like he'd shot them from his finger in a stream. "How are you doing, Mr. Brock?"

"Better than you, I'd say," Brock said. "Glad to hear you're keeping your head about you, though. You look a little less ragged than the others wandering around the scene."

Scott froze, looking around suddenly. "How did you know that?"

"You're on the news," Brock said, and Scott turned to see a reporter doing a live shot just behind him. "I'm glad you're all right, but uh … you do seem to keep showing up where the trouble is in this town."

"Yeah," Scott said. "Funny how that keeps happening."

"Maybe it's the company you keep."

"Well, I have been associating with some unsavory types of late," Scott said, looking up, hoping to see some sign of Sienna. She wasn't there, of course, and hadn't been for a while.

"Well, I'm glad you're all right, m'boy," Brock said, and he sounded genuine. "You weren't staying at the Luxuriant, were you?"

"No," Scott said, shaking his head. "I wasn't."

"Oh, good," Brock said. "I was gonna offer to let you stay with me if you needed. I'd get out of downtown as soon as you can, though. Sun's going to be up in a few hours, and … well, the traffic's gonna be a real bear today, I'm guessing. Might want to hunker down."

"I'll be out of here as soon as I can," Scott said, not fully absorbing the words. "Thank you for worrying." He lifted the phone away from his ear long enough to check the time. "What are you doing up at three in the morning?"

Brock laughed, deep and hearty. "I've been accused of being a vampire. I don't sleep much, see. I was going over some numbers with the TV on in the background when I saw the emergency bulletin. Interrupted my regularly scheduled rerun of *Empty Nest*."

"Oh," Scott said, "that's a real tragedy."

"I think," Brock said, "that what's happening there is the real tragedy. You sound a little shell-shocked. You're running on adrenaline and too little sleep. Do yourself a favor and get back to bed for a while. And tomorrow—get out of LA. You don't need any more of this trouble."

"I'll definitely take that under advisement," Scott said numbly.

"Just a friendly suggestion from an old man who doesn't want to see anyone get hurt," Brock said. "Take care, Scott."

"You too, Mr. Brock," Scott said, and the line went dead.

"Was that your daddy?" a voice from behind him asked. Scott spun to see Guy Friday standing behind him, arms folded, the new bodyguard, Butler, a pace behind him.

"No," Scott said, not really sure how to take that. "It was a—it was the guy who I came to LA to meet."

"David Boreanaz?" Friday asked. He sounded serious.

"What?" Scott frowned. "No. What are you two doing here? Shouldn't you be rushing Kat to safety?"

"Yeah, about that," Butler said, stepping up. "Your girl came and took her away. Flew off into the eastern sky. Kinda like riding off into the sunset, but you know—in reverse."

"Riding off into the sunrise," Guy Friday said, nodding, "but sunrise isn't until 6:17 a.m. today." He cocked his head. "Though, if she continues to go east, she'll meet the sun earlier, like—"

"Where'd she go?" Scott asked, cutting to the quick. "Also ..." His voice dripped with loathing, "she's not 'my girl.' Or my anything."

"No idea," Butler said, "other than east." He looked around and caught sight of the news camera in the background, then fussed with his hair for a second. "You think they're recording right now?"

"Yeah, they're live," Scott said absently, his mind on other things. "Why'd Sienna take Kat?"

"They had a quarrel," Guy Friday pronounced, arms still

folded. "On the roof. She called the blond girl—"

"You know what time local sunrise is to the minute but you can't remember the name of the woman you're protecting?" Butler asked.

"—selfish and dragged her off," Friday said. "I think she's going to murder her. Probably in the desert."

"Oh, man." Butler looked genuinely distressed. "That's going to look bad on my bodyguard resume."

"Also," Scott said, feeling a creeping sense of horror, "there would be a dead woman, which—I can't tell from either of your reactions, but I think—is a horrible thing to have happen."

Butler looked around uneasily. "I gotta be honest ... who's going to notice one more corpse after this? I mean ... like half the illuminati did not make it out of that party. They're all pancaked on the ground floor of Luxuriant. I mean, the Marvel guys got picked up by Sienna, but I think I saw the DC execs running for the elevator, which means—I think that's probably the end of the Superman and Batman franchises for a while."

"Like Zack Snyder didn't already accomplish that," Friday said.

"I doubt Sienna's going to kill Kat," Scott said, pausing after he said it. "Probably not, anyway."

"You didn't hear what she said to her," Butler said nervously.

"Hey." Another voice caused Scott to turn. Steven Clayton was standing right next to him, covered in dust. "What's up?"

"We were just discussing whether Sienna flew off to kill Kat," Scott said acidly. "What do you want?"

"Has anyone tried calling her?" Steven asked, stepping into the circle.

Scott froze for just a second. "No. No, we haven't."

Steven looked around at them. "Mind if I give it a try?"

"You don't need my permission," Scott said, giving him a

decent glare. He couldn't decide why he didn't like this guy, but he didn't.

"No, but I need her number," Steven said slickly, not breaking away from Scott's glare. "You know, if you don't want to call her yourself."

"No, I don't want to call her myself," Scott said, thumbing his phone open and scrolling to her number in his contacts. "Knock yourself out." He held up the screen so Steven could see it.

Butler sashayed around with his own phone in hand. "I'm just gonna go ahead and get those digits, too … maybe her firm is hiring, since I'm probably going to have a hard time explaining to other potential employers how I just lost my protectee."

"You think *she'll* understand?" Scott had a hard time not laughing.

"Well, she's the one who did it, so … yes." Butler focused on the number, keying it into his own phone. "On the other hand, I could just try and switch tracks, maybe use this as an opportunity to seek out some more traditional roles … never hurts to keep all your options open, though."

Steven already his phone up to his ear, and Scott could faintly hear the ringing. He heard the voicemail pick up, too, a few seconds later. Scott smiled bitterly. "I wouldn't count on a call back anytime soon, either, if I were you."

"Thanks for the advice," Steven said, smiling politely, not showing a tooth. "Hey, Sienna," he said, leaving a message, "Scott and the gang just told me you got out with Kat. I made it out before Redbeard blew the place, but uh … I'm kinda searching for the next move here." He looked around. "Cops don't seem to have a clue, but I'm guessing he made it out. Probably heading back to his base, wherever that is. Snake to his hole and all that. Anyway …" He paused, lips twisting in a frown, "… let me know you're okay, please, whenever you land. I'll be waiting for your call." He hung up and pulled the phone away from his ear.

"Dude, you got mad screen presence," Butler said, staring at him. "Who's your coach?"

"What?" Steven looked like he was coming out of a long sleep then ignored Butler entirely. "What are you guys going to do?"

"I'm gonna try and get seen on the news," Butler said, running fingers through his hair and then looking at them. "I need more dust to look like I was actually in this thing, don't I? We didn't get hit with the cloud up on the roof, and I didn't get soaked like the others." He craned his neck to look at another camera filming an interview a hundred feet away. "Holy shit, that's Joseph Gordon Levitt, isn't it?" He wandered off toward the interview, stopping to run his hands over a piece of rubble and then through his hair.

"What are the rest of you doing?" Steven amended, looking more than a little pissed off.

"I'm going to the Santa Monica pier," Guy Friday said with a shrug. "Call me if you need me." He turned around and left, walking straight out of the police line without anyone trying to stop him.

"Why does that guy always wear a mask?" Steven asked, watching him go. "He looks like the Gimp." He refocused on Scott. "What about you?"

"I'm ..." Scott gave that a thought and looked around. The scene—the wreckage—the people—it was all just a raging storm inside him, a liquid tornado in his chest. Before it had just seemed like clouds were rolling through his head, but now there was a solid form to it, a force, an emotion that hadn't been there before.

It was like he'd found something he'd lost.

"I want to kill this guy," he said, almost whispering. His eyes fell on the rubble. "I want to find him and kill him."

"I understand that fully," Steven said, his own gaze settling on the destroyed hotel. "Where do we start?"

And now Scott was back to blank clouds, formless and unsure. "I don't know," he said.

74.

Kat

When the sun rose, they were over the desert, flying toward the orange orb that was breaking over the horizon. Kat was cold and shivering and had been for well over an hour, the chill having seeped into her bones. Sienna wasn't saying anything and hadn't since they'd left the rooftop pool deck behind. She might as well have been a plane carrying Kat for all the talking she was doing, just a silent force propelling her through the dawn air.

"Where are we going?" Kat asked, her voice scratchy. They were only a few thousand feet up, and green, brushy vegetation speckled white, dusty ground below. It looked like bushes planted in white sands.

Sienna didn't answer. Kat turned around far enough to see that she was still there—obviously, since she had her hands firmly anchored on Kat's person. She held at her a little bit of distance, though, to keep from touching her skin. Sienna's hands were bunched up against the fabric of Kat's dress, perfectly balancing her at the midsection. "Where are you taking me?" Kat asked again, louder this time, but her voice just as hoarse. She needed a drink. The air at this altitude had utterly dried her out.

"Far away from LA," Sienna answered at last, sounding a little scratchy herself. There were clouds ahead. Big, white, fluffy ones, and they were headed straight for them, the orange light of the sun lighting them up.

"I don't want to leave," Kat said, her voice breaking.

"You don't have a choice," Sienna said.

"Because you're kidnapping me," Kat said, a little defiantly. She'd been stewing in this for over an hour and she was ready to just let her have it. If Sienna planned to kill her, there wasn't going to be much Kat could do about it in any case. Sienna was stronger, faster, meaner. "Are you going to kill me?"

"No, I'm not going to kill you, Kat," Sienna said, her ire rising with her voice, "and screw you for suggesting it. I'm just removing you from the situation. Which is what I should have done yesterday, before I remembered you're a selfish little cow who doesn't give a damn about anyone but herself."

The words stung, and so did the cold air. Kat had already been seeping tears from the speed of wind that was hitting her in the face, but this spurred a new round. "That's not true," she said quietly.

"What do you care about, Kat?" Sienna asked, throwing it down like a challenge. "Other than your own worthless neck? Do you give a damn about anyone? Like any of the people who died tonight because you decided you needed to party more than other people needed to keep breathing?"

"I didn't know that would happen," Kat said. "I thought we could just show up for an hour and no one would know until later—"

"Don't give me that," Sienna said, and the ground started to grow larger, the green brush below getting bigger. "Just like the party, and just like MacArthur Park, right? You were trending on Twitter. Everyone knew you were there. Redbeard could have found you if he'd been blind." The desert sands were growing larger, too, along with the spaces between the green bushes and the white ground that filled her sight all the way to the horizon. "You are an attention whore, and you were doing what you did best—getting attention."

"I need to set an example," Kat said. "People look up to me. I'm an entertainer—"

"You have no talent at all," Sienna snapped. "You're famous, essentially, for being an idiot that knew me once upon a time."

"I'm not an idiot," Kat said, flush running over her cheeks, "and you're wrong. I get millions of people to tune in to me every week because they want to see the lifestyle I'm living, they aspire to it—the glitz, the glamour—and it inspires them. I'm an example to little girls—"

"Of what you can accomplish without any actual talent, or bravery, or having to show up and go do real work, just by showing your ass on national television—"

"I do not show my ass on—"

"I've seen the vacation photos," Sienna said. "You show your ass in every way possible, even when you're not on camera. I mean, really, Taggert—"

"Screw you!" Kat shot at her. She squirmed against Sienna's invasive grasp; the fingers against her torso felt like aliens or worms, unpleasant invaders. "You don't know what it's like—"

"Knock it off or I'll let go," Sienna said, the ground looming ever closer. "And instead of just being in exile for a while, you can try and scrape yourself off the desert sands for the last five minutes of your stupid life."

"Why are you always so mean?" Kat asked, growing very still. "You always just say … just the most horrible things."

Sienna did not answer for a long minute, sweeping ever closer to the ground. "Because for as long as I've known you," she said at last, "you were everything I wanted to be— pretty, loved, liked—and because when I was as low as I could get, when I didn't have a friend left in the world, you stabbed me in the back by airing my personal confessions to the world, Kat."

"I didn't know—"

Sienna let her loose, and the surprising shock of being up in the air without any support, without anything below her and no one to hold her up took over. "AHH!" Kat screamed, eyes snapping as wide as they could, taking in the vast desert beneath her, looking for the nearest help she could find, reaching out a hand—

She seized control of a thorny bush below, a brambly bit of greenery that had deep roots designed to drink every drop of liquid they could on the desperately rare occasions when it rained. She pushed the reservoirs within the plant, taking control of the shoots, reaching up—

They caught her nimbly, softly, moving down as she fell, absorbing the impact into the bush. It caught her as lightly as if a pair of arms had reached out to catch a child dropped from six inches of height. She turned the course sideways and the plant nudged her bare feet into the sand, pushing her upright gently.

"You're life and I'm death, do you get that?" Sienna loomed over her, floating six feet off the ground. "You're the tall, willowy, classic beauty that everyone thinks is hot, and I'm short, squat and not exactly shaped like a model, okay? You were always so sweet to everybody, and you didn't think deep thoughts or constantly worry about the fate of the world and everyone liked you anyway. And me?" She made an ugly face and looked resentfully at the rising sun. "No matter what I've done since I beat Sovereign, since I became a so-called 'celebrity' … it's all turned to vinegar. People hate me, and I can't … I can't control my anger a lot of the time, okay? I'm inappropriately violent. I order a tall mocha with whip and the barista makes a face when he hands it to me, I imagine myself driving his stupid nose into the countertop— and I could do it. Now, ninety-nine percent of the time I don't, and when I do, it's always to some asshole who's hurt people, like Eric Simmons, who had just wrecked a subway train full of people after trying to rob the Federal Reserve."

Her smile grew bitter as she looked straight at Kat. "But I don't get credit for that. Instead I get a thousand think pieces written about how I'm a menace, and they use the incident at the campus with the Russians to reinforce the argument that I'm brutal dictator who doesn't know how to do anything but kill people. Our little phone call, edited for 'clarity,'" she made air quotations, "didn't help."

"I told you I didn't have anything to do with that," Kat said.

"Yeah," Sienna replied, "and you didn't have anything to do with going ahead on the *Vanity Fair* shoot yesterday that cost a bunch of people their lives, and you definitely didn't know that going to the party last night would kill—hell, I don't even know, but probably hundreds." She shook her head. "The thing that burns me ..." She glared right at Kat. "You weren't being brave and we both know it. You were being selfish. But everyone's going to say you were being brave, because they love you and hate me, and that's just the way it is."

"That's not my fault, either," Kat said numbly.

"It's a little your fault."

"I didn't lead you into talking about how you killed those Russians," Kat said. "I didn't bait you into talking about smacking around Eric Simmons, and when we did talk about it, I at least acknowledged the other circumstances, what with him saying what he did to that waitress—"

"And none of that made the cut," Sienna crossed her arms and looked away, still hovering in the dawn air, "so you get no points with me."

"None of it would have mattered anyway," Kat said. "People don't hate you because you beat the shit out of Eric Simmons or killed a bunch of Russians who were staging a jailbreak of dangerous prisoners."

"Really?" The sarcasm dripped off Sienna's words. "Then please, oh expert, tell me why they hate me—in your opinion."

"Because you're such a bitch," Kat shot at her. "I mean, *really*. Normal people don't kill, okay? They don't shoot people, they don't beat people with their bare hands, they don't set fire to them with superpowers—none of that happens in civilized society. And if they have to do any of those things, they damned sure don't mouth off to Gail Roth and come off like a psycho afterward. You're your own worst enemy." Kat folded her own arms. She doubted Sienna was going to *get* any of this, it would just roll off her like a punch to the face. And that girl could take a punch. "You look like a lunatic all the time. You're mad at me because I'm pretty and put together and try to act in a way that makes people like me—"

"'Act' being both the operative word and one of the things that irritates me most about you, yes."

"Well, it's a full-time job acting like you're a well-socialized human being when you're dealing with the press, okay?" Kat exploded. "Because they're busy trying to find every little speck of dirt they can, and you're busy looking like there's none, like you've never taken a dump in your entire life. It's inhuman, and the sport we make in this country of trying to raise people up before we find their flaws and tear them down so we can burn them in effigy? Dodging that is a full-time job, too, and you treat it like it's a—like it's—like it's nothing. You don't worry about it. You don't try to be likable and you wonder why people don't like you?"

"I don't wonder that hard, okay? It may not be one of my powers, but self-awareness isn't something I'm utterly short of."

"Well, you gripe about it like it's the thing you want most," Kat said, "but you don't act like it matters at all. You've got this defiance about you, like, 'I'm going to be who I'm going to be,'" Kat waved her hands at Sienna, "but you get mad when people don't like who you are. Well … stop acting like a shrew and a bully to everyone."

"I'm that way mostly to you."

"You're that way mostly to everyone," Kat said. "Steven is the only person I've seen you interact with since you got here that you didn't fill full of barbs. You—you got in an argument with the president at his own fundraiser, for crying out loud—"

"He's a dick."

"Yes, everyone's a dick but you," Kat said, feeling the fight ebb out of her. "You're the only sane, non-cantankerous person in the world." She leaned closer and looked up at Sienna. "Or maybe your godlike powers make you the most irritable, impatient—"

"Did you miss it when I admitted I had anger issues?"

"—and thanks a hell of a lot for bringing me out here where I'm safe from everything but the cacti," Kat said, falling right down into the soft sand.

"You can control the cacti, can't you?" Sienna asked, looking to the horizon. "You should be safe from them, too."

"If I don't get a skinny latte soon," Kat said, sighing, "I'm going to impale myself on the needles, so no, I'm not safe from them." She looked around. "Where did you even bring me? Arizona?"

Sienna showed a hint of guilt at that. "Not quite."

"Are we in Mexico?" Kat looked around as though a Mariachi band might jump out from behind the brush.

"Come on," Sienna said, hovering closer to her, extending her arms.

"Can we go home now?" Kat asked, pushing herself up, sand drifting out of the folds of her dress.

"No."

"Come on," Kat said as Sienna spun her around and lifted her up again. "I just … just take me home. I'll hide until—"

"Until what?" Sienna asked acidly. "Until I deal with this problem for you? That's another reason I don't like you."

"Do you dislike all the people you have to protect?" Kat

asked, resignedly. "Because that would explain why you act the way you do to so many—"

"Oh, shut up." And they flew off into the eastern sky.

75.

Karl

Once Karl had found a car and driven home, it didn't take much for him realize that the police had compromised his bolt-hole. Normally, one would find a police patrol in Elysium maybe once a month. The LAPD didn't come to Elysium unless they were called, and when they did, it was in force.

He passed three cruisers once he got off the freeway, just maneuvering around to some of the local restaurants, picking up drive-thru. As he drew closer to the bolt-hole, he suddenly he realized the pedestrians were gone, gone, gone. The herd was thin, even for this early in the morning, and that wasn't normal, either.

Ergo, cops were in force in the neighborhood, and why would they do that?

He pulled over into a parking lot outside an old, abandoned K-Mart. There were a few other stores still hanging on in this strip mall, but not many. He let his stolen Buick idle with the AC blowing while he dialed his phone and waited for an answer, his eyes scanning the rearview mirrors all the while. A cop car went past on the road, and he didn't think it was one of the ones he'd seen before. He could see the old-style lights on the outline of the car's roof.

This was just ...

It was so …

Perfect.

When the answer came on the other end of the line, Karl couldn't help letting the smile creep into his voice. "The cops found the bolt-hole."

There was a moment's hesitation on the other end. "You ready?"

"I am as ready as I could ever be," Karl said, feeling like his chest was swelling with the excitement. "It's all taken care of. All I need now is the last element, and we're good."

"Well," his benefactor said, "it sounds like you should get to work, then."

"I want to wait until daybreak," Karl said, still smiling. "Whole lot of people are going to die today. I want the cameras to catch as many of them dying as possible."

"I know." There was a pause, and he could almost imagine his backer grinning. "You're excited, aren't you?"

"I am. Can't imagine anything sweeter," Karl said. "This is goodbye, then."

"Goodbye, Karl. You'll do fine, and you know where to go after this."

"I do," Karl said, the excitement causing him to tap his fingers on the wheel. "So long, sir." And he hung up.

It was time.

This was what he'd been waiting for.

Now he'd get everything he'd ever wanted, and whether he walked out the other side or not … his benefactor would make sure that no one—NO ONE—would ever forget his name.

76.

Sienna

Kat was screaming when we came shooting down out of the clouds at our destination, which was so very not helpful but was such a Kat thing to do.

I guess, if I'd been trying to be fair, I might have conceded that we were approaching the ground at something on the order of three hundred miles an hour and cut her a little slack, but I still wasn't feeling terribly generous toward her, so I just concentrated on the speck of green grass streaking up toward us incredibly fast and sped up.

We screamed to a stop—well, she screamed, and I clamped a hand over her mouth for the last hundred feet—in the backyard of a small house. Kat was wriggling, but not thrashing, which was fortunate for her since I was only holding her with one hand. I brought us from three hundred miles per hour to zero pretty fast, and she snapped in my arms as I braced her, absorbing as much of the shock as I could. When we were motionless, a foot above the ground, I pulled my hand off her mouth heard her making a, "Huhhhhhhhhhhh," kind of whining and breathing sound.

"You all right?" I asked, gently lowering her feet to the ground.

She wobbled on unsteady legs for less than a second before she collapsed on the lawn. "N ... No, I am not all right," she said in a whisper. She looked around at the fenced-in yard around us. "Where are we?"

"Austin, Texas," I said, taking a quick glance at my phone to make sure I had it right. I did. I'd been checking it regularly before we made our final approach, looking at my GPS to be sure I didn't miss our stop.

"Why?" she asked, twisting around to look at me. "Why would you bring me to Texas?"

"Well, it's far from California for everyone who can't break the sound barrier at will," I said, looking around. The sun was up here, but not by too much. "You should be safe."

"You're just going to drop me off in some random yard?" Kat's jaw fell in disbelief. "Do you think I won't—what, I won't catch the first flight to LA?"

"No," I said. "I don't think you will."

Her eyes burned with resentment. "Well, I will. You can't stop me."

"I'm not going to even try," I said, and looked up when I saw motion at the sliding glass door to the house. "I'll leave that to them." I nodded as the door slid open.

"What the hell are you doing?" Reed hissed, stepping out onto a slab of concrete that comprised a patio. Augustus Coleman was peering out from behind his shoulder, eyes foggy with sleep and mouth open in a yawn, or maybe shock.

"Sorry to interrupt your boys' club poker night," I said. I grabbed Kat under the arm, hauling her to her feet and breaking skin contact in less than a second. "But I've got more work for you."

"More work?" Reed did not look happy. "We've been trying to catch a positive ID on Grayson Dieter for days—"

"We've been on our asses for days," Augustus said from behind him. "Taking shifts staring out the front window. Most boring assignment ever. I caught up on my homework on day one, and I've been waiting for Monday to come so they'll email me more so I have something to do besides watch his ass make little baby tornadoes on the coffee table."

Augustus nodded at Kat. "What's this?" He blinked. "Wait … is that …?"

Reed just rolled his eyes. "Now you want us to do stakeout and babysitting?"

"Dude, that's Kat Forrest," Augustus said, elbowing him hard in the ribs. He stepped out onto the patio, and I realized he was in his boxers and a t-shirt. "What's up?" he asked, nodding at her, smiling a little stupidly.

"Augustus," I said, looking meaningfully at his attire.

He got the hint in a second. "Oh! Oh, shit!" He disappeared back into the house.

Reed was slightly better dressed, at least, wearing jeans with his t-shirt. "She can't stay here," he said.

"It's funny you say that," I bumped Kat forward, and she started walking toward the patio like she was being forced to at gunpoint, "because here I thought I was your boss—"

"Ungh," Reed made a sound like a zombie in the dark. "You always do this when we butt heads over decisions, you pull the 'I'm your boss' card—"

"Just another reason why people don't like you," Kat said, a little sing-songy, either because she was gloating or because she was woozy from our rapid descent. Which I had done so as not to tip off the subject of the stakeout, by the way, not just to make Kat nauseous and scared. That was just a fringe benefit.

"Shut up," Reed and I said at the same time. His hair was still short from where it had been burned off a few months earlier, and at the moment he looked like the firebomb had taken his humor with it. "We're busy here," he said.

"You're watching a house for hours a day," I said as Kat and I stepped onto the patio. "You can watch her, too."

"I don't really need to be watched," Kat said, "I need to get back to LA—"

"So that more people can die on the altar of your career?" I eyed her with an unforgiving look. "How about 'no'?"

"I need to do press," she protested, crossing into whining

and making my ears feel like they were ready to bleed. "Disappearing right now is—"

"Wow," Reed said, cutting her off, "you really are shallow and vapid now. I argued for you, you know." He shook his head. "When Sienna said you were a total write-off as a human being."

"Thanks," Kat said, clearly meaning anything but. "But I don't need your approval."

"Okay, I'll watch her," Reed said, meeting my eyes, all trace of resistance gone.

"Knew I could count on you." I snapped my fingers and pointed at him, "Bro."

"Yeah, don't do that." Reed shook his head. "You can't pull it off."

My phone buzzed in my pocket and I went to check the caller ID. "Zollers," I said in pleasant surprise. "You mind getting her something to eat?"

"I'm not hungry," Kat said irritably, "and this is kidnapping, you know."

"Katrina Forrest," Reed said, once again rolling his eyes, "for your own protection and that of others, you are under arrest under the authority of the Metahuman Policing and Threat Response—"

"I know the name of the agency," Kat snapped as Reed took her arm in hand and I answered my phone.

"Hey yo," I said, looking out over the Austin morning. It was already kinda balmy, the sun shining and the air dry.

"Hey," Dr. Zollers said. "How are you doing?"

"I just had Kat placed into protective custody after physically hauling her out of Los Angeles," I said as Reed shut the sliding glass door behind him, giving me the illusion of privacy. "So ... I've had better and worse days, really."

"Did you enjoy that?" Zollers asked, slipping immediately into therapist mode.

"Uhmm ..." I gave it some thought. "Not really. We had a lovely argument in the middle of the desert, but frankly, I

could have done without it. It didn't exactly give me closure."
I paused. "Say, you're not just calling because I didn't book a
session this week, did you?"

"Well, as much fun as it is running a startup practice," he
said, and I could hear him smiling with just a hint of strain,
"no, I'm not so desperate for a paycheck that I need to bill
you for this—though it is going to come in at a special rate of
eight hundred dollars per hour—"

"You know I'd pay it," I said seriously.

"I know you would," he said. "But I'm just concerned by
what I've picked up in your emotional state, that's all. Also,
the news. This ... this villain you're up against ..."

"He's a doozy, isn't he?" I stared hard at the horizon, the
blue sky and fluffy white clouds. "He just ... man, he hates.
He's like a world champion hater. I don't like Kat or what
she does for a living, but this dude irrationally hates her with
a force that I can't even muster for Old Man Winter at this
point. Possibly for my first date the other night, though ..."

"He does seem like an injustice collector," Zollers said.
"Just from what I've seen on TV, anyhow. His exchanges
with you, documented on YouTube—"

"How is it that YouTube is like the historical archive of
my life?"

"—and you're right, he's furious about some past issues,
possibly related to his clash with Augustus."

"Yeah," I said. "I'll talk to Augustus about that in a
minute."

"Don't expect him to be much help," Zollers said. "I
took a look at the file the agency has—"

"How did you—" It only took me a second. "Never
mind. Stupid question."

"—and this Redbeard, as you've taken to calling him ...
he merits a line, and I don't think it's because Augustus
forgot him. It's because he only dealt with him for sixty
seconds or less."

"Yeah," I said, shaking my head. "Redbeard nearly killed

his girlfriend, and Augustus buried him. Now he's back, five months later, and he's mad about—well, everything."

"What you should consider," Zollers said, smooth as ever, "is what happened in the interim."

"Well, clearly Redbeard went crazy—"

"No, I mean—what do you think happened to him next?"

I shrugged even though he couldn't see me. "He probably found a tunnel and—"

"It could be," Zollers said, "but I looked at the geography, and I don't think there's much in the way of tunnels beneath Augustus's neighborhood, which is where that clash happened."

"Well, he had to get out of the ground somehow," I said, frowning. "He couldn't just—" I stopped. "Could he?"

"It's funny you ask," Zollers said, and I heard the sound of shuffling paper at his end. "I have a report here about a starvation-thin white man with an overgrown red beard and long hair turning up in the Indian Ocean, picked up by a passing freighter. They didn't know what to make of him."

"As one doesn't, when picking up a red-haired hobo-looking fellow in the middle of the Indian Ocean." I pondered it for a minute in the silence of the morning. "You think he drifted through the whole damned earth?"

"I suspect, yes," Zollers said. "He's a meta, probably pretty far up on the power scale"

"But he'd need to eat," I said, not believing it. "To drink. To breathe."

"When I was doing my practice at the Directorate, before you showed up," Zollers said, starting to lecture, "Dr. Sessions ran across a meta who had been entombed for a hundred years. No air, no water, no food."

"Uhhh ... I don't like where this is going ..."

"He seemed dead," Zollers went on, "like he was in a suspended state. We never did find out what type he was, because when Sessions and Perugini went to perform the autopsy—"

"Really, really don't like where this is going."

"—he sprang to life, scaring the hell out of both of them," Zollers said. "Now, he died shortly thereafter—"

"Of shock?"

"Of a scalpel to the eye. Dr. Perugini … she's not the sort you want to mess with."

"I called that even before there was an imminent danger of her becoming my sis-in-law." I hoped Reed was eavesdropping and heard that.

"Anyhow," Zollers said, "when Sessions did the autopsy, he speculated that the man first fed off all his fat reserves, and after that, his brain entered a state of—well, oxygen deprivation and malnutrition, as well as—"

"I get the gist," I said, definitely feeling skeeved out. "And now I know more about torturing a metahuman than I really wanted to."

"I'm sure the Nazis performed experiments of that sort that were probably even less humane," Zollers said. "In any case, this meta—he was mad by the time Perugini and Sessions revived him. Crazy. His brain lacked vital nutrients in addition to oxygen, and he was permanently damaged in a way that affected his cognitive function. He must have been high on the power scale as well, because we have very clearly documented cases of metahumans dying of oxygen deprivation."

"Remind me to avoid accidentally locking myself in a coffin."

"I thought you already slept in one during the day," Zollers deadpanned.

"Nice." I puckered my lips. "So Redbeard's genuinely crazy in addition to feeling wronged by me and Kat, for undefined reasons."

"He may not need clearly defined reasons, and that's the point. His mind is not functioning in a logical fashion."

"Neither is Kat's. Hey, maybe she's starved herself, too—"

"Sienna."

"Well, it's a possibility," I said, knowing that it wasn't. "Have you seen her bony ass?" I gave us a moment. "This guy's not going to stop, is he?"

"He's fixated on both of you," Zollers said. "He's failed a few times in trying to end at least Kat, if not both of you. But he won't be done until he's killed you."

I didn't bother to mention that he hadn't failed that hard, since Redbeard actually had killed me once already. That was the sort of thing I generally preferred to spring on my friends in person. "Well, he's going to have a hard time getting hold of Kat," I said. "But me … I'm going to have to go after him."

"Be careful when you do," Zollers said, and I could feel the sense of worry through the phone, "because in addition to being crazy as hell, he likely wants nothing more than to see you bleed and die in front of the whole wide world … a repayment for the sins he imagines you've committed against him."

77.

I stayed outside for a few minutes after I hung up with Zollers, just staring into the sky, hoping for an answer to come streaking down and hit me in the forehead. Unfortunately, it did not, and after less than sixty seconds, a little voice piped up from inside me instead.

You were awfully hard on Klementina, Aleksandr Gavrikov said quietly. Yes, he practically whispered in my head, which was a lot nicer than the shit that Bjorn or Wolfe usually pulled, two men who spectacularly failed at "indoor voice."

"For f—" I let out a hiss of exasperation. "She doesn't even like to be called Klementina anymore, Gavrikov. She doesn't remember you, or her life before. It's all gone. All that's left is Kat." I stared at a cloud shaped like a kidney. "Stupid, selfish, Kat."

You didn't know Klementina, Gavrikov said. *She was not selfish. Wounded, yes. Damaged, perhaps—*

"Your sister is damaged, all right. I'd help inflict more, if I weren't trying to self-improve."

—but not selfish. Never selfish.

"Times change," I said. "People change. She's changed, trust me."

She has the power to heal, to give life, Gavrikov said.

"Well, she's dealing out more death than me, lately," I said, tapping my foot on the thin grass. "And that takes some doing."

She is merely trying to do what—

"What she wants," I said, cutting him off pretty harshly. "She's doing what she wants, not what's right. Therefore, she is selfish."

We all want what we want.

"Yes," I said, losing patience, "but we don't all start getting people killed to get it, do we? There's the selfish thing again, see. Reasonable people are willing to maybe back it off when people start dying for what they want. You don't even have to be a hero to do that; you just have to not be a totally self-centered asshole."

There is still good in her.

"Yeah, well, I don't see it," I said, tilting my head back and looking up, "but maybe I'm the wrong person to be looking."

"Is that self-pity I hear?" Reed's voice came from behind me and I spun to see him standing at the sliding glass door, closing it quietly behind him.

"It's ..." I searched for an answer and did not find a good one. "Probably."

"Why ever would you feel sorry for yourself?" Reed asked. "It's not as though your life isn't completely perfect, every moment a blissful treasure free of stress and worry—"

"Where's Kat?" I asked, turning my attention back to my brother with a surge of alarm.

"Relax," he said, "Augustus is keeping two very watchful eyes on her."

"Probably also keeping a very drooling tongue on her as well."

"I don't rule that out," Reed said, "he does seem a bit starstruck." He took a couple steps off the patio into the yard. "You talking to the voices in your head?"

"Just the one that's pleading for clemency for Kat," I said, tapping my skull with my index finger a little too hard. Ouch. "What is it about brothers that blinds them to their sisters' faults?" I smirked at him as I asked.

He gave me a wary eye. "I don't think that's a universal thing."

"No?"

"Yeah, I got a really long list of yours. It's not something I can travel with, though, because the airlines dock you if you fly with a suitcase over 50 pounds—"

I raised my hand to playfully swat at him and gave him plenty of time to cringe away. "Love does tend to blind us," he said finally, continuing to get closer to me. "To faults, I mean. Probably why people who love themselves so much don't realize how shitty they are."

"I don't love myself enough to ignore how shitty I am," I said, uncomfortable with the sudden self-reflection. "I mean ... I know why people hate me. Kat busted me over the head with it, but she didn't really tell me anything I didn't already know."

"What'd she say?" Reed asked, eyes full of concern.

"Ohh ..." I played it back in my head. "I don't know. Something about not being attentive to others, but I wasn't really listening ..." I flashed a grin at him. "She said ... I kill people. Lots of people. And I've got powers. And I'm cold and mean ... yadda yadda, you know all this."

"Well," Reed said, slipping his thumbs in his pockets like a hillbilly with a pair of overalls, "if it makes you feel better ... you're less of those things lately, in my estimation."

"I'm trying," I said softly. I actually was, at least to the people I cared about.

"I know you are," he said. He put an arm around my shoulder and pulled me close. He smelled like queso and salsa, like freshly chopped onions, and I wrinkled my nose but didn't say anything. "Change isn't easy."

"Scott figured it out," I said. "The memory thing."

"Ouch. He mad?"

"Is the Pacific Ocean filled with water?"

"I don't know, you've seen it more recently than I have, and supposedly there's a drought."

"It's still there," I assured him. "And ... yeah. He's not happy."

"You didn't expect him to take it with grace and aplomb, did you?"

"I didn't expect to have to deal with it yet, if ever," I said with a sigh. "I know, I know ... I said I'd tell him, and I always meant to, but, you know ... later."

"You should tell him how it happened," Reed said, every muscle tense.

"I don't want to," I said and buried my face in his side. "And I damned sure don't want to do it before I find this Redbeard bastard and cathartically skin him alive."

"You need to tell him," Reed said. "The how is the context. If you don't tell him the how, he's going to be mad forever."

"I'm not sure he's going to get any happier after I tell him—" I sighed. "I'd rather start with something easier, like saying I'm sorry to J.J."

"What'd you do to my homie?" he asked with a frown.

"He probably thinks I accused him of bestiality."

"Does he think that *because* you accused him of bestiality?"

"... Maybe."

Reed let out a sigh. "You are getting better, but ... yeah, you should apologize for that, too. And tell Scott."

"Uhhh," I groaned, "making amends to people is hard. Screwing them up is just so much easier." My phone buzzed, and I lifted it up to see another text from Dick-O. "And it comes so naturally to me, because so many people clearly just want me to go human wrecking ball on them."

Ricardo

You are as glorious as the sunrise, and you burn my loins as though I had exposed myself to you all the day, without protection.

"What the hell?" Reed stared at my phone. "Who sent you *that*?"

"My new boyfriend," I said, hiding a smirk. "We might

just be married inside a month. For the money, naturally."

"And divorced in two?"

"Please, I'm not Kim Kardashian. Besides, I don't believe in divorce," I said with a straight face. "Murder, though—"

"I think I might approve, in this case." He made a gesture at the phone. "So what's your next move? How are you going to get this guy?" He waved off my phone. "Not *that* guy. Please, please, don't ever get *that* guy. Redbeard, I meant."

"I don't know," I said, staring at the sun, enjoying having my brother just stand there with me, like I wasn't alone for a few minutes. "I really don't."

78.

Scott

Scott found himself by the beach before dawn. Steven Clayton had tagged along, not that Scott had done much to protest the movie star hanging around with him. Clayton seemed hung up on Sienna, which stuck in Scott's craw, but what was he going to do? Deck the guy? He had an earnestness about him, and Scott was torn between warning him off and encouraging him, not sure whether he wanted to see Clayton get burned by Sienna or not.

"First time on the coast?" Steven asked, staring out at the Pacific with him.

"No." Scott shook his head. "I've been to LA a couple times before."

"I don't really like this town," Steven said, staring out at the indigo sky, still deep and dark, the sun yet to rise.

"Then why don't you leave?" Scott asked with a scoff. "You're kind of on top of the world, aren't you?"

"One person's top of the world is another person's bottom," Steven said with a shrug. "It's all perspective."

"What kind of screwed-up perspective do you have to have to see Mr. Hollywood, *People's* Sexiest Man, blah blah, as on the bottom of anything other than a neverending pile of sexy women?" Scott barely kept himself from laughing.

"Maybe I don't want sex and money in my life," Steven

said flatly.

"Every man wants sex and money."

"Well, I don't *just* want sex and money, okay?" Steven asked, now sounding a little annoyed.

Scott held his peace for a moment. "Sex, money and ... fame?"

"Not really."

"Drugs?"

Clayton gave him a hard look. "No."

"Because the fame gets you money, which can buy the drugs and—"

"I want a life, okay?" Clayton said, finally losing his patience. "Wife, kids ... you know?" He frowned. "And no drugs. Maybe a beer or two from time to time, but that's it."

Scott felt a rush of inexplicable anger. "You could find that wife and kids thing a lot of places other than here, if you put that in the deck above money, sex and fame."

"I like playing other people," Steven pulled his arms close to him, hugging himself against the wind that blew in off the ocean. "You know? Acting ... I really love it. The actual work. Have since I was a kid in a school play. Even the physical part of it, there's this satisfaction to getting in there in your stunts—"

"Yeah, I don't need to hear about that," Scott said, looking at the dark horizon. "I've done enough stunts of my own for one night."

"Jumping off a building without a wire or a parachute," Steven said, cocking his head, "that's a new one. I think I would have let my double handle that one."

"I don't have a double and this isn't a movie," Scott said. "Maybe you should go home."

"It's not that easy," Steven said.

"We came here in your car," Scott said dismissively. "You just go over there and start it up, drive off. I won't mind, I promise. This isn't your deal."

"It's not yours either," Steven said. "This guy—Redbeard

or whatever—he's not even after you." Clayton stretched, then shivered. "Man. This weather."

"Too cold for you?" Scott asked.

"It shouldn't be," Steven said. "I'm from Alaska. We have summer nights colder than this. But I've been down here a few years now, and maybe my blood got thin or something … I dunno. I guess I adapted. But one thing that hasn't happened, in all the time I've been here … I haven't forgotten how I was raised." He looked straight at Scott. "Bad things happen every day. Here, in this city, elsewhere in the world. It'd take a mightier man than me to feel like he could jump in and change things everywhere." He shook his head. "But this guy, Redbeard … he's killed people right in front of me. I don't need to feel like I can change the world to know that I've crossed him, I've hurt him, and this problem—this one, singular problem—I can help solve."

"This isn't going to go down like you think it will," Scott said. "These fights … they pretty much never get settled by straight up gunplay. It comes down to it, it's almost always powers that win the day."

"Well, I don't have powers," Steven said, "but I do have a gun and I've wounded this guy a few times with it. If I can wound him a little more, maybe open up the field for you guys … I'd consider that my civic duty. And I can't walk away from it."

"You might end up regretting that," Scott said, looking out over the ocean and extending his hand, subtly drawing water out and toward him. *Better replenish the stock*, he figured.

"I think I'd regret it more if I didn't see this through."

Scott blinked. "Yeah. I think I feel the same." *Even knowing Sienna is in this.*

79.

Kat

The house was a dive, a dump, a craphole. It didn't look like it had been redone since the 1970s, with its crappy, faded wood paneling on every wall, and baseboards that looked so weathered they might have been carved a century before the house's construction. She sat in the front room staring at the house across the street with Augustus, whom she had certainly heard about on TV and whatnot, though she hadn't met him until a few minutes earlier. He was a handsome enough guy, though really young, and he was obviously trying hard to split his focus between watching the house across the street and paying attention to her. Which was cute.

"So you've been working with Sienna for a few months now?" she asked, really pouring the honey into it.

"Yeah," he said, nodding, glancing at her and then back to the house. They were looking out on the street through a gap in the curtains occupied by white sheers. "When did she come to Atlanta? June, I guess ... anyway, not long."

"Mmhmm," Kat said with a nod, like she knew something he didn't.

"You know, my mom watches your show," Augustus said, looking out of the corner of his eye. "I, uh ... I've watched it, too."

"Well, thank you," she said. "We really work hard on

turning out an entertaining product."

"Well, you nailed that," Augustus said, staring out the window. "Lots of people must be watching." He fiddled with a pair of binoculars on a table, nearly knocking them over through nervous clumsiness.

She giggled disarmingly, trying to get him to relax. He looked up sheepishly. "It's okay," she said. "You don't have to be nervous. I don't bite." *I'm not Sienna*, she didn't say.

"Naw, I know that," he said, taking her seriously. "I, just, y'know ... you're famous and stuff."

She puffed up a little bit at that. "You seem awfully sensible," she said with a smile, "and I'm not just telling you that because you're a fan." She put a hand on his arm and ran it down to his elbow. He looked like he might jump out of his skin, and she lowered her voice. "Why's a bright guy like you in this?" She tilted her head toward the back of the house. "You know ... with Sienna."

He stared at her blankly. "Well ... because she's a hero, of course."

Kat's smile fled, and she snorted inadvertently. "Oh," she said, not really sure what to say. "Okay. That's it?"

"Well, the agency's paying for me to go to college," Augustus said, "but ... yeah. Financial incentive aside, I believe in what we're doing here. I believe in Sienna, in what she tries to accomplish." A hint of uncertainty ran across his young face. "Why did you leave?"

Kat felt herself slip into a performance answer that had nuggets of honesty couched in it. "You don't get what you want when you're running with her." A bristling feeling ran along her back and down the hairs on her arm that didn't even exist because she had them waxed off, dammit. "With Sienna it's all sacrifice and the job and doing ..." She drifted off and lost the thread.

"What's right?" Augustus asked, filling it in for her. He raised an eyebrow. "That's so horrible," he said, letting it drip with irony.

"I don't mean it like that," Kat said, shaking her head. "The way she does things, the way she runs things ... it's like living in hell. You don't get to live your life—"

"It's not been so bad for me," Augustus said with a shrug. "Though I tend to miss some classes here and there on assignment."

"Well, it was that bad for me," Kat sniffed. "You're not going to get rich working for the agency."

"Most people don't get rich at all, statistically speaking." He smiled. "Most of us are content to try and live our lives and hope to get merely ahead, rather than rich." He nodded deferentially. "Present company excluded, of course. I mean, obviously, you figured it out, cracked the 'rich' code."

"Yeah, I, uh," Kat fumbled, "I ... things are going well."

"You got what you wanted," Augustus said with a nod and a smile. "Swimming pools and, uh ... reality TV stars, I guess. Do you have a Ferrari? Because I would maybe consider selling out a little bit for—"

"No," she said, thinking of Taggert. She shuddered mildly, which was strange. "My agent has a ... he's got a ... I don't know, it's a Ferrari. He took me for a ride in it a few times ... before." She blinked. "When we first got to know each other and ..."

"Oh, that sounds impressive," Augustus said. "It's cool that he'd do that for you. Sounds nice."

"Well, he's ..." Kat's lip twitched. "I think he was just trying to ... impress me in order to ..." She rubbed her forehead.

"You okay?" Augustus asked.

A cold, clammy feeling ran down Kat's entire body. "I'm being used, aren't I?" It wasn't a question.

"Uhhh ..." Augustus looked around like he was in the middle of an ocean, sinking, and he needed to find a life preserver. "I don't ... uh ..."

"He used me," Kat said, a nauseous feeling crept into her stomach. "He used me and I let him. I let him because I thought—I thought—that I'd get what I wanted. That he'd make the connections, the introductions, that I'd have a career, and everyone would know me, that they'd ..." She felt cold chills run down her back. "I thought ... it would feel different. That this change would be ... that this time it would feel ... more right."

"What's wrong about it?" Augustus asked. "You got, like ... a dynamite house—"

"It's cold," Kat said, staring out the window.

"I ... never heard that about California—"

"It's me and a film crew and a bunch of people that rotate in and out of my life on filming days and never show up when the camera isn't rolling if they don't want to talk about a business deal." Kat swallowed hard. "Days when there's no filming, it's like ..." She rubbed her face. "I tweeted that I was ... hanging out down one of the local restaurants ... just hanging out ... because I ..." Her face crumpled, though she tried to act, tried to keep it straight, "... I didn't want eat lunch alone again. I just wanted people to ... anyone to ..." She rubbed her eyes. "And people showed up, thank God, because ... we hadn't been filming for a month, and—and—and ... I don't think I had a conversation with anyone other than my driver during that time, and it was before the Bruces, my bodyguards ..."

"So ... you're lonely," Augustus said carefully, almost like the words were a chemical mixture that might blow up in his face.

"Oh, God, yes," Kat said, realizing the truth of it. "All the time. How can you be surrounded by people ... have the cameras—have them yell, 'Cut!' and then no one talks to you until they start rolling again, except to give a little direction? How does that happen?"

"Uhmm ... because you don't have any friends?" Augustus asked, wide-eyed. His eyes got bigger. "I'm sorry, I didn't mean to—"

"To tell the truth?" Kat asked, stunned, staring straight

ahead. "I *don't* have any actual friends. Why has that been so hard to say? So ... hard to realize?" She put her face in her hands. "I busted Sienna so hard on the fact that people don't like her, but they supposedly like me, and I'm more alone than she is."

"I feel like I should get you some help," Augustus said, standing abruptly. "You want me to call Dr. Zollers for you?"

She sniffed and looked up. "Dr. Zollers? He's back?"

"Yeah," Augustus nodded so hard it looked like his head would spring off. He looked desperately uncomfortable at Kat's display of emotion. "I can call him. This is not even a thing. I'll even pay for your therapy session if you—"

Kat sniffed, staring out the window, and caught motion in front of the house across the way. "Hey, were you watching this house for someone?"

Augustus turned and peered out. "Yeah, we're—Oh, oh! That's him! That's Grayson Dieter, he's the—that's the guy we're here to apprehend!" He spun in excitement, as though looking for Reed, and, not finding him, locked wide eyes on Kat. "I gotta get Reed. We need to move on this—but if I shout, he'll hear, because he's a meta—"

Kat stood and vaulted over a nearby couch as she went for the front door. She paused at the handle as she turned it, and it sprung open. "Get him, go. I'll follow this guy." And she plunged out the door before Augustus could respond.

The air was warm and the sun was like fuel for her soul. She walked down the house's short driveway with a spring in her step. This was natural. This was normal. This wasn't the half-assed walk down the driveway of her house in LA in the mornings, a fight against gravity just to get out of bed and propel herself into action for the cameras.

This was real. This was important. There was a fugitive not a hundred feet away from her.

She looked him over as he walked down his own short driveway at a hurried pace. His shoulders were hunched, hands driven into his pockets, his dark brown hair long and hanging over his eyes. He was glancing around furtively, as if someone might jump out at him any minute now.

He rotated his head to look at her, catching her motion as he stepped across the lawn toward the sidewalk, and did a double take. When he saw her, his eyes went wide and his mouth dropped open, and she knew she'd been recognized.

"Grayson Dieter!" she shouted, her voice crackling with authority over the quiet Austin neighborhood, "Stop where you are and put your hands in the air!"

Dieter looked dumbstruck, frozen on the grass, hands still jammed in his pockets. He stood like that for a solid second before his meta reflexes caught up with him and he started to run.

Kat threw out a hand by instinct, feeling the woven roots of the grass beneath Dieter's feet. She commanded them, roots that were adapted to the dry climate, grass that wasn't dying of thirst, and she compelled it to action.

Before Dieter even took a step, the grass had lashed across his feet, rooting him to the earth. Dieter's eyes got even wider as he lost his balance and fell forward, jaw meeting sidewalk because his hands were trapped in his pants pockets.

Kat sprinted across the street as Dieter lay there, dazed, and she flipped him onto his back. He stared at her with glazed eyes that snapped into focus, and he ripped his hands from his pockets—

Kat snapped a hard punch into his jaw, rocking his head back into the concrete sidewalk. *That's for you, Taggert, for using me.*

She followed it with another, seizing his t-shirt collar with her other hand and yanking him back up like a punching bag attached to a chain. She hit him again, and again, and again, and again—

"Whoa!" Sienna's voice flooded Kat's consciousness as hands seized her and pulled her roughly off of Grayson

Dieter. She looked down and saw a bloodied, mangled face, bones broken and eyes rolled up in his head. "Holy shit, Kat, what the hell did you do?" Sienna asked, pushing her out of the way.

"I stopped him," Kat said, staring down at the damage to Grayson Dieter's face. She raised a finger to point at him and realized her knuckles were bloody, skinned from the force of the blows she'd rained down him. "Right?"

"Oh, you stopped him all right," Augustus said, trotting up as Reed landed in a gust of wind a few paces ahead of him. "You damned near killed him, also, but you definitely stopped him."

Kat stared at her knuckles, at the breaks in the skin that gently oozed blood. "Oh. Oh my."

"Uhh," Reed said, kneeling next to Dieter, "I ... don't know if this guy's going to make it to the hospital. That's a skull fracture, and he's—"

"Oh, shush, Mr. Dr. Perugini," Sienna said, folding her arms in front of her, and looking straight at Kat. "Kat ... do your thing."

Kat blinked. "You ... want me to finish him off?"

Sienna's jaw dropped slightly. "No. I want you to heal him, which is your thing. If I wanted him beaten to death, I would have said it was time to do '*my* thing.'"

"Apparently, 'your thing' isn't just yours anymore," Augustus said, looking at Grayson Dieter with more than a little alarm. "Because ... I mean, *damn*. She racked him up."

"Oh," Kat said, "right." She advanced on Dieter slowly, looking down at the bloodied, battered face. "I guess I should ..."

"Yeah," Sienna said, "I guess you should."

Kat knelt, looking at Dieter all the while. His eyes were rolled back in his head, his tongue looked like it had fallen back in his throat, his mouth open and most of his teeth missing. "Did I really do that?" she whispered.

"Well, I damned sure didn't," Sienna muttered. "For

once."

Kat put a hand on Dieter's jaw, felt that strange crawl down her skin, that bizarre tingle that she never really felt anymore. It wasn't like nerves or chills. It was a warm feeling, a lovely one, really, like stepping next to a fire on a cold night, or diving into the ocean on the hottest day of summer.

Her skin flushed and the energy flowed to the tips of her fingers, down into the jaw of Grayson Dieter. He groaned and his muscles contracted, his bloodied wounds knitting together like a perfect CGI demo. His eyes rolled forward and he looked around, his jaw assuming its normal shape and teeth sprouting from the empty, bloody spots in his gums.

"What ... the hell ...?" Grayson Dieter asked, looking at the faces around him in surprise.

"Yeah, you're under arrest," Sienna said, stepping forward and hauling Dieter to his feet just so she could kick him down to his knees. She held out a hand and Reed stepped up, slapping cuffs onto Dieter's wrists.

"Wha ...?" Dieter mumbled, looking around in alarm. "Where'd that ..." he locked eyes with Kat. "Get her away from me!"

"Yeah, I'm on that," Augustus said, dragging Dieter to his feet as Reed closed the cuffs on his other wrist. "Come on, Grayson. You've been a shy boy lately, keeping your head down. I can see why you wanted to do that now, getting your ass kicked by a 98-pound little white girl? Man, you gotta be embarrassed as hell right now ..." Reed followed behind, casting a look at Sienna and Kat both, inclining his head as he walked away. There was something being communicated between he and Sienna, and Kat picked it up even though she couldn't tell what was being said.

Sienna, for her part, just stared at Kat, blinking every so often. It was the only sign Kat had that she wasn't being watched by a statue or a dead person. "Nicely done," Sienna finally said, nodding once at Kat, then walking off back across the street.

Kat just stood there, basking in the strange, warm glow that ran through her skin. "It really was," she said. Because for the first time in a long time, she knew she'd done right.

80.

Sienna

I was still shaking my head from Kat beating our perp when I remembered I had things to do. Nothing like watching the declawed kitten kick some ass to remind you that other asses were waiting for you to kick them as well.

She did well, Gavrikov said.

Yeah, I replied silently. *Probably just looking to blow off some steam.*

Perhaps, he replied.

I shook that one off and grabbed my cell phone, vaulting straight over the house and landing in the backyard, my own private refuge. I could hear Augustus still chiding Grayson Dieter as he herded him inside. He and Reed would need to make arrangements for transporting Dieter back to our prison in Minnesota at the ruins of the old campus. And Kat would probably have to go with them, for safety. Hers, clearly. Definitely not Dieter's. She'd really pounded the hell out of that guy.

I ignored the voicemail I'd acquired from an unknown number and looked at the contact I'd pulled up, taking a deep breath. "All right, J.J.," I muttered and hit the dial button, pressing the cold screen to my cheek in the warm morning air.

"Hello," came the deflated answer on the fourth ring. I

could tell just by listening to him that he'd clearly been warring with himself on even answering. "What do you want?"

"I wanted to say I'm sorry," I said, my eyes rolling painfully as I coughed out my apology. "I was needlessly cruel in what I said, and it was wrong, and I regret it. You're a valuable member of our team, and without you, we'd be spinning uselessly, like a futzed compass, on more occasions than I can count."

There was a giant, gaping silence. I waited, listening. "J.J.?" I finally asked.

"I'm just waiting for your request," J.J. said, clearly filled with suspicion.

"No requests," I said. "Just an apology. I'll let you go." I started to hang up.

"Waiiiiit," J.J. said. "You weren't calling me for info? You always call me for info, for hacking—"

"Because I can't do any of those things myself," I explained. "I'm useless with tech and you know it. But I don't have a technical issue now, and I assume if you had anything to share regarding our perp, you'd have pushed it through channels, so … no, I was just calling to apologize. That was it, and I'm done, so …"

"Huh." He sounded actually dumbstruck. "That is so weird."

A little tiny flash of annoyance coupled with embarrassment ran through me. "Me apologizing to you is weird?" I paused. "Right. It is weird."

"Well, yeah, that," he said, not decreasing my annoyance, "but I was actually mustering up the courage to call you when you rang."

I clutched the phone tighter. "You were? Not a social call, I assume."

"Hahah, no, you wouldn't be first on my list if—uh, I mean … no. It wasn't." I heard the tapping of keys in the background of the call. "I got an anonymous email a few minutes ago that kind of laid out what's going on in LA."

"What?" I squinted, looking up into the sunny day. "What are you talking about?"

"Someone's laid out the plan behind this Redbeard guy—real name Karl Nash, by the way," J.J. said. "And what's going on here is ... well, there's more to it than we thought."

81.

I stood in stark silence in the house in Austin, surrounded by Augustus, Reed, Kat, and Grayson Dieter, who was watching us while doing his best impersonation of a picture on the wall, silent and motionless. He watched Kat with frightened eyes the whole time, though.

"Wait," Augustus said, looking at me with a puzzled gaze, trying to sort through what I'd just told him, "so this isn't just a crazy guy on a rampage, in the classic manner of young, socially awkward and/or mentally ill young white men?"

"Hey," Reed said, frowning.

"No," I said. "Karl Nash—that's Redbeard's name—he is crazy, socially awkward and on a rampage. But he's also got a backer and a plan."

"Dude's been causing a lot of seemingly random havoc for a man with a plan," Augustus said.

"It hasn't been that random, though," I said. "He planned out the hotel attack and the one on MacArthur Park to cause maximum casualties."

"But there are easier ways to kill a whole bunch of people if you're a meta," Reed said. "I mean, the guy probably proved it with his impromptu train massacre, didn't he? That was more lethal than anything except the Luxuriant attack."

Kat was watching us all hash it through, as quiet as Dieter. "If he just wanted to kill people, why target me?" Her eyes flashed, and she glanced at me for just a second. "I mean … us. What's the plan there?"

"Well, according to J.J.'s source," I said, still puzzling over why someone would have sent us this heads up, "Nash—Redbeard—"

"I don't like that name for him," Reed said, shaking his head.

"Feels like it's not menacing enough," Augustus agreed.

"Guys," I snapped. "Explaining the big scheme here. How about you both zip it and debate supervillain names on your flight back to MSP?"

"Sorry," Reed said. "So what's his play?"

"There's this neighborhood," I said, still trying to wrap my brain around everything J.J. had said to me, "called Elysium. Great location, but it was built in like, the forties and it's become a real crime-ridden mess—"

"As all great havens of the Greek dead do, given time," Reed cracked.

"—anyway, Nash's backer is setting up to provoke another rampage right there in Elysium," I said. "They're hoping to draw me into a fight—"

"They want to get into a fight with you?" Augustus asked, mouth slightly agape. "That is *the* worst plan ever. Do they not know how that always turns out?"

"Yes, Karl is likely to die," I said, "but you have to keep in mind, he doesn't care. He's a nihilistic, mentally damaged glory-killer who just wants people to remember his name when he's dead. He wants to be noticed, to be the center of attention, and to be remembered so bad that he's willing to go out in a blaze of glory in order to make that happen." I took a deep breath.

"So what's that get his backer?" Reed asked with a shrug. "I mean, other than this neighborhood—Elysium—leveled to the ground?"

"That's what it gets him," I said, my lips pressed tightly together.

Augustus got it first. "Because if the neighborhood gets

leveled in a meta fight—"

"Acts of gods," Reed said, understanding washing over him. "The residents' homeowners insurance won't pay—"

"And this guy comes in with cash and buys them out," I said. "That's why Karl has been using explosives so much. He's planted explosives under every house, and so even if the fight doesn't destroy it all, the insurance companies are going to claim it's all in the same big shit pie and deny the claims. These people will be left with plots of empty land and not a dime of recompense—assuming they survive."

"That's dirty," Augustus said, shaking his head. "I bet you anything the kingpin behind this got his idea from what happened to my neighborhood, because if not for Cavanagh shelling out to rebuild our houses before he died, we would have been in the same situation."

"Wow," Reed said, shaking his head. "Why is it always land schemes in LA?"

"Have you seen the price of a three-bedroom out there?" Kat asked, scoffing. "This is gonna be like printing your own money. The price of land in that neighborhood is going to triple or quadruple overnight. Elysium is between the beach and downtown, right off a major freeway—it's the best location you could ask for, and all it needs is to be completely destroyed and rebuilt." She made a face. "That's so evil, driving people out of their homes ... but—"

"Don't finish that thought," I said, shaking my head at her. "I need to stop this from happening."

"How?" Reed asked. "I mean ... how do you stop the invisible man?"

"All due credit to Wells, he's not invisible," Augustus said, "he can just, y'know, make parts of himself pass through solid matter. He's more like 'The Ephemeral Man.' 'The Substanceless Man'?" He frowned. "'The Ghost'?"

"Pretty sure that last one's been done to death," Reed said with a frown. "Only utter hacks would name a character 'The Ghost.'"

"Speaking of people without substance," I said, "you two need to take Kat with you back to Minnesota."

"I'm sitting right here," Kat said, going from zero to outraged in a heartbeat. "And I'm not going with them."

"Fine, you can stay here in Austin," I said.

"I need to come with you," she said, with a different kind of fervor than she'd exhibited in the desert.

"Look," I said, sighing, "let me take care of this, and then you can go back to your life and your cameras and whatever, okay?"

"No." She shook her head. "This is my responsibility."

I froze in the middle of constructing my next argument. "Whaaa …?"

"For whatever reason," Kat said, bowing her head, "this—I don't want to call him by his name, that's giving him too much credit—Redbeard—he picked me as a target." Her head came up, and there was a lot of anger in those green eyes. "He killed … so many people trying to get to me. I may have been a secondary or a publicity target or whatever in the eyes of his backer, but this guy made it personal. This is my responsibility, and I can't just hide my face while people are dying."

I stared at her. "Are you just blowing smoke up my ass?"

"What?" She frowned. "No. Why would I …?"

"To be 'brave,'" I said, using the air quotes. "Like you said before."

"I don't …" Kat looked away. "No, not like that. No cameras, no … Hollywood bullshit." She looked back up, determined. "I want to help you stop this guy." She brought up her bloody knuckles. "I want to make him go solid and beat his ass."

Grayson Dieter made a pained noise and his chair scuffed the floor as he scooted back from Kat and hit the wall. "Now that's brave," Augustus said, clamping on Dieter's shoulder to stop his pointless, fearful slide.

"Kat," I said, looking right at her. "This could … this guy

is serious. He wants to kill you, and this is his last act. You could die. That'd put a pretty definite end to your career. I mean, you've led us into a few stupid things the last few days, but I don't for a minute believe you actually want to die."

She pushed the hair back off her forehead. "I don't want to die. But worse than that is the thought of living and knowing I could have helped put this ... this scum away, and I just sat idly by while he destroyed a whole neighborhood. I can't do that anymore. It's not about me, it's not about being seen ... it's about doing the right thing."

"Well, okay then," I said, nodding. "I guess we need to get back to California and beat old Karl like the red-headed sonofabitch that he is."

82.

Scott

"Hey," Steven said, answering his phone and flipping on the speaker. "How's it going?"

Scott stood back, glancing at the screen. It had Sienna's name on it, and the sound of wind rushing came out over the speaker. "Hey, I got your message," Sienna's voice crackled, then lowered. "Stop writhing around like an angry baby."

Steven looked at Scott, eyebrows creased, perplexed. "Uh … okay?"

"Not you," Sienna's voice rang through, clearer now even in spite of the sound of wind. "I was talking to Kat. Stop it."

"I'm not writhing!" Kat shouted in the background. "You're holding me with one arm, and it's awkward. I feel like you're going to drop me."

"I *am* going to drop you if you don't stop writhing, and then you'll be sitting this fight out with a cactus up your skinny ass."

"I would make the cactus dodge out of the way."

"You couldn't move the cactus far enough away, I would aim you right square at the damned thing—"

"Umm, hello?" Steven asked experimentally. "Where are you?"

"Yes. Sorry," Sienna said. "We're on our way back to LA right now."

"Both of you?" Scott asked, his voice breaking unexpectedly in the middle. Where had that come from?

"Who is that?" Sienna asked, a little tinny.

"It's Scott." Scott stared at the phone, waiting for a response.

"Oh. Well. Good," it came at last. "Because we've got a major problem and, uh … we could use all the help we can get."

Scott stared at the phone skeptically, but Steven spoke before he could answer. "What's going on?"

"Redbeard's got a final attack planned," Sienna said. "He and his backer—"

"This guy's got a backer?" Steven asked.

"Like an executive producer!" Kat called out in the background.

Steven met Scott's eyes in the silence. "Yeah," Steven said finally into the awkwardness that followed, "I got that. Who is it?"

"Uhmm," Sienna said, clearly thinking about it, "J.J. told me the name, but I don't … I hadn't heard the name before. Buchanan … uh … Beverton? No, that's not it."

"Buchanan Brock?" Scott asked, blinking away his surprise.

"Wait, you know the bad guy?" Kat asked over the crackling speaker.

"He's the reason I'm out here," Scott said, meeting Steven's eyebrow-raised gaze. "He wanted a business deal with my father, so I came out here to negotiate."

"Well, he's pulling Redbeard's strings," Sienna said. "He's been running this show from the start. They're planning to start a fight with me in the Elysium neighborhood so he can come in and buy the place up at discount prices when all those peoples' homeowners insurances deny their claims."

"That can't be," Scott said, shaking his head. "I met with him just before …" The cold realization washed over him. "Just before the first attack on Kat. I was literally shaking his hand when I saw her and went over. Redbeard came at her like two seconds later. Damn."

"And you, naturally," Sienna said, "pulled the panic button and called in the cavalry—namely me, which was what he wanted all along."

"Even now," Scott said, bitterness rolling through him as he shook his head in disgust, "people are using me to get to you."

"Don't feel too bad," she said, "it wasn't like he wanted me as a person, either. He just wanted me to come to town because of the destruction I bring everywhere I go."

"Tell me about it," Scott said, looking pointedly in warning at Steven, who looked coolly unmoved.

"So Buchanan Brock is the bad guy in all this," Steven said. "He was at the president's fundraiser at Anna Vargas's house, too, just before that went to hell."

"He called me after the Luxuriant disaster," Scott said, shaking his head. "Yeah. I should have known. He wasn't just being a nice guy; he's tangled in this mess all the way."

"He's not the imminent threat, though," Sienna said. "That's Redbeard. He's got Elysium wired to blow and he's probably going to start the show any second now."

"How do we stop him?" Steven asked, concern furrowing his brow.

Silence filled the air. "This guy wants attention, right?" Kat asked over the crackling speaker.

"Yeah ..." Sienna said.

"So, if we don't give it to him ..."

"He's just gonna make louder and louder noises until he gets it," Scott said. "And he's certainly shown he's not afraid to make big noises with those bombs of his."

"Yeah, but what if we actively drove any attention away?" Kat asked, her voice run through with a hope Scott couldn't recall hearing from her in a long while.

"Uh, Kat," Steven said, frowning, "one of the defining characteristics of the press is that no matter how ugly the shitshot, they want pics and video of every single turd. People don't look away from that sort of thing, and this guy is promising spectacle. Bombs going off in any neighborhood are going to get their attention pretty definitely, whether we want them to or not."

"Then we need to make sure they don't go off," Scott said, jumping right to the conclusion.

"Scott," Sienna said, adding more than a little condescension, "it takes like, a second to press a detonator. Less if you're a meta. How are we supposed to stop him from doing that this time?"

"It's simple." Scott blinked, and once more, the answer came him as if handed out of the fog that had settled on his mind. "We do what Kat suggested ... and then we give him exactly what he wants ..."

83.

Karl

The hour was almost at hand, and Karl was ready. He had his master detonator on hand, the one wired to all the houses in the Elysium neighborhood, and he was ready to pull the trigger. The only thing he had to do first was get some attention.

The sun was coming up, and he was leaned back against the headrest in the car. It had been a sleepless, listless, restless few hours. He'd gone through the burgers, all of them, figuring if he was going to have a last meal, it should be a good one, so he'd eaten every last bit of what he'd taken from Amy the burger chef, including the now-soggy fries.

He was stuffed and feeling sick, but he couldn't sleep because of excitement and anticipation. It was like waiting for Christmas as a kid, he thought, though he couldn't really remember that.

If there was a downer in all this, a regret he had, it was that Kat Forrest was going to skate out of this mess. That was a bummer. She should have died, he should have ripped her guts out, but she was a coward, so that wasn't going to happen. Sienna Nealon had gotten her out once and for all, he would bet on that. No, he'd have to settle for Nealon. She'd come like a dog when he rang the bell and started killing cops, of that he was sure.

He took a deep breath through his nose, ran his fingers over the smooth interior of the Buick. He was sick of this car. He'd want to make sure he got it close to the explosions when the time came, just for a little extra collateral damage. Because he could, and it'd be fun and satisfying. Not as satisfying as killing a mess of cops, but still …

Another deep breath. The moment was almost here.

84.

Sienna

I dropped off Kat where she asked me to as soon as I got back to LA and set about my work, streaking across the sky around downtown, phone in hand, seeking out my first target. In truth, I didn't really need my phone for this one, so I dropped it at the top of the US Bank Tower and shot off toward the Hollywood Hills to get down to business.

The sun was barely up, but it wasn't like the Hollywood sign was really difficult to see, probably even in the dark. I lingered in the sky overhead for about two minutes, making crazy loop-de-loops like I was trying to dodge something, and flinging fire from my hands, shooting a foe that wasn't there. I tossed in a few nets of light for the sake of being flashy, then sighed, knowing I couldn't postpone this next part any longer.

I realigned, heading up into the sky out of easy view of cameras, and focused in on the white letters of the sign. They looked … big, even from up here. They also looked solid, which was the part that worried me more than the size, but this was no time to be a coward.

"Be brave," I said almost mockingly, like I was saying it to Kat or something.

And then I came shooting at them at subsonic speed, bracing myself.

Wolfe, I said.

No problem, he replied, and I cringed as I rocketed closer.

There are nine letters in Hollywood, and I felt every damned one of them as I smashed through the supports of the Hollywood sign at high speed, ripping it apart and sending pieces rolling down the hill.

Me, I went rolling, too, but through the sky in an end-over-end flight, my head aching and spinning. I looked back and saw the sign utterly destroyed, falling down the hill in a shattered mess.

I righted myself and shot off into the sky again, gaining altitude and hopefully escaping the cell phone cameras that were doubtless filming the destruction I'd just wrought.

"One down," I muttered, still feeling the aches from that one. I hated this plan, but I didn't have a better one, so I zoomed back to the US Bank tower to collect my phone for the next part of it.

85.

My next target was a little harder to find. I used my GPS to hone in on 6925 Hollywood Boulevard, then snuck up on Grauman's Chinese Theater from behind. I left my cell phone on top of the roof before scooting about six blocks north and then going into the sky again. I did another aerial acrobatics display, shooting fire and light at my unseen pursuer, putting on a damned good stunt show, if I say so myself, and then I zoomed down and buzzed Hollywood Boulevard, pulling up hard into the clouds just above Grauman's box office after I found my target landing zone.

I took a moment for a breather while I was safely nestled in the clouds. Stunt flying was not the easiest work, and shooting fire and light was kind of tiring, too. Plus, it lacked the joyful exuberance of actually pounding the stuffing out of a worthy enemy.

Still, it had to be done.

My moment's respite ended, I dropped out of the clouds, limp as though I'd been knocked out, face down in a hard, plummeting fall.

I did steer a little bit, because I could do it without looking like anything other than a rag doll, and as a result, I landed exactly where I meant to, smashing the shit out of the Hollywood Walk of Fame star I'd targeted.

It was Godzilla's. I figured he'd understand seemingly random destruction better than anyone. Other than maybe

Sean Penn.

I lay insensate on Godzilla's shattered star, letting people take video and pictures of my 'unconscious' body for about twenty seconds while I let Wolfe's powers heal the minimal damage I'd just done. Strangely, no one tried to render any help, and I didn't hear anyone call 911. Lots of sounds of pictures being taken, though.

This effing town, I tell ya.

I blinked my eyes, spitting out blood and putting on my best determined look. I staggered to my feet and spat on the sidewalk. "Son of a bitch," I said, loud and clear, and zoomed back into the sky.

I stealthily retrieved my phone and moved on, ignoring the ache in my back from the landing. Naturally, Scott would have come up with a plan that both made sense and caused me pain. The jackass. I flew on to my final target, just wanting to get this over already so I could get back to battering people who actually deserved it instead of beating the hell out of myself.

86.

Scott

"I hope this works," Scott said, riding shotgun as Steven steered the car down the freeway at a few miles per hour. They'd done their part, made a scene at the beach, staged a little metahuman drama using Scott's powers, enough to get people wondering what the hell was going on, hopefully draw some press. That coupled with Sienna's maneuvers …

Scott sighed as Steven hit the brakes again. They weren't exactly moving fast, and there was a hell of a backup as far as he could see. It wasn't even seven o'clock yet. "Though I'd have more hope if we could get there …"

"It's Los Angeles," Steven said with more than a little impatience of his own. He jerked the wheel to the right and rode the shoulder for three hundred yards before hitting an exit that did not say anything about the Elysium neighborhood. When Scott looked at him questioningly, the actor shrugged. "I don't think the freeway's going to do much moving this morning. Back streets are probably a better bet since we're still about two miles from Elysium."

"Okay," Scott said, hanging onto the hand rest as Steven jerked the wheel and made an illegal right turn. Horns honked and the actor looked decidedly unimpressed. "Don't get us killed on the way there, please."

"I will take that under advisement," Steven said, driving

like he was in a movie. Damn, Scott thought, watching someone else do something awfully similar three lanes away in a bright red sports car, what is it with this town?

87.

Sienna

I thought about trying to light the La Brea tar pits on fire, but decided that "ecological disaster" was a step above what I was aiming here for, so instead I made a horrendous crash landing in front of Griffith Observatory, creating enough work to keep the gardening staff rolling in overtime for six months.

It hurt, ripping across the lawn, twisting my limbs as I came down, listening to bones break and reset, to nerves cry out and then stop as Wolfe's power healed them. I'd done this much the same as I'd done the other landings, except this time I skidded for about a hundred yards. Or at least it felt like a hundred yards. Or maybe a hundred miles.

"Ouch," I said, rolling limply around my landing sight. The camera phones were out again, but at least these people had the grace not to stick them directly in my face. Maybe they just knew how to use the zoom feature. "I am so going to kick your ass for this," I said, plenty loud enough for them to hear me, and I looked into the sky above as I said it.

That's right, Hollywood. You got me to act. Way to bring out the lying liar in me.

I peeled myself out of the dirt, brushed myself off, cast a scathing look at the empty sky above, and zoomed off toward the heavens. I'd made enough of a mess to get the

Los Angeles press chasing its own tail in three different locales around the city. Hopefully that coupled with the tipoff I'd given to Detective Waters about what was coming would keep them busy.

I'd done absolutely everything I could to clear out the Elysium neighborhood of the kind of trouble and attention that Karl Nash was looking for.

All that was left was to go to Elysium and confront Redbeard, and make sure that attention-seeking whore regretted ever getting mine.

88.

Karl

The cops went screaming past in a line of patrol cars just as Karl was about to pull out to start his attack. There was no mistaking what had happened.

Someone had just captured the spotlight he intended for himself.

Karl's jaw tightened as he watched the last in the line of cars go by, its lights disappearing under a freeway overpass, the sound of the siren fading into the distance. He didn't care for this at all. He clenched his teeth and clamped his hands on the steering wheel to keep them from shaking.

Who would dare …?

It was probably nothing. Just some punk who'd done something stupid, no big deal. Whatever had happened, the cops probably thought it was him. When they realized he wasn't involved, they'd come rushing back, especially if he gave them a solid reason for doing so. And he had a pretty good one in mind.

89.

Taggert

Aaron Taggert had had a marvelous few days. His number one star was absent after a horrendous, sympathy-and-awe inducing incident that had resulted in widespread destruction and the death of more of his rival producers than he could count, her recently completed *Vanity Fair* shoot had come back full of beautiful, breathtaking pictures, and better than that, he'd gotten laid last night by a nineteen year-old production assistant who had bragged about being a gymnast in high school. He hadn't even had to try very hard on that one, no booze, no pills, nothing but a few idle promises about what he could do for her, and she'd done for him plenty enough to give him a great big capper on his week.

Yeah, it was a good life. That bodyguard he'd hired for Kitten had predictably sucked, completely inadequate to the task, but he looked good to Kitten, and that was what had mattered.

Taggert had his suspicions that Kitten was fine, of course, based on everything he'd heard from the production crew on location, but even if she turned up dead, the second season of *Beyond Human* was already in the can, and with the death of so many big wheels on the scripted side of Hollywood in the Luxuriant disaster, his star was about to rise, big time. There was a void to fill, after all, and he was just the guy to fill it.

Just like I did with that nineteen year-old last night, he thought with a guffaw. What was her name again? Ehh, it didn't matter.

He left his production office with a song in his heart. The sky was the limit, no possibility too far-fetched after last night. He was gonna make so much scratch he might as well have his own mint. But there was nothing else to do today except "participate" in the mourning by being seen at all the right funerals and wakes. Hands would be shaken, ideas would be batted back and forth in whispers, because the scraps needed to be collected. This town didn't stop for anyone, after all.

He thought about taking the SUV, especially since Kitten wouldn't be needing it or the driver, but this was a day where he actually felt like driving, so Taggert headed down to the garage in his production office, keys in hand, ready to take his prize for a spin. Hell, it was older than the women he'd bedded for the last few years, he thought with a laugh. Prettier and less needy, too.

He looked around at the spot where his 1961 Ferrari Spyder had been parked. It was empty.

"What the hell?" Aaron Taggert muttered to himself.

90.

Sienna

When Scott had said that we were going to give Redbeard what he wanted, I'd assumed he meant feeding Kat to him as some sort of bait. Now, I wasn't merciless enough to think we'd, y'know, stand idly by while he skinned her alive or anything ...

Probably. We probably wouldn't do that.

Anyway, I'd started listening to his plan with the preconceived notion that he was counting on ol' Karl to want to kill Kat so badly he'd suspend all reason to do so. He had, after all, seemed to fixate on her above all else.

But Scott—wisely, annoyingly—had pointed out that really, Kat was likely the first-string target all this time because Brock had wanted to draw me out here to LA and thought—annoyingly, rightly—that Kat plus Scott would get that job done. And here I was in Tinseltown, so I guess I was the stupid one for stumbling ass over teakettle right into that trap. Me and my dumb nobility and stuff, making me all predictable.

So anyway, Scott then pointed out that, really, Kat coming back after the Luxuriant would really just throw up a giant red flag for anyone with half a brain. And we had to assume that in spite of whatever neurological damage ol' Redbeard had suffered, he still at least *had* a brain. Therefore, putting her front and center as bait would probably raise Karl's worry level when we needed the bastard lulled.

Oh, I wanted to kill Scott. So badly. Because of course, he'd gone and used reason, and suggested that the only person that Redbeard would REALLY, REALLY want to kill that would actually come after him would be—

—naturally—

me.

And so I found myself flying low and slow a few hundred feet above the Elysium neighborhood, working a steady course toward Redbeard's bolt-hole, which, if Detective Waters had done her job by now, would be empty, along with every house for a block in every direction (because of the bombs he'd planted in his own house, duh).

It was by no means a perfect plan, seeing as the rest of the neighborhood, still occupied, was probably still laced with massive amounts of explosives, but it had all the crazy elements needed—bait, in the form of me, a trap, in the form of the others, and prey, in the form of Redbeard.

Now all I had to do was hope it came together in the least deadly way possible for the people left in the neighborhood.

91.

Karl

She was just flying overhead like an invitation offered right to him, and he drove after her as quickly as he could.

He could see where she was going, of course—right to his old hidey-hole, probably looking for a clue as to his whereabouts. She was so dumb, she was practically fumbling about in the dark without a clue where the light switch was. He watched her descend over the house, coming down to the earth slowly, wafting, gravity causing her to drift downward. He watched her go, driving after her, slow enough not to attract attention.

The neighborhood was quiet, only a few people walking around here and there. Karl had a grin that stretched across his face and hurt the corners of his mouth. He parked a half block away from the house, and she just stood there in the middle of the street for a minute, staring at the house like it was going to blow up on her.

He wouldn't do that, though. No, she needed to suffer more. An explosion would end it entirely too quickly, and he didn't intend to let her off that lightly. Not since Kat Forrest—that bitch—had gotten away.

She started toward the house, and he got out of the car, leaving the door open as he stalked down the block. He watched Sienna Nealon disappear down the side of the house behind the wall that separated his yard from the neighbor's.

Karl came around the corner of the wall that stretched along the front of the neighbor's house and peeked after her. She was just walking down the side of the house, stalking near-silently along the overgrown lawn, peeking in a window.

This was going to be beautiful.

Karl snuck along the other side of the wall, heavy with dried-out foliage shadowing the ground beneath him, his head out of phase and stuck through so he could watch her. He went quickly, trusting that his footsteps would be hidden enough by the wall separating them to throw off her suspicion. The wall between the yards was about six feet high, a concrete, cinder block creation that had been painted white once upon a time but now was cracked and fading. Karl stalked along quickly, gaining ground on her, his head leaning through the wall just enough to keep an eye on her.

She paused and he froze, her back tensing through her crumpled suit as she looked around to either side. Karl dodged through the wall and minded his footsteps, careful to stick to the loosest patches of grass. He listened for her, trying to tell if she was moving, turning around, trying to see if someone was stalking her.

If she thought she was about to surprise him, she had another thing coming.

Karl braced himself just on the other side of the wall from where he'd seen her. She hadn't taken a single step, hadn't moved at all, based on sound. She was just standing there on the other side of the wall, though she probably wouldn't be for much longer. Now was the time to act, now was the time to—

Karl lunged through the wall, turning himself insubstantial as he passed through, the bottoms of his feet going solid again as soon as he was through. He sprang out into daylight—

And caught Sienna Nealon with her back turned.

Karl smiled uncontrollably and plunged his hand into her

back, turning it solid as he reached her heart. This was the end of her, he thought as his fingers turned solid and he ripped open the muscle that let her live.

This was the end, at last.

92.

Scott

Steven took them through the Elysium neighborhood, flying around corners at high speed, rushing for the rendezvous. "Make it. Make it in time," Steven was muttering under his breath.

Scott was trying to decide if that was something he was rooting for, too, his fingers pressed into the leather padding on the car's door. He still wasn't sure.

93.

Sienna

When someone sticks their damned fingers into your heart, it hurts. A lot. In fact, it's usually a fatal sort of injury, so maybe you could just imagine how much it hurts, since most people wouldn't live enough to tell that it hurts. It does. Lots and lots.

Fortunately, I was not a normal person, and more than just being abnormal on my own, I also carried with me the power to summon a crazy serial killer who could heal more wounds than time alone.

See, Wolfe said, *for that insult I should just let you die.*

My old response would have been something along the lines of, *Fine, we'll all die together, then, crazy*, because Wolfe was really kind of chickenshit about "dying" again. He wasn't exactly living it up in my head, but apparently going into the great beyond was a little much for him to contemplate.

But I'm trying to be the new me, Sienna 2.0, kinder and gentler, so instead, what I said was, *Pretty please, Wolfe? With sugar on top? Heal me?*

And grudgingly, he said, with a growl that hinted he was a little taken off guard, *All right …*

The torn and shredded, painful muscle that was my heart closed up around Redbeard's fingers, and my ribcage started to heal around his arm. He grunted in surprise, and I knew I had him, though probably not for long.

Gavrikov, I said to myself and was rewarded with an angry curse in Russian, apparently directed at Redbeard, but which he would not hear, or even understand if he had. *Yob' tvoyu mat!* Gavrikov yelled in my skull, apparently not happy with ol' Red targeting his sister. I surged into the sky, dragging Redbeard with me, his fingers still in my heart muscle, his arm buried in my back up to the wrist.

"Wheeeee!" I yelled as I surged into the sky, Redbeard stuck with me as I zoomed two hundred feet into the air. I twisted my head around to look at him. He looked appropriately scared shitless. "Bet you weren't counting on that when you went to kill me. That's called the tables turning, you m—"

Redbeard went insubstantial and the holes he was holding open in my heart and back were suddenly vacant, causing me pain again, as well as a sudden desire to black out. It also caused him to drop, a very frightened look in his eyes. I would have enjoyed it, but I was busy bleeding out.

Wolfe ...

Mmmm, on it. Now go eat his eyes.

"I'm not *that* hungry," I said, regaining my strength. "Also, he looks unwashed."

More spice for the—

EWWWWWWWWWWWW.

Redbeard came in for a hard landing on the roof of his bolt-hole, and suddenly that already-discounted house was due for a pricing adjustment. I wondered at first why he would have bothered going solid, and then I realized he was probably using the marginally less hard material used in the roof to soften his landing, because otherwise he would have come crashing right onto the concrete sub-floor of the foundation with only a little carpet to maybe break the fall.

I went after him, but slower, hoping that he'd done a real number on himself, or better still, been knocked unconscious. Unfortunately, I couldn't see very well because of the curtains. The hole in the roof was a big shadowy pit without a hint of what lay within.

"Oh, these are always the best situations," I muttered to myself as I descended into the house. The sky was a little cloudy, occluding a lot of the light that would have been visible at this time of morning. The sun wasn't totally up just yet, so it wasn't as bright as it had been the last few days. I squinted into the dark, just hoping Redbeard was a puddle on the floor, but knowing that a fall from that height was probably not enough to kill him. I actually had no idea how his power would work in relation to falls; for all I know he'd opted to go insubstantial after crashing through the roof and was halfway to China by now.

I flipped upside down and stuck my head into the house first, experimentally, figuring it'd be better if a) I could see and b) if he had to jump to throw a punch at me. What I saw when my eyes adjusted a second or so later did not fill me with warm, happy feelings.

He'd landed in here, all right. The floor was busted up enough that I could tell he'd impacted, in between all the pieces of roof debris that were scattered on the tile. He was also not here any longer, which was more vexing.

"How are you still alive?" Karl's voice echoed through the house.

"I could ask you the same," I said, trying to triangulate his location. "But for me, it's like that old Nietzsche quote— 'That which does not kill me really, really pisses me off.'"

He didn't respond to my obvious misquotation, but I heard him moving around in the shadowy house. I looked around, trying to figure out which direction he was going to come at me from. I pulled out Shadow and readied myself, keeping my gun hidden out of sight so that he wouldn't see it coming when I started shooting at him.

"It doesn't matter how angry you are," he said from somewhere off to my left, "it's a pittance compared to how pissed off I am. Righteous indignation—"

"'Righteous' might be overselling it, loser."

"—fuels the soul," he said, getting way overdramatic. "It inflames the spirit. Those who are wronged but are given the course to redress those wrongs—"

I yawned theatrically, making it last like, ten seconds. That shut him up. "I'm not in the mood for a lecture, okay? Let's just cut to the chase and fight to the death already."

"It's a common characteristic of the oppressors to try and dismiss the grievances of the oppressed," Redbeard hissed from somewhere in the dark.

"And it's a common characteristic of infants who don't get their way to throw a tantrum, too," I said, glancing around. "You're a little older and a little more powerful than most of them, though, so naturally your tantrum has to have deadly consequences for people who have had nothing to do with your sad and pathetic self-inflicted butt hurt. Just use the toilet brush for its intended purpose and stop experimenting already—"

"You have no idea what I've been through."

"Uhm, the earth?" I asked. "Of course, if you were a man about it you'd just bury your inability to function in everyday life inside and deal with it instead of blowing up like a volcano, thrashing around and hurting others. You want attention, like a toddler, you want someone to notice you," I made my voice do that baby-talk thing, "to tell you you're soooo pathetic, and of course it's okay to be angry, little baby, to validate you and make you famous, because no one ever paid attention to you before. You want your face on a thousand channels, your name whispered in awe. Congrats, Redbeard, you've got a god complex, and you've confused notoriety and infamy as something actually desirable. It's the least of your problems, but it's causing most of ours."

"You don't know me," he spat, stepping out of the darkness. "You know nothing about me."

"You think I don't know anything about how shitty life can be?" I pointed a hand at my chest. "Moi? You think I

369

don't know anything of hurt, you who just put a hand through my freaking heart and ripped it open? I know pain, asshole." I glared at him. "I know more about pain than you ever will, but it's not a competition, is it? Because here's the difference between you and me—you want to be a victim—"

"And you make victims," he shot at me.

"—and I refuse to be one," I said.

"Oh, classic," he said with a sneer. "Your argument is 'bad shit happens, get over it'? Typical oppressor."

"Whine and lash out," I said, "typical baby." I took aim at his feet and shot.

He flinched slightly. "I've decreased the amount of flesh that I've made substantial to only a few microns. That won't work anymore. It's like pinpricks."

"I agree you're probably carrying a pin prick," I said, saving my ammo for later. "But anything else you said, I'm tuning out."

His face twisted. "You think you can ignore me?"

"Well, I'm not going to give you any more attention than I need to in order to deal with you, I can tell you that much."

"You keep telling me I'm having a tantrum," he said with a furious satisfaction, "but you're ignoring the fact that I've killed hundreds of people."

"And you've done it for truly glorious reasons," I said, nodding my head, "You're not even a proper nihilist. I mean, carrying out a real estate scheme for a guy like Buchanan Brock … that's righteous."

Redbeard flushed, and I could tell I'd scored a direct hit. "It's not like that."

"Oh, it is," I said, keeping a straight face. "You're blathering on about changing the world, but really all you care about is changing the property values of this area for an already wealthy real estate tycoon."

Redbeard backpedaled. "You don't understand. He provided the explosives so that I could change the world—"

"He provided the explosives so that you'd work for him,

you corporate shill," I said, and I could tell I was fishing with dynamite. Redbeard's face was horrified, his internal motivation compromised in the worst way. "You act like you're some glorious fighter for the common people or whatever—honestly, it's all a bit blurry and crazyass to me— but really, you work for the highest bidder. I mean … you're not even planning to really go out in the blaze of glory here in the neighborhood, are you?" I smirked at his horror. "You're gonna … what? Get on a private plane and go somewhere sunny, aren't you?"

"No," he shook his head in fury. "I mean—I'm going to change things—"

"You're going to change the size of your bank account, but I doubt the world is going to go rolling off its axis because you move a few zeroes into your assets column."

"You don't understand anything," Redbeard said, near tears. "Not anything!"

"Yeah, you're upset because I totally don't get you," I said with my usual dollop of sarcasm. "Or, alternatively, you're currently mad enough to cry because I'm calling you out on all your bullshit instead of building you up like the news media has been doing—lionizing you into this spooky guy with a cause and a crusade. You're just a paid hack, another guy with a job who's sold out his so-called principles for the almighty dollar, another whining crybaby who can't get his shit together enough to—you know what? Screw it. You're not even worth talking to." And I drifted out of the hole in his roof.

Now this was the moment of calculated risk, because he could easily go and be a shit head, decide he'd had enough, and blow the whole neighborhood. But at the same time, letting him stand there, insubstantial, going back and forth forever was not something that was going to result in victory for me and my team. In fact, the longer I insulted him, the more likely it was that he'd eventually get itchy and pull the detonator before I could stop him, because, let's face it, I wasn't going to be able to stop insulting him. It just wasn't in my nature to let this spoiled brat vent his spleen about his— whatever without continuously shitting all over him about his massive life failures.

Yeah, I know. I'm meeting with a therapist weekly for a reason. I am also NOT ONE for the same reason.

I drifted out onto the front lawn, listening to the revving of an engine down the block. I whistled a jaunty tune as I went, my feet setting back down on grass as I walked for the street. I glanced back and saw Redbeard come shuffling out of the wall of the house, staring after me, mouth slightly open in disbelief that I'd walked away from him.

"Where are you going?" he asked. He sounded insulted. Good.

"Away from you," I said. "You need a therapist, not a superhero."

He gawked at me. "I'm—I'm going to destroy—"

"Yeah, yeah," I waved him off, rolling my eyes. "But I can't make you turn solid for a fight, so why am I wasting my time?"

"I'm going to do it," he said, but his voice sounded flimsy.

"I'm sure you will," I said, shrugging, "as soon as the cameras show up, because you're such a confident guy that you'd do it for nothing but love of the game—oh, wait, that's right. You're actually doing it for attention and for your boss, neither of whom is going to be served by having this go down without a huge meta battle that gets on all the TV networks first." I glanced up and down the street. "Seems the TV news hasn't gotten the message. Maybe you should have scheduled a press conference."

"They'll be here," he said. It was probably the first time he'd voiced optimism in a while, because he sounded so pathetic about it.

"Probably not," I said. "I staged some fights at major LA landmarks this morning to get their attention. I doubt they've noticed a squabble here in Elysium, especially since there aren't any cops around for miles." I shrugged. "Maybe if you blow something up it'll get their attention, but—say, all the bombs in the neighborhood aren't attached to one detonator, are they? Because then that probably won't allow for using it as an attention-getter …"

He flushed, glancing down at his belt, telling me exactly where the location of the detonator was. Redbeard was clearly not the brightest bulb in the Christmas tree, and the way his brain was chunking along, his thoughts visible on his face, I couldn't help but feel I'd gotten into a battle of wits with an unarmed man. Getting attention was his number one motive, and he needed to be seen doing meta shit before blowing up the neighborhood, but he'd failed to kill me, which—I mean, displaying my corpse on the end of his fist would have probably been worth a YouTube video or twelve. People on the street would have been lining up to film that, but like at everything else in his life, he'd failed.

Sooo … what was a loser to do next? Just give up on his dreams and run away? That would have been the smart play, maybe blowing up the neighborhood out of spite on the way out. It would have messed with Brock's plan, not having evidence of acts of gods for insurance to deny the claims, but Karl Nash could have still gotten some infamy, albeit without any live video footage of him being a megalomaniacal destructive asshole and displaying all his personality defects to the world.

But then, that was his problem. He had to be seen, he had to be infamous, he had to be known. It was like the call of the wild to his coyote heart, the number one motivation. He needed to not only blow shit up, he wanted to be known for doing it, because it was the only way his cold and craven heart would feel like he'd taken actual revenge.

I could see the emotions playing across his face as he tried to figure out what to do next. Silently, I was egging him on, because I'd planned this much out in advance and already knew the logical answer. Crazy people don't generally jump to the most logical answer, though, so I waited to see if he'd get to it.

"I'm going to kill you," he said, face twisting even harder into hate, and my previously wounded heart sang. Oh, good. He got there, finally. "I'm going to make a mess of you, and people are going to film it, I'm going to film it, and the whole world is going to see."

Uh, yeah. Yay. I guess.

He came at me in a menacing walk, and I stood my ground defiantly, letting him know I wasn't scared of him. Which … I mostly wasn't. Mostly. I mean, the guy could technically put his hand through my brain and kill me, and he was holding it out, the skin fading slightly as he advanced on me, as inevitable as the rain anywhere but in LA.

Okay, maybe I was a little afraid.

94.

Kat

Kat shifted the car into gear. It had been years since she'd driven a stick shift, or even since she'd driven herself at all. She'd stalled the car multiple times, the transmission grinding and guttering as she failed to shift it at the appropriate times, the engine racing and screaming.

That was all fine with her, though. It was Taggert's car, after all. His precious baby, his vintage Ferrari.

She had parked on the street, waiting for Sienna to show, and now there she was, backing slowly toward the street. Redbeard stepped into sight, anger on his face like a cloud of pestilence, advancing on the "helpless" Sienna.

Kat hit the accelerator, listened to the transmission scream at her again and she frantically shifted up to prevent another stall. It did, however, cause Redbeard to look up and see her, his eyes narrowing as he tried to figure out what he was looking at.

"Hold that pose, asshole," she said. She thrust a hand forward, seizing the roots of the grass beneath Redbeard's feet and causing them to reach upward to grab him just like she'd done to Grayson Dieter. His feet may not have been wholly there, but he was walking on something, and the roots found the thin soles and wrapped them up tight as Redbeard jerked in surprise at the unexpected resistance, looking up at her with his eyes now wide as she drove the Ferrari right at him in a hard slide, jamming the brakes as she mounted the curb and went onto the lawn.

95.

Sienna

I wasn't going to be hiring Kat as my driver anytime soon, I knew that much as I saw the old Ferrari come shooting at Redbeard. She hit the curb hard enough to rip off the bumper, but even that didn't slow her down. The sports car hit a hard skid and came at my opponent sideways. I could have sworn I saw the grass beneath it rippling as the car slid into the space where Redbeard was standing, his hands thrown up defensively even as he faded out of phase in panic.

So, he did react emotionally. That was helpful.

When Kat came to a skidding halt, the Ferrari was parked with Redbeard sticking right out of the roof from chest up, hands still thrown out in front of him, his eyes closed. Kat kicked open the door and bailed out the side before Redbeard recovered—quite wisely for her, I thought.

"Sienna, now!" she shouted, and I obliged her.

Gavrikov, I said, and threw a hand up, blasting a round of flame into the gas tank.

The Ferrari blew up as Kat rolled toward me, a billowing cloud of fire blasting out of the body and chassis of the sweet, exquisitely cared-for classic. I would have felt really, really guilty about it if I hadn't known it was Taggert's car and that my destroying it meant he'd get zero replacement costs from the insurance company. Acts of gods, that's right. Thank you, Redbeard, for providing me and Kat a moment of sweet, sweet vengeance in the midst of this battle. Lemonade from lemons and all that.

I didn't expect the sudden explosion of the gasoline to kill Redbeard, and I wasn't terribly surprised when it didn't. It wasn't even that big of an explosion, actually, more of a WHOOOOOOOMP! as the tank went up. It certainly didn't blow up like in the movies, or like any of Redbeard's targets did. It was quieter, less percussive, but the flames were pretty hot.

Kat crawled to her feet and looked back at our little neighborhood barbecue, stunned, her mouth open.

"Don't go catatonic on me now, Cameron," I shot at her.

She blinked at me and got off her knees. "Do you think—"

"No," Redbeard said, stepping out of the fire, the soles of his feet black. Dude needed a shoe store.

"Have you ever thought about wearing something with heels?" I asked, genuinely curious. "Feels like it would solve some of your problems—"

Another squeal of tires came from down the street, and this time, like a trained sucker, Redbeard looked again. Another sports car came shooting to a stop a few feet short of hitting me, and Scott popped out, hands up. "What's up?" he asked, mostly for effect, I suspected.

"The number of points on Kat's license," I answered honestly.

"I'm gonna kill you all," Redbeard said, sounding a little more unhinged.

"You've done a smashing job of it so far," I said, watching out of the corner of my eye as Steven got out of his car, a little slower than Scott, obviously, but holding his Glock in his hands, waiting for a chance to shoot Redbeard in the feet, plainly. Or elsewhere.

With the flaming sports car as his backdrop, Redbeard

looked a little shadowed, the fire dancing behind him. It would have been a cool shot in an action movie, but because it was overcast, it came off a little muted and—

Ugh. I have to get out of this town.

"I got this," Scott said, nodding at Redbeard, a little tension on display in his rugged jawline.

"You've got a handful of nothing," Redbeard growled back.

"That should be the title of your autobiography," I said helpfully. "Which no one will read."

When Redbeard turned to retort to me, Scott blasted at him with a full force water wash from both hands. Redbeard saw it coming out of the corner of his eye and started to smirk as he opened his mouth to say something, but shut it as the water washed his feet out from underneath him and he faceplanted in the newly created mud with a splash.

"Nice one, waterboy," Steven said.

Kat threw out her hands like she was conducting a symphony, and I watched green and brown roots burst out of the sodden, muddy ground and seize Redbeard by his newly solid hands. He stared dully at them for a moment and then pulled them free, looking angrily at all of us, his skin going ghostly again.

That was when I knew we had him.

He had panicked earlier when the car was coming and gone insubstantial. Now, when threatened with the possibility of falling through the earth when Scott took his feet from beneath him, he'd gone solid through and through. That told me he was operating purely on instinct when he was fighting. It wasn't training, it wasn't smarts, it was a really angry guy who had some damned helpful powers that he didn't fully control, especially when emotion got involved—specifically fear and anger. It made me wonder if he'd been shifting states when I was taunting him in the dark. I suspected it did.

And boy, did I know how to stir those emotions.

"What a chickenshit," I said, rolling my eyes. "Your

power is such a perfect illustration of who you are—you have no ability to touch or influence the world around you. You're a nothing. You don't even really exist—and when I kill you, it'll be like you were never here at all."

Redbeard's complexion reddened slightly. "You think that hurts my feelings?"

"Yes, you ginormous baby," I shot back. "I think you've known it all along, which is why you're continuing to have these little tantrums. You've got colic and you want mommy to pat you on the back and make it all better."

He wavered a little, the disgust rolling off him as he went insubstantial again after that slight return to form. "You're nothing but a bunch of hot air."

I nodded at Scott and he shot out with another fierce burst of water that took Redbeard's feet from underneath him again, creating another mud puddle that Redbeard splashed in as he landed, his face now twisting with fury—

Just as I shot a flaming burst at the water beneath his face. It flash-boiled and he flinched as it spattered like a shotgun burst, angry red marks springing up all over his face like teenage acne, the blisters already starting to form. "I make hot air," I said, "because technically boiling water is—"

He hissed like the puddle had when I nuked it, springing back to his feet, more angry than wounded, though he was clearly hurting from the attack. He took another step forward and Kat seized his feet, stalling him for a second as he raged again, ripping the roots free with an angry kick. "You look like a stomping child," I said. "How appropriate."

I guessed he was about two more good insults from completely losing his shit, because his face went even redder. He had mud and burns on his face and hands, he was wavering, his appearance rippling as he shifted phases, and I could tell he was—as Zollers had accused me of in the past—stuffing resentment. That's not healthy, I'm told. I was equally sure Redbeard planned to release that unhealthy emotion on me—or another target—at his earliest

380

convenience. "You bitch," he said simply.

"No, you bitch," I said, "and whine, and moan, and complain, and grouse—"

He reddened and flickered again. One more good insult would get him. Maybe two bad ones.

"You're all nothing," he said, more to reassure himself than anything, I was sure.

"No," Kat said, her head held high, "you're nothing. We are famous. We're everything you wish you could be—and nothing that you are ... loser."

I wouldn't have thought that it would be Kat—daffy, frivolous Kat—who would put a serious villain like Redbeard (and for all my insults, he'd done serious damage and was a serious villain) over the edge. But it must have been something about the classic high-school popular girl way she delivered that line, because it sent Karl Nash over the edge like she'd nailed his ass with a sports car going a hundred miles an hour and he was solid as a normal human being.

The reaction was immediate; I could see his pupils dilate from where I stood. He was still a little slumped from where he'd been warring with her grass root snares, but he snapped up immediately like he'd had his tail plugged into an electrical outlet. He looked at her with wide, furious eyes and his lips pushed together so hard that they went pale. He reached down and fumbled at his belt, rummaging until he came up with the prize—

The detonator.

Wolfe, I said, *Gavrikov, Eve, Bjorn—*

I blasted Redbeard right in the eyes with a net of light as I simultaneously hit him with the warmind. The net hit dead on, his upper face disappearing behind a blinding strip like someone had bound a blindfold made of pure, iridescent light around his eyes. He staggered as though I'd punched him from both the blinding light shining into his retinas and the dark mental attack I was subjecting him to.

That was all a distraction, though.

I shot forward at just under sonic speed, channeling the power of Wolfe as I went. I caught the subtle ripple through Redbeard's chest that told me he was solid for a second, out of control of his own body, and I took full advantage.

I came down with every bit of strength I had, raising my hand and lowering it in a flash, turning the underside of my flattened hand to an iron-like consistency with Wolfe's power and hours of beating my various limbs against a giant block of steel. It was tiresome work, but it tended to pay off in moments like this, when I matched my hand against Redbeard's wrist at something like three hundred and fifty miles an hour—

And I sheared his hand off in the middle of his forearm.

I caught the falling hand and stepped back, prying it loose of the detonator just in case, holding the little plastic nob in my own and taking his hand by the wrist in my other like a bad prop comic.

Redbeard staggered back, turning insubstantial again. The net of concentrated light fell off his eyes and he blinked repeatedly as he stumbled backward toward the flaming wreckage of Taggert's car. He squinted and stared out at us as he recovered his sight, trying to figure out what had just happened. Based on the look on his face, the pain of his severed limb hadn't quite hit him yet.

"Hi," I said, waving his own hand at him.

I don't normally glory in the misery of others, but watching his brain catch up with the fact that he'd just suffered an amputation was pretty damned hilarious, if you're starved for entertainment like most of America. I mean, people watched Kat live her meaningless life in their spare time. That's not any sicker than waving someone's amputated hand at them.

"What the—" Karl said, looking down at his forearm in shock. "You—you—"

"'You hero,'" I finished for him, waving his hand like it was one of those little novelty flags on the fourth of July.

"'You winner.' 'You star—'"

"You b—"

"You already used that one," I said with a roll of the eyes. Okay, I'll admit it, sometimes I do glory in the misery of others. I'll add it to the list of things to change about myself. But tomorrow. I held up the detonator and flash-burned it out of existence by heating it to four thousand degrees in the course of less than a second. "Come up with something new already. It's not like you're handicapped—" I held up my hand in front of my mouth, mockingly, asshole that I am. "Oops. Too soon?"

"You Skywalkered me," Redbeard said limply, and he looked all used up, like he was ready to just fade into the earth.

I'll admit it, I got offended by that. "Wait, you're casting *me* as Vader? Are you serious?"

He just stared at his missing hand, his skin rippling as he shifted in and out of phase. "I … I was gonna …" It was almost enough to make me feel sorry for him.

But then I remembered that he'd killed more innocent people than I could count, and my inner b-word came rising right back to the surface.

I stalked toward him, vaporizing his disembodied hand before his eyes as he watched, tearfully. "No one will remember your name," I said, and he looked at me, dazed. "No one will know who you are. No one is watching you now, no one will see what you've done. When I report this little incident, it's going to be without acknowledging you as anything other than a rabid dog that needed to be put down. What you have done is beyond the pale, who you have become is subhuman. However you think you were wronged, the wrongs you did in return more than tipped the scales."

"You can't hide it," Redbeard said, thinly satisfied smile peeking out of his lips beneath the cold resignation. "If you just kill me, the world will always wonder."

I thought about that for a second. "You're right,

Redbeard—"

"Say my name," he said, face darkening. "I know you know it."

"You're not worthy of that recognition, Heisenberg," I said coldly, looking right back at him. "You have no soul, no humanity."

"Neither do you," he shot back. "Everybody says so."

"Unlike you," I said, shrugging, "I never put much stock in the opinions of the masses." I glanced back. "Anyone got a phone?"

"Uh, yeah," Steven pulled his out, and so did Scott. "Why?"

"You might want to record this," I said, smiling coldly as I turned back to Redbeard. "For posterity. And as a warning to others who think this chickenheart is some kind of hero."

"I am a hero," Redbeard said, still flickering. "I am—"

I'd had about enough of his shit so I let loose the fire.

It blossomed out and consumed him before he could pull himself out of the physical realm. I knew he wanted to say his name, but the pain was swift and sudden, and his voice was consumed by fires hungry for oxygen. Karl Nash died over the course of about ten seconds as the flame raged over him, consuming him, turning him crispy and burnt. His screams and cries were pitiful, the sort of disgusting, heartbreaking noises that might even have moved me to tears if I hadn't been doing everything I could to hold back the tide by playing a little video in my head of all the horrors he'd done.

"Who's Vader now, asshole?" I asked as his body was turned to ash, to smoke, to dust. I kept my voice even only through the most extreme effort. In truth, I wanted to go home and curl up in the fetal position, but I just kept my face straight and lowered my hand as the final scream of the man who would forever be known to the public as Redbeard echoed in my ears.

And as his last scream died with him, I stood there,

listening to another cry rising in my head—that of the humanity most people denied even existed in me. It was a cry of desperation inside me, the hope that the horror I had just committed would serve as a warning to any future copycats seeking glory that there was no glory to be found here at all.

96.

"So he's definitely dead?" Detective Waters asked, looking at me skeptically.

"The video already has like ten thousand views on YouTube," Kat said, playing with my phone. She glanced up at me. "You should not read the comments."

I wanted to sigh, but I didn't. I'd known what I was in for when I'd made my choice. I looked at Waters instead. "He's definitely dead. Vaporized, no remains, no way to tell who he was."

She raised an eyebrow at me. "You sure that was the best way to go?"

I looked around. The neighborhood was still standing, the fires that had destroyed Taggert's car were out, Steven was leaning against his own ride, and Scott was ... well, he was doing his damnedest not to even look at me. "You know as well as I do that with these types, copycats are a real danger. Keeping him anonymous and making sure his death had no glamour to it seemed like the way to send him off the stage."

"You make it sound like this was all a play," Waters said, harrumphing her disdain as she made notes in her notebook.

"In his mind," I said, "it was all drama. Some people think being in front of a big audience, on TV, is some kind of a good thing, regardless of how you got there. They're so desperate for any kind of attention that they're willing to debase themselves and lose their humanity just to have people see their stupid face and know their name."

"Okay," Kat said, and her face was flushed, eyes all narrowed, fuming as she looked at me, "I get it. I've been dumb—in your opinion."

"I wasn't talking about y—" I frowned. "Though I guess that does apply, doesn't it?"

She looked like she'd never been amused and never would be. Sour does not begin to describe it. "You—"

She was interrupted by a car screeching to a halt. I turned to see a taxi stop a hundred feet away and Guy Friday come springing out. "Federal Agent!" he shouted at the taxi driver in lieu, I suspected, of paying his fare. He ran over to us. "I missed it all, didn't I?" He was already grown to supersize, slapping a ham-like fist into the palm of his other hand. "Man. You should have called. I would have made sure and Team Rocketed this bastard." He stared at us, waiting for the joke to land. "Like … Team Rocket's blasting off again?"

I blinked. "Nice one, Yancy." I turned my attention back to Waters. "So … Redbeard had a backer. Guy named Buchanan Brock."

"Buck Brock?" She looked up at me from her notebook. "I know of him. He human or one of yours?"

I eyed her, deciding to let that one pass. "Human, so far as I know."

"Got an address on him?" she asked.

"I've got one," Scott said, finally breaking his silence. He shuffled over to us, stiffly, like he was aching all over, and held out his cell phone. "Here's his number, here's his office."

"I'll get him picked up," Waters said.

"Be careful with that one," I said, "he's one of the president's donors. Got a lot of connections."

"I could go help," Guy Friday said to Detective Waters. "Just in case he's not human."

She gave him the once over, in his giant form. "All right." She waved him to follow, and he trotted after her like a loyal dog. She stopped, turned and looked back at me as the first news van came rolling up. "We're not done with you yet, you know. Don't go running off until we get things wrapped up, okay?"

I frowned at the sight of the press, knowing that I was due a good pillorying for how I'd handled this one. "Of course you're not done with me." I lowered my voice to a sarcastic whisper. "Because getting the hell out of town before this thing explodes in my face would make my life way, way too easy."

"Ooh, you got a text message," Kat said, slipping my phone into my palm. It buzzed again in my grip.

Ricardo

My heart and loins are aflame for you in much the same way as that man you set on fire. I know that you, too, must feel the burn in your—

My eyes forced themselves shut of their own accord, probably in hopes of unseeing what I'd just seen. Didn't help. With them closed, I had a vision of Dick-o fanning himself. It was not pleasant. "Dick, if only I could do to you what I just did to Redbeard, you might stand a chance of making me happy."

"Who is this Ricardo?" Steven asked, sidling up to me and looking at my phone now that Waters had walked away. The scene was buzzing with patrol officers, but they didn't exactly have it cordoned off yet.

"Just some Dick," I said.

"Can I have your phone back?" Kat asked, looking at me with hopeful eyes.

"Don't you want to go give an interview or twelve?" I asked, nodding at the press already starting to butt up against the police perimeter.

"Oh, right," she said and off she went. She'd just been through a hotel collapse, a multi-state flight, a car accident and a fight with Redbeard, and her hair looked totally fine. Her dress was even still in good condition. Some people get all the luck, or the glamour, or something. She wandered off in her bare feet, blades of grass tilting toward her where they sprang up from cracks in the pavement.

"That girl's destined to make some poor bastard really miserable," Steven observed, watching her with a visible cringe.

"She's not that bad," I said half-heartedly. He gave me a sympathetic smile. "What are you doing sticking your neck out on this, Hollywood? Aren't you famous enough without boosting your box office cred by being all crazy and dangerous?"

"Well, I decided to generate some controversy, see," Steven said, not quite keeping a straight face. "I know, I know—the traditional wisdom says scandals are the way to go. Maybe do what Flannery did, run in with the law, have a big pile of drugs, but I just—I can't handle my liquor, I'm not really into narcotics—"

"What are you doing in this town again?"

"—so I decided to try old-fashioned guts and glory," he said with a smile. "I figure it's something different for this age."

"Hmph," I said, shaking my head. "You better be careful. People might go thinking you're a real-deal hero."

"I'd settle for you thinking it," he said with a smile. "So … what do you think?"

"I think you live in LA, and if I ever come back to this town again, it'll be too soon," I said with a little grimace of my own. "Sorry."

"Wow," he said with a little laugh. "Shot down. That's … I forgot what that felt like."

"If it makes you feel better," I said, trying to be a little consoling, "I can honestly say that it's not you, it actually is me." I put my hands uneasily in my jean pockets. "I'm a wreck, Steven. I haven't had a healthy relationship in years," I looked at Scott, who was lurking nearby, definitely in listening distance, but he wasn't looking at me, "I'm a public menace, and, uhm … you really don't want to be near me for the next few months, because this thing I just did—it's not going to play well in the press." Or anywhere else, really. I'd just documented myself roasting another human being alive and had it posted on the internet. This put even my past YouTube videos to shame for sheer, nasty brutality.

"I think you might have made the right call," he said. "These guys—these—what did you call them?"

"Injustice collectors," I said. "That's what the FBI calls them."

"Yeah, them," he said, "when they get to go out in a blaze of glory, it probably appeals to the impressionable idiots just like them." He shuddered. "I don't think seeing one of their own get roasted like fresh venison on an open fire is going to inspire anyone to step up and copycat, that's for sure. And otherwise, this guy … I mean, if he'd pulled off what he planned to …" He shuddered again.

"Yeah," I looked around the neighborhood. "I don't even know what they're going to do about that. There's got to be more unexploded bombs buried in the ground here than a World War II battlefield in 1945. Pretty sure that's not going to push property values in the direction Brock was hoping for."

"They'll get 'em out somehow," he offered hopefully. I didn't quite share his optimism. He looked me straight in the eye. "So no chance, huh?"

"For us?" I pretended to give it a moment's thought. "Chalk this up to another bad decision for me on a whole pile of them, but … I gotta say no. I need to work on me for a while before I go inflicting myself on anyone else."

"You've always been nice to me," he said with a smile.

"You barely know me," I said with one of my own. "Also, you're kinda hot. Aren't you used to being treated differently?"

He nodded. "That's a good point." His eyes twinkled. "Let me know if you change your mind."

"Why are you pushing so hard on this?" I asked as he started to turn away. "I know I'm nothing special in the looks department—"

"Yeah," he said, cutting me off, "I don't agree with you there. You never wear make-up or do your hair, and you still look pretty nice to my eyes. Plus," his smile disappeared and he got serious, "there's that whole fact that … fifty, sixty years ago … back when we saw things a little more black and white, before all the shades of grey crept in … you would have been a hero, period, full stop, no questions asked."

"I kinda like the shades of grey," I said, trying to force a smile and failing. "I hate to think what I would have been like if I was never challenged on my … my bullshit, let's call it. My out of control …" I lowered my eyes. "Well, some of the questionable things I've done. I'd probably be like—"

"A goddess?" Now he was smiling again. "Handing down commands from on high?"

"Something like that," I said and extended my hand. He took it and shook it, and leaned in to give me a quick peck on the cheek.

"It was nice to meet you, Sienna Nealon," he said. "And if you ever do come back to LA—"

"If it's up to me, I won't, no offense."

"Yeah, terrible weather," he said, looking around, "awful food—"

"Lovely traffic, such wonderful, deep and considerate people—"

He grinned. "Take care of yourself. Maybe go a little easier on those flaws you see in the mirror—'cause I don't see 'em like you do." He walked away, and I watched him.

I didn't need to see the flaws when I looked in the mirror. I turned my head and saw Kat gushing to a TV reporter, putting a hand on hers, complimenting her on something or another, being nice, looking personable, and giving an interview that beat the hell out of the confrontational mess I'd put up when questioned by Gail Roth all those years ago.

No, I didn't need to look in the mirror to see my flaws. I'd be seeing them on every TV station for the foreseeable future, that much was certain. I listened in, just for a second, to try and hear what Kat was saying to the reporters in the cluster.

"Sienna's a real hero," Kat said, "and this entire city would have been destroyed if not for her. I'd be dead. Like, for real. She saved my life and she stopped Redbeard, and I think she sent a really solid message to all these sick people who think that this is the way to get famous, and she did it by—you know, like really taking the burden on herself. She's such a hero. I couldn't even imagine having to go through what she's gone through, or having to be as brave as she's been over some of the things people have said about her—"

Damn.

Are we sure there's a drought going on in Los Angeles? Because my eyes just watered. Must be the humidity.

97.

Scott

The scene was a loose sort of chaos, and Scott felt lost in the clamor. It wasn't the press or the violence that had discombobulated him. It was the voice in his head that reminded him that, in spite of whatever victory he'd been part of today, he was still missing something.

Something big.

It buzzed in his head as he listened to Kat talk to the press. She was giving tireless interviews, one after another, and the things she was saying about Sienna made him nearly sick on the spot.

"She's lying, you know," he said, certain that Sienna was still lingering behind him.

"I know," came the answer, her voice quiet enough that even a boom mic wouldn't have caught it.

Scott whirled around and saw her sitting there with her arms folded, leaning against a parked police cruiser, the wreckage of Taggert's car still smoking behind her. "You're not a hero. You burned that guy to death—"

"For a reason."

"Because it's who you are," he said, controlling his anger just barely. He held up a hand and water vapor wafted off it. "What you told Steven, about not wanting to live in a world where you wouldn't be held accountable ... you're kidding yourself. That's like, your fantasy."

"I thought you didn't know me anymore," she said, and sounded … hurt?

"I know enough," he said, looking away from her. "I know enough to know I don't want to be around you. That I don't trust you." Now he looked her in the eye, but she dropped her gaze. "I may have helped you today, but we're not okay. And we're never going to be okay again." He held up one finger and pointed it right at her. "Don't ever call me asking for help again." He started to walk away.

"I never have," she said quietly. He did not turn, just kept walking, past the police line, ignoring the reporters. He broke into a run, not entirely caring where he ended up, just knowing he needed to get away from here—and from her.

98.

Sienna

I hung around the scene after Scott told me off. No one heard, but it was still embarrassing. Well deserved, probably, but still embarrassing. I leaned against a police cruiser's hood, feeling the dry air on my face, wondering if he'd taken the minuscule amount of moisture in the air with him when he'd stormed off. Probably not, but I imagined him doing it like a lover packing his things and slamming the door behind him after a tense argument.

It didn't take much imagination to come up with that simile, because I'd seen him do it before, in almost exactly that way.

My phone rang, and I didn't even want to look at who it was. Probably Dick, seeing how my luck was going at the moment.

It wasn't. It was Phillips. Better or worse? I dunno, you decide.

"Yeah, what?" I asked, not half as nastily as I would have a few days earlier. I was too tired to be snarky.

"Did you know—uh, Friday—went with the LAPD to arrest the human suspect behind this attack?" Phillips opened with this, so naturally my stomach tensed in anticipation of terrible news, like that Friday had accidentally caught a bullet to the head or something. Wait, would that be terrible?

"Yeah," I said, still feeling tense. "Why, what did—"

"The guy," Phillips said, "Brock. He resisted arrest. Got killed in the attempt."

I sat in silence for a moment, still tense. Not fully certain, but my buttcheeks might have creased the cop car's hood. "He did what?"

"He pulled a Sienna," Phillips said, not sounding sarcastic in tone but damned sure being it. "Buchanan Brock is dead. I guess the guy took a shot at the LAPD detective who was accompanying Friday on the arrest."

"Why do you call him Friday if you know his real name?" I asked, rubbing my head.

"Because I'm talking to you and that's what you call him."

"Don't pander to me," I said, sighing. "So … the only living witness to the scheme is dead. Nice wrap-up of that particular loose end."

"Big shooter like that," Phillips said, "his lawyers would have had him out of jail in an hour. He'd never have seen the inside of a cell."

"Someone said the same thing about Edward Cavanagh," I recalled. "Funny how that ended up being true, too, though he at least went out via a stroke."

"You have a strange definition for what constitutes funny," Phillips said, "but then again, you did just burn a man to death, so we'll all chalk it up to PTSD and move on."

"You know what else is funny?" I asked.

"In your current state of mind, probably *Paul Blart: Mall Cop 8*."

I ignored that rather malicious piece of character assassination. "Cavanagh and Brock had something in common—both of them were pretty big donors to President Harmon's campaign."

"I don't find that very funny."

"Really?" I asked. "Because unlike *Paul Blart 8*, I think it's hilarious."

"You'd probably find it less funny if you pulled yourself

away from searching for yourself on YouTube and looked for Buchanan Brock," Phillips said. He sounded a little too satisfied for anyone's own good.

"Why?" I asked. "What would I find?"

"You lacking an internet connection?" he snarked.

"Yeah, this shitty government cell phone plan has the worst service," I volleyed back. "What am I missing?"

"A video that's not nearly as appealing to your sensibilities," Phillips said, "as the one you recorded today. It's footage of a verbal altercation in which President Harmon ripped Buchanan Brock a new one at that fundraiser you were at the other night."

"The one that ended in tears and death and explosions?" I asked, my brow furrowing all on its own. Brock and the president had a public falling out?

"As all parties that you attend seem to, yes."

That hurt because it was true. "Well, isn't that convenient," I said, frowning.

"It was posted days ago," Phillips said. "Stop jumping to conclusions."

"Pffft," I said. "I have no need to jump to conclusions. I can fly."

"Yeah, well," Phillips said, "your business in LA is concluded, so why don't you fly on home? And stay away from the press."

"Fine," I said, jaded. Like there was any danger of me talking to the press about anything, ever.

"You realize what you've done?" Phillips asked, and I could tell he was winding things up.

"Well, I made a big mess." Again.

"You executed a terrorist who had murdered hundreds, a man no one else could stop." Phillips didn't sound pleased. Ever. And he didn't sound pleased now, either, but ...

He did sound less pissed than usual.

"You probably just won President Harmon re-election," Phillips finished. "You validated the faith he placed in you.

Good job. Hurry home." And of course, then he hung up.

"Shit," I said to no one in particular. I looked around the scene one last time, pocketed my cell phone, and rocketed off into the sky.

99.

Kat

It took her a few hours to disentangle herself from the press. She didn't want to leave them, and they didn't want her to leave until they'd asked, "one more question!" She took a lot of "one more questions," but finally, they reached their end, and so did she, heading home in the back of a police cruiser that dropped her off in front of her rented mansion.

She walked up the drive after vaulting the gate because she couldn't remember the code. Dan the driver always opened it for her, but he hadn't shown up to collect her, and she hadn't bothered to call—not that she knew his number anyway.

The SUV was parked on the driveway up by the house. Sprinklers were going on the lawn, watering the lush, green grass, the spritzing sound in the quiet evening.

Kat stood out front for a few minutes and just looked at the house. It was all glorious architecture and curves and arches; it could have been transplanted from Italy straight to southern California. It was beautiful, there was no doubt. But as she stood there, she had to ask …

Is this what you really want?

She took a breath of the cool night air, feeling just a hint of humidity. She walked across the grass, still barefoot, and felt its caress, dancing across the soles of her feet. She could feel the carpet of greenery all the way to its roots, kept artificially alive by desperate measures in this place that hadn't seen a genuine rainfall in forever.

She opened the front door and found it unlocked. She stepped inside and there was silence.

No camera crews.

No fans.

No one excited to see her.

"There you are," Taggert said, stepping around the corner into the entry, face radiating fury.

"Here I am," Kat said, standing in the entryway on the hard tile, the bottoms of her feet already missing the grass she'd left behind.

"You wrecked my car." He said it in silent accusation, but with hints of utter disgust, like she'd done the most horrible thing imaginable.

"Yeah," she said, and it came out in a pleased, exultant rush, pulling a smile. "Well, I mean, technically, I'd blame it on Redbeard, but … yeah." She couldn't control the smile.

Taggert towered over her, and he loomed closer, the smell of liquor wafting off him. "Do you have any idea how much that car cost?"

"As many times as you've bragged about it, I should," she said, her smile turning to one of hard satisfaction at his reaction.

"You silly little bitch," he said, eyes darkening. "It's worth more than you are."

"I've made you enough to buy several of them," she said, feeling her own face darken in response. "Don't be overly dramatic, Aaron. It's why you don't do 'on-camera.' You're such a ham."

"How's this for ham?" he asked and raised a hand to hit her. He brought it down swiftly, aimed right at her cheek in a hard slap.

She caught it, spun him around, and slung him headfirst into a wall. With a crash, he broke through the plaster, and lodged there up to his shoulders, his body stuck in place. She kicked him lightly in the ass and he jumped, his body jerking with his head still buried in the wall.

"I don't like you, Aaron," she said, as though she were just deciding this for herself. "I don't like being called 'Kitten.' I don't like being used. And I don't like what I've let you turn me into." She kicked him in the ass again, relatively lightly—hard enough to bruise but not to break bones. "So ... screw you. And to hell with this town."

"Where are you going?" he asked, trying to pull himself out of the hole.

"Away," she said, heading for her bedroom. It took her less than three minutes to pack everything she wanted to take with her.

By the time she got back, Taggert had just gotten his head out of the wall. He had blood running down his neck where the studs had eaten into the skin behind his ears, and his face was flushed under the plaster dust that coated it like he'd stuck his head in a bowl of coke. "You silly little ... you're nothing without me, you know that?"

"I was a person long before I met you," she said, a little rush of rebellion giving her strength. "But since I've known you, I haven't been a very good one." She made a face. "Good luck, Aaron. I'm sure you'll do just fine without me."

"You'll be a nobody without me."

"Oh, I don't know about that," she said coyly. "I was thinking of writing a tell-all book describing our time together." She grinned nastily. "I think there might be a few people who'd be interested in hearing that story, don't you? Maybe a few ... sexual harassment lawyers?"

His face paled under the layer of plaster dust. "You wouldn't."

She paused, dropping the suitcase at the door and tracing her steps back to him—perfectly poised, like walking the catwalk, never breaking eye contact with him the whole way. She smiled dangerously, and leaned in to whisper in his ear.

"I would. I could. And more than that ... I just put your head through a wall and kicked your ass not even trying." She pulled back so she could look him straight in the eye. "If you push me ... I'll do worse than just sue you. You'll be walking next a tree one day and it'll just ... strangle you. Oops."

He adjusted his tie-less collar. "You think you can threaten me? You've been hanging out with Sienna Nealon too long. It's like you're adopting the worst personality traits of that psychotic lunatic. You're gonna go follow her? Well, go on then. Good riddance. You'll probably be just like her in a year."

Kat looked straight at him and didn't blink until he did. "I've been called worse," she said, and picked up her suitcase before walking out the door. She never did look back.

100.

Scott

He sat on the beach as the sun faded into the west. The wind whipped quietly around him, the taste of the salt air so strong he could practically taste it on his tongue. The sky was a bright orange, the yellow disc of the sun slipping below the horizon as he watched it go, wondering what the night would bring.

"So?" a voice asked as he felt someone sit down next to him. He turned his head to see his own face, his own self standing there next to him. "What now?"

"I don't know," he told himself and stared off into the sunset. "I just ... don't know."

101.

Sienna

I found my house still standing when I got home, which was always a good sign. Ariadne wasn't home when I landed in the back yard, but I had a hidden key, and so all was good. I showered and cooled off and relaxed for a little bit, watching some news coverage to wind down at the end of my day.

When the knock came at the door a few hours later, I assumed it was Ariadne coming back.

It wasn't.

"Hey," Kat said, breezing in with a suitcase in her messed-up dress that she had been wearing for who-knew-how-many hours at this point. She just came right on in and I didn't stop her, because … well, because I was too busy being stunned.

"Kat," I said as she plopped down on my loveseat, "what are you doing here?"

"I left LA," she said, positioning herself next to me like she was giving a confessional-booth interview to a cameraman. "You know, the time had just come for me to realize that as a person, I wasn't making headway there. You know, that fame really wasn't what I wanted."

"Uhm …" I stared at her. "What … do you want?" Dammit, I played right into interviewing her.

"I want to work on not being a shitty person," she said,

looking right at me. "Like you are!"

I tried really hard to take that as a compliment. "Thanks." I looked down and realized ... why was her suitcase in my living room? I pointed at it. "Uhh ... you're not here to—"

"No," she said with a shake of the head, a little trace of pity for poor me, "I've got a room at the Marquette, but since your house is right on the way from the airport ..." She probably wasn't trying to be haughty, but it sure came out that way. She straightened up in her seat. "I wanted to talk to you."

I closed the door, since it appeared she wasn't going to be leaving immediately. "About ...?" I waited, and could tell she was struggling with what she wanted to say. "If it's about me being a shitty person, you kind of already dropped that bomb."

"It's about what you did to Scott," she said, and she looked right at me. Right through me, really, and I felt like I'd been caught red-handed.

"What about ... it?" I asked, feeling distinctly gobsmacked, my knees a little weak.

"What did you do to him?" she asked, green eyes shining in the dim light of my living room.

"I, uh ..." I took a couple wooden steps away from my front door and made my way toward the couch. This was a heavy topic, one that made my knees feel a little weak and weary. "That's kind of personal, Kat, and—no offense, but last time I spilled my guts about personal feelings to you, I got slam-hammered for months afterward about it."

"'Slam-hammered' is not a thing," she said. She lowered her voice. "And there's no phones here. No cameras. No recordings." She sounded soft and sincere. "Just you and me."

I wavered, not sure what to say. I had never truly confessed what happened with Scott before. Oh, people knew. Reed knew—at least the net result, when it was all said and done, and some of the edges around the thing. He knew enough to think less of me and with some reason. But that wasn't the story.

Zollers knew exactly what had happened, because he'd read it out of my head. But he hadn't had to ask, and I hadn't had to speak it aloud.

Never.

I sat down heavily, the couch absorbing my fall. I stared into the distance, wondering exactly what the hell I was thinking. "No phones?" I asked. "No cameras?"

She pulled out her phone and lit it up, hitting the power button. It went dark. "Just you and me," she said again, "and I get the feeling ... maybe you need to tell someone about this."

This was the thing that reporters—and America, actually—loved about Kat. When she wasn't being a self-centered cow, she could be the warmest person ever, someone who, when her attention was focused on you, seemed to bring life to a cold and empty room.

"We ..." I started and stopped, trying to figure out how to say what I needed to say. "It didn't go well, Scott and I," I finally decided to say, like that was a news flash to anyone. Kat, to her credit, didn't say anything; she just kept those big green eyes on me and kept listening. "Okay, it didn't only not go well ... it went ... horribly, after you left."

"I figured," she said, in a voice of pure understanding. "What happened?"

"We fought," I said honestly. "I mean, after you and Janus took off." She blanched a little at the use of her ex's name. "It was a steady stream of people leaving. Scott was ... one of the first, but he didn't leave town or anything. Just ... didn't want to be in the meta policing business anymore, he said. I think the war ... what we had to do ... I mean, you remember. He was waffling toward the end anyway, and he pulled it together for the fight with Sovereign, because of what it meant to him personally, but ..."

"He was out," she said quietly.

"Yeah," I said. "But he was ... so supportive of me continuing ... at first. We were still together even though he quit the job, and I thought ... we could be apart at work like everybody else and together ... well, you know. But it didn't work that way.

"Once everyone left, it was down to me and Reed to do it all." I was leaning forward, and I couldn't look at her for more than a few seconds at a time. "And we did, but ... it meant a lot of late nights. A lot of calls to go around the country, even out of the country ... and Scott's ... understanding ... faded pretty quickly. He was working normal hours with his dad's company, and I was ... not."

Kat nodded her head. "Your job became your life."

"It took over everything," I said, like I was doing my very own confessional-booth interview. "All my time. All my attention. Even when I was with him, I was pondering cases." I blushed. "I'm not a good investigator, Kat. I'm a good ass-beater. It's probably why I couldn't figure out the angle behind Redbeard and Brock's plan without someone anonymously tipping us off." I frowned, that particular mystery prickling at me. "But I have to investigate for the job, and it ... well, it takes time. It takes a lot of ... mental energy, seeing the things we see, dealing with the people we deal with. It burns the humanity out of you, dealing with the worst our kind has to offer. I was thinking about work constantly."

"He resented it," she said.

"Boy, did he," I said.

"He's the jealous type," she said, sounding almost apologetic about it. "I knew that from how he acted when I couldn't remember him."

"Yeah," I said softly. "Well. It all came to a head the night I blew the interview with Gail Roth."

"No," she said, putting her hand up to her chest. She looked stunned in just the right way, and if she was acting, she'd upped her game.

I nodded. "It exploded like Redbeard had put a bomb in it. I made myself look stupid in front of the whole country, and that night—that very night—we had our biggest argument ever.

"Don't get me wrong," I said, "we'd been having them for a while, this progressively escalating series of problems. We'd start the fight over stupid little things and soon enough it'd double back to the same thing as always—I wasn't there for him, ever." I rubbed my forehead. "Of course I'd throw right back that he wasn't there for me, ever, on the job, when I actually needed him, and ... that didn't really help.

"'It's like you don't even care anymore,' he said." I stared blankly ahead. "He accused me of just ... giving it all to the job. Of choosing it over him, every time. And ... I did," I said, nodding along with my confession. "Every time. Because there was no one else to do it, I said." I looked right at her. "I'm supposed to be this super powerful person, but sometimes ... when I watch someone like Redbeard kill people and I can't do anything about it ... I realize how powerless I really am in this world." My voice sounded empty and haunted, even to me. "How could I walk away from that? Knowing what it might cost in lives? Knowing that what happened in LA, if left to someone else other than me, might have ended with that whole neighborhood getting blown sky high? How many people do you think would have died if that had happened?"

"Thousands," Kat said with certainty. "Thousands and thousands."

"He never got that," I said. "He looked right at me, looked me the eyes, the man who helped me—us—win the war against Sovereign ... and I could tell that he'd just lost the righteous feeling, that he didn't think it was worth the sacrifice anymore." I met her eyes for a blink. "I told him he should just go. Just ... be rid of me, that he'd never get to have a normal life with me, because ..." I held up a hand and stared at it. "I can't touch anyone for very long without hurting them … but I can't keep my hands to myself, either. That's the job, isn't it? Keep trying to … to do the opposite of Redbeard. I keep trying to influence things, to shape them, to make them better by taking the bad guys who want to shape them badly out of the game. I'm sculpting the world anew with my own hands, but I can't … touch it." I blinked, and my vision blurred. "He said … he said he couldn't cut the cord. 'I can't just stop loving you,' he said, 'even if I wish I could'."

I blinked and felt hot liquid stream down my cheek. "And I heard that in my head, and stinging from getting my ass kicked on national TV by Gail Roth, I just did what I always do, and tried to make it right. I kissed him, I touched him, and we …" I swallowed hard. "We … you know." I choked up. "And in the middle of it … I put my fingers softly on his forehead, and left them there just a few seconds longer than I needed to … and took every single memory of *us* away from him so he could move on." I smacked my dry lips together. "I did what he couldn't. I tried to give him …" I blinked, and my cheeks ran afresh. "I tried to set him free."

"You made yourself a prisoner in the process, though, didn't you?" Kat asked, and I blinked in surprise. "Now you've got the memories for both of you. And you can't get rid of them, can you?"

"No," I said, and the tears came streaming down my cheeks again. "I'll never forget. I have to remember it all— the pain, the tears, the good times and the break-up … for both of us."

102.

A week later, on election night, Ariadne and I were watching with mounting unease as the returns rolled in on TV. I'd started the evening thinking maybe I'd want popcorn, heavily buttered and guilt-free, but by this point I was just wanting booze, also guilt-free.

"It's not decided yet," Ariadne said, watching me out of the corner of her eye as we sat in the living room, the TV tuned to one of the news channels.

They had the electoral map up, and it wasn't looking so hot for Senator Robb Foreman. He'd need to swing a lot of states to pull this one off. "It may not be over," I said, "but the fat lady is definitely warming up."

Ariadne just pursed her lips in worry and didn't say anything. We'd both voted that morning and kind of puttered around aimlessly waiting for the serious coverage to start pouring in about five. When it had, I know I wasn't the only one thinking about pouring a drink in order to deal with it. Ariadne's face had a flushed, worried quality all night. "Hard to believe the polls swung ten points in one week," she said, not putting the blame exactly where it belonged.

She didn't have to. The blame was sitting right here, in my chair, without her needing to do any shifting. By burning Redbeard to death I'd suddenly put my horrendous and violent nature to work for the American people in the best possible way. Naturally, Gerry Harmon had been quick to tout his not firing me over the last year plus as a vote of confidence that had paid off, and somehow, the media that had been wanting me to spontaneously combust in a tank of gasoline only a few weeks ago was singing my praises so effusively my mother would have preemptively slapped me just to keep me humble after hearing all of it. You know, if she were still alive.

Even his prior relationship with Brock hadn't stuck to Harmon. Whoever had filmed that YouTube video of him ripping the hell out of Brock had some serious prescience, I'd give them that. I'd watched it a couple times, and it was a nasty piece of work, with the president practically cutting a campaign ad right there under the portico at Anna Vargas's house and using a stunned Buchanan Brock as the perfect prop. The man had stood there and taken the president's vicious tirade with only a little sputtering and some ineffectual replies.

Best of all for Harmon, even absent the knowledge that Brock was a dirty bastard, it was the sort of thing that played well. He'd ripped him for being a greedy piece of shit, and naturally, press digging on Brock had revealed ... well, he was a greedy piece of shit with dirty deals in every corner of LA. If there was an odious dollar to be made, Brock was all over it, from running a scam charity to backing a super-dicey hedge fund that dodged the hell out of taxes using every loophole known to man and apparently a few that weren't even known to the IRS until now.

Yep, that had been worth a ten-point swing in the polls in seven days. And the worst part was, I had to sit back and watch it shift knowing that if I said a damned word, not only would the landscape shift underneath me, but well, let's face it—I'd just burned a man to death on video. There would be consequences, no matter how, uh, pure my intent was in doing so.

"Uh oh," Ariadne said, drawing my attention back to the television.

"And with 51 percent of the vote in," the anchor said, "we are now prepared to call the state of California for President Gerard Harmon, which gives him—"

I clicked off the television before he could finish. "The whole damned ballgame," I said in disgust.

Ariadne gave me a smile of sympathy mingled with dread. "Maybe it won't be that bad."

"Oh, you think?" I ask, giving her the side-eye. "I don't care how much I just helped him. My days have been numbered for a year. I guarantee you I'm out plus or minus a month from inauguration day."

"It's not like you haven't known this was coming," she said, still sympathetic.

"It's not like I have anywhere else to go," I said snottily, as my phone began to buzz on the arm of the couch. I looked down at it and frowned, gun-shy that it might be a text from Dick-o. J.J. had shown me how to block his calls and texts, but I still lived with the PTSD of thinking he'd send me a dick pic—errr, the kind that didn't involve his face, I should clarify.

It wasn't him calling. It was a 202 number. I held it up and showed Ariadne.

She frowned. "Who's calling you from Washington, DC?"

I shrugged and hit the answer button. There was only one way to find out. "Hello?"

"Please hold for the President of the United States," came a woman's very steady, very perfunctory voice on the other end of the call.

"Shit," I said, "it's Harmon."

Ariadne's eyes went wide. "President Harmon?"

"No, Dan Harmon, the creator of *Community*. We're in the same anger management group—yes, Gerry Effing Harmon—"

"That's still *President* Gerry Effing Harmon, thanks to you," came Gerry Harmon's energetic voice crackling through the line with more than a little amusement. "How are you doing this evening, Miss Nealon?"

"Peachy," I said. "I guess congratulations are in order."

"Yes, I'm having my people send you that fruit basket," he said, oh-so-full of helpful irony. "I know, I know, you haven't quite made it the hundred and twenty days yet, but after what you did stopping that lunatic in LA, I feel like special thanks are in order."

"You're welcome," I said, not really feeling it. "Though I have to admit, I'm a little surprised you're calling me ... what, ten seconds after the victory was announced."

"Well, when you owe someone as much as I owe you, it pays to show a little appreciation," Harmon said, smarmy as ever. "But you're right, I've got speeches to make, an agenda to shape. This is going to go down as a landslide, you know. I'll have long coattails tonight, and it's all thanks to you."

I had a feeling he didn't mean that, but he was being a politician and blowing smoke straight up my ass. My ass, ever health-conscious, did not appreciate the secondhand smoke. "You're welcome," I said again, not meaning it any more than the first time, but strangely unable to come up with some way to insult the man who'd just won an overwhelming victory because I'd set someone on fire publicly.

Yeah. You come up with something to say in that situation, because I came up with nada.

"Well, good evening to you, Ms. Nealon," President Harmon said. "I hope you have an excellent rest of your night."

"How likely do you rate that?" I asked, just being honest.

"Oh, I'm sure it's low," he said jovially. "By the way ... your agency is being merged with the FBI."

I felt like someone had whacked me in the back of the head and knocked my eyes out of their sockets. "Excuse me?"

"Yes, you'll be in DC soon," he said casually.

"Um, I live in Minneapolis," I said. "Not really planning

to move."

"Of course not," he said as though it were obvious. "That's your choice, naturally. I can't blame you. Many, many people consider themselves rooted to a place for one reason or another. But either way, I wish you the best of luck."

"Thanks," I said, and realized he'd hung up. "Asshole," I said, pulling the phone away from my ear.

"What was that?" Ariadne asked, staring at me in concern.

"We're being folded into the FBI," I said, frowning. "They're moving operations to DC."

"He called to tell you that himself?" Ariadne looked slightly impressed. "Tonight?"

"No, he called to gloat," I said. "He just tossed that last bit in because he hadn't had enough good news for tonight, he also needed to guarantee I wasn't going to be around to screw up the rest of his administration." I grabbed the TV remote and started to throw it, then thought the better of it. Showering us both in shattered plastic chips was not a wise way to vent my anger. I let it drop to the couch, and saw small cracks in the side where I'd squeezed it. "I'm going to bed."

"Good call, I guess," Ariadne said, sounding shell-shocked. "I ... might stay up a little while, ponder over the ... well ... this."

"Being jobless?" I stood. "We could move, I guess."

She looked right at me, and I detected nervousness. "We could."

"I don't want to move. You?"

"No." She shook her head.

I sighed and left her, heading to my childhood room, where I climbed into my childhood bed and felt ... well, very much like a child, out of control of my own world, my own destiny ... still. I tossed and turned, clutching at my pillow, worrying that I was about to be out of a job, and that the purpose I'd poured my life into, the one that I'd pushed

Scott aside for, was about to be taken away from me, ripped out of my hands by someone more powerful than me.

I tossed around like that for hours, my insides roiling like a storm. The only real job I'd ever had, the only one I thought I was any good at, was about to be yanked out of my hands.

I stared at the ceiling like I was a kid again, feeling like I was trapped in my room, trapped in my own house … trapped in my own life, with no way to escape.

On second thought…the more things change, the more they stay the same.

Ugh, change.

Epilogue

The White House
Washington, DC

President Gerry Harmon could not recall the last time Amanda Brackett had smiled before this week, but it had been a while. His Chief of Staff's moods changed with the polls, and so naturally, she'd been sour for a bit before now.

"You've got your speech?" Brackett asked, the faint trace of a smile playing over her lips.

"I do," Harmon said with a smile. He felt just as mellow now as he had while losing, but then, he'd been in a good mood for a little while before the shift in polls.

"Know it by heart?"

"I know the sentiments by heart," Harmon said, waving a hand. "It's mostly ... let's face it, it's a puff speech, not a policy speech." Those would come later.

"Mmhmm." Brackett gave him a little of that no-nonsense frown, which was something she employed quite a bit in her capacity as Chief of Staff. "You came within a whisker's edge. You know that, right?"

"Of losing?" Harmon looked in the mirror and straightened his bow tie. He always went with the classics, and his tux was a perfect representation of that. "It wasn't as close as you think."

"If not for that Nealon girl—"

"Who you wanted me to fire," Harmon said with a satisfied smile. It wasn't smug the way he did it, more like a polite reminder to Amanda that he wasn't an idiot, that he had some idea of what he was doing.

"Hm," Brackett said. "And what about Brock?" She fixed her gaze on him. "That could have been a disaster."

"And yet it all turned out in our favor," he said, turning away from the mirror, his bowtie straight. She didn't think it was, he could tell, but it was.

"Because of an anonymous tip," Brackett said. "A sudden, fortuitous anonymous tip." She stared right at him. "And an untraceable one, as I understand it."

"Yes," Harmon said, nodding along, "indeed. Fortune smiles." He arched his eyebrows and started for the door, knowing she'd hit him with it before he made it out.

"Did you tip them off?" Brackett asked.

Harmon paused before the door to the Oval Office and turned smoothly back to her. "Why, Amanda, are you asking me if I personally sent an email regarding one of our ... greedier, less ethical donors, unearthing one of his less savory schemes that involved the slaughter of our constituents in order to make a whole oodle of money?" He straightened. "Why, if I had known, it was certainly my duty to inform the duly constituted authorities."

"You are the duly constituted authorities," she said, impassive. "It was a good play. Especially distancing yourself from him in public before it came out."

"Buck Brock was an easy target," Harmon said. "He was only connected to us because he wanted power and influence, and he confused money with that. A common error."

"Still," she said, playing it a little cool, "I'd pay folding money to know how you figured that one out."

Gerry Harmon smiled at his Chief of Staff. "The thing about people and secrets is ... everybody thinks they've got secrets, and nobody realizes that ... nothing is secret. The world has changed in the last five years, and the biggest secret ever kept was exposed … there are gods among us. Some piker idiot with a land scheme that hinges on mass murder? That's a petty secret. There are bigger ones still out there." He stopped theatrically. His eyes danced; he was natural speech-giver, and loved playing to an audience.

"Yes?" Amanda Brackett was nothing if not a game audience for him. That was part of the reason he kept her on, even in spite of her dour and sour self. "What are they?"

"They don't call them secrets for nothing, Amanda," Harmon said. He held the door open for his Chief of Staff. "Oh, and now that we're done with Nealon … get her out. She knows it's coming. Preferably wait until after inauguration, just to give the press some room to forget, but before we have any more … incidents."

Brackett nodded. "Will do, sir. How do you want it handled?"

Harmon smiled. "She called me a dick. Handle it … however you think appropriate. Use your imagination." And with a parting smile, he left to go address his crowd, to give the speech he had in his pocket, and to celebrate his third—and final—term.

Sienna Nealon returns in

PAINKILLER

Out of the Box
Book Eight

Coming April 12, 2016!

Author's Note

If you want to know when future books become available, take sixty seconds and sign up for my NEW RELEASE EMAIL ALERTS by visiting my website at www.robertjcrane.com. Don't let the caps lock scare you; I don't sell your information and I only send out emails when I have a new book out. The reason you should sign up for this is because I don't like to set release dates (it's this whole thing, you can find an answer on my website in the FAQ section), and even if you're following me on Facebook (robertJcrane (Author)) or Twitter (@robertJcrane), it's easy to miss my book announcements because…well, because social media is an imprecise thing.

Come join the discussion on my website: http://www.robertjcrane.com !

Cheers,
Robert J. Crane

ACKNOWLEDGMENTS

Editorial/Literary Janitorial duties performed by Sarah Barbour and Jeffrey Bryan. Final proofing was handle by Jo Evans. Any errors you see in the text, however, are the result of me rejecting changes.

The cover was masterfully designed by Karri Klawiter.

Jennifer Ellison, who provided excellent feedback as both a first reader and an LA resident so I (hopefully) didn't make too much of an ass of myself in trying to get a feel for the locale.

As always, thanks to my parents, my kids and my wife, for helping me keep things together.

Other Works by Robert J. Crane

The Sanctuary Series
Epic Fantasy

Defender: The Sanctuary Series, Volume One
Avenger: The Sanctuary Series, Volume Two
Champion: The Sanctuary Series, Volume Three
Crusader: The Sanctuary Series, Volume Four
Sanctuary Tales, Volume One - A Short Story Collection
Thy Father's Shadow: The Sanctuary Series, Volume 4.5
Master: The Sanctuary Series, Volume Five
Fated in Darkness: The Sanctuary Series, Volume 5.5
Warlord: The Sanctuary Series, Volume Six
Heretic: The Sanctuary Series, Volume Seven* (Coming
      March 15, 2016!)
Legend: The Sanctuary Series, Volume Eight* (Coming
      June 14, 2016!)

The Girl in the Box
and
Out of the Box
Contemporary Urban Fantasy

Alone: The Girl in the Box, Book 1
Untouched: The Girl in the Box, Book 2
Soulless: The Girl in the Box, Book 3
Family: The Girl in the Box, Book 4
Omega: The Girl in the Box, Book 5
Broken: The Girl in the Box, Book 6
Enemies: The Girl in the Box, Book 7
Legacy: The Girl in the Box, Book 8
Destiny: The Girl in the Box, Book 9
Power: The Girl in the Box, Book 10

Limitless: Out of the Box, Book 1
In the Wind: Out of the Box, Book 2
Ruthless: Out of the Box, Book 3
Grounded: Out of the Box, Book 4
Tormented: Out of the Box, Book 5
Vengeful: Out of the Box, Book 6
Sea Change: Out of the Box, Book 7
Painkiller: Out of the Box, Book 8* (Coming April 12, 2016!)
Masks: Out of the Box, Book 9* (Coming July 12, 2016!)

Southern Watch
Contemporary Urban Fantasy

Called: Southern Watch, Book 1
Depths: Southern Watch, Book 2
Corrupted: Southern Watch, Book 3
Unearthed: Southern Watch, Book 4
Legion: Southern Watch, Book 5* (Coming in 2016!)

* Forthcoming and subject to change